Woe in Total Darkness

SEM THORNWOOD

Sem Thornwood

Woe in Total Darkness

Sem Thornwood

Copyright © 2022 by Sem Thornwood

All rights are reserved. No part of this publication may be reproduced, stored in a retrieval system, or transmitted in any form or by any means, electronic, mechanical, photocopying, recording, or otherwise, without prior permission or written consent of the publisher, except in the case of brief quotation embodied in critical reviews, and other noncommercial uses permitted by copyright law.

This is a work of fiction. Names, characters, business, events, and incidents are either products of the author's imagination or used in a fictional manner

Woe in Total Darkness

Trigger Warning

This book is intended for an adult audience and includes graphic sexual scenes, graphic violence and profanity. Also has themes that might be upsetting or triggering for some people including trauma, family problems, death, loss of a loved one, complications at birth, and chronic illness.

If you think my trigger warning is misleading or lacking, you can reach out to semcheery@gmail.com

Sem Thornwood

Woe in Total Darkness

To the little girl who dreamed of becoming an author,
We did it.

THE CONTINENT

Moon Palace

MOON

Holly Mountains

Sun Pal

S

ISLE OF AE

Wolf Mountains

The Boulder

MAINLANDS

OM

Lake Luna

SHIFTER TERRITORY

HANATE

Giant Territory

GREEN BAY

Palace of Mirria

EELIE KINGDOM

Lake Gleo

D LANDS

mple of Tisasa

Sem Thornwood

Prologue

Luran

I look out the window, eyeing the capital of Sun Khanate. Stone buildings fill most of my vision. The streets are densely crowded despite the late hour, and the Folk here are dressed too colorfully and seem happy for no reason at all.

In the distance I can see the sandy hills of the desert. They are kept away by the walls that surround the city. One strong wind and a sandstorm appear almost too easily.

I hate the desert.

Slowly, I spread my black wings and draw them close. They still ache from the long road I had to fly. Even the base of my horns throbs from the wind I had to face on the road. All of that just so I could be in a meeting room in this god-awful city.

One golden stamped letter was enough for me to come. King Luran Haliyes of the Moonfolk Lands, Master of the Moonshine, and Lightbringer of the Dark Nights was lured by that one small sun-shaped stamp.

She sent me a letter saying we needed a meeting and I flew in without thinking.

I hate being here and the topic we have to discuss. More than that, I hate leaving her. I hate everything about this situation, but I can never deny her anything.

I have the power of Moonshine in my veins. I am the light in the darkest hour. Yet it is not enough. I always crave sunshine. I always crave her. She feels like soft silk under my hands, tastes like citrus on my tongue, and sounds sweet like warm honey.

"Where did the accident happen?" I ask, even though I know the answer by now, just so I can hear her voice.

But my plans fail. The voice that fills my ears doesn't belong to my sweet lover. It is the voice of the only other person in the room. "This is the third time you are asking," she says with her annoying voice.

Mav K'rra is the reason she is not in my arms right now.

Even though I don't want to see the face of the Seelie Queen, I turn away from the window. Mav sits across the table from me. Her rich green skin is smooth, and she is wearing yellow flowers in her white hair like a savage. *Because she is a savage*, I remind myself. She is a Seelie.

Enough of a reason to hate her.

"I forgot," I deadpan towards Mav. The Seelie Queen is young. I knew her mother better, and I used to hate her as well. Seelies always demand things just like she is doing right now. Just like she has been doing since she took the throne.

I turn my attention away from her just to supress the need to behead her on the spot. Instead, I look at the person my question was actually intended to. I drink in the only thing that can calm me at the moment.

Khan Güne Mitharaus looks at me with soft, golden eyes. Her eyes shine like the sun while mine shine like the moon. My skin is dark like my ancestors', and hers is tanned from the desert sun. Her red hair is braided down one shoulder, and her white horns appear delicate. She mostly looks relaxed, but I can tell she is not from the stiffness of her red wings.

"Close to the Northern border," she answers. "Soldiers from a caravanserai realized the shadows from afar. They realized it must be a Patch of Darkness. When they reached there, a monster came from the Patch, and thank Tisasa, they were able to kill it.

Woe in Total Darkness

Afterward, I sent sun spheres to close it. Everything is okay now, but the curse is getting out of control." Her beautiful eyes fill with terror.

The Darkness Curse has been here for a while, but the worst of it was always at the Seelie Lands. Güne only had them close to the Southern border where they didn't pose a big threat to her lands. They never jumped this far. They never scared Güne so much.

But this changes everything.

"Curse has been out of control for a while," Mav says. "You just didn't want to acknowledge it because all of it happened in my lands. You thought it could not harm you."

It is true, but I will not accept it out loud. Mav wanted our help since the first Patch appeared in the southern part of the Seelie Lands. We didn't know what it was in the beginning, but it sucked all the light around it and horrible monsters born from it. We called them Patches after a while and realized that they could only be killed with light powers. Only Güne's Sunshine and my Moonshine were able to close those Patches.

Since we were not able to go all the Patches ourselves we perfected a method of capturing the light. We put it in small glass spheres so others could use it to close those Patches. Güne made more spheres than I did. She has always been better than me at using our powers.

But long story short, we didn't leave Mav on her own. So, I ask, "We did help you didn't we, Mav?"

She looks angry – her mother was not this fiery. She shakes her head. "Do you think the light spheres you send are enough? They are not the real thing. It takes too many of them to close off a Patch, and you always send less than we need."

"It is not only your problem," argues Güne. "Patches are ruining my lands as well."

To that, fire lit up Seelie Queen's eyes. "I am getting the worst of it, Güne. I don't even get the help that I need. I know you don't care about a Seelie dying, but the Patch hurts our crops. We all need those. What does it do to your land? Burns up your precious sand?"

Güne's eyes widen, and my jaw flexes at those words. I know she is right about the crops. That is the only reason I bothered to send her moon spheres. All three lands depend on each other. We all need everything we can get from the Trade Road. No food sounds much more horrifying than a Seelie death.

"Calm down, Mav!" I say with a harsh voice. Sand is sacred to the Sunfolk. It is sacred to Güne. I won't let a lowly creature insult it like that.

To my surprise, she actually does. Her eyes turn down, and shoulders shrink. "It is going to hurt the things you care about soon," she murmurs.

And unfortunately, I know she is right. If the Darkness jumps to the North, it can kill more than Seelies.

A dead Seelie means dead labor, but a dead Feyada means someone I failed to protect.

I need to fix things. I know if I truly try, I can fix it. This is just darkness, and I am as bright as the full moon.

Güne is as bright as the sun.

We can make it.

But we need to be smart about this. We need a plan.

"Is there any news about the Curser?" I ask.

Mav shakes her head absently. "I don't think they are doing this. This is something big. This is the work of a God. Curser is just using it to their advantage. They do not matter."

From a political view, it does matter. They are getting stronger every day by using religion and tales about the Patches. Even if they didn't create this curse, they are still getting strong because of it. I can light up the darkness but fighting off a cult is very different.

I want to tell all this to Mav, but a knock cuts me off. Before any of us can answer, the door opens, and a Sun Soldier wearing a chained facepiece steps into the room. His face is emotionless, but his body is tense. Everybody knows that we shouldn't be interrupted, so I understand something bad has happened.

"What is it?" I ask with a voice of steel. I can feel the worry of both females around me as well.

Woe in Total Darkness

"We got a signal." The soldier swallows uncomfortably. "Moon Palace is under attack."

Blood rushes to my head. For a second, I think I am hearing him wrong. For a second, I wish for him to be joking. But I know it is neither.

Years after, I leave my palace, and it is under attack. There is no time to think, no time to consider who is behind it.

My daughter is in the palace. My heir, my princess.

I look at the terrified eyes of Güne. She looks like she is about to faint. Her son is in the palace too.

There is no time to waste.

I step closer as Güne stands up, and without caring about Mav or the soldier, I kiss her forehead affectionately. I whisper into her hair, "I am going to save them."

Then I jump out of the window, starting my journey once more. I fly as fast as I can because Moon Palace carries such treasures. I cannot lose my daughter, but more importantly, I cannot lose Güne's smiles.

I have to save them.

1

Zuraya

I resist the urge to shield my eyes from the shining sun. It is more than I am used to, but I want to get the full experience. I want to feel the sun all over me. Even my black wings are spread out around me as I lay on the meadows.

The Moon Kingdom are usually chilly with the ocean wind. I enjoy the chill. I love going to the rocky beach and breathing in the ocean air. It mostly sticks to my skin. I never minded it until a few years ago when someone told me I smelled like a mermaid.

No one wants to smell like a mermaid: the savage killers of the sea.

Qyron told me their opinions didn't matter, and I didn't smell like a mermaid. I told him he could not know that.

Opinions of the palace never mattered to Qyron, but it does to me. Their approval matters since I will be their queen one day. I need them to love and respect me.

I need to work on my reputation, unlike my best friend.

So, I always carry chamomile oil with me. I apply some on the back of my ears and a lot on my long, dark brown horns. It relieves some of the tension too.

I touch my horns absently and feel how hot they are. I am not used to this weather. In the North, this much sun means everybody

Woe in Total Darkness

gets to go out and be lazy. That is what we are doing even though the sun doesn't mean the same thing to Qyron.

I look over at my best friend, lying next to me. His orange color wings are spread out just like mine, and his right one overlaps with my left one just so we can get a little closer. He watches the sky with a small smile on his lips. I know he doesn't like to close his eyes a lot. I also know his pale horns – weirdly even paler than his skin tone – are not as hot as mine. He looks very unbothered by the sun.

Qyron carries the sunshine inside him, just like his mother Güne and his annoying sister.

"Does this remind you of home?" I sign in the air, as close to his eyesight as possible. When he looks at me with furrowed brows, I repeat the motions.

Qyron's lips upturn in amusement and his cheekbones are glimmering under the sun from all the glitter he applied. *"Little sun is not enough for that, My Heart."* He turns back to the sky with a blissful face, like he is remembering the home he hasn't visited for years. His hands stay in the air to keep signing to me. *"Desert sun burns down your skin, filling your blood with warmth. The feeling of sand under your feet and your hands is indescribable. There is no good sand in here."*

He looks sad, and my chest squeezes at the sight. My love for Qyron is greater than most things. He is my best friend.

Qyron does visit the Sun Khanate from time to time, but it is never too much. When the Darkness Curse emerged twelve years ago, his mother sent him here so he could be safe. His twin sister Lenora, who is the heir to the throne, stayed back, and Qyron became a permanent resident of the Moon Palace.

I don't usually ask him if he misses his home or his sister. I know he does. But I also know he wouldn't want to leave me even though there is no good sand here.

We only have it on the beach, and it is wet, muddy, and white. I don't remember visiting the desert, but I know Qyron has a jar full of desert sand in his room. It feels much different than the mud near the ocean. It feels like happiness, and everything good.

It feels like Qyron.

At this moment, I don't want to ask him if he misses his home, but the look on his face is no longer peaceful. There is a yearning there.

So, I ask about something I know he loves. *"How is your sister?"*

Qyron turns to me. His face is still not filled with joy, but there is excitement in his glowing orange eyes. He lies half atop his wing. His red hair is disheveled, and his freckles spread on his face and arms perfectly. His skin glows a faint yellow light. He looks like pure sunshine, and I can understand why so many people are head over heels for him.

But I know he would be more handsome if he was happy. I need to make him happy.

"She is coming here," Qyron signs with one hand since the other one is busy propping his body up.

Normally that would surprise me. Princess Lenora never leaves the Sun Khanate. I think she hasn't visited here in seven years. She prefers to stay in her territory and show people what a great heir she is.

Princess Lenora is doing what I am doing, but from what I hear, she is just doing it much better than me.

Master of the Moonshine and Sunshine are the two halves of a whole. I know when I get my throne, I will need to have a close relationship with her. I know we need to get along, but I have never tried to do it before. Being close to Qyron felt like enough, even though I knew it was not. He is not an heir. He has Sunshine but not like his twin sister.

No one can shine like Princess Lenora.

At least, that's what I have been hearing my whole life.

I never told Qyron, but I kind of hate her. I know it is stupid since I don't know her, but I cannot help myself. I feel like she just has everything I want in life. She has Qyron as a brother, and she has the love of her people. She makes it look so easy while I am struggling every day and night.

Sometimes I wonder if her pulse also picks up when she thinks about the future or breathing gets hard every night when she closes her eyes. It seems like wishful thinking.

I never minded her not visiting and the news of her arrival would be surprising and slightly irritating if it was any other time, but now it is not. I know why she is coming.

Everyone is coming to the Moon Kingdom.

Because of the wedding. It is a wedding no one can afford to miss.

My wedding.

The thought makes me feel a little sick, but I try to ignore it. Every bride gets nervous before her wedding anyway. It is not about me. It is okay.

"It is going to be a great wedding," I murmur. I don't sign it. Those words are more for me than Qyron.

But he still understands since he can lipread. He nudges my shoulder with his wing and signs, *"It is going to be amazing."*

I don't know if he is saying that just to make me feel good or it is actually a prophecy since he is a seer. I want to ask even though I know he doesn't like it.

Before my fingers can form the words, he leans down to kiss my cheek. He unleashes his power through his lips just a little bit. I feel a little tingle from the Sunshine and, in return, free my own light to my cheek. Sun meets the moon.

One warm and sweet, the other cool and fresh

It is almost a game for us now. Our powers are opposites, but they are also the same. I can feel how they push each other, but they also complement. I can feel it not only on my skin but on my whole body. I can even feel it in the air around me.

It is strange, but it is also sweet.

I smile at the genuine look on his face. I am grateful to have him in my life. Without him, I would be twice as nervous. I need him by my side every step of the way.

That reminds me of a question Qyron has not yet answered. My features turn serious, and I prop myself on my elbow to get eye to eye with him and sign with my free hand, *"Are you coming to my mating ball?"*

Qyron lets himself fall back to the floor and closes his eyes. I know he does this to shut me off and I hate it.

"You are closing my sun," he says, softly slurring in certain parts. He also doesn't change from sign to speaking unless he is trying to avoid me

I tower over him and spread my wings to block off his sun more. I poke him in the chest, his thin yellow tunic making it very easy. I keep repeating my question, "Are you coming to my mating ball?" It doesn't matter if he cannot hear it. I want to annoy him.

He tries to push off my hand, but after a few tries, he just opens his eyes and gives me a frustrated look. I am still repeating the question. Now he knows I am not giving up before getting an answer.

Qyron rolls his eyes and finally answers. *"I don't want to."*

My throat tightens. *"Why?"*

Qyron flashes an easy-going smile. *"Because it is not something as dirty as it sounds?"*

I roll my eyes and let my disappointment appear on my face. I know he likes to joke about the name, but it is nothing obscene. *"It is like a wedding."*

"I am coming to the wedding."

Everybody is coming to the wedding. As my best friend, he needs to come to the mating ball as well.

My wedding is going to be according to Feyada traditions. It will be in the Moon Palace, and almost the whole Isle of Ae will care about that. Feyada traditions dominate everybody's lives.

Still, the Shifters want a mating ball. It is their tradition, and they will count that as the real wedding. According to them, after the mating ball, the alliance between Shifters and the Moon Kingdom is going to be set.

I am happy with honoring their traditions, but I need my best friend with me as I do it.

He always dodged the question, but I thought it was just a play. He needs to be there for me. *"Are you really not coming?"*

"It is in the Shifter Territory."

I know what he means. He is a Mitharaus, and Shifters are not very fond of Sunfolk. But it doesn't matter because he will be my guest. So, I just play stupid. *"You love Shifters. You slept with all the Shifters in the Moon Palace."* Except one. Thank Tisasa.

"And you think that is not going to cause a scandal at the ball?"

"You are coming!" I sign with a hard face. I am not getting married without Qyron there.

He holds his hand, about to answer me with a bored face, but then his eyes focus on something behind me, and they light up. The side of his lips rises. I know that look on his face. It is a frequent one. It is the face he gets right before he mocks someone. "Your puppy is here," he says. He usually uses his voice to mock.

My shoulders fall. He dodged the topic again, but I cannot even focus on that. I look back to see a black wolf running from the palace towards us. From here, he doesn't look so huge, but I know when I stay next to him, I need to crack my neck just to see his face. I am a little short, but still, he is enormous. He can shred anyone to pieces, and I feel like he would do that to Qyron if I was not in the picture.

But I *am* in the picture, and Qyron's words really annoy me. I turn back to him and slap his shoulder. *"You cannot call Shifters puppies, Qyron. It is racist."*

"I am not calling Shifters puppies. I am calling him a puppy." As he signs "him," he points to the wolf, like he can poke him all the way from here.

I roll my eyes for maybe the hundredth time today and rise from my spot to make my way down. I want to meet him halfway. More than that, I want to meet him far away from Qyron. I cannot take their bantering now.

I walk bare feet. My wings flutter as I jump big steps downhill. I know despite everything, I look very graceful in my light blue dress. It is a skill I spent years perfecting. I need to look elegant, like the moon, at all times.

As we come close, his body starts changing. He shifts. The huge wolf form transforms into something that looks a lot like an Earthling. Maybe he also looks like me – a Feyada – minus the wings and the horns, of course.

I know some find the lack of them very unattractive. *How can you find a wingless male handsome?* They never say it to my face, but I know they want to ask it.

Honestly, I don't mind it. His personality makes up for his lack of wings and horns for me. I also like to watch him shift because I don't like the wolf form as much. I would never tell him that, but it intimidates me.

His naked form appears just a few feet away from me. My eyes take in his body. His skin is naturally tanned. He doesn't need sun. His chest and abs are rock-hard. He has a trail of hair going down to his most private place.

It is a sight that can leave anyone breathless. Of course, it has the same effect on me. After all he is Rionn Ay Ujk, Alpha Shifter, Ruler of the Shifter Territory, and most importantly, my fiancée.

I look up at his face when we are closer. His dark hair is disheveled, and his eyes are dark with amusement. He always knows how good he looks and what type of effect he has over everyone.

He unties the pants from his arm and quickly pulls them over his legs as I take the last few steps between us. A huge smile appears on my face. I wrap my arms around his shoulders. "You don't have to dress on my account," I say jokingly and brush his nose with mine.

Rionn bites my bottom lip. "I am not dressing up for you," he whispers to my lips playfully, but a second later, his eyes lift to something behind me, and they harden at once. "I am dressing up for him."

I don't need to look back to know who he is talking about, but I still do. My best friend watches us with a mocking smile on his lips. There is also a challenge in his eyes. Looking back, I see that Rionn's eyes mirror that challenge.

It is always a fight for them and I hate it. I hate when they are like this.

I capture Rionn's chin and turn his face back to me. "Please don't," I say with a pleading voice, and his eyes soften on me. He doesn't like to make me sad, but he cannot stop being rivals with my best friend either. That is his only unperfect trait.

Rionn kisses my forehead and brushes away my dark braids to kiss my naked shoulder. "I am sorry, My Moon."

I soften under his touch because he apologized even though his word of endearment is a very unoriginal one. There is no need to be snotty about it. "You two are the most important people in my life. I want you to get along."

Rionn's body goes rigid, and I cannot even fathom how did I cause it. His next words explain as he deadpans, "It is nice to know I am sharing my fiancée's heart with another."

I want to scream.

I love Rionn, but Qyron is my best friend. I don't want Rionn to be jealous of him. I don't want us to have fights over stupid things like these. I just want to be happy with him. He is going to be my husband after all. We need to find a way to be happy.

My hands go even lower on his torso, and this time I kiss him. I nibble his sharp jaw, and he doesn't stop me. After years of being together, I found out this usually works best. "You know it is not like that." I kiss his lips and whisper, "Just try to get along with him."

The hardness in Rionn's eyes remains. He doesn't soften for me. So, I kiss his scowl again. When it remains, my lips pull into a smile, and I kiss him again. And again. And again.

I kiss him until his lips twitch and his arms around my waist tighten.

"You are killing me, Zuraya," he growls to my neck, biting the skin softly.

I giggle, happy that we are not fighting anymore. Touches and kisses always work. "I won't kill you. I am going to marry you."

This makes him kiss my lips. He looks happy. We should be happy. Our mating ball is in a few days. Nothing should ruin our happiness.

As he kisses me, fire builds inside my stomach. I am not very fond of sex but I like making Rionn happy since he makes me happy in other ways. I also want to have sex right now because when I focus on that, I usually cannot focus on my other problems. I really need to concentrate to get some pleasure out of it.

"Not here," he growls.

I want him to not care, but I understand. We shouldn't be seen doing obscene things.

I hate this too. Not because I cannot keep my hands off of him but because I want to feel ordinary sometimes. I want to experience things I am not allowed to.

But I know I can never have.

"Go to my room?" I ask. I never let him stay in my room because that would be inappropriate, but I do smuggle him there from time to time. Keeping a guy happy without sex is impossible, so I do find ways.

Rionn kisses my temple again and gives me a heart-stopping smile. "I was hoping you say that."

I smile back and let him pull me back towards the Moon Palace. I know everything is going to be okay when we are tangled under the sheets. He is going to be lost in his pleasure and I will get rid of my stressful thoughts.

I have Rionn and Qyron in my life. I have my father's approval as a princess, and when the time comes, I will have my people's acceptance as a queen.

My life is perfect, just like it should be, and nothing can ruin perfection.

2

Lenora

I swing my sword at the monster, cutting one of its mandibles. The ugly thing screams in pain. Its voice is high enough to rupture my eardrums. It is a nasty one.

Monsters coming from the Patches are always ugly, but usually similar to each other. At this point, I know how to fight all of them. This one is new, though. It looks like a giant spider, but it has a torso similar to my kind. Its legs are also much more bendable.

It is nasty, but not immortal.

I can fucking kill this thing.

I focus on my power. I can feel it filling my body. Sunshine is running in my veins instead of blood. My body is so hot with the sun power that I don't even feel the heat of the desert. I just feel the pure light my body is radiating. I can shine from every pore on my body, but the source always feels like my heart. It feels like Tisasa took the sun from the sky and put it inside my chest.

It is a maddening feeling.

I let it pour from my palms to the ancient glass sword. My soldiers are tiring the creature. They are doing a good job. I know they can kill it on their own even if I wasn't here , but it would be much more complex.

These darkness creatures melt under my Sunshine.

Warm light shines from my sword as I swing it again. I cut off a leg. Then another.

The Creature trashes on the ground. My nose and mouth are protected with a cloth mask, but my eyes fill with sand. The screams hurt my ears, and I notice my soldiers trying to block the sound out.

I don't bother.

I open my wings and fly toward the creature's head. It jumps to catch me as I rise, and he stabs my leg with his remaining mandible. The pain doesn't even make me flinch as I cut off that mandible while the tip is still stuck to my leg. Next, I stab my sword to its head, all the way down to his chin. It has a big head, but nothing my sword cannot handle.

The creature gives one last shriek and collapses on the sand. My body sways in the air since I am still holding onto my sword. Usually I am stronger, but something affects my balance. My wings feel weak for some reason, but I still manage to step on the creature's head and pull off my sword. I fly down to the surface. It is more complicated than it should have been.

"General," someone calls to me. When I look up, I see my soldiers. Two Earthlings and one Feyada all run toward me. The owner of the voice is the Feyada, Hashim. He pulls down his mask and hood. He looks worried.

There is nothing to be worried about. I killed the creature. Now I only need to close the Patch, and we are done with this. We can go back to the palace.

"General," Hashim repeats when he is closer to me. "Are you okay?"

My skin feels wet, but it is not so weird. Sweat is normal. *Am I more sweaty than usual? Am I injured?*

I know I need to check myself after fights. I can feel pain. I can feel so much pain, but it doesn't bother me as much. I am always in pain, so I cannot always tell when some new pain adds to that.

I look down to asses my body and see the source of worry on my soldiers' faces. The mandible is still stuck to my calf. I try to focus

Woe in Total Darkness

if it hurts, but it gives something much worse than pain. It's stuck to a vein. Darkness creatures shouldn't touch your veins.

I understand why my wings feel weak. My whole body feels weak. My chest is too tight for my lungs. I immediately reach and pull out the mandible, not caring how dizzy it makes me. I think I am going to faint. Now I *know* I am sweating more than usual. Darkness is creeping into me.

"General, let's go to the healer," Hashim says pleadingly.

I shake my head absently. I turn back to where the creature came from. In the middle of the desert, an area is completely buried in darkness. No light can creep inside it. Only my power can close it, ruin it.

I need to close it.

Hashim says something behind me, but I block him out. I take a step toward the Patch of Darkness. And collapse on the floor.

"Fuck," Hashim hisses and then lifts me in his arms. He starts running to the cart we came in. "Qassandra!" he shouts.

I need to close the Patch.

I feel horrible.

Darkness trying to reach inside me. Fucking curse is all over my leg. It usually wants blood, energy, and life. But I know it wants my light. It wants to consume it all.

"Lay her in the cart," I hear Andy's calm voice. She is always calm. A good trait to have in a healer.

Andy is an Earthling. She doesn't have magic, but I trust her. I trust her to save me. I cannot die. If I die, everybody dies. I cannot go before I end this fucking curse.

Everybody is counting on me.

"Andy," I manage when they lay me down inside the cart. My throat feels dry, and my wings feel cramped up. "I cannot die."

She doesn't look at my sweating face, though. All her focus is on my leg. I cannot breathe but she is so calm. I imagine what will happen if she needs to cut off my leg. How much time will it take to train a fake leg?

Andy brushes something over my skin, and I recognize my own power. She is using light from a sun sphere I made. She always uses them to get rid of the curse. They don't always work. The mandible was inside my leg for too long.

I know it is not going to work.

"Tell me something," I plea.

Andy assesses my leg for a second more, and then her big dark eyes come to mine. "I think you can save the leg, Len."

"Me?" She is the healer.

"Bleeding keeps the curse from entering your system, but it is too deep to treat with a sun sphere. You need to fight it from inside with your power."

I grit my teeth. I would have done it long ago if I could. Darkness is attacking my power. I can't reach it. "I can't," I say breathlessly. Pain from the curse is probably the only kind of pain that can affect me.

Andy looks a little worried, but she is still calm. "If I make you bleed more the blood might keep the darkness out for a short while. You need to call your light."

That makes sense. "Do it."

Andy's eyes fill with concern. "It is going to hurt," she says.

"It won't," I answer. "Nothing can hurt me. Do it."

Andy reaches to Hashim's belt for his knife and orders, "Hold her shoulders." I don't need it, but Hashim still pushes my shoulders down to the cart floor. Andy then starts cutting. I can feel the flesh of my leg splitting open. I can feel the terrible pain.

But I remain still.

The blood loss makes me dizzy, but I still reach into my power. It starts from my heart, and I send it to my leg. I don't look down, but I know my blood shines like it is coated with gold.

I send all my power there despite the resistance. Pain doesn't make me even flinch. I just fight. I surround the darkness with sun and suffocate it. It hurts but it also feels good. Fight always feels good.

I only stop when there is no longer a push against my light. I know the curse is all gone now.

"All good," Andy assures me even though I know it. Hashim exhales a deep breath, and I am happy that my soldiers are at ease.

Woe in Total Darkness

I should never be the reason for their concerns. I am strong. I don't need their worry.

I am General Lenora Mitharaus; I don't have the luxury of having people worry over me

Without warning, I feel a needle stab my leg. "I am stitching you up, and then we are going to the Palace."

My mouth twitches. It is cute that she thinks she can order me around.

I don't say anything, though. I focus on my breathing as Andy fixes my leg. I can feel the pain from the cut and from the needle. Most think I cannot feel pain. Some think I cannot feel anything. It is not true at all.

I feel everything.

I am in constant pain. I learned how to deal with it. A new cut on my body is just an addition to my continuous suffering. Sometimes I cannot even notice, and it is easy to keep a straight face when I do notice. I don't ignore my pain. I just know how resist.

My best skill is being strong.

Hard like the desert, undefeated like the sun.

I wait until she is done stitching, and then I sit up. Andy immediately tries to push me back. "Just lay down, Len. We'll take you back to the palace."

I remain upright. She cannot physically push me. It is impossible. I look at the Patch and stand up from the cart with my good leg. "I need to heal the darkness," I murmur.

Andy again says something and reaches for my wrist, but all my focus is on the Patch. I pull my hand away. "I am your General Qassandra," I say with a stern voice and move towards my destination.

No one else tries to stop me. My command is the law.

"You are gonna split your stitches," calls Andy. Her voice does something to me, and I look back to see her a few feet away from the Darkness. She looks broken, but her eyes carry worry. I didn't fuck up too much with my words then. Andy is my friend. I don't want to hurt her, but I must close the Patch. I cannot leave before I do.

I nod at her and take my next steps more carefully. It is good to be vary of my leg.

When I take a step inside the pitch-black darkness, my breath hitches. I have done this so many times, but it still fills my body with dread. All the curse surrounds me, and I feel like it is biting my skin all over. It hurts more than any other thing. It hurts so much that I am actually aware of it. All the other pain in my body feels like nothing compared to this.

I try to take a deep breath. It is heavy inside the darkness, but I manage. I fill my lungs with the horrible air and reach into my heart again. I free the light inside me. It is different than what I did for my leg. This time I shine all over. I can even feel it on the tips of my hair.

The Darkness is trying to swallow my power, but it is impossible. I am not a Feyada at this moment. I am pure sunshine. My light slices the Darkness slowly but effectively. The Patch fills with the sun. The air around me gets warm and sweet. It is like heaven.

It also hurts.

My power burns the curse around me, and I can feel every attack on my power deep inside my chest. It is a good kind of pain, though. I like this pain. It feels like a victory, even though I know this is not the end. This is not the last Patch I will have to close.

I cannot focus on that. Every destruction feels like a rebirth.

Just when my last rebirth ends and the darkness is cleared around me, I fall face-first to the ground. Sand fills my mouth, and my body feels too weak. Despite all, I smile and let my eyes close.

I did it.

———— (————

Bang!

The world is dark but too loud. It is uncomfortably loud.

Bang!

My headaches and the sound creates an earthquake inside my head. I can feel my fucking horns shaking because of it.

Bang!

Woe in Total Darkness

I slowly open my eyes and try to understand my surroundings. The last thing I remember is the dark against my light. I was in the desert. Now I am in my room, but I feel too tired, and the loud noise is not stopping.

I flutter my eyes open and see my gold covered bedroom. I am wearing a sleep shirt, and my leg is bandaged. My body feels drained, and someone keeps knocking at my door.

That is what the loud noise is.

But the knocking is too consistent. It is not normal even if the person doesn't know I am beaten up. Who would even dare to disturb me like this? They must have a death wish.

I do have odalisques like every royal in the palace, but unlike some, I don't like to have them in my space all the time. I also don't like to share my bed with them like some do. So, I know no one can open that door except me. I almost wish I had used the extra room in my chamber for one of my odalisques.

I carefully get up from the bed as the knocking grows even more demanding. I just want to rush there and curse, but I keep my steps slow and careful. I can't feel how bad my wound is. I don't want to pull the stitches.

When I reach the door, I open it with my messy hair, half-transparent night shirt, and my bloodied bandage. If they care about my state, it is their own problem.

To my shock, there stands a court guard with a terrified face. He is wearing pure white fabrics with sun pins on both his shoulders. His dark curls are trimmed close to his head. He is a good-looking Earthling. My mom chooses them specifically and thinks looks are more important than skills. Honestly, they don't need to be too skilled anyway. Sun Army is always out there to keep the dangers away from the Capital. They are mainly here to serve. They are no different than odalisque, but they show status. Everyone can send an odalisque to my room, but only a few people can send a court guard.

Despite knowing those few people, I still ask, "What the fuck are you doing?"

He swallows visibly. "General, Her Excellency the Khan wants to see you."

This is weird. My mother so rarely wants to see me. We need to work together sometimes, but even then, we try to manage it without crossing paths. The only times we actually meet up are the dinners my dad organizes. He wants us to have a close relationship, and I attend those dinners for his sake. I don't know why my mother attends, given she doesn't like my dad either.

"Did she say why?" I ask and point to my bandages. "You see, I am not really in a condition to leave my room."

The guard lets himself to look at my leg. "She is aware, General. The court was deeply sorry to hear what happened. Yet the Khan still wants to see you."

I rub my sleepy eyes and then rub my temples. My mother has the worst timing in the world. I feel like she is doing this just to torment me. "Did she say why?" I ask again. Maybe I don't need to go.

"She was angry at you for your absence," the guard says. When he sees the confusion on my face, he further explains, "Because you didn't attend the celebration of Beg Mallari tonight."

How the fuck could I attend a celebration when I was unconscious? I want to scream at the guard, but I know he cannot comfort me. He can give me answers, though. I know Beg Mallari. She is the Beg of a large land close to the Giant Territory. I don't know what happened there, and it concerns me.

"What did Beg Mallari do that needed to be celebrated?" I ask.

The guard looks a little concerned but still answers, "She joined us in the court."

A welcome celebration. "What a fucking accomplishment." I try so hard to keep from exploding. She wants to see me because I didn't attend a welcome celebration? My mother is definitely crazy.

Unfortunately, she is also the Khan. I cannot say no to her.

"Tell her I am coming as quickly as possible," I say, accepting my fate.

After closing the door to the guard's face, I turn to my room. I know I need to look at least a bit presentable. My mother values these things, and the less hate I see in her eyes is better. So, I wear a white dress with a golden belt, praying Tisasa for my leg to not bleed through to the white fabric. The dress makes the golden

Woe in Total Darkness

tattoos on my arms visible. They are traditional to the Isle and the Sunfolk but my mother still looks at them like they are the stamp of me choosing the Army over my royal duties. She likes to act like the Isle would be okay without my efforts.

I braid my blonde hair since my mother hates it. I don't have the fire-red hair of the Mitharaus family. Instead, I have my father's dark blonde locks. My mother acts like I did that on purpose in her womb just to despise her.

I don't have time to put anything on my face, but that is not a problem. My mother finds me quite ugly, even with longer lashes or blusher cheeks. I find my strong cheekbones and large lips okay, actually, but my mother believes a princess should have delicate lips and a soft round face. She also doesn't like my sunburnt skin. I always got a tan easier than my mother or my brother, but it is also because I am out fighting monsters almost every day. She lost all her tan by not leaving the palace for seven years and despises mine even more.

Lastly, I put on a golden headpiece to draw attention away from my horns. They are white like my mother's and make it obvious how my skin color changed due to the sun. One might think my mother praises me on my horns since they are milky white, but that is a wrong assumption. My horns are smaller compared to most Feyada. Short horns are considered ugly in any part of the Isle.

As I fit the golden headpiece, I remember a distant memory. I remember my twin brother Qyron with his long, proud horns. My mother loved those just like she loved everything about Qyron. One day my brother realized how I was sad because of my short horns, and he filed his own to match mine. My mother was furious.

When they grew back, he filed them again.

I smile at the memory. I miss Qyron.

Quickly shaking my head, I get rid of those thoughts. It is not the time to dive deep into distant memories. I focus on my destination and leave. I want to run towards my mother's chamber, but I know it is not good for my leg. I don't want to prolong the healing time, but more importantly, I don't want to visit my mother in a bloodied dress.

Luckily when I reach the chamber, the guards take me inside at once since she is already waiting for me. It is absolutely the worst when my mom decides to make me wait for no reason. She does a lot of things just to despise me because she believes I do it too.

I don't.

I do my fucking best to make her happy.

Her odalisque takes me to her private room, and I find my mom facing the window, watching the brutal sands instead of looking at me.

I am okay with it. If she doesn't look at me, I won't have to see the disapproval in her gaze. I calmly take a seat on one of the golden-colored chairs without bothering with a courtesy. She wants her subjects to kneel for her. That is something I will never do for anyone. "You wanted to see me, my Khan." She doesn't like it when I call her mother, so I try to avoid it.

A mocking sound leaves her lips. "I didn't want to see you, Lenora. You pushed me to have this conversation."

"I did?"

My mother turns to me this time with huge eyes like I asked the most stupid question in the world. The white and yellow fabric flows around her lithe, delicate body. The red feathers in her wings are combed perfectly, and the horns on her head are glittering. She is wearing a more oversized golden headpiece than me, and her red hair flows down her boney shoulder.

Güne Mitharaus is the definition of perfection, and the most imperfect thing about her is me, her daughter.

"You haven't joined the celebration for Beg Mallari. Did you think I was just going to let it pass? You have obligations as the Princess."

And in her eyes, I will never be able to fulfill those obligations, but I am still her heir. It is killing her.

She is killing me.

I take a deep breath and explain in my calmest voice. I don't want to fight. "I couldn't attend because I was unconscious."

Woe in Total Darkness

My mom again laughs in that mocking way. "It is always excuses with you, Lenora."

This time I cannot stay calm. I get on my feet. "I was attacked by a Darkness creature and almost died. Yet you are upset I didn't dance for your friend's arrival?"

My mother looks at me with disappointment. "I let you know she was coming weeks ago. You should have never even left the palace today. Sometimes you forget you are a princess before a general .

"I am the General," I say harshly. She acts like this is just a fun little game. "I wish you appreciated it more since your khanate is safe because of me. This whole fucking Isle is safe because of me!"

"You are exaggerating, Lenora. Your powers make it easy to fight off the Darkness."

"Then why don't you do it?" I almost scream in her face. I can take her words, but I cannot take that look. It is the reason I see her so very little. I cannot bear how much she hates me, while I cannot stop loving her.

She is my mother.

My mother shakes her head with disgust and makes it so hard to keep tears in. She gazes off the window and murmurs, "Why can't you be more like him?"

Him.

My twin Qyron.

My mother's precious child.

I swallow all my pain. I used to cry in front of my mother. It only disgusted her more, so I stopped. I tried to be strong for her. I tried to be perfect. I managed to gain everybody's love in this nation but the one who bore me.

"I am not him," I say with a stern voice. "I will never be him. I am Lenora Mitharaus, the General of the Sun Army, fucking Lightbringer. I am your daughter and your heir, and I will never be Qyron, mom."

A sob escapes my mother's lips at the name of my brother. She misses him. I miss him too, but she cannot keep searching for him in me. I will never be him. I can never be.

Hate pools her eyes. She keeps quiet, but I know what she is thinking. She wishes Qyron was the older one. She wishes he was here instead of me.

We both have yellow-orange eyes that look like flames, like the sun. Hers are bloodshot when she finally looks at me and talks. "You *are* my heir. You are the Princess Lenora Mitharaus of the Sun Khanate. So, next time I expect you to fulfill your duties as the Princess. Don't disappoint me." Then she turns back to the window, disregarding my existence. "You can leave now. Your dress looks ridiculous anyway."

I look down instinctively at my dress and see all the red on the skirt. White fabric is sticking to my bloodied bandages. I know she will never ask if I am okay.

Yet it still hurts.

Leaving my mother's chamber, I run to my room, not caring if I rip open my stitches. I don't care about anything. I just want to reach my room and open my secret drawer. There stands a silver ring I cannot wear around anyone. A simple crescent on a simple band. It is a ring from Moon Kingdom.

I just take it, press it against my chest, and cry to my pillow.

I wish I could hate my mother. I wish I could hate Qyron for everything. But I don't.

I can't.

My love for them is beyond reason. Qyron more than my mother. I miss him more and more every day. I want him here. I want him to see me like this. I want my brother to hug me and console me.

Unfortunately, I know it will not happen, and when I wake up from the sleep I fell while crying, I will still hate myself for everything.

3

Zuraya

It is dark. So dark.

The world doesn't get dark around me. I am the Moon.

It is cold. So cold.

I shouldn't feel cold. My veins are filled with cool light anyway.

I can't see. I can't breathe. I can't move.

It's not real. I know it's not. I know it too well. For the last seven years, I have had this horrible dream almost every night.

Impossible to wake up unless someone shakes me awake.

Impossible to bear.

I don't feel pain, but it is even worse. I *need* to feel pain. I want to shine, but I can't. It should hurt me. It doesn't make sense like this, and it makes everything even worse.

My eyes feel like they are sewn shut. Sometimes I can open them. I don't remember seeing a lot, though. Sometimes I see chains on my ankles, on my wrists. Sometimes I see an Earthling with red hair sitting across from me. I want to talk to them. I want to ask how I can escape. Maybe this is a punishment from Tisasa. I am not religious, but I am ready to do anything that Earthling tells me to get rid of this.

I have Tisasa's power. Her Moonshine. Maybe she wants it back. I will give it back just to escape.

But I can't *escape.*

They came for me in the dark seven years ago. Their wings were strapped to their backs. Their faces were covered in shadows. They came to my room while dad was away. They closed my mouth and held my arms and legs.

They wanted to take me.

Kill me.

But I shone. I shone so brightly. I blinded their eyes. I broke their bones. I made them writhe in pain. I made them beg for mercy.

I did it despite never learning how to.

By the time dad came, they were dead. I was safe.

Not really.

I don't get these nightmares when I am sleeping next to Rionn. I want to get rid of them, but I sometimes send Rionn away for some reason. Sometimes I say no even though he only wants to hold me in my sleep.

A side of me says that maybe I want the nightmares. Maybe I want to remember the darkness. Maybe I want to be in the darkness, shackled and alone. I want to remember what kind of pain they would inflict on me if I didn't shine.

Maybe...

I don't know.

I know that I scream through the nightmares. I scream until I am awake. My throat always hurt the next day.

The darkness surrounds me, restricting my vision. I want to move and fly off, but my shackles are so tight and I cannot feel my wings.

I want to go.

Leave.

Escape.

Woe in Total Darkness

Then I feel a gentle hand over my head. I press into it. I try to understand who it is, what it is. That takes me off from one darkness to another. Only now, it is not silent.

I am screaming in my bed, covered in sweat. It is dark but only for a second. A warm light appears next to me when I open my eyes. So different than the cool, white light of mine.

I look up to see the source even though I already know. It is warm and yellow and orange and soothing. It is Qyron.

"It is okay," he signs. *"You are awake."*

He is the only one who can't hear my screams in the whole palace. But he is always the one answering them.

"Stay with me?" I ask. I usually use my Moonshine to make my hands visible in the dark, but I am too shaken to do that right now. It doesn't matter anyway. He knows I am going to want this.

Qyron nods and gets under the covers with me. He is still shining dimly because he knows darkness makes me nervous. He is warm when he wraps me in his arms. Too warm for my chilly body, but I don't care. He also doesn't care that I am covered in sweat and that I will kick him away in my sleep. He only squeezes me and kisses one of my dark braids close to my scalp.

"I am here," he whispers with a raspy voice. He is terrible at whispering, but I don't care about that either. I am just grateful he is here for me.

I close my eyes smiling, and draft off in my best friend's arms.

———— ☾ ————

In the morning, I once again open my eyes to the sunlight, but this time the source is not Qyron.

Light fills my bedroom through many windows. I never use curtains because I love the moon being the last thing touching my body and the sun being the first.

Qyron is no longer holding me; in fact, I am lying face down in a weird way. I can't see him, but I know he is still here. My foot is touching his hairy calf, and I can feel his wing poking my shoulder.

He always sleeps more than me. Once, he told me that there was nothing that could make him wake up. Sunshine doesn't bother him since he is filled with it, and he cannot hear any sounds. He said that his body was made for sleeping.

I like to get more sleep as well, but I need to start getting ready. My trip to Shifter Territory has been planned for a while, but I haven't packed yet. I wanted to make sure Qyron was coming first. Because he caved only yesterday, I have very little time.

Rionn wants to leave tomorrow.

As I try to peel my body off the bed so I can call servants to help me, the door to my bedroom opens. There are guards in the royal wing, and I know only a few people can come to my room through those guards. I don't know a lot who can barge into my room since my servants must be present in the antechamber.

Before I can even turn my sleepy eyes to the entrance and see who it is, his voice fills the room, "Zuraya?"

I finally manage to sit up and rub my eyes happily. I love when Rionn comes to see me first thing in the morning. It is so caring. He looks so handsome like always. I remind myself how lucky I am to have a fiancé this perfect. I should be the happiest Feyada in the whole Isle.

"What the fuck is this?" he growls next, and my eyes fully open. My smile disappears.

He is looking at Qyron's sleeping form on the bed. My best friend is not even close to being awake. He is oblivious to the furious eyes focused on him.

The hate in my fiancée's eyes irritates me just like always. "What?" I ask with a shrug. I have never hidden the fact that Qyron slept in my bed from time to time. I never told him when it happened, and he never found him like this, but he was aware that this was happening. I never lied.

"*What?*" Rion repeats with a mocking voice. His pupils are dilated, making him look intimidating beyond imagination. He is dangerous.

However, I still step off the bed to get closer to him because he is also my future husband. I cannot let things crumble.

Woe in Total Darkness

Qyron shifts in the bed, murmuring nonsense, but I don't look back at him. My focus is solely on Rionn. He is being unreasonable, but I try to be patient because I don't want him to be mad. Not this close to our mating ceremony.

Just when I am about to talk, Rionn explodes again. "I just found my fiancée in bed with another, Zuraya! And you act like it is nothing?"

I fight so hard not to roll my eyes. He actually acts like he caught me cheating on him. "Because it is nothing," I defend. "It is just Qyron. He came because I had a nightmare."

"You had a nightmare?" Rionn asks, and something soft touches his voice. I can see he is still angry, but he also knows how horrible my nightmares are. He knows I get them when I am alone. I can see how my terror hurts him.

Rionn cups my cheeks, and desperation fills his eyes. "Call for me then, My Moon. Let me be the one to soothe you. Don't shatter my heart."

I want to tell him I don't. I want to tell him he is being ridiculous, being jealous of my childhood friend. I want to tell him I love him. But before I can, I hear Qyron getting onto his feet, and Rionn's eyes fill with fire once more.

Why is this making him mad? Why can't he be happy just because I am happy?

"Get the fuck out of here!" he growls to Qyron.

"Rionn!"

My best friend seems not distressed at all. He smiles, looks down at his shoes, and says, "Trouble," failing at keeping his voice low. Then he makes his way outside.

"Why are you always doing this?" I ask Rionn, almost wincing at the desperation in my voice. I put my hands on his chest, and Moonshine dimly lit up my palms in an attempt to calm his heart. I wish I was better at using my powers like that.

Rionn closes his eyes for a few seconds as he swallows. When those dark irises appear again, he doesn't look angry. He looks... defeated.

I want to throw up.

"I am not doing anything, Zuraya," he says. "You are kicking me off your room for no reason and seek another for comfort. I want to be the one to heal you. I want to be next to you, but you always want *him* instead of me. I thought it would change with time. I kept silent for so long but I cannot do this anymore."

No.

We are only a few days away from our mating ball, and he wants to break up with me. No amount of moonshine can defeat the darkness his words create.

I can feel tears in my eyes. "Don't do this to me, Rionn. I love you. I have given you everything. My heart, my soul, my body. You can't let me go."

"You love me, " he whispers softly like he cannot believe it. There is pain in his eyes, in his voice as he asks, "And do you love Qyron?"

"Of course," I answer without hesitation, even though it fills his eyes with more agony . I cannot lie about this. "But it is different. You know it is different."

He takes a step back, so my hands no longer touch his chest. My light dims, and my hands drop to my sides. "I can't keep letting you ruin me just because I love you, Zuraya."

Now tears slide down to my cheeks. "Are you leaving me? Is this the end? Right before our wedding?" It is a horrible scandal.

He swallows hard, but his knuckles brush away my tears. Just the ghost of a touch. "Our marriage is not only dependent on our feelings, Zuraya. We will marry, but I have to make sure if this is just a political alliance or a real marriage."

My heart squeezes. My brows come together. "What do you mean?"

"It is forbidden for Sunshine heir and Moonshine heir to marry. I must ensure you didn't choose me just because I was the next best thing. I need to make sure this is not something to make Shifters loyal to the crown."

I rub my hand over my heart. It hurts. I need to calm it. "How can you even say such a thing? I love you, Rionn." He has always been so good to me. A perfect match. How can I not love him?

He doesn't look like a man who wants to leave me. He looks like his heart is rotting but it doesn't stop him.

Rionn kisses my right cheek, capturing my tear. Then he presses his perfect lips to mine. When he pulls back, he is still close.

"I just need time," he whispers. "Can you give me that?"

I don't want to but that is my only option to fix things. "Yes."

"I will leave for the Shifter Territory today. You will come when you are ready, and we will talk, okay?"

I nod. "Okay." My voice is too small. I can't manage more than one sentence.

Rionn leans down again and kisses my lips softly. "I love you," he whispers.

"I love you," I echo almosy instinctively.

And then he leaves.

My tears take over as I fall back onto my bed. My perfect plans for a perfect future is ruined. Everybody told me how lucky I was to have Rionn as a fiancé. I told myself how lucky I was to find love in such a good match, but if he stops loving me, no love will remain in our relationship.

And that will not be perfect at all.

4

Lenora

I am reading a letter from a Beg in my bed. A Northern Beg, I can tell without checking because their problems are not life-threatening. They are mad that Seelie goods are constantly being delivered with a delay. Trade Road is not as swift as it used to be.

It is because the Patches keep appearing closer and closer to the Trade Road. The Seelie Kingdom already has too many Patches ruining their crops. I try to travel there from time to time, but mostly they need to fix the Patches with their sun sphere stocks; which are hard to come because I am the only one supplying them. My mother cannot bother helping the Seelie Queen.

I throw the letter into the unimportant pile. Someone else can write back to the Beg telling them their rose water stocks are going to be filled soon enough. The only ones I will reply myself are the ones concerning real problems. Northern folk doesn't have many of those since a Patch almost never appeared past Sun Palace.

"Do we have to check all these letters ourselves?" Andy asks from her spot on the foot of my bed.

"You were the one who wanted to help," I reply without even looking up. Her yellow dress looks more fitting for a night out, and her black locks are so long that they brush the pile of letters next to

Woe in Total Darkness

her. It is clear that she didn't want to spend her night like this, but she also didn't want to leave me alone.

Andy throws a letter into the unimportant pile, and her deepless black. I can see the glitter she put on her shoulders and arms. Her skin is much darker than mine, but it has a paleness. Her black hair also has silver strands. Anyone can tell that she is not Sunfolk.

Andy pouts her full lips, and I see more glitter. "How many odalisques do you have that can do this?"

I throw another letter and answer. "Too many, but I have none that I trust."

"You are being ridiculous," she says. "Even your mom lets her odalisques answer her letters."

I already know this. Most royals do like that. Odalisques are not like servants or chambermaids. They are bright Feyadas and Earthlings. They get an education in the palace and are mostly loyal. They don't feel less than the royals because they can gain power and land if they are clever enough. They can even father an heir like my dad, who was my grandmother's odalisque years ago when he caught my mother's attention.

Still, I cannot risk it.

"Honestly, my mother gets less secretive letters than I do."

Andy rolls her eyes like I am exaggerating, but she knows I am right. My mother is ruling a country, but I am keeping every creature on this Isle alive.

"All I see is ungrateful Northerners," Andy murmurs. "And it is public knowledge."

I chuckle at her words. It is mostly nonsense. I went through most of it last night, and it was so boring I fell asleep surrounded by letters. Yet, I still need to check all of them. "I need to read them too in case there is unusual activity in the North. I don't want anyone to know if a Patch has appeared there. Secrecy is important."

Dark doe eyes turn to me, and I look down to not see their skepticism. I try to focus on the letter in my hands, but I can feel everything going on inside Andy's head.

"This is about the Curser, isn't it?" she questions. I glance up to the sympathetic eyes staring at me. "You believe they have followers in the Sun Palace? It is impossible, Len."

"Years ago, we thought the Darkness Curse was impossible too. We thought no power was stronger than Sunshine or Moonshine. But look where we are."

This time Andy crawls toward me on the bed and touches my arm. "Len, you cannot live in fear. Do you even believe they did this? You believe the Curser created this curse?"

"I don't know," I confess. Andy's touch is comforting, but this is not a worry I can just let go. This is the mission of my life.

I cannot trust anyone.

But I trust Andy.

Only because I trust her do I let her utter those next words. "What if it really is Tisasa? What if we are fighting this all wrong?" Because if the Curser didn't do this, it must be the Goddess' doing.

Andy asking this doesn't bother me, but the whole idea does. "I prefer to think it is not."

"Why not?"

I bit down my bottom lip. I don't know if I ever spilled my guts about this to anyone, but I know if I am going to be honest with someone, it will be Andy. "Because I can fight the Curser. They are a Feyada, an Earthling, or something else, but they are someone I can fight. I can be secretive to get around their cult. I can search for them, and when I find them, I can just snap their neck and end all this fucking rapture. No more darkness. No more deaths." The idea that it will still go on after I kill the Curser is terrifying.

Andy gives me a warm smile. "You will end this, Len. If it was work of the Goddess, Seelies would have known."

Despite all the pain she carries inside, Qassandra Andino is great at making people feel good. I sometimes wonder if that is the gift of a healer.

I take comfort in her confidence. When the curse first started, Seelies believed it must be the work of Tisasa because the Patches

Woe in Total Darkness

started close to the Sacred Lands. They made sacrifices to the Goddess and performed rituals to apologize for whatever we did to cause her this much anger.

All that answered them was silence.

The former Seelie Queen was sure that it was not Tisasa's doing. They determined the curse was related to Tisasa's powers, just like my Sunshine and Haliyes family's Moonshine.

Maybe because it makes sense, or maybe because it is the easier truth to swallow

But I have no time to dwell on it. I am neither a Seelie priestess nor religious. I am merely the Lightbringer.

I raise my walls again so Andy cannot see so deep into my soul and then I reach for another letter. "Let's finish these. I need to have dinner with my parents."

Andy doesn't push it, instead goes back to her pile like nothing happened. It is one of the many reasons I like her so much.

"You father's request?" she asks.

Of course, it is. He desires a better relationship between my mother and me. We never accomplish anything in that regard, but that never dimmed my father's hope.

The corners of my lips tick up with the thought of my dad, but it is cut short because of Andy's shriek. "Oh, my Goddess!"

Her voice is surprised but thankfully not terrified. She is looking at a letter with huge eyes, and her lips are pressed together in an attempt to not laugh. I have no idea what can be this funny.

Before I can even ask, she looks up and answers for me. "This is a love letter."

Shit.

I immediately reach in an attempt to pull the letter from her grip, but Andy jumps to her feet, her eyes still locked on the paper. She looks way too amused.

I know which letter it is. I know every word that is written on that paper. I also know it shouldn't be on the unread pile. I had already read that letter a few times last night but apparently misplaced it when I fell asleep.

Stupid. Stupid move.

"It is not a love letter," I say. It is a love letter, but maybe it is not the most romantic one. I would not know since I only got those from one person and one person only. So, it is my best attempt.

When Andy gives me an unbelieving look, I understand that it is a pitiful attempt. She quickly looks back at the letter, but then the mockery in her eyes fills her voice as she starts reading out loud. "There is not one night that passes without me yearning for the honey smell of your warm skin." She looks back at me with an open mouth. "You say this is not a love letter?"

I shrug. "It is not love. It is just lust."

"Who even is this?" Andy asks and looks at the name. Only then do I realize her easy-going tone was apparent because she didn't check the name. The second she reads it, her face goes a little pale.

"He is not like them," I say immediately. I step off the bed to touch Andy. This time it is my turn to comfort her. "He is not like the Shifters who hurt you. He is not like the Alpha before him."

Andy closes her eyes and nods. "I know," she murmurs. "I know he is not like his uncle. I know he changed a lot of laws that used to make it easy for them to hurt me."

I wrap my arms around her. It is not something I do a lot, but the mention of her past always burns my heart. I wish I could go back in time and save her. I wish I could have saved her way before my mother did. Way before any damage was done.

"I know there are good ones. I know not all Shifters have a thing for girls who have been kissed by the moon," she says, referring to the paleness touching all of her dark features. "Or a thing for little girls."

I kiss both of her cheeks. "I am sorry," I say. "I wish I could find them all and give them the most painful death."

Andy nods with a small smile. "I know." She hugs me close for a few seconds, but when she pulls back, her smile is bigger, and she dabs at her wet eyes. "I don't want to talk about that. I don't want them to ruin my night."

I don't want that either. "We can talk about whatever you want." I might even ditch the letters to go out with her. This is more important than any letter.

Woe in Total Darkness

"Tell me how this happened," Andy says, waving the letter in her hand. Some sadness lingers in her eyes, but she also looks playful. She wants to be able to do this without getting sad.

Because of this, I didn't tell her. I was worried it might upset her, "It is not a very serious thing," which is true.

Andy pulls me to the bed so we can sit while she laughs. "Well, I hope so. I mean, are you aware of how messy this is?"

"Of course I am." I have been aware since the first time he kissed me.

"Tell me how it happened," Andy pushes again. I can see the excitement in her eyes. She is not the most adventurous when it comes to love and sex herself, but she loves to gossip about it.

I know at this point, I cannot step back. I hope that maybe finally telling someone will help me. "It started when I visited the Shifter Territory."

"That was months ago."

I nod. It was. "I was dealing with a Patch closer to there, and then Rionn Ay Ujk invited me since I have never visited and was trying to have a better relationship with the Sun Khanate. I went just to see how they were doing. I stayed there for a week, and we spent every day together. First, he showed me around, telling me about the Shifters' state. It was all normal, but then he kissed me, and we spent the last three days in his bed." I look away. "And maybe out of his bed."

Andy playfully pushes me. "Oh, great, Tisasa. You are so bad, Len."

"I feel awful," I reply though I am not sure if that is true.

"No, no," Andy shakes her head. "You wanted to have some fun. No one can shame you for it. If you ask me, you deserve it. I know you can barely find time for yourself."

She is right. If it is a decision between my pleasure and the safety of people, I will always choose the latter. I can never see myself as more important than the ones I am obligated to protect. But I also know no one will shame me for that. There is a much bigger reason.

Also, it was not just momentary fun. "I kept answering his letter afterward. At the moment, I thought that it was just a one-time thing, but the letters made it bigger."

Andy gives me a dreamy look but her body is a little tense. "Are you in love with him?"

"No," I answer quickly. I knew she was going to ask that. Andy believes in love. She is marveled at the idea of love. I believe it exists as well, but I don't think it is ever going to happen for me. I am also very sure what is happening between Rionn and me is not love.

At least, it is not for me.

"I am not in love with him. I am aware our relationship is forbidden and too messy to even bother." I look at Andy with pleading eyes. Pleading for her to understand. "But I also don't want to end it."

She looks at me for a few seconds, and the understanding slowly fills her eyes. She sees how much I need this. She sees why I need these letters and someone to be amazed by me for anything other than my heroic accomplishments. Then she hugs me and whispers. "I won't tell a soul."

"I know." It is better than a thank you because I always know. I can trust Andy.

When she pulls back, there is a naughty expression on her face, and I am grateful for it. "You know what will improve your mood?"

"A night out in the city?" I guess, with a smile.

Andy jumps on the bed, making some of the letters fly off to the floor, "Exactly!"

I giggle at her enthusiasm. After a quick look at all the letters, I nod. "We will go out after my dinner."

———— ᴄ ————

Every time my dad invites me to have dinner with him and my mother, I become a believer and pray to Tisasa to end the night's torture quickly.

This night is no different.

Woe in Total Darkness

At least my outfit is acceptable to my mother. I am wearing a red dress with golden linings; my blonde hair is styled nicely by Andy as I read a few more letters. My shoulders and eyelids are shining with golden glitter. I am wearing a crown circling my head instead of a huge headpiece like my mother, but she doesn't look very displeased.

My dad seems more than happy to have me for dinner.

For the longest time, I wondered why my mom accepts his invitations. I value my dad's happiness. I love my dad. I know my mom doesn't. She never looks at him with any amount of love. Yet she endures these dinners with me just because he wants it.

It used to be a big mystery to me.

My dad Rasol is my mother's only concubine. He is the only one that fathered her children, and if rumors are true, he is the only one who ever shared her bed. Still, she has no love for him.

However, my dad has plenty of love for my mom. The look of adoration he gave her never changed since my childhood. He loves her despite everything, and I know he will keep loving her until his dying breath.

Because of this, my mother wants to please him. I don't know the details of her feelings toward my dad, but even if she hates him, she wants his love. She is afraid of losing the only person who loves her unconditionally.

So, she accepts his invitations.

"How is your leg doing, Lenny?" My dad asks with a kind smile. He is the only one calling me Lenny these days. Qyron used to call me that once upon a time as well.

I return his smile. "Excellent. I am back on working."

I look more like my dad than my mother with my tan skin, shorter horns, and blonde hair, but I don't think my smile can ever be as bright as his.

Before my dad can answer, my mom chimes in, "How perfect."

I try to contain my shock. She never even cared about my injury. "Thank you, my Khan."

She nods approvingly and looks at my father. "See Rasol? I told you she must have been fine by now."

"You were talking about me?" This one is not surprising, but my mother looks a little too enthusiastic.

She can only say "Yes," before my father cuts her. "Maybe this is not the time for that talk, My Light. We are having a family dinner."

My mother smiles at my dad, but it is all fake. So fake that I wonder how my dad can still love this woman. "Well, we are the royal family. Our family dinners can include political matters."

That gets my attention. "What is it?" I might dislike my mother, but if there is an important matter, I rather know it sooner than later. I can just make it up to my father after I learn what it is.

My mother seems pleased. "You are expected in the Moon Palace."

I already have plans to travel to the Moon Kingdom but not yet. I always try to visit different parts of the Island, but I was never invited explicitly to the Moon Palace. It sounds sketchy. I already have a guess. "Is this about the Princess?"

"Why does it matter?" she asks in a defensive tone. "King Luran personally invited you. You should get ready as soon as possible. Maybe tomorrow?"

"Tomorrow?" I look at her with wide eyes. There is not a chance I can leave that soon. I have too many things to deal with, mainly because my leg only recently healed, and it put me back on my work.

My mother must have known this. She most likely doesn't care.

"Why not?" she asks, a little too aggressive. Her jawline is sharp, and I can see her delicate fingers shake slightly.

My eyes narrow on her stiff form. "You know more than you share, mother."

Fury touches her eyes more because of the word "mother" rather than my accusation. "It doesn't matter. You will learn when you go there, Lenora."

My father puts his hands on her shoulders in an attempt to soothe her. "My Light, maybe it is better to let Lenora choose the time. She knows her schedule best."

Woe in Total Darkness

My mother looks at my dad, ready to cry. "You don't understand, Rasol. This might mean..." a sob escapes her before she can continue, and my father hugs her close.

"I understand, My Love. I understand better than anyone," he soothes her.

My throat tightens at the sight. I remember the last time I saw my mom cry this hard. It reminds me of my biggest shame.

I cannot take this.

I stand up from my chair, looking anywhere but my parents. "I will leave as soon as I can. No sooner." I don't want to be harsh, but I cannot let her use me.

My heavy schedule doesn't have time to waste on Zuraya Haliyes.

"You are heartless," my mother shouts at me while her face is still buried in my dad's chest.

I don't flinch.

My dad looks up with a soft expression, but I can also see the deep woe in his eyes. All this pain is no different than the one I feel in my heart. Yet they only want each other. I am not a part of this.

I am just a horrible reminder.

"You can leave, Lenny," my father says. He means well, but it still hurts.

So, I leave without a word. When I reach my room with Qassandra in it, I ask for the best eyedrop that can make me forget. That is the only way I can cope with the memories.

5

Zuraya

Cold is all around me. I am surrounded by ice and dark.

It is so unnatural.

My ankles are wrapped in cold. Cold is lining up the floor.

I should ache. I can even feel where I should ache. My arms, my legs, my chest.

My back.

Oh, great, Tisasa, my back feels so light. There should be some pain in there. I want to feel pain. I want to ache.

If I do, this will be real. If this is real, I can free myself.

Reality should come to find me.

I open my eyes so I can see. I want to see that Earthling with auburn hair. I want to ask them what this is. I want to talk to them. If I can see them, if I can hear them, they will be real.

I need it.

Rionn's missing body sends me here. He is not there to wake me up. His body can save me. He should be sleeping beside me at all times.

My eyelids flutter open. It is dark and it is blurry. I cannot find the Earthling lying across from me. Their body is missing. The comfort they radiate is gone. It feels so close to the end.

Woe in Total Darkness

Why are they gone?

I need *something*.

I need to shine.

I need to break free.

Just as I try to scream, warm hands wrap around me. My eyes open. A bright light saves me from the nightmare. I let myself into his warmth. He is my only comfort.

———— c ————

"Why am I even coming with you?" Qyron asks for the hundredth time across from me in the royal carriage. He asked it too many times before we left the palace and didn't stop when our journey began. At this point, I know he is only doing it to distract me because we are too close to our destination. He cannot go back now.

I answer, *"Because you are my best friend."*

"He left because of me, and you are bringing me along?"

It does seem stupid when he puts it like that, but it is not. After Rionn left, I was miserable, but I also didn't want to sweep things under the rug. If I am going to marry him, we need to solve this for good.

With a determined look, I sign, *"He needs to understand you will always be at my side. If he cannot accept it, then maybe we shouldn't marry."*

Qyron's orange eyes widen, and I realize what I have just said. Our relationship is rocky, but our marriage is another thing. It is not dependent on our relationship.

But it should be.

"Are you going to break off the engagement?" Qyron seems calm, but I can tell it is all an act. To his credit, I don't think anyone can stay calm after those words.

I look outside for a second, thinking. I never said it out loud because I am hopeful that we are going to make up. We love each other. We must stay strong. But deep down, I know if our marriage is not going to be real, I don't want it.

53

I said yes to Rionn because he was the type of guy who would make anyone happy, not because I saw him beneficial to the crown. I want to believe I still live for myself just a little. I want someone to love me.

When I look back at Qyron, my body has no strength, so instead of signing, I say, "Would it be horrible if I do?"

Qyron's lips tighten. I know the answer. I know I have to marry him anyway, so the best I can do is to pray he was as miserable as me these last three days.

I need to trust his love.

I think about the start of our relationship. Secret rendezvouses in the Moon Palace garden and our long talks. I think about the first time Rionn told me he loved me next to the ocean and how he proposed at the same spot one year later. I remember how everyone swooned when I talked about our dates.

However, I also remember something else. I remember the annoyance in his eyes every time he came to see me, and Qyron was right there. He always wanted me all to himself, and I never considered it could be this difficult.

I sign with dread in my chest, *"Would you prefer if I never agreed to marry him?"*

Qyron looks at me with soft eyes and reaches for my hands as he shakes his head. "You love him," he says. He seems to believe it too.

Tears fill my eyes. I know Qyron doesn't like my fiancé, but still, this is his only response. My happiness is the only thing that matters.

It is the only thing I ever wished from Rionn.

I only hold my best friend's hands and wonder why Rionn's suspicions are not accurate. Why can this not be the only thing I want? Even though it makes me feel bad, I cannot stop. And I just hope Rionn will act exactly the same as Qyron.

Woe in Total Darkness

Before our carriage even starts slowing down, I hear the music. It is my first clue that we are almost there. And I immediately stuck my nose to the window to see.

Shifter territory is so very green. It is a mass of rocks and caves in the middle of a beautiful forest.

Now I can see the *Boulder.* It is part of a mountain range, but it looks like a hill of rocks. Boulder is the home to the royal family of the Shifters, a palace carved inside an enormous mountain.

It is Rionn's home.

With every passing second, the music gets louder, and I can better see the crowd in front of the palace. I had visited the Shifter Territory before but was never greeted with music and a crowd this size.

However, I never visited as Rionn's fiancée.

Excitement fills my heart, and suddenly I can see the drums I have been hearing. Shifters are dancing and singing to the rhythm, which is absolutely beautiful.

A smile spreads to my face, and I turn to Qyron. *"They are singing."*

He laughs. *"I can feel it."*

Oh right. It is really loud and getting louder.

When our carriage starts to slow down, and I am able to see the passageway people created from the road to the gates of the Boulder, some anxiety joins my excitement. When I visited before, I only wanted to impress them as their future queen, but now I am also going to be the wife of their Alpha. I know they care about that more.

I swallow thickly and reach for my shoes. I can impress them. I know what they are expecting of me. I quickly unlace them as I mentally prep myself.

Qyron's hand wraps around my wrist, but I don't stop. So, he says, "What are you doing?" a little too loud.

After I push off my first shoe, I look up at my friend and sign, *"Shifters value the bond between the Earth and the creatures. Being bare feet is important, especially in celebrations."*

Qyron looks both impressed and proud of me. Instead of saying anything further, he helps me shrug off my other shoe and then takes off his own. I hear him murmur, "Wearing my best shoes was a mistake," and it puts a smile on my face despite the nerves.

Our carriage stops, and I take a deep breath. *Tisasa, help me make this right.*

I feel Qyron's hand on my arm, and when I look at him, there is an encouraging smile on his face. *"Give them a show,"* he signs, and I nod with a smile of my own. I get power from my best friend. I am dressed in light blue fabrics, and the only make-up I have is the silver paint on my eyelids. I have the moonlight. I possess everything that can impress Shifters, yet I don't have Qyron's confidence. I take a look at his clothes. He is dressed in an orange tunic and ridiculous golden pants. His eyelids, temples, lips, and tips of his fingers are all painted with golden glitter. He is hated by these creatures as Sunfolk, but I know he is going to walk with a charming smile on his face.

If he can do it, I can do it too.

I squeeze his hand for a moment to get confidence and smile when the carriage door opens for me. I step down to the grass with bare feet. Before I can even look around, someone greets me, "Welcome to the Boulder Princess."

Relief touches my chest when I turn towards the familiar golden skin and long brown hair. "Nyko, I am happy to be here," I answer Rionn's Beta and press my forehead to his in Shifter greeting.

When I pull back, Nyko gives me an impressed look, but then his eyes go to Qyron as he leaves the carriage. He looks tense for a moment, but then his smile looks as genuine as it can be. "Prince Qyron, we are happy to see you. I hope your first visit to the Boulder will be satisfactory."

Qyron thanks him with a polite nod and then looks around. A way is cleared for me to walk toward the palace, but there are Shifters all around. I look at them and try to understand what they are seeing. Some of them are in their wolf form, so it is tough to read their expressions, and some of them are lost in the music. It is a lively melody that fills up your soul with too many emotions.

Woe in Total Darkness

Nyko points to the cleared-out pathway. "Let's walk, Princess. Alpha is waiting at the gates."

Those words take my breath away, and I look straight ahead. Between all the crowd, all the festives he is here. Right at the gateway of the Boulder, my fiancé is waiting for me with all his glory.

Rionn is almost naked like most of the other Shifters. His chest is decorated with charm necklaces, and the only thing hiding his manhood is a tiny loincloth. He looks too damn handsome, and I realize how stupid I will look if I ever cancel the engagement.

He looks at me with pride and happiness in his eyes. I can see even from here. He is happy to see me.

Thank Tisasa.

I can't help but smile at the sight of him, and at the same time, I start to shine. It is only sundown and not too dark, but it must be visible because I hear some people gasp. I only look away from Rionn to give them my smiles.

I start walking while still shining with my Moonshine. I want them to see me as worthy of their Alpha. I see how they dance and have fun. I see young and old. I see a lot of couples.

No, not couples. Mates.

My focus drifts to them more as I keep walking. The mating bond for Shifters is something special. It is destined. The bond is so strong that I can feel it around some of them.

Oh, Tisasa, I can *smell* it in the air.

Some of those mates are both Shifters, but I see a few that are Shifter-Earthling pairings. Earthlings are only accepted here if they are a mate, and they can only be a mate if they are kissed by the moon. I can recognise them instantly. Even the ones with darker skin and darker hair have a paleness like a silver fog is surrounding them. I don't know if it is easy for everyone or if my power is recognizing their uniqueness.

Or maybe I recognize them because they are the only ones that are not Shifters. They are an exception to a rule. They are special.

I am special too, because of my power. I only hope the white light radiating from my skin is going to be enough to impress them because I have no other trick.

I am not Rionn's mate. I will never be.

But I will be his wife and want to be loved by his people.

Fortunately, I don't see anyone looking at me with hate. Some of them who are on the pathway reach for me, and I kindly press my forehead with theirs in greeting. I accept their kind words. With every other act of acceptance, my heart flutters more, and with every step closer to the love of my life, my throat tightens.

At last, I come face to face with Rionn. Our eyes meet when there are only a few more steps between us. I look at him with such yearning and see the same in his dark eyes. Unfortunately, I am also aware of how we left things. I take those last steps wondering how I should behave. How should I greet him?

But before I can even make up my mind, Rionn closes the gap between us, and his strong arms go around me. He presses me to his naked chest as my knees weaken and bury his face into my neck. I hug him back. I hug him with so much relief.

Rion smells my skin, my braids like he needs it more than air, and then whispers words meant only for my ears, "I missed you."

I caress his soft, short hair. "I missed you too."

There are many more things to say, but it is not the time. For now, I just want to know he still loves me. When I look at him our bodies are still flushed together, and his expression is so soft on me.

Without thinking I cup his neck and kiss him. This is my way of making sure everything is okay.

Just as my lips brush his soft ones, Rionn pulls me closer to his body with his hands on my waist. He kisses me sweet and deep. I kiss him hoping to forget all the nights I cried over his departure.

It is just like nothing happened. I know I cannot act like this forever. I have to point out how much he hurt me. We need to talk.

Just not right now. Right now, we can just be lovers.

Woe in Total Darkness

Only when we are apart, do I realize the cheering around us from the Shifters.

Rionn smiles his beautiful smile, and I flush read. I want to hide my face in his neck. "I didn't even consider if it was appropriate."

He chuckles and brushes his lips to mine in a quick kiss. "This is not the pretentious Moon Palace, My Moon. We kiss whenever we want to."

I don't even argue with his insult because the Moon Court really is stuck up about public displays of affection. I am not the biggest fan of kissing, but the idea of being so free here excites me. "Well, that can get addicting," I giggle, and Rionn joins me.

My fiancé still holds me close, but his eyes shift to something behind me for a moment, and I feel his muscles tense. I know he is looking at Qyron, and I pray to Tisasa for him to be civil to not say anything. At least give me a chance to talk to him first.

Sunfolk are already hated enough by Shifters. A repellent welcome will not be beneficial for anyone. It will push all the Shifters to be inhospitable against my best friend, and that is the last thing I want at my wedding.

Because of all this, when Rionn says, "Qyron," with a harsh voice, I get anxious. I want to plea him with my eyes, but he doesn't look at me. Even his arms unwrap around my body, and dread fills my heart. He only accepted me because he thought I had left Qyron behind? Was the kiss a lie?

But before my mind can whirl around all those questions, Rionn does something that knocks the Moonshine out of me. He slowly signs to Qyron as he talks. *"I am glad to see you here."*

Right after, his eyes find mine, and I know why. He wants confirmation for his signing. He is not fluent, and he did mess up the sign for glad. Thus it doesn't bother me. It shows that it was not a planned answer. It was not a play. He did this genuinely.

I smile brightly at him and slowly show him the right sign for glad and whisper, "Glad."

Though he knows Qyron can lip-read, he quickly signs the same words again, this time does it right. When I look back, Qyron has a soft smile on his face as well. *"Happy to be here,"* he answers with sign and speech at the same time.

Sem Thornwood

Rionn merely gives him a curt nod. I know they are not magically going to be best friends. I know some hate still lingers in both of their hearts, but I am over the moon that they are choosing to be polite for my sake.

It is a good start.

One of Rionn's hands come to the small of my back like he didn't want to stay too long without touching me, but his eyes are on the horizon. He looks at my other companions, the soldiers who are waiting a few feet away from us. His brows furrow as he looks back at me. "General didn't come with you?"

I can see the anger in his dark eyes even though there was no danger in the path we followed. There is no danger in the Moon Kingdom. The rest of the Isle can be considered pretty safe as well. Still, Rionn worries, and that warms my chest.

I pat his shoulder in an attempt to calm him. "His wife is heavily pregnant. She says any day now, so he didn't want to risk it."

Darkness doesn't leave Rionn's eyes, but then I hear Nyko's cheery voice, "Doesn't pregnancies have a due date?"

I roll my eyes at him playfully. I want to say how clueless males are, but this is a different situation than that, so I explain, "Princess Maha is a Seelie, and General Archard is a Feyada. Interbreed pregnancies are hard to grasp."

"Oh, so that is going to happen to you as well."

Rionn softly growls to his friend, and I tense a little. Thankfully my fiancé saves me. "Let's show you your rooms. You must be tired."

"Not so much." I fluttered my wings. "I didn't fly the way."

Qyron came closer to the entrance. "Talk for yourself."

I giggle and let our hosts lead the way. I want a tour, want to meet the people but I need to go to my room. I need to talk to Rionn, alone.

As we walk deeper into the palace, I look around me with amazement. We are not visiting the rooms, but it still looks astonishing. The dips and ridges of the walls are different shades of grey and brown; at some points, I swear it shines. It is also possible to see different types of ivies curl around the spurs of the rock.

Woe in Total Darkness

"It is even more beautiful than the last time I visited."

Rionn smiles at me brightly, and he looks proud of his home. "We found the biggest beds for your rooms in the palace." He nudges one of my tightly gathered wings.

"Am I not staying in your room?" I whisper softly. Is that a bad sign?

"It is against the tradition."

My chest still feels tight. When I am close to him. It is easy to feel his love when he touches and kisses me. When we are apart, I cannot be so sure of it. That is the reason I always welcome his touch even though it is not always pleasurable.

I try to keep a bright face since we are not alone, but before I can adjust my small smile, Rionn laces his fingers with mine, giving me a possessive look. "You will move into my room after the mating ceremony." He whispers the next part to my ear in a husky tone. "Until then, I will sleep in your bed."

Oh.

I can't help but smile at that. We should respect the traditions. I will respect any tradition as long as we can find a loophole to be together.

"Nyko, can you show the Prince his room?" Rionn asks when we reach the second floor.

I reach and squeeze Qyron's hand. He gives me a smirk right before Nyko takes him to the opposite side of the hallway. With a hand on my waist, Rionn takes me to a room with a driftwood door.

I remember staying in the Boulder. I know good rooms have windows looking at the woods or the rocky cliffs on the ocean side. I also know the decoration is mostly made from stone, wood, and skins.

I am impressed by the beauty of my room from the moment I step inside.

The walls are filled with traditional artwork, and I can see some blue from the window. I can even smell the ocean. There is no silver and diamond décor filling the room like it is back in the Moon Palace. There is beautifully done pottery, stones of all colors, different type of plants, and furs that I don't even know where they came from.

This place is not made for a refugee breed. Shifters are the real owners of all these lands, and it shows. It is all-natural.

I delicately touch a white fur blanket on my bed. It is smaller than my normal bed but enough. "This is beautiful," I murmur.

"Only the best for you," Rionn comes closer and touches the sensitive inside part of my wing, making me shiver.

"Rionn," I say with a breathy tone I only use beyond closed doors. A sound I only create for my lover. He looks at me with lust in his eyes. His fingers are still on my wings. He is the only one who knows my body like this and the only one I let touch me like this. However, I know it is not the time. I catch his wrist and bring his fingers from my wing to my lips. "We need to talk."

Dread replaces the lust in his eyes. He hesitantly touches his knuckles to my cheek. "I know," he whispers. "I was just trying to postpone it as much as possible."

I shake my head. "No. Don't do that. We cannot really fix this if we don't talk about it."

Rionn nods, but his eyes don't look like he accepts my answer. "I made a mistake, Zuraya. I was so fucking mad, and I made a mistake. Every night I spent away from you pained me. I am sorry."

Tears well in my eyes. In the carriage, I was expecting him to be still mad. I thought maybe he hated me now. But the guy in front of me looks at me with real hurt in his eyes. He looks like a person who is ready to fight for his love.

"Why were you so mad?" I ask and put my hands under the charm necklaces he wears right over his naked chest.

He doesn't step back from me, but his chiseled jaw clenches anyway. "I was jealous, Zuraya. Too fucking jealous."

I already know that. I don't want this answer. I want something deeper. "Why? Qyron is my best friend. Why can't you accept it?"

Shifters have strong bonds of family and friendship. Rionn and Nyko can be even closer than I and Qyron. I know he understands the concept. I also know I never gave him a reason to doubt our

Woe in Total Darkness

friendship. He never liked Qyron much, but it shouldn't lead to him thinking he was going to seduce me just to despise him. He also shouldn't believe I am going to be seduced by someone just like that.

He was supposed to trust me.

And I can see he wants to. He wants to believe me and trust me. I just need to see what is keeping him away. What is putting these crazy ideas in his head to make him constantly jealous of my best friend?

"You are the Moon," he says, his black eyes desperate. "And he is the Sun."

Such a simple answer, but he says it like it should explain it all.

It doesn't. Our ancestors took their powers from Tisasa herself. The power of both day and night. The power of a Goddess. The source is the same but there is no connection.

Does Rionn think something different about it? Does the power mean love to him?

It is also against the rules for us to be together even though he is not the heir and his sister is, the rule still applies.

"I don't understand," I say with furrowed burrows.

Rionn looks pained, like I should have already understood and kissed him better. "You are the opposites but also the same. Different sides of the same coin."

My eyes flutter at his words. I have heard that before. *Different sides of the same coin.* I know it is a popular saying amongst the natives of these lands. Seelies, Giants, and Shifters use it for a lot of things, but there is a specific thing Shifters use this saying for.

Mates.

For all their lives, Shifters search for their fated mates. A mate means forever.

And I am not Rion's mate. I can never be.

"Feyadas don't have mates."

"I know this," he rasps. "I know, but I cannot stop myself. That is how I grew up. That is what your powers remind me, and it makes me so fucking jealous."

My chest tightens. I understand. He thinks that I am going to leave him for Qyron one day because he is my mate. I understand it too well that it brings hurtful thoughts. So, I let it free, "Will you leave me if you ever find your mate?"

Rionn's eyes harden on me. He swallows thickly before looking away from my troubled face. "I never will find my mate. It is a curse."

Only it is not. "It is a prophecy." My voice cracks.

"Zuraya," he turns towards me. His cheekbones are sharp, but I can see his eyes are slightly shiny and soft. He cups my face delicately with his strong hands. "No one in my family ever found their mate. Since I was a little boy, I knew I was not going to as well. I never looked for a mate. I never even looked for love, but I still found it with you. I don't want a mate. I only want you."

Those words break the knot around my heart. "I only want you too, Rionn."

"I know."

I shake my head. "No, you don't really understand. I will never leave you for someone else. I will never cheat on you as well. Not with Qyron or with anyone else. I love you." Because as everyone says he is my perfect match.

His eyes dip to my lips. "I love you too, Zuraya. I will always love you."

For some reason, he doesn't kiss me, and I realize he is waiting for me. I wanted to push it away. I wanted to talk first, and he gave me as much as I needed. He is letting me choose when to kiss him. It is sweet so I give him what he wants.

I rise on my tiptoes and brush my lips to his. "Please make love to me now. I missed you too much."

"Thank Tisasa," he growls and then impales his lips to mine. I want him to pour all his love into me.

All my life, I have always wanted love. I wanted one thing I do for myself. Because of that I never want to believe my relationship with Rionn is only political. I need something just for me.

That is why I let him take me to bed and act like I enjoy it more than I do. It is not his fault. He does everything to make me feel good. I am just not into it as much as he is, but I will do it to make him happy. He is the only thing I am allowed to have for myself.

If I can't make him love me enough then I have nothing.

6

Zuraya

Dark and cold.

The only thing I can feel is dread.

Woe.

Everything good and bright has been taken away from me. I need them back.

I know I am in Rionn's arms. I don't usually come here when I am in his arms.

His love should protect me.

He should save me from here.

He should help me shine through this darkness and be free.

Please, I think into the darkness. S*ave me.*

———☾———

Shifter celebrations are so much better than Feyada celebrations.

Maybe it is because everything is new to me, but I don't remember ever having this much fun. It could also be because this is my wedding and I am not just a guest. Either way, our mating ceremony is going amazingly.

We had the actual ceremony in the first moments of the dark. When the moon filled the night sky Rionn and I sat in front of an elder Shifter. He bound our hands together with colorful bands and blessed our union using various incense. We only looked into each other's eyes and answered yes when the elder wanted our vows. There were no long vows like the Feyada weddings. Rionn told me it exists, but it is more private. Couples would make those vows to each other when they were in private on their wedding night. I was wondering what he was going to vow to me tonight, but he said we didn't need to do that since we were going to make those vows at our wedding very soon.

After the elder declared us mates, we touched our foreheads together and then kissed. After the ceremony, the celebration began.

I am sitting in a circle of Shifters, all laughing and drinking heavy kumis. I know kumis is a traditional drink for the natives of the Island. They also drink it during the daytime, but the celebrations require heavy kumis.

When they first served the drink to us, I was a little skeptical, but Qyron happily gulped down his first cup. Apparently, they drink this in the Sun Khanate. I, on the other hand, never had it before.

It tastes nice, but it feels stronger than wine.

I am wearing very little as it is the tradition, but I still didn't feel comfortable not covering my breasts. A small vest protects my chest from exposure, and I am also wearing a small leather skirt that is decorated with beads. I also have too many bracelets and too many necklaces. All of them represent different types of things and are basically the Shifter's version of a wedding dress. Also, they drew different patterns on my skin with colorful dyes.

I actually like it. I look very colorful with all the beads. If you ignore my wings and horns, I look just like another Shifter.

Luckily my piercings fit here perfectly. It is a custom Moonfolk got from the Shifters, but no one in the Moon Palace has as many piercings as me. I wanted to do it to be able to represent every kind that lives in the Moon Kingdom.

And I feel so accepted among these people. Rionn is in another circle having a talk, and when our gazes line up, he gives me a happy, proud smile. He loves seeing me like this in his home, surrounded by his family.

Everything had been so great. He was even very kind to Qyron. I hope it will persist when we return to the Moon Palace. I want to live in this dream forever.

I was worried that Shifters were going to treat Qyron badly, but thankfully I was wrong. Shifters are not very fond of the Sunfolk because they are only seen as invaders. The sun power does not carry respect around the Shifters, so they don't get the treatment the Moonfolk gets.

But it is almost impossible not to love Qyron. He has been friendly to everyone since we came, so people requited his good behavior. Also, he knows more about the native culture than I do. When the Feyadas came to the Island, we took different paths. The Moon Kingdom revolved around the culture we remembered from the Mainlands, but the Sun Khanate was open for change. They accepted a lot of aspects of the Seelie culture.

Thus Qyron feels closer to these people than I do. He understands them better. He automates with such ease that I am sometimes jealous.

But he has always been like this. Nothing can ruin that confidence and that cocky attitude.

I see my best friend chugging kumis with a few Shifters in the far corner of the main saloon. I turn back to the middle-aged couple in my circle with a joyful smile as they are narrating the story of how they met.

I quickly realized that there are three very popular activities to do in a mating ceremony. Drinking yourself into oblivion, dancing as you sing, and sharing love stories. I don't want to drink too much since I want to remember this happy day. I already did the dancing part, and I feel like joining these circles is important to be seen as one of the Shifters.

I want to put my best game out there for them to love me.

So far, it has been going well.

The Shifter called Omana wraps an arm around her small blonde mate. Their legs are already intertwined. "Nina and I realized we were mates fifty years ago," she starts.

"Fifty-one," Nina corrects with a look, and the whole circle chuckles.

Mating stories are new to me, but I can see I am not the only one interested in the story. Most of the circle is unmated Shifters. I cannot always tell, but they don't have any visible tattoos that circle around their arms like Omana and Nina has. I learned that not all mated couples get tattoos. Northern tradition is to get a piercing to honor the union. Most Moonfolk does that, but I know it is different in the Desert and beyond. Sunfolk and the Seelies put great importance on tattoos. Apparently, Shifters grew away from the tattoo traditions but still do it for their fated mates.

"We were friends since childhood," Omana continues, one hand playing with her mate's hair. "In our teenage years, we fell in love. I mean, how could I resist her charm?"

Nina giggles. "I would wake up early every day just to look pretty."

"You are always pretty."

Nina kisses the tip of Omana's nose, and warmth fills my chest. It is such a refreshment from the Moon Palace. I enjoy seeing their love.

"When did you understand?" asks a young Shifter with his heart in his eyes.

They come back from their little love-drunk moment and turn back to the circle. Omana says, "The first time I kissed her. We were friends, and then we fell in love, but it took us some time to kiss. One day we were lying in the forest, watching the stars. She looked so beautiful that I knew I needed to kiss her. So, I did, and then it happened."

"We just felt it. The bond snapped into place. We were mated," Nina adds.

I am amazed by the story but also a little confused. Before I can even say anything, another confused Shifter asks, "How did you know?"

They chuckle a little. "Well, it is hard to describe," Omana says. "You look, and that person becomes the center of the world for you. I felt like our souls were connected. She was mine, and I was hers. There was no question about it." She looks at her mate with so much love I don't think I have ever seen a look that strong. "I loved her before, but when the mating bond formed, it was so much more than that. I knew that I cannot exist without her by my side."

Nina kisses her mate, and everybody in our circle swoons by their love. This time I know it is not even about Shifters being okay with public affection. If someone looked at me like that and said those words, I would have kissed them even in the Moon Palace throne room.

Maybe I would even like kissing if I had what they have.

I think if Rionn ever looked at me like that. Unfortunately, I know the answers. He didn't, and he won't. I am not his mate.

He can exist without me.

Pain spreads to my chest, and I excuse myself from the group. I climb to one of the small stalls. I don't think they can be called balconies since they are too small and more buried into the mountain than a balcony would. They are just tiny rooms that are half open and high up in the palace. It is hard to see it from the inside since the entrances are carved very tight. It is so small that I have a hard time getting there with my wings. I don't think three Feyadas can fit into one stall.

Luckily I know no one is going to leave the celebration to come here. Shifters like looking at the night sky but prefer to do it from the cave entrance, or they just go to the woods. Stalls are safe for me.

When I step inside and cool, fresh air touches my skin, I take a deep breath. I let my facial muscles relax. I don't have to smile. It feels freeing.

I look up at the stars. At the moon.

I feel strong. I feel unbreakable. Even though it is not true.

I told Rionn it doesn't matter that we are not mates. Feyadas don't have mates. It was never something I cared about. After hearing that story, though...

How does it feel to have a mate? Can our love even be compared to a mating bond?

Woe in Total Darkness

And suddenly, I understand everything. I genuinely understand why he was always so jealous. After learning how strong the mating bond is, it makes so much more sense. You cannot keep someone just with love if they find that bond.

He didn't want to lose me. He wanted to stop the bond from forming.

That is a stupid thought, though. A bond cannot be formed between Qyron and me. We are the two sides of the same coin because of our powers, but that is different. Feyadas don't have mates. Only the natives of the Island have mates.

I bit down my lip with a horrible realization. Natives of these lands have mates, and our powers also come from the Isle.

In the middle of my small terror, a sound startles me. "Zuraya?"

I turn back and see pale skin with gold glitter all over. I see hair that looks auburn because of the dark. I see eyes bright like the sun. Qyron is frowning down at me.

I didn't hear him come because, unlike everybody else, he doesn't wear these necklaces and bracelets that jingle. He is dressed in his casual, white robes, only showing more skin than usual.

Maybe I should be surprised that he followed me. I should be surprised that he is right here, just as I was thinking about him. But I don't.

Qyron always knows when I am distressed. He always knows when I need him.

And right now, I need him.

I wrap my arms around him and bury my face into his chest. He doesn't hesitate and hugs me back. He smells like citrus. He smells so familiar and safe. He smells like he is a part of me.

"What happened?" he asks with his voice since my face is buried in his warm chest. He is always so warm. He always makes me feel so happy.

Is it possible that I was so blind?

He is my friend.

But what if he is more?

Sem Thornwood

I cannot even answer. I just shook my head against his skin, and he didn't ask anything more. He just hugs me closer.

I just want what I saw downstairs. I want how Omana looked at Nina. It was a big unknown to me, but now that I have seen it, how can I turn away from it? How can I settle for less?

I need to know.

I pull back and look at Qyron's concerned face. He is my best friend. I never saw him as anything other than my best friend. Rionn's concerns were always so ridiculous to me. I never loved him like that.

Yet I need to know.

Omana said she knew when she first kissed Nina. I never kissed Qyron. I never had a reason to kiss Qyron.

Now I do.

I look up at his face. He doesn't shine right now, but his skin is still pale in the darkness. His cheekbones are sharp, and his lips look so soft. He looks so handsome. It is not a surprise. He was always handsome. Everybody always drooled over his beauty. To me, it never mattered.

He was always just a friend. Now I look at his worried expression and want to know if I was wrong. If we were too blind to see.

I don't even dare to whisper the words. I can't. So, I sign, *"Can I kiss you?"*

It is basically my wedding night, and I am trying to kiss another person. It is as horrible as it sounds, but I need to know. I cannot live the rest of my life wondering.

Thankfully Qyron doesn't look at me with judgment. He doesn't even look surprised. He is just giving me that soft look he gives when he comes to wake me up from a nightmare. He looks at me like he is always going to be here when I need him.

"Why?" he signs.

"I need to know."

My words don't make sense but still, understanding dawns on Qyron's eyes. He always understands me the best. His power lets him see the future and control his mind, but sometimes I feel like he can read my mind.

Woe in Total Darkness

That is beyond his powers. That should mean something else.

Qyron nods slowly, and then one hand cups my cheek, and the other goes to my waist. I wrap my arms around his neck and throw my head back, letting him kiss me.

His soft lips close over mine softly. Different from the hungry kisses I am used to from Rionn. This kiss is so soft.

I can feel his heat wrapping around me. His touch on my cheek and waist feels so familiar. We had never kissed before, but he is my best friend. Nothing feels weird.

His lips move over mine slowly. Such a lovely kiss. He is too experienced to be not good at this. He kisses with skill.

It is a great kiss.

I am the first one to pull back. I need air. He kissed me breathless.

Qyron rests his forehead on mine, and our horns softly click. I giggle, but both of us are still breathing heavily. I close my eyes and savor the moment. I know Qyron is doing the same.

When I pull back, my hands are still on his neck. He still looks so handsome. His hair is slightly more messed up, and his lips are swollen. I try to see something more. I try to feel something more. I want to feel the bond.

Though all I see is my best friend.

It was a great kiss but it didn't make me feel anything. It didn't change anything.

A sad smile appears on my face, and I pull my hands just so I can sign, *"It is not it."*

Qyron brushes his lips to mine quickly. *"I love you,"* he signs with one hand, his face serious. Then he smiles. *"But it is not it."*

This time I giggle. Not with sadness. I needed to know, and now at least, I do. *"Worth a shot,"* I sign, and we laugh together.

Now I don't need to live wondering if Qyron is my mate. I can feel the sadness deep down. Knowing I will never have what Omana and Nina have is dreadful, but I have to accept it. It was just a theory.

Feyadas don't have mates.

But maybe love can be enough. I can be happy forever with Rionn's love.

I don't need a mate. I have everything a person can ever want.

7

Lenora

I watch as they put my journey belongings into the cart. Earthling soldiers are next to their *davakas*. All of their gear is up, and their wings are tucked in nicely. *Davakas* are actually birds, but their wings are not good for flying. The best they can do is jump high. I don't know if it is because of their long legs or long necks, but they are still good for traveling. They are not strong enough to carry Feyadas, but Earthlings have no problem using them. Northern people are not very familiar with them, but they are the best ride in the desert.

The cart is pulled by desert foxes. They are stronger than *davakas* but hard to gear up for the Earthlings. We only use them for carts and carriages.

There are no carriages. My mom told me to get some of my odalisques with me to the Moon Palace, but there is no need. I am not planning to stay long, and despite my mother's wish, this is not a royal journey for me. I am going there as the General of the Sun Army.

I am going there as the Lightbringer. A name I share with the Moon King.

People don't call him Lightbringer anymore. Maybe Moonfolk do. I have no idea. Just like my mom, he is too busy sitting in his glorious palace. We are lucky if we get any moon spheres from him.

Seelies don't get even one a month anymore. It fucking bugs me.

I feel my jaw flex. I don't want to make my soldiers worry. I try to relax and look to my right to focus on something else. Andy is with me, watching the group get ready to leave. She is the only person I would have requested a carriage for.

"You sure you don't want to come?" I ask even though I did before. Maybe she changed her mind. This is her last chance to come. The Feyada soldiers and I will go tomorrow, but it is only because we are faster with our wings. This group will wait for us close to the Moon Palace, and tomorrow we will arrive there together.

Andy looks at me with a flat face. She is trying hard to hide her emotions. "I want to be at your side. I can feel it is going to be quite the entrance."

I chuckle. "I hope so. My mother is going to be very angry. She gifted me a golden dress to go with my Princess headpiece. She wants them to think I am the prettiest thing on the Isle."

That has never been a title of mine. It belonged to another. Still does.

I cannot be delicate like the moon, showing all the pretty colors while they look at me with awe. I cannot make them fall in love with me with just one look. I am not that person. I am not her.

I am still living in Qyron's shadow. I cannot also live in *her* shadow. We are too different, and they have to see that. I am strong, unbreakable like the sun. I am their protector. I am a soldier princess, not a pretty little thing for them to look at.

They are going to understand how much they need me.

When I feel my jaw flex again, Andy laughs and brings me back to reality. "I suppose you are not going to wear those."

"Of course not." I am not disregarding the biggest part of my life. I am a soldier. If they don't like the way I am, they can go fuck themselves. "I am wearing white robes and a facepiece."

I don't wear those while fighting, but for special occasions that is my uniform. I know it does not fit the Moon Palace, and that makes me even more excited to wear it.

A smile pulls my lips, and I let it. "Let them see how people who protect them from the darkness look like."

"Fuck," Andy curses. "Now, I really want to come."

I look at the soldiers that are getting into their *davakas* with worry. "I can stop them for you. You can go in the cart, or we can arrange a carriage. Hell, I'll carry you with us tomorrow."

Andy rolled her eyes at me. "The last time I flew with you, I almost puked."

Yeah, I usually forget Earthlings have more sensitive stomachs than us. "What about the carriage?"

This time she doesn't joke or hide her emotions. Worry fills her eyes, and her lips press into a thin line. "Did you get a letter from Rionn?"

It is a question, but it is also enough of an answer. I know why she hesitates. I know why she is staying back. So I answer, "Yes," knowing what that means.

"What did he say?"

"He told me how much he misses the golden hue of my hair," I say with a playful smile just so I can ease her worry. I don't like it when she gets lost in distant memories. I need her here safe and happy. I want to protect her from her past.

I can see a threatening smile, so she bites down her bottom lip, but there is still worry in her eyes. "And?"

I take a deep breath. "And how happy he is that we are going to see each other in the Moon Palace. He and his group will be there before me."

Andy nods. She looks so tense. I know going back to the Moon Kingdom is hard for her. I knew it since my mother rescued her on a trip she made there. I think she would have been okay with me on her side, but even I cannot make her go to a place where she can see a Shifter, not after everything they have done to her.

She can stay back here safe and sound, away from her childhood memories.

I swallow the lump in my throat and attempt to lighten the mood at least for a bit, "He is very excited to taste me again, you know. Not my words, his."

Andy looks distressed for a second, but then she playfully attacks me and bites my shoulder. As I give a loud "Ow," she throws her head back and laughs. "I cannot blame him," when she looks back at me, her eyes look joyful. "You taste amazing, General."

I look at the faint bite mark on my arm. She really went for a taste there. "I fight hundreds of dark creatures without losing a limb, and in the end, my healer is the one who takes a bite out of me. How ironic."

"I am full of surprises," she teases.

An Earthling soldier shouts from the top of his *davaka,* "General, we are ready to leave."

I look up to see it is Kunter. He is a trusted soldier and leading the group. My mother doesn't think Earthling soldiers are very valuable, but after I became the General, Kunter and a few other Earthlings jumped levels in the army.

I put my left fist over my heart and then lift the same hand in the sky with my palm open. "See you soon, Kunter."

His face is serious, but his eyes are warm as he answers, "See you, General." Then he leads the group as they leave the tall walls of the Sun Palace.

Andy watches them leave next to me. "They should be in the Moon Palace by tomorrow before dinnertime."

I nod. "The rest of us will take off tomorrow morning. I am planning to take only a few breaks. We will probably be there at night."

"Few breaks, huh? I am almost going to think you are excited to leave."

I don't try to contain my smile, and it spreads on my face as I turn back to the palace. Andy follows me. I answer her, "Maybe I am excited."

Andy nudges me with her hip. "Is that anything to do with Rionn?" she says his name in a whisper.

Woe in Total Darkness

That thought only comes to me with the question. I am actually pleased that I am going to see Rionn. I like the attention he is giving me. He is nice to talk to and nice to fuck. Also, I know he will not expect anything serious from me. I don't have to see him every day since he is living away, and there is no way in hell for us to be really together.

Rionn is complicated, but he is also safe. With him, I don't have to fear over my heart. My heart can only belong to my mission until this fucking curse is broken.

So Andy's heart-eyed guess is not true. He is not the reason I am excited to go. "There is something else."

Andy looks impatient. "Tell me."

I stop in the middle of the hallway and look around to make sure no one is in earshot. "If the King personally invited me, this means he really needs me. He is going to want something from me. He must be desperate." I smirk. "I am going to use his desperation against him."

Andy's eyes fill with understanding. "Moon spheres," she mumbles. They are much more powerful against the Darkness than sun spheres. If the King sends enough of them, I can cut down my mission and focus on getting to the root of this.

He has one thing I desperately need, so in exchange for that, I am ready to do anything he so desperately needs from me.

8

Zuraya

This is happening much more than usual. I shouldn't have this nightmare this much.

I survived years ago. They wanted to drag me into the darkness, but they failed.

They failed.

I want to breathe. I want this to end.

Rionn will wake me soon. He will see me trashing, and he will wake me. His warm body will replace this cold soon.

He cannot make it stop, though. I will always keep coming back here.

To the cold.

To the chains.

To the darkness.

―――☾―――

"I cannot believe you haven't popped up yet!" I say and sign simultaneously, looking at Maha's now huge belly.

She sighs, rubbing her naked swollen flesh. *"Me too."* She also signs her words. When we are spending time with royalty in the

Woe in Total Darkness

Moon Palace, Qyron usually needs to lip-read since Moonfolk doesn't know sign language. That is one of the reasons we love spending time with Maha. She is not Moonfolk. She is a Seelie Princess and knows sign maybe even better than Qyron. It is one of her native languages.

"What if you get into labor during the wedding?" Qyron asks, and I know if the ladies and lords surrounding us in the garden understood the sign, they would gasp at the question.

"I am so scared of that happening," signs Maha, and she, in fact, looks scared. Seelie Princess has one of the kindest hearts I came to know, so she probably thinks her labor is going to overshadow my wedding. She is afraid of stealing my thunder.

It is an unnecessary concern. At this point, seeing Maha finally give birth will make me happier than ever. She looks like she is really uncomfortable in her pregnancy.

I give her a warm smile to ease her concerns. "I already had one wedding. We need some new activities for the second one, right?"

I, Qyron, and Maha laugh at that, but the royals don't look too amused. They always try to spend time with us. Two princesses and one prince is a company they cannot pass, but they are not always in line with our humor.

We never send them away, though, especially when we are out in the open. Sometimes the three of us plan private activities in one of our rooms but other than that, we let the royal Moonfolk surround us. It is crucial to have a good relationship with them.

Maybe Qyron and Maha can risk it, but I cannot. I need them to love me.

As we sit joyfully in the garden with two pet foxes running around, they seem like they love me. I am creating an alliance between the Moonfolk and the Shifters. My very fun wedding is tomorrow, and I am out here blessing their warm day with my presence.

"Mating ball is not a wedding, Princess," someone says. I cannot even remember her name, but I know she is the third child of a Lord. All her life is going to be about having fun and eventually trying to climb up with marriage because her family will not give her much.

I don't show her any of my real feelings. She is someone who will be elated just being close to me. I cannot risk losing their unreasonable love. So, I smile. "Well, it bonded the Shifters to our Kingdom tighter, and it's all that matters, isn't it?"

Almost everyone around us cheer at my words, and Qyron gives me an amused look. Whenever I act for the crowd, he gives me that look. It is almost like he is telling me how much of a fool I am for trying to please them.

He will never understand. He doesn't need to be loved by the people.

That's why I try my best to ignore those looks.

He doesn't know what it is to be me.

Maha doesn't either. She is the little sister to the Seelie Queen Mav. Yet she doesn't make fun of me like Qyron. I don't think she can make fun of anyone. She is a very fragile and kind soul. I still have no idea how she fell for General Archard.

"It looks like the baby dropped, though," I comment on Maha's pregnancy again. I actually have no idea if it really did, but it is a safe topic.

Maha again rubs her belly. Despite today being sunny, I am still wearing a long-sleeved dress. Seelies are always more resistant to the weather. Maha is wearing a green dress that is only a shade darker than her skin. It covers her breasts, but her huge belly is naked for everyone to see. Her white hair is long and strands fuzzy. Her hair is adorned with daisies. Some Feyadas consider it a barbarian thing, but it is only because of their racism against the Seelies. I think the flowers in her hair look very pretty. I can also smell lilies on her. I know she put the scent on her horns. Even though our horns are different, I learned that trick from her. No one called me a barbarian when I put chamomile oil on my horns.

I hate when I hear people talk behind her back. I pray that she never hears any. She doesn't deserve it.

"At this point, I cannot say anything. This pregnancy goes weird in every way." Maha looks at Qyron with pleading eyes. *"Can't you see when he is going to come out?"*

Qyron looks at her belly like it is going to help. I know looking will not help his seeing. He usually sees randomly. The future shows itself to him almost every minute. I haven't even seen him get lost in a vision. People who encounter other seers always say Qyron is the most natural they have seen.

But he cannot see anything about Maha's baby. He tried before.

Despite anything, I can see him trying again. He tries to put on a playful smile even though I know it concerns him. *"It can mean they are going to be a seer."*

To that, she looks excited. *"Really?"*

"Yes. I heard how a seer's destiny might be unavailable to another one."

Maha looks down at her bump with a smile. When I look at Qyron, he winks at me. I don't know if what he said was true or not, but it makes Maha happy, and it is all that matters. There is no need to put her under more stress. Qyron is always good at calming people.

"Ah!" Maha grunts suddenly, and everybody in the circle leans toward her. Qyron even jumps to his feet.

"Are you okay, Maha?" I ask with so many other people.

She smiles sweetly. "Yes, yes, don't worry. False contractions. I just need to lay down a bit."

Qyron gets closer. *"What can I do?"*

Maha reaches out to him from the pillows she was leaning on. "Help me up. I cannot move being this huge."

When Qyron reaches for her hands, a voice steals Maha's attention, "I'll get her."

We all look at the Feyada walking towards us with worry in his eyes and even Qyron's attention shifts towards him. His wings are slightly open in a possessive gesture. His auburn hair is perfectly combed back, and his horns are taller than anyone I have ever seen. His dark skin is a little lighter than mine, but he doesn't shine since his body has no glitter. He looks hard and scary.

Still, Maha gets the most beautiful smile at the sight of him. "Davon," she says joyfully.

General Davon Archard comes next to his wife and kneels. His attention is fully on her. His face is hard as stone. "Are you well, My Flower?"

"Yes. Just false contractions."

Archard lifts a brow. "False?"

Maha rolls her eyes. "It has been like this for days. You know it."

"I just want to make sure you are well," Archard says, and his hand absently rubs his wife's belly.

For a second, Maha looks up at the group, and her face turns a darker shade of green from embarrassment. I know everybody is looking at them with longing. Everybody is amazed by how a hard man like Archard is so soft with Maha.

Their story is famous, from the Moon Palace to the Sacred Lands. It is exquisite.

A Seelie Princess and Feyada General. Something that should have been impossible. Though they made it happen. They stood against the traditions and got married. Their love defeated all their enemies.

I cannot stop but be amazed by it myself.

What a love. And without a mating bond. My heart fills with hope and warmth, and everything good.

It is possible.

Archard lifts Maha to her feet and wraps an arm around her waist. "Want me to carry you, Love?"

"No, no, walking is good."

He lifts a brow skeptically. Maha can barely walk these days.

She throws her head back to look at her husband. Maha is tall like most Seelie, but Davon Archard is unbelievably big. His wing size is almost double of mine. It is weird that he doesn't have a known family history with many unique traits. He is a Moonfolk with red hair, for Tisasa's sake.

Unfortunately, no one knows his family history because he is an orphan. An orphan who managed to climb this high in the Moon Kingdom and married a Seelie princess.

He is not my favorite person with his cold demeanor, but I respect him greatly.

In the end, Maha gives all her weight to her husband and takes a step. "You can carry me when we reach the stairs."

Woe in Total Darkness

"Deal," Archard says with a small smile, but when he looks back at the group, his expression hardens at once. He gives those soft looks and smiles to Maha alone.

He looks at us like he wants to kill us. Even his respectful nod to me feels like a threat.

I feel like he has a monster inside of him, and his wife is the only thing keeping it locked in.

Thank Tisasa for Maha.

For more reasons than one.

———— ᴄ ————

As dinnertime comes close, fewer people stay with us in the garden. The weather also gets colder. I make one of my chambermaids bring me a coat. Yet I still stay in the garden. I missed just sitting here with Qyron. Our trip to the Shifter Territory was tiresome. We need some rest.

After the long day, even our pet foxes are tired. Many royals excuse themselves, no doubt, to get ready for dinner, and the foxes lay in our laps.

"You are not getting ready for dinner?" Qyron asks, scratching the back of Surya's head.

I smirk. *"I am going to be so ready for tomorrow's dinner, so I am keeping it casual tonight."*

Qyron smiles but then the smile changes. It is such a small thing, but I can see it dim. "Rionn's coming."

Oh.

Well, at least he didn't call him a puppy this time. Progress.

Rionn and Qyron were not as hostile to each other after the mating ceremony. I am happy about it, but I also cannot stop thinking about what would have happened if Rionn knew I kissed Qyron. I haven't told him because I really didn't want to push the progress back.

It is best to keep it a secret. It didn't mean anything anyway. Kisses never mean anything to me.

I relax in my chair. There is nothing to worry about. Everything is going according to my way.

I just smile and look out to the palace where my fiancé is coming toward us in his Earthling form. "Why are you still here?" he yells as he comes.

"Weather is nice today," I answer.

Rionn gives me a skeptical look and comes closer to wrap his arms around me. "Is that why you are wearing a coat?"

"Okay, we are just being lazy."

He nibbles my jaw playfully, then pulls back so Qyron can also understand what he is saying. "We have many important guests tonight."

That makes Qyron straighten. "Did the Sunfolk group come?"

Rionn nods. "They newly arrived."

"Was my sister with them?"

Rionn pulls me away from the chair and sits on it himself, placing me on his lap, my back to him. Only then does he answers, "Lenora?"

I can see Qyron putting so much effort not to roll his eyes. "Yes, Princess Lenora Mitharaus, my only sister. She has blonde hair and the same sun eyes as me."

I feel Rionn's fingers flex on my thigh. "I know how Lenora looks like."

Qyron gets to his feet. "So, is she here?"

"No," my fiancé answers and presses a kiss to my neck. "They came on *davatas*. Feyadas must be here later tonight."

I relax with the answer. I knew Lenora was coming for the wedding. I actually thought she was going to be here earlier. I am thankful that she is not. I don't want to see the perfect princess so soon. She has everything I work so hard for.

She is always better than me.

This time I want to be better. This is my wedding. The best is to avoid her as much as possible.

Unfortunately, it is always hard to keep her away from my mind even if she is physically not here. It is going to be hard but I need to do it for Qyron's sake.

Woe in Total Darkness

He loves her so much. Sometimes I also feel insecure, wondering if he loves her more than me. I don't have any siblings. I only have Qyron, while he has a twin. A perfect, loveable twin.

Life is easier when I act like she doesn't exist. I haven't seen her for many years. I thought I would when Maha married but she didn't attend the wedding.

Even though she will attend mine, I will not let her ruin my day.

I press myself back to Rionn, wanting his warmth.

"I should go welcome them," Qyron signs to me.

I understand. He probably misses his home way more than he shows. *"Of course."*

When he leaves, it is only Rionn and me. I turn in his hold and smile. "I missed you."

He kisses my cheek. "I always miss you."

"We should probably get ready for dinner, right?"

Rionn gets a naughty look in his eyes and squeezes my thigh. "Maybe we can manage some extra activity before that."

I giggle. "Well, don't tire yourself so much, Alpha. I am planning to keep you in bed for days after the wedding." I can think of many things I will enjoy more, but I am also aware that is what is expected of a newlywed couple.

"Just like you did after the mating ceremony?" He asks.

"Exactly like that."

Rionn presses a kiss to my heated cheek. "You know we can start it tonight,"

I actually might prefer making love to Rionn to a dinner where I most likely will see Lenora Mitharaus but there are things I am obligated to do. The mating ceremony was for us. I did it to make Rionn happy and to connect with his people, but the wedding is different. I need to have a great big wedding where I can impress the whole Isle. They have to be amazed. They have to love me for it.

It is something I cannot run away from. I need to oblige to tradition.

I nudge Rionn's nose with mine, hiding all my worries. I am good at that. "We should stay separated before the wedding. No one told you? We will sleep in different beds for the last time tonight."

Some concern appears on his face, and he holds my face tenderly. "Are you sure? I know your nightmares are getting worse."

They are getting worse, and the idea of sleeping alone terrifies me. So my real plan is not to sleep alone. I want to sleep with Qyron because he is the one who can fight my nightmares the best. I want us to have one last night together. I want a farewell to my best friend.

But I cannot tell that to Rionn. "I want to do it. I can handle it, I promise."

The concern doesn't go away, but Rionn forces a smile for my sake. I know he doesn't want to say no to me. "Okay, My Moon," he says and continues with a husky tone, "After tonight, I will always be with you anyway. I will fight your nightmares for you."

I smile and kiss him, hoping he is strong enough to defeat the darkness.

I hope at least someone is.

9

Lenora

We start our descent when I spot the perfectly white walls of the Moon Palace through the clouds. We had to take more stops than I anticipated. We needed to change clothes. The Moon Kingdom is so fucking cold.

It doesn't have the rush of the desert. It feels too strange.

I don't belong here.

This is the land of the beautiful and graceful princess. I am not built for that.

This is no place for a fighter. There are not even any Patches of Darkness. The moon illuminates the whole city. I don't think there is anything for me here.

I have no purpose.

I feel empty.

But still, I go. I can take something from here. I can benefit from this. I just need to focus. Some fights need to be won over tasty meals and wine. I cannot stab every problem with my sword. I need to be a princess.

A soldier but also a politician. I need to be the princess my people need.

Sem Thornwood

I can do this.

When we touch the ground, I try so hard not to let my wings relax. I just want to let them down after all that flying, but that is a look I cannot afford. So, my wings stay erect behind me. I also cover the exhaustion from my face. There is a certain way a soldier is expected to look, and even though normally I am not very strict on it, I am now. I believe the actions show success more than the appearances, but I am in a place almost everybody sees me as a princess before a soldier. I need to impress them for them to respect me as the General of the Sun Army.

Moonfolk loves appearances, after all.

Because it is late at night, there are only a few servants and soldiers to welcome us. All my work seems unnecessary against this small crowd, but then a figure appears in the doorway. He is tall, even taller than King Luran. Auburn wings folded on his back, and his same-color hair is a little messy. His brown eyes, which are surrounded by thick lashes, are only a shade lighter than his skin.

It has been a while, but he is impossible to not recognize. "General Archard," I greet. "How nice of you to come out at this late hour to greet me."

He gives a hard look at my mockery. "It wasn't my decision."

Before I can ask, another person appears next to him. She is jumping more than walking toward me, one hand supporting her swollen belly, and there is a huge grin on her face. Archard's hand wraps around his wife's arm. "My Flower, please."

Her attention turns to him from me, and her green eyes widen. "Oh right, no jumping. Sorry."

Archard only puts a small kiss on her cheek as an answer. It is so unbelievable how careful he is with her. I always thought he was worse than me when it came to our job. I care about it so much that nothing can compare. I thought Archard was like me.

Obviously, I am wrong. I realized it when I attended their wedding. He even looks at her in a different way. It is wonderful.

All the hardness disappears from my face as I look at Maha. She is a source of joy. I take longer steps so she won't jump again. She looks like she might bust even under her white nightdress.

Woe in Total Darkness

When I am in front of her, I cup her neck and press my forehead to hers. She is only a little shorter than me. Our horns touch with the movement as well. I know this is not an appropriate greeting in the Moon Kingdom, but neither of us is Moonfolk. Only her husband is.

"I haven't seen you in so long, Lenora," Maha chirps when we pull back.

I nod in agreement, and my eyes go to her belly. "You are huge!"

Maha smiles proudly and Archard rubs her waist with affection. "I know, right! I think it has wings. Seelie babies are not this big. They do most of their growing up after birth."

"At least Seelies have large birth canals. There are horrible stories about Earthlings trying to birth to winged babies."

This doesn't scare off Maha. I wouldn't have said it if I thought it would anyway. She just gives me a determined look. "I can do it. I am stronger than I look."

Before I can say it, Archard murmurs, "You definitely are."

Maha gets a huge grin and looks at her husband with her heart in her eyes. Archard is not my favorite person, but I am happy he is with Maha. He makes her really happy, and Maha definitely deserves it.

I never believed Archard would go against his king, but he did it for Maha. It made me respect him more than anything he ever did.

I guess the last time I saw Maha was at her wedding. She was happy back then, and she is happy now.

Also, among everyone who can welcome me into this palace, she is at the top of my list.

Things that start well go well. This is going to be a successful trip.

———❡———

The warmth of the welcome Maha provided disappears more quickly than I guess. As a servant shows me my chamber, I require odalisque to settle down since I haven't brought any of my own.

The young Feyada male looks at me like I have two heads. "We do not have odalisque in the Moon Palace, Princess. I might advise you about a few clubs in the city, though."

For a second, I don't understand, but then I see the redness creeping into his neck and ears. He is a believer in ridiculous rumors about the Sun Palace. He thinks I am asking for a whore.

"By odalisque, I meant chambermaid. I need to settle."

"Oh," he says, turning even redder. "Of course, Princess." He looks uncertain for a second but then adds, "Still, I should warn you that chambermaids are different than odalisque in some matters."

"Don't worry. I know." They are definitely different in many ways, but it is not the way he thinks. Odalisque is not obligated to sleep with anyone, just like chambermaids. Though an odalisque sleeping with a royal is not a scandal. They are not mere servants. They are part of the court and have great potential.

They are something the Northerners will not understand.

Only thing I say to the servant as he shows me my room is, "You may call me General Len and not Princess."

I need them to understand that. I need to force them to respect me even though they will never respect the culture I come from.

Thankfully two chambermaids come and help me settle into my room. I don't keep them long. I am already tired from the flight. I remove my light flying gear and my robes in exchange for a sleep shirt. I am extremely hungry, but it is better to just sleep. I will see King Luran in the morning. I need to be ready.

Just before I can get into bed, a knock comes from the door. Since I sent back the guards, it is already locked. I don't like anyone in my business, so no one should wait at my door. I open the door myself and see my second welcomer this night.

Rionn Ay Ujk is standing in my doorway with a pot in his hands. He is a bit taller than me and much broader. His black hair is perfectly made. I can tell he didn't come out of bed. He was already waiting for me. He is wearing black pants and a black shirt. So unlike Shifters. He is more clothed than I have ever seen him.

His throat moves up and down as his eyes look at me with fascination. "General," he nods.

Woe in Total Darkness

I cannot even stay serious. So much has happened. So much is upon my shoulders. I need a friend. I need to relieve tension.

A grin appears on my face. "Did you miss me, Rionn?"

His dark eyes turn playful. "I thought my letters made it quite obvious."

"Apparently not enough." *Give me more.*

"Maybe I can show it to you if you welcome me inside."

A laugh escapes, and I step aside for him to get in. When he does, I close and lock the door again. I am planning to keep him here for a little. I am tired, but I need this more. I need a distraction.

Rionn is the best at that.

He puts the pot on the desk. "I brought you soup. You must be hungry."

I am hungry, but not just for food. I don't want to think about anything. Thankfully when I kiss Rionn he kisses me back and he lets me pull him to the bed. I don't have to fight him for dominance. He knows that is the only way I like it.

I have no feelings for him like Andy predicted but sometimes I just need a warm body to erase my pain. It is not always so easy to get exactly what I want. Rionn is good at providing it.

It is just skin on skin. Nothing more.

But I like how he is also trying to be a friend. After our playing in the sheet is done, he puts back on his pants. I wear my nightshirt again, and we sit at the table. He watches me with the remaining pleasure in his eyes as I eat.

"How is your soup?" Rionn asks.

I give him a smirk. "Cold."

His only chuckles.

I take a spoonful of my cold soup. The food still feels good. Having Rion watch me with hungry eyes is good too, but I need something different from him now. We are both here for a purpose, and he arrived earlier. "So, tell me. What does King Luran want?"

He lifts one dark eyebrow. "Why do you think I know?"

Sem Thornwood

There is no debate. For whatever reason, I am here. He is here for the same. The Moon King has something going on, and even though I am sure he is going to share it with me tomorrow, I want some insight now. I want to be ready for whatever he is going to throw at me.

"You know," I push.

He thinks for a moment, like considering the consequences of telling me, but then he speaks, "It is about the Princess."

"Princess?" I guessed but it still sounds too absurd.

Rionn's dark eyes focus on me. "Princess Zuraya."

Even though I knew it was her, the name still makes me go rigid. I don't want to think about her. I don't want to talk about her. Most importantly, I don't want to guess what the King might want from me concerning her.

Princess Zuraya is someone I want to bury, but apparently, she is the only way I will be able to bargain with the King. I take a deep breath and say, "Tell me."

10

Zuraya

It is not dark. A candle is shining dimly in my room. I draw shapes in the air with my hand and make them shine. Everything is okay.

It is okay because I am awake. I cannot go to sleep.

I am so afraid of not waking up and going back to that darkness. I am not strong enough for that.

As I try to gather my courage to close my eyes, I hear the creaking of my door. I look up, holding my hand for the light, even though the candle is enough to light Qyron's form. He sneakily gets into my room. I can tell he is walking on his tiptoes. He has his tricks to be silent, but they usually don't work on me. I can feel his presence even if I cannot hear him.

"You awake," he signs before getting in the bed with me. *"I guessed it."*

"You did?" I smile. He knows me so well.

"You have a wedding tomorrow. You must be freaking out."

"I am already married. Nothing to worry about."

Qyron gives me a no-nonsense look. It has little to do with the marriage. Being with Rionn doesn't scare me, but I feel overwhelmed. I just know if I close my eyes, I will be sucked into the dark and cold. I don't want to let myself go. I want to stay on my guard. Otherwise, I'll fall hard.

I cannot afford a fall. I am Princess Zuraya Haliyes.

But I don't want to tell those to Qyron. I know he already knows, anyway. I attempt to change the subject. *"Has your sister arrived?"*

He gives me a look like he knows what I am doing, but he also cannot help his smile. *"She is here,"* he signs, and my heart squeezes. I don't want to share him with her.

I wish Qyron was my sibling. I wish Princess Lenora never existed. She is the constant reminder that Qyron is not really mine. He is not Moonfolk. He is only here as a guest. He has a family back in the desert. I am not his whole life while he is mine.

It is unhealthy, but I cannot help it. I want one thing I love to be only mine.

"You must be happy." I try my best to have a genuine smile.

Qyron's skin glows, making my expression even more visible, and he lifts a brow. *"You made me get along with Rionn. You have to get along with Lenora."*

He is absolutely right, but I don't want to accept it. *"Can I do that tomorrow? I am not in the mood now."*

He grins. *"Absolutely."*

I am telling the truth. I will put in an effort to get along with Lenora. I will do it for Qyron. I just don't want to think about it now. I want to just stay in the moment with my best friend.

I want to relax.

To sleep.

"Do you have a vision?" I ask. I rarely ask him that. The whole world is bugging him enough. But now I just need it. I need the comfort of knowing.

For a moment, he looks at me with sad eyes but then smiles. *"It is all going to be good. I can feel it."*

"Feel or see?"

"Why not both?"

I smile and wiggle in bed to get closer to him. I put a hand between our faces, and he puts his own over it. Our fingers intertwine. It feels so familiar.

We would lie like this when we were little. When Qyron was a scared eight-year-old, and I was his seven-year-old savior. He was sent away here, far from his home, his family, his twin. Meant to be mine.

The Southern side of the Isle was dangerous because of the Patches of Darkness. I have never seen one, but I couldn't find it in me to hate them. They brought me Qyron. We would have never been best friends if not for them.

Back then, we didn't care about the Patches. We didn't care about the person behind it, who was called the Curser. We were safe in the Moon Kingdom. We were two lonely kids who found each other. Qyron taught me sign language. I let him stay late at my room. I let him sleep in my bed, holding my hand just like right now. We became each other's home.

A safe haven.

Without him, I'll crumble.

We have slept together like this almost every night since then. He was right here in my bed the night they came. The night that still gives me nightmares.

"Do you remember?" I whisper, my skin dimly shining.

Qyron's eyes fill with tears. *"I cannot forget."*

I don't know if he has nightmares like me or if his demons come to him in different forms. He never tells me. He never wants to talk about that night. We survived, but he acted like we didn't. I do my best to not remind him.

But I need to let it out.

"I should have seen it," Qyron signs with regret in his eyes. Even years later, that look is the same. I watched him blame himself over it for days. My words never made anything better. No harm was done. We were okay.

Still, Qyron never stopped feeling guilty.

Everybody asked him about it. How in the world did our perfect seer miss the attack? How did Qyron fail?

They wanted to know. We never told them the truth.

It didn't matter. Everything was okay.

"We were kids," I try to soothe him. We were thirteen and fourteen when the attack happened. It was not his fault, and I hate seeing him like this. It doesn't fit his sunshine.

Qyron shakes his head. *"We were kids doing things they weren't supposed to."*

No, we were just kids trying to have fun. We felt alone. We only had each other. Either of us didn't know it could be harmful. We thought we were safe in the Moon Palace. Curser and his followers were not in the North. They could not touch us.

We didn't know they could come into my room that night.

Qyron's eyes lose focus for a moment, like he is still in this bed but at another time. He is in another reality. "Things could have been so much different," he murmurs so quietly that I almost don't hear it.

I squeeze his hand. *"I don't want it. This is the most perfect version of my life."*

A sad little smile pulls on his lips, but I can feel his affection all over me. *"It is, isn't it?"*

I nod and get even closer to him. I want to make him happy.

"I wish I could have protected you that night, Zuraya."

I shake my head and kiss the hand that covers mine. When I put my head back on my pillow, I remember years ago. I remember the night we slept like this and what we told each other before we went to sleep every night. We never did after the attack.

But it shouldn't matter. An attack cannot touch us. They failed, and we won. Curser or the Darkness cannot touch us anymore.

I take a deep breath, but before I can move, Qyron almost reads my mind. He signs the words he told me every night instead of the good night when we were little, *"You are my heart."*

I smile and sign my answer, *"You are my breath."*

We cannot exist without each other and will never need to.

Our heads come closer, and we both close our eyes. For the first time in a long time, I believe the nightmares will not come tonight. Qyron will protect me from them.

Tonight, I am going to be rescued from the darkness.

11

Zuraya

It is dark.
It is cold.
It feels too real.
Oh, Tisasa, why does this feel so real? It is just a nightmare. I wasn't supposed to have one tonight. Qyron was supposed to protect me.
I don't want to be here.
I try to open my eyes. It is easier than before. Almost too easy.
Earthling across from me is still gone. It is only me in this very tiny room. My ankles hurt from the ice wrapped around them. I try to move. That is not too easy, but I manage enough to feel the coldness surrounding them. It is shackled. I am naked and shackled in this room.
I want to wake up.
I close my eyes, squeeze and open them again, but it doesn't work. I am still in this hellish place. The air is so moist. It is so heavy. I feel like my magic is struggling, just like my body. This room is worse than a prison. It eats me from the inside. I cannot stay here longer.
I need help.

Please wake me up.

Just when I close my eyes again, I hear distant sounds. Such low noise. It is not like Qyron's sweet whispers trying to wake me up. It is coming from outside the room. Chatter, whispers, footsteps, and everything else I cannot understand.

Please, I plea, even though I cannot speak. *Whoever you are, just wake me up.*

My eyes feel heavy, and the sounds get louder. I feel so weak. I don't want to be weak. Something I don't know is coming here. I cannot let go, just like I did years ago.

I cannot let sleep capture me.

I need to fight. Are they here to hurt me?

Please don't hurt me.

I just want to wake up.

Where is Qyron? He should be next to me. He should stop them. He should wake me up. We are not kids anymore. We are not weak.

Protect me, please. Don't let them touch me again.

A sob catches in my throat, but I am even too tired to cry. I cannot even manage that. *Please don't let them take me.*

They are here to take me.

The room is moist, but my eyes are even more now. My cheeks are wet with tears. Everything around me is both dark and blurry. My back aches with lightness, my ankles burn, and my body is too damn weak. I cannot escape this I am bound.

Someone, please rescue me.

I cannot take this anymore.

When I lose hope, I see a light. It is bright and warm. I can even see it with my bad vision.

It is beautiful.

I want to hold onto it. I want it to save me, but just when a figure forms in the light, my eyelids close shut. I fall back to sleep.

Back to the dark.

—— c ——

Woe in Total Darkness

I don't wake up in my room. I don't wake up to Qyron.

My consciousness comes back to me slowly. I feel so tired, so heavy. My back still aches, and my ankles are burning. I feel sick. My head is spinning even though my eyes are closed.

I can feel a hard surface under me. I am lying face down. I am not naked like I was in my dream, but I don't feel my soft nightshirt either. There is only a heavy cloak over me, covering my body.

And most importantly, the floor is moving. It is making me sicker.

Where the fuck am I?

Panic settles in slowly. I try to open my eyes. I try to listen. I need to understand where I am. I need to act quickly. This is not good. I need to be in my bed.

"I don't feel good about holding her like this," says an unfamiliar voice. He doesn't sound harmful, but I cannot be sure.

Then someone speaks much closer to me. Voice is feminine but also hard and absolutely flawless. "She will get her bed before she can open her eyes. It is okay."

Oh, my Goddess, where am I?

Actually, now that I am awake, I can tell. I still feel dizzy, but I can tell that I am in a cart or a carriage. The important question is where are we going because clearly, they are taking me somewhere. It almost feels like all those years ago. Even though they never got to take me, I feel like I am living this moment for the second time.

Everything feels so horrifyingly familiar.

I push my body and manage to flutter open my eyes. I see a set of brown boots in front of my face. I cannot focus on the condition of my body, and my sight is not very clear because I am still too dizzy. Despite it all, I gather my courage and look up at the owner of the shoes. I am faced with probably the most glorious being I have ever seen.

She is a Feyada. She has broad shoulders under her white robes and light golden armor. She has delicate white horns, and all of the skin I can see is covered with freckles. Her face is hard as stone, and when she looks right at me, my heart stops.

101

Her glory scares me. She looks powerful. I don't know how I can fight her.

I barely see the side of her lips tip up before she mocks, "Look at that. Princess is awake."

I don't know if I should ask something or try to attack her. But we are not alone in this cart. I am not even good at fighting. This is a losing battle from the beginning. Tears fill my eyes at feeling so helpless.

I wonder who they are. I cannot see her very well. I don't know her voice. Are they working for Curser? Are they the same people who came seven years ago?

No, that is impossible. Those people were executed alongside Curser. He is gone. The Darkness is gone. This cannot be real.

"Where are we going?" I ask with a hoarse voice. I don't know how that is going to help me. I am desperate, and I feel too numb to freak out.

She looks away from me. Her whole body is tense. "Home."

Home?

Whose home?

I cannot even say anything else because that was not the answer I was expecting from her. I wanted something helpful. She is being too weird. She looks like someone who lost even though she successfully kidnapped me.

It is an impossible situation, and my body is throbbing.

I focus on her face. Why is she not happy? I am here lying at her feet, helpless. What more does she want?

Then a thought comes to me. I remember how I was not alone in my bedroom. It was the same as years ago. Qyron was there with me. He is not now.

A horrible feeling fills my chest, and I blink a few times before looking up at her. She still has all the glory I spotted before, but there is also something else. This time I can see the color of her eyes. They are like melted gold, like a flaming fire.

They are just like the sun.

My heart beats so hard in my chest, and tears sprang to my cheeks. I use all my power to stand up, at least on my knees. My body feels too light, but I have to do this. I clutch her knees to stay upright. And then I scream, "What have you done to him?"

Her body turns even tenser, and she looks at me like I am crazy. She looks at me like she is not the one who is kidnapping me. I hate her.

"What have you done to Qyron?" I scream again, and she looks angry. I don't care. I need to know. I need to know what she did to her twin brother. "Where is he, Lenora?"

"Shut up and lay back down," she snarls. Her orange eyes are burning with rage at me.

It doesn't stop me. Only the answer will stop me. I try my best to reach into her face to scratch her skin, but someone holds me back from my waist. It feels good to have support to stand, but I cannot reach her face. She doesn't even flinch at my attempt to assault her. She is too cocky.

Why is she doing this? She should be on our side.

What does she want from me?

"General, maybe you should use your power," someone suggests. I have no idea who the General is, but when I turn to him, I see him looking at Lenora. Is she a General in this religious cult?

I shake my head. Confusion is wrapped around my weak body. I don't want her to use her powers because I know I cannot resist. I know she can shut down my brain. I cannot let her do that. I have to fight back. I need to get free.

I want to go back to my palace.

Today is my wedding day. Someone must be searching for me.

"If you attack, I'll attack back," I warn even though I cannot feel my magic at all. There is all darkness inside me. My heart is all dimmed.

Lenora smiles, but there is no joy on her face. "You think I need my fucking power to knock you out?"

I cannot answer that, so I push my other question, "Where is Qyron?"

"Don't speak of his name!" she sneers.

"What have you done to him, Lenora?" I shout again. "He trusted you. What have you done to Qyron? Why did you fail him? How can you..."

I cannot finish my words because Lenora punches me in the face. Her fiery eyes fill with pain as much as anger. She doesn't even give me time to think. She just swings, and the force is so strong that I am surprised for a few seconds before my body meets the floor, and my eyes close again, looking at the Sun Princess's feet.

———*———

The second time I open my eyes, it feels more peaceful. I am not on a cart, but instead, I am wrapped around with softness. It is quiet too. However, my vision is still blurry, and my body still doesn't feel quite like mine. Also, my cheek aches.

Oh, Tisasa, what is happening?

I forcefully flutter my lashes, trying to get my vision back. My body feels so weird. It is not only pain. I feel light.

When I can actually see around me, I realize I am safely tucked in my bed, inside my room. Everything looks familiar. I force my body to get up, and the second my head leaves the pillow, I start spinning. I feel drunk.

But I am at home.

Did someone save me?

What happened?

I want to know. I want all the answers. For a second, I think about yelling for a chambermaid, but I cannot trust them yet. I cannot trust anything or anyone. I need to figure out what is happening.

I try to lift my body off of the familiar bed. I feel light but trying to get up is almost impossible. I have no strength. My arms and legs scream from the pain as I peel my limbs off the linens and let the covers fall off my body.

My eyes barely look down my body. I see the blue fabric. I cannot recall this nightgown, but it is not my biggest worry. I need to move. I need answers.

Woe in Total Darkness

My knees shake when I finally put my feet on the floor. The cool marble feels familiar. I am back at home. I am safe. Yet nothing feels right. I want to disregard everything as a nightmare. I want to believe it was caused by my negative feelings towards Lenora Mitharaus, and it was all in my head.

But for some reason, it doesn't sound right.

I hardly take a step. My eyes can see better now, but I cannot find my balance. Walking feels so wrong. I can only take three steps before I stumble onto the floor, hitting my knees hard on the surface. A cry comes to my lips, but I force it down. I cannot make a sound before I am sure it is safe.

I raise my head with tears in my eyes but the second I look up, I freeze. I can see myself in the floor-length mirror. It is far away, but it doesn't matter. I look horrible. My neat braids are gone, and my hair looks oily and dirty. My skin is ashen. My piercings are nowhere to be seen. One of my horns is broken from the tip. I look like I came back from the dead.

However, none of those are important. I barely notice them because there is something much more important.

I don't have my wings.

My eyes sting, and I try to move my wings. I can swear I feel them.

They don't move.

Ragged breaths leave me, and I crane my neck. I don't see them. My hand goes to my back, and the only thing I feel is bumps of already healed wounds.

I can't think, and I can't move.

I just scream. Tears leave my eyes as I sob. I want to wake up from this. I want Qyron to save me from this hell. This cannot be real.

Two chambermaids rush into the room, no doubt hearing my sobs. I cannot even see their faces from my tears. I cannot take this. It is more painful than all the nightmares I had. I need to wake up.

Maids try to hold my body that shakes from the sobs. "Princess, what happened?" they ask, and I wonder if they are stupid. *Isn't it obvious what happened? How can she ask me that?*

"Qyron," I manage to say between sobs. Whatever this is, nightmare or reality, he is the person I need. I cannot go through this on my own. I need my best friend.

"What?" says the maid.

"Get me, Qyron," I continue crying. I repeat it over and over again. "Please."

They don't answer me. Why is no one answering me? What did Lenora do to me?

"Please," I beg again. I'll die if I need to do this alone.

"Princess, do you want me to get your father?"

"I want Qyron."

She stays silent again for a while, and I cry even harder. "I am sorry, Princess, but I cannot do that."

Why? I want to ask why. I want to yell at her with all my might, but I cannot. I am so empty.

I cannot fight her, so this time I ask for the next person I can think of. "Rionn. Get me, Rionn, then." My sobs stop with the feeling of helplessness, but my tears keep falling down my cheeks to my neck.

After a few seconds, the maid asks, "Rionn Ay Ujk?"

"Yes," I cry softly. "Please get my fiancé."

12

Lenora

I stay in front of the stone archway. My hands curl into fists and then open to flex. Again. And again. This place always made me nervous. My heart beats so fast that I can hear it in my ears. Zuraya's words made everything even harder.

I wish I had come here more in the last seven years. I wish I had visited my brother more. It makes my heart ache because I know what Zuraya said is the truth. Qyron always trusted me. He always trusted me, and I failed him. Visiting here reminds me of that.

Princess Lenora Mitharaus, Heir of Sunshine, General of the Sun Army, the Lightbringer couldn't save her brother.

My biggest failure. My biggest mistake.

I wish I could take it back. And for a few hopeful, stupid hours, I believed I could. Moon King decided to see me in private hurriedly. He told me he had intel about the location of the Princess. He wanted me to save her. In return, he was going to give me all the moon spheres I desired.

Of course, I agreed, but my mind was not focused on the Princess. It was not even focused on the moon spheres. I had only one thought, and it was finding Qyron alongside Zuraya.

Even though I knew it was not possible.

For the last seven years, Zuraya has been missing.

Qyron was *dead.*

My throat tightens with the thought. I still cannot accept that he is gone. Every night I fall asleep thinking he might come back tomorrow.

He never does.

With a deep inhale, I step inside the tomb. This one is smaller than the one back home. No one knows which one really holds his body but my mom. She wanted to have two tombs because both of these places were his home. I know he loved the desert, but he also loved these lands. Despite everything, he was happy here. He was happy with Zuraya.

Sometimes I still feel so jealous of her. She got to have him more than I did. She got the love I deserved.

I don't even have many memories of him when he was older. Yet I can recall almost everything when we were little. I remember having classes together with him every day. I remember how my mother always preferred him, but I was never jealous. I would choose him over me too.

I remember once my mother took him out of classes for a trip around the desert. Qyron wanted me to join, but mother didn't let me come. She said I was the heir and I needed those classes more than Qyron. She took him from me as he looked at me with sorrow. The next day when they came back, he made me sneak out of the class, and we played around as he told me everything he saw.

I can feel tears fill my eyes. There is not a day I don't miss my brother.

There is not a moment I don't wish it was me instead of him.

Carefully I reach and touch the words carved into the stone. *Prince Qyron Mitharaus, Blessed with Sunshine.*

I wonder if he really feels blessed right now. If he can feel anything at all. I want to believe it. I want to believe there is something after death, and he is happy there. My logic never accepts the concept of an afterlife, but I always force myself because I don't want to admit that he is just dirt now.

Woe in Total Darkness

He deserved better.

Without even realizing it, tears start to slide down my cheeks. I don't try to stop it. I don't try to look tough. I am sad because I lost him, and I am not ashamed. Anyone would be sad over losing someone like Qyron.

I kneel next to the stone that is supposedly covering his body. I press my forehead to the cold surface. Rubies and emeralds dug into my skin. It is a pretty tomb. Qyron would have liked it. Unfortunately, it doesn't matter.

I cry softly, touching the stone. I want him back. I want a miracle. Everything would have been better if he had been here. No one believed Zuraya could be found as well. Why can't Qyron come back too? Why is life so unfair? I'd give everything to see him one more time. Just to hold him or tell him how much I loved him.

I know I didn't say it enough.

We had so little time.

"Len?" I hear a worried familiar voice. My eyes open, but I hardly move my head as I look at Rionn. He looks tense before coming to kneel next to me. A strong hand closes over my shoulder. "Are you okay?"

No, I want to scream. I am never okay. There is nothing out there to make me feel okay. I am so sad and tired, and I am slowly vanishing. I want one good thing to happen.

I want a miracle.

Until that happens, I am not okay.

Still, I answer with a soft, "Yes." I cannot imagine saying anything else.

"I was worried about you," he says gently. He doesn't need to be gentle or seek me out. We are not friends. We just fuck sometimes, but we are nothing. He needs to understand that for everyone's sake. But before I can even open my mouth, he continues. "You seemed out of your mind back there."

That gets my attention. It is about our mission, and he is gently saying I sucked. I don't have the luxury to suck. With an angry face, I turn to him. Drying tears on my cheeks most likely making me look even scarier. "What do you mean?"

"You seemed too excited to get into that shed. Even after we found the Princess, you didn't calm. You sent her off and kept checking around. That was not a job for a General. You acted like a newbie."

My power boils inside me. "I saved the Princess."

"With luck."

"Don't fucking question my methods, Rionn. You have no authority to do that." I can feel my palms burn with the Sunshine.

Something flashes in Rionn's eyes, but he is better than me at keeping his cool. It is annoying. "You were looking for him," he says softly. He says it like he understands, but he can't. No one can understand this pain.

I close my eyes and bite down my bottom lip. I don't answer him because I don't want to lie. I just want some peace with my brother. I want to be left alone with him. I visit his tomb back home, but for some reason, I feel like his body is actually here. This means more to me. "Just leave me alone," I whisper so softly that I am not sure if he even hears me.

Anyway, before he can react in any way, a feminine voice calls out shyly, "Sir Alpha?"

I cringe inwardly. He is just the Alpha, but some of the Moon Court has a tendency to be stupid. Unlike me, Rionn doesn't care and turns to the maid in blue robes. "Yes?"

When she doesn't answer right away, I look at her too. I am strangely intrigued. She twists her fingers nervously. "The Princess wanted to see you," she says, looking between us.

I am surprised that she woke up this early. I actually wanted to be there when she woke. I wanted to be the first person to talk to her. I need her intel.

But I am still baffled by the request.

"She wanted me?" Rionn asks, confused.

Maid nods, but I can see that she is no less surprised. "First, she wanted to see Prince Qyron," she swallows, and an angry pain stabs my chest. "Then she said she wanted to see Rionn Ay Ujk."

I look at him with furrowed brows. "Why would she want to see you?"

Woe in Total Darkness

"I have no idea. I don't think she saw me; even if she did, she could not know me. We never met."

I lick my teeth and murmur, "Interesting." There is something weird going on, and I need to know. My assignment might not be done yet, so I stand up and brush away dust from my knees and let my power free on my skin so the sunshine can dry the tears on my cheeks. I look at Rionn. "I'll come with. Let's go."

———c———

I follow the maid with Rionn alongside me. I have been to Princess's room before, but I don't remember. When we reached the palace, I let Davon carry her. After she railed me up to punch her, I wanted to stay away.

Moon King can still get mad at me for that punch. It was a stupid move on my part, but Qyron is always a very delicate subject for me.

Anyway, I feel things are more complicated than me punching his little girl. Whatever reason Zuraya called Rionn for is going to be enough to make us forget any other problem out there.

When we reach the big door with silver linings, the chambermaid turns to us with some worry in her eyes. "She was a little out of it when I left her."

I almost roll my eyes. "She was imprisoned for seven years. What were you expecting?" The maid keeps looking at me with huge eyes, so I sigh and point to the door with my chin. "Open it."

She seems not sure but still complies. I step inside the large room, but Rionn looks undecided at the archway. My eyes travel along the white walls and the big bed in the middle of the room. Blue and white curtains are flying all around the room with the wind. And I see Princess Zuraya. She is sitting on the floor, curled up to herself. Next to her, there is a large mirror, but I can only tell from the corner of it because the rest has been covered with fabric. It is not so hard to guess what happened.

I was expecting to find Zuraya in bad condition. She was going to look older than her pictures, and she was probably going to be tortured. I knew some damage was done, but I was not expecting to find her without wings. That even shocked me.

Cutting off a Feyada's wings is no normal thing. Our wings are not just another limb. They are sacred. They separate us from the rest of the creatures on the Isle. Most Feyadas prefer death over losing their wings.

Not me, though. I find it stupid to put so much value into any body part.

But I know it must hurt Zuraya. I am curious about when they cut her wings. I want to know how much time she had to get used to it. She looks so broken. For some reason, it feels weird. I thought she would be more of a fighter.

Why she still looks so shattered after being rescued?

As I watch her with wonder Princess looks up at me, and her blue eyes fill with hatred. "Why are you here?" she asks. With the next words, her voice cracks, "What did you do to me?"

Tisasa, she really looks hurt. I know the punch was a horrible move, but I am surprised she is holding a grudge for a single punch after being saved from seven years of hell. I don't want to hurt her further. Now that she is not using Qyron's name, I realize how horrible she looks. I don't want to break her. I have never been someone to attack the weak. With a deep inhale, I say, "I am sorry. It was a heat-of-the-moment thing. It is my fault."

Zuraya looks at me like she cannot believe my words. "What are you talking about?" She looks like she cried so hard not so long ago and is so close to crying again.

"The punch," I answer, but I am not so sure anymore.

Tears fill Zuraya's eyes, and she looks at me like I am making fun of her. I can even manage to hurt her when I am not trying. It is a foreign feeling. A sob leaves her, "You cut off my wings!"

What?

"Why the fuck would I cut your wings." *I saved you.*

Zuraya shakes her head. "Why are you here?" she cries. "I didn't ask for you."

At that moment, the person she asked for decides to step inside the room. Rionn comes in and gives me a look that mirrors my own confusion. We both don't know what is happening here.

What have they done to you, Zuraya?

Just a second later, I hear Zuraya's gasp. I look at her and see that she is still teary. There is no more hatred, though. Her eyes have already left me, and now she is focused on Rionn. She looks at him like he is the real savior, like he saved her from me. Her bottom lip trembles and she gets onto her feet in a second. "Rionn," she says with a shaky but grateful voice, and she walks to him with wobbly legs. She manages to get close, and before taking the last few steps, she collapses. Her arms go around Rionn, and she holds him tightly. Her head is buried into his chest, inhaling his scent.

All the while, Rionn stays like a statue and looks at me with huge eyes. Unfortunately, I am just as confused as he is.

13

Zuraya

I hold Rionn close. So close.

He is the only thing keeping me together. His presence assures me that everything is okay. If he is here, everything must be okay. He can save me from this nightmare.

"Rionn," I murmur into his chest. He is so warm and so familiar. Except he is really not. He is my Rionn, but he doesn't hug me back. He is just tense.

I pull back to look at his face and find him looking at Lenora with furrowed brows. "Rionn," I say again. This time he looks at me, but there is no love or softness in his dark eyes. He looks at me like I am a stranger. My heart hurts at his expression. "What is wrong?" I ask. *What did I do?*

His throat moves up and down, and he shakes his head. "I am sorry, Princess, but I am just confused. Why did you call for me?"

Because they didn't let me get Qyron.

I don't say those words. It will only make Rionn mad. However, a side of me wants him to get angry at that because it will feel familiar. It will seem real.

"Who would I call if not you? I wanted Qyron and you. Why is it surprising?"

Woe in Total Darkness

This time Lenora speaks before Rionn can even react. "You called for Qyron?" Her voice stiff.

I look at her with hostility. I have always hated Lenora Mitharaus but never as much as I do at this moment. Whatever is happening to me is all her fault. I am sure of it. "Of course I did. He might be your brother but he is also my best friend."

I expect her to get angry. I want her to burn with the knowledge that Qyron is mine. Yet she doesn't. She only looks at me a little dumbfounded. It bothers me. She did all of this. How dare she acts surprised.

"What did they do to you?" she asks with narrowed eyes.

A joyless laugh escapes me. "Who are you talking about? Just tell me what did *you* do to me!" I am so angry that my whole body trembles. I hold onto Rionn's rigid form.

"I saved you," she says softly.

My blood boils inside me. The chill of the moonshine is nowhere to be found. Tears prick my eyes for the millionth time, and I yell at the Sun Princess, "You cut off my wings!"

She might as well just kill me. It would be less painful. She stole everything from me.

A Feyada without wings is nothing.

"Why the fuck would I cut off your wings?"

Tears slid down my cheeks. "I don't know," I mumble. "Just tell me what is happening. I am so confused. Please help me." I hate begging her, but I have no options left. Rionn is extremely quiet and distant. Qyron is not here. I just want to know.

Lenora nods, and there is understanding in her golden gaze. I hate it more than everything. I don't want her to pity me. I don't want her gentleness.

Unfortunately, I need it.

"Maybe we should sit down," she says, and her eyes lift to Rionn just for a second. That second is enough for him to get me into the couch. Lenora follows suit and sits on a chair. She doesn't look threatening right now. I would never guess she was the one who punched me in the face. Right now, she only looks curious.

"Tell me what you know, Princess," she demands. "Not what you assume but what you know so I can help you."

She is the one who should speak. She should tell me whatever is going on. I want to yell at her face, but Sun Princess is my only way to get answers.

Before I can speak, Rionn asks with uncertainty, "Should I leave?"

"No!" we say at the same time. My hand goes to clutch his arm, and my nails dig into his skin. "Why are you acting like this?" I ask with blurry eyes. He is my only anchor in this nightmare, and he is being so damn unreliable. I want my Rionn back.

"I am sorry," he says, and for a moment, he looks genuinely sorry for me. However, the next second I realize it is more of a pity than sadness. "I really don't know why you would need me."

My mouth falls open, and words die on my tongue. How can I even answer that? It should be pretty clear why I want him here.

"Please sit down, Rionn," Lenora cuts in, and he listens. Since they came, he always listened to her. It is another weird thing I cannot comprehend. Rionn should keep me above the Sun Princess.

When I realize Lenora is looking at me expectedly, I clear my throat. I want to tell her that she kidnapped me and cut off my wings, but they are assumptions. She didn't want those. She wanted facts. So I spit out the biggest fact there is. "Today is my wedding day," I murmur. I turn my head towards Rionn. "Today was our wedding day."

His dark eyes widen, and Lenora says, "What?" a little too roughly. *How can she not know?*

"What does this mean, Rionn?" She asks, her voice almost accusing.

Rionn's rounded eyes turn to her from me. "I have no idea what she is talking about. I promise," he says, and my heart drops.

This is really a nightmare.

"How can you say such a thing, Rionn? We have been engaged for almost two years. We already had our mating ceremony. Today was our wedding day. Everybody came to the Moon Palace for this occasion." I turn to Lenora with pleading eyes. "You came here to attend the wedding."

She looks sad, so sad. I want to punch that expression away from her face. I want to do it harder than she punched me. I try to reach my power. I am gifted. I can make her body hurt without lifting a finger.

I cannot do it, though.

Everything I have valued in my life are falling apart, and I don't even understand how.

Lenora shakes her head. "I didn't come for the wedding Zuraya. Rionn didn't come for the wedding. General Davon got intel about your location, so your father called for all the great warriors on the Isle. We came here to save you, to bring you home."

Her words don't make sense. Rionn has been here for me. Qyron told me Lenora came for the wedding. Lenora is not a great warrior, anyway. She is a princess just like me, and that's all.

She is lying.

I can use all those facts against her, but there is something much more evident. "I have always been here, Lenora. I have been at home."

She nibbles her bottom lip nervously, almost torturing the skin with her teeth. She is also torturing me with her dragging. Then she spits it out, "You have not been here for the last seven years, Zuraya. You were kidnapped."

My eyes widen at her words, but it doesn't make any sense. I have been here. How can I be kidnapped and not know it? I was always here. I never left.

She is wrong.

"Is this supposed to be a joke?" I choke. I always hated Lenora Mitharaus for being perfect, but I never would have guessed she was also this cruel. How can she hurt me this much with her lies?

Lenora looks in a loss for words. She doesn't look at me like it is a joke. Then she has to be crazy. She cannot expect me to believe I was kidnapped and didn't know about it for seven years.

I feel Rionn's arm loosely wrap around my middle as Lenora stays silent. Her eyes follow the movement with an alert, but I don't focus on her. I just turn to the love of my life. The look he gives me is soft, but it is so different than how he normally looks at me.

"She is telling the truth," he whispers. "The Curser attacked the Moon Palace seven years ago and kidnapped you. That's why I was confused. We have never met."

"But we did," I insist with teary eyes. They cannot be serious. "I survived that attack. The Curser died."

Lenora cuts in as tears leave my eyes. "Zuraya, I swear I will find out what they did to you. We will figure this out, but I need time. Will you let me put you to sleep?"

Sleep?

My heart pounds in my chest. She wants to use her power over me, manipulate my mind to close off.

I don't want that. I cannot give up. I might lose my wings and half of a horn and everything I believed, but I won't be weak. I still have some fight in me. I can still wake up from this nightmare. I can do anything. I just need one tiny favor.

I just need him.

"Qyron," I say softly and try not to notice how Lenora tenses. "Just let me see Qyron."

Lenora's jaw flexes, and she answers roughly, "I can't do that."

I want to yell and cry, but I don't think those will work on the Sun Princess. I need to be smart to get Qyron. "I have known him longer than seven years. Maybe Rionn doesn't remember me, but he will. He was my best friend before I got kidnapped too." Lenora stays silent, looking very uncomfortable, and another possibility clogs my throat. "Was he also kidnapped? He was with me the night they came to take me. I remember that. If you also rescued him and think keeping us apart is a good idea, it is not. I am sure you have your reasons, Lenora, but you cannot separate us. We need each other."

Lenora shakes her head like none of my words mean anything. She doesn't look disapproving or angry. She looks sad. I cannot figure her out. "You cannot see Qyron," she says, looking away.

"Why?" I ask with a broken voice. "You cannot keep him away from me, Lenora."

"I am not," she murmurs and then looks at me with orange eyes, Qyron's eyes. "I cannot make you see him. It is not in my power."

I want to say *everything is in your power*, even though I know she has her superiors too. She looks so powerful that my brain doesn't want to believe she cannot do anything.

"Who is stopping you?" I ask. "Tell me, and I'll talk to them. I need Qyron."

Lenora gives me a broken look, and I can almost swear she has tears in her eyes, just like mine. Before I can be sure, she answers me, "I cannot let you see Qyron because he is *dead.*"

And with those words, my heart shatters all over the floor.

14

Lenora

I left Zuraya's room.

Maybe I should have stayed and calmed her. Maybe I should have helped her with her pain. However, I didn't. It is not my responsibility. I cannot stay around her just to watch the pain I went through seven years ago all over again.

I don't want Qyron in my brain more than he already is. I cannot cry while there are people out there who trust me to keep them safe.

Qyron would have understood.

She doesn't want me anyway. She requested Rionn. It's his problem to solve. It is King Luran's problem more than anyone's. I'll gladly let them handle it while I go back to the Desert with my moon spheres to fight the Darkness Curse and hunt the Curser. With Zuraya's rescue, we might be able to get closer to catching them.

I will be in touch with General Archard about that, but right now, all I want to do is go back home. I don't like this damp weather here. I need to go back to the Desert.

When the Moon King granted me his presence two days ago, I made sure our agreement let me go back home as soon as possible. I hated being here. So when he told me about the rescue mission, I had my own requirements.

I told him I wanted moon spheres in return, for the Seelie Lands and for me.

It was a cocky move. King Luran is a man who takes without needing to give. Yet he didn't seem surprised after I also refused to kneel for him. He might be a strong warrior once upon a time, but he lost his title to me. Now people call me the Lightbringer.

I only kneel for people who earned my respect, and King Luran definitely didn't.

The only good thing is that he agreed to my terms. Bring back the Moon Princess and get the moon spheres.

Now I wait in his antechamber for a meeting. I came here straight from Zuraya's room, but King Luran didn't accept me right away. He wanted to see his daughter since she was awake now. I didn't have the heart to tell him she was not in the position to be seen. I only hoped her father would make her feel better. Though I doubt that. As far as I remember, he was not a very present father. He was more of a King.

Still, I am sure he must be more loving than my mother. At least he doesn't hate his own daughter. He wanted to find her.

I think my mother would have been happy if I went missing.

She even told me that. When Qyron died, she told me she wished it was me instead. It hurt so much at that time. Honestly, it still hurts to this day, but I am better at ignoring the sting. I am no stranger to pain, after all.

As I sit on the comfortable blue chair, the door opens harshly, and I almost jump. King Luran enters the room looking like he wants to rip someone in half. Maybe me? He looks angry but still graceful. I am almost sure it is a Haliyes quality. His short braids are tight, and his black wings are slightly open.

I watch him with wide eyes from my seat. Davon Archard and Rionn follows after him. The General looks worried, and the Alpha looks a little lost. Honestly, I am lost too.

I open my mouth to say something but Archard's hard brown eyes stop me. Then he makes a move with his chin, and I understand I need to stand up. Normally I wouldn't care, but the King's condition makes me confused enough to follow orders.

King Luran stands in front of the window and looks outside for a second. No one dares to say a word, and I wish I knew what the fuck happened. I just want to take my moon spheres and leave.

He turns to us and pinches the bridge of his nose, then nervously touches the piercing in his right eyebrow. His strong features look so tight with worry and anger. He looks like he is about to blow, and just a second later, he does, "What the fuck happened to her?"

His judgment makes my muscles tense. "She has been a prisoner for seven years. Were you expecting everything to be normal?"

"She is traumatized, Your Majesty. I am sure she will be better with the right treatment." Archard says, almost trying to soften my words.

I don't want anyone to ever soften my words.

Fortunately, I manage to keep my growl inside. It would only make the situation more complicated. I need to be in my political form, not my soldier form. It is easy to mix them sometimes.

The Moon King directly looks at me like Archard didn't even speak. "I was expecting her to be happy to be rescued. Of course, I knew she was going to be traumatized and tortured. I was expecting the lack of wings would be the worst thing."

I wonder how seven years of torture can be not worse than clipped wings. But the Haliyes family is all about appearances. I sometimes think my mother is like them in that regard. They care about how they look so much that she needs to be the perfect Feyada princess to be satisfactory.

But surely, he doesn't expect her to be that only seconds after the rescue. I am not sure, though.

"She is sad. Give her time," I say with a voice that is a little too harsh. King Luran's disappointment makes me want to defend Zuraya. I am no stranger to harsh treatment, but he is not being understanding at all.

King Luran shakes his head and throws himself onto a couch. The rest of us remain standing for some reason. "It is not normal," he murmurs. "I was expecting her to be hurt, but I thought she was

Woe in Total Darkness

going to be happy to be free after all. Whatever they did to her broke her much more than I guessed. She told me she would rather go back instead of living in a world where Qyron is dead."

Those words pierce my heart. I remember feeling like that. "She will learn to live with it."

The King looks at me with pleading eyes. "What have they done to her? She acts like being free here is worse than being back there. She keeps talking nonsense."

I am not exactly sure about her words either, but luckily Rionn clears his throat to speak. "I think they put a spell around her. For seven years, she was in a dream." His eyes turn to me. "Can't you give people daydreams, separate them from reality? Your mind manipulation is capable of that, right?"

I think for a second. What he says makes sense. Zuraya never knew she was kidnapped. Her words can be a result of heavy trauma. She might have created a world in her head to survive all the pain they gave her, but it doesn't explain how she put a man she didn't know in there. She knew Rionn instantly. The world in her head seems too real. It could have been created by someone else.

There is only one problem. "For seven years?" I ask.

"Is it not possible?" Rionn asks in return, and I look at him like he is stupid. It is a complex power to master.

King Luran doesn't see my look and instead answers Rionn himself. "It is not. Not even Güne can do it."

The mention of my mother makes my jaw flex, but I don't say anything. What he says is true anyway. Even my mother cannot do that.

I shrug with a new thought. "Maybe they didn't need to do it for seven years."

"What do you mean?" Luran asks.

"At first, I thought this might be caused by her trauma, and it can still be. Maybe they somehow used a type of spell on her and left the rest to her mind. Maybe she created everything in her head. She started living in this dream instead of feeling the torture. She did it to survive."

Rionn looks impressed. "And she did survive."

King Luran swallows thickly but looks even more disappointed. "But now she is shattering apart."

A bad taste fills my mouth at his words. I thought he would be happy to finally have his daughter back, but the happiness seems so far away from him at this point. Instead, he is disappointed because she is not the princess he hoped for.

Maybe I was wrong, and King Luran is no better than my mother after all.

Zuraya doesn't even have another parent to soften the blow. Her mother died when she was pretty young. I have never actually known her, but at this point, I like to think she was kind. Zuraya deserves someone kind.

"It has been hard on her. Give her time to heal."

"Do you think it is possible for her to heal? Can she ever be the Moon Princess my people want?"

My face hardens. He disgusts me. "Of course, she can. How can you give up on your own daughter so fast? She just needs time and the right treatment. She can be better than you can even imagine."

"Is that so?" he murmurs with sudden interest and surprise. It is not very common for me to defend anyone with this passion, especially someone I despised when I had actually known her. So, his surprise is understandable, but I know there is something else. I know something bad is coming even before he opens his mouth and says, "Well, then, you will be the one who fixes her, Sun Princess."

He almost spits my title because he knows I prefer to be called General. He wants to rile me up. He wants to make me do everything for him. Just like my fucking mother.

Unfortunately, I am not going to say yes to everything he commands like the rest of the population. I say, "No."

"No?" He asks, almost offended. I am also offended because he has the audacity to look surprised at my reaction.

"I already completed what you asked of me. I did my end of the bargain, so now it is time for yours. Give me my moon spheres so I

Woe in Total Darkness

can go back to the Desert, and you can enjoy the reunion with your daughter."

He thinks for a long moment, and his moonshine eyes fill with evil every passing second. In the end, he looks at me with mischief. "I won't give you the moon spheres."

"You agreed to it." Thankfully I made the agreement in front of an audience, and his obsession with looking good is enough to protect me in that regard.

"I agreed to give you 100 moon spheres if you rescue the Moon Princess," he says, and I just stand there confused. That is what I fucking did. I rescued his daughter for less than a year's supply of moon spheres. It is nothing compared to what he is getting out of the agreement.

However, he doesn't let me answer him. "The girl you brought back is not the Moon Princess. She might be my daughter, Zuraya Haliyes, but I wanted the Moon Princess. You must hold your side of the bargain and make him the princess I desire."

My jaw flexes, and my short nails bury in my palms, almost slicing the skin. A fire is burning inside me as I spit, "You are a shitty father."

He doesn't even seem a bit affected by those words. He is definitely no different than my mother. It makes me mad, but it also makes me sad. After everything, Zuraya doesn't deserve this garbage of a person as a parent. I look at the other two people in the room, who have been awfully quiet. Archard's face is drained of emotions, and Rionn looks shocked at the King's cruelty. Shifter culture will never let someone treat family like this.

Still, I know I will not get any support. Rionn is honest about his tradition, but he is also a good politician. He will not argue with the Moon King to defend Sunfolk. He might like me in the sheets, but he can still hate me in a meeting.

I am not expecting him to defend me anyway.

I stand firm in front of the unaffected King Luran. He only has a sinister shimmer in his eyes. He doesn't care for my insult. Instead, he says, "I will give you 200 moons spheres if you can convince people that she is the Moon Princess at her name-day celebration in four months' time. I don't care how you do it. If you do it, I promise not to be hard with the negotiations. You will be able to get more help from me in the future, more moon spheres."

I grit my teeth. I hate this man. I hate this land. The idea of spending most of my time here for four months sounds like hell. Being near someone mourning Qyron sounds like dying. However, I know what I have to do. I know how important the Moon King's help is.

I only think about the people who need me and not for myself but for the folk, I answer, "Yes."

15

Zuraya

I don't know how long it has been. It must be a few days, but I have no idea how much. I didn't leave the window-side much anyway. I look into the familiar view, and I force myself to sleep right here when the pain is too much. I am afraid to get into my bed. It is where I have been attacked. It could be where Qyron was killed.

I can never be able to get into that bed ever again.

I don't want to be here. I want to go back to where I was happy. It was my wedding. Rionn knew me, and Qyron was alive.

They say I was rescued. I don't feel rescued.

How can they do this to me? Lenora brought me back to this horrible reality, and my dad requested it. I wish they had failed. I wish I had just stayed in that dream.

Dream. That's what I heard maids call it. They think I am so out of it, so they don't bother being silent around me. I can hear all their gossip. I let them wash me and braid my hair. I don't try talking to them. I don't try talking to anyone. All I want is to be left alone. Everything about this world gives me pain.

I don't have Qyron, and I don't have Rionn. My father cannot even stand to look at me. I have no one I can hold onto.

I might as well be dead.

The best I can do is act like I am dead. I just live as an empty shell. Still, I am not as empty as the chambermaids think I am. They treat me like a small kid, like I am made of glass. I hate their pitying looks. Staying silent and ignoring is easier.

I listen to the gossip, though. Hearing about the world from their lips might be the only thing still keeping me alive. Thanks to them, I know Lenora left almost immediately after our last interaction, and for some reason, it disappoints me that she is no longer here. She put me in this hell and just fled. If she had been here, maybe I could have punched her. I would show my anger, which sounds better than feeling so empty.

Also, deep down, I feel like she is the only person who can understand the pain of losing Qyron. My pain goes even deeper than this, but I think maybe sharing that grief might have helped me.

However, I only want someone to fight for me because I have no will to fight for myself. Lenora seems like a strong person. I think she could actually win if she did fight for me.

I also know Rionn didn't leave, but his presence cannot make me excited. I would prefer Lenora over him because at least seeing Lenora doesn't hurt me. She can look at me with hate, and I still won't care.

It is different with Rionn.

Every time he doesn't look at me with love, I break a little more. I see him and want to take shelter in his presence from my pain, but he doesn't know who I am. I cannot even blame him for it. He cannot jump into comforting a stranger and act like he is her lover.

Unfortunately, I cannot accept that fact. I cannot accept he doesn't know me. When I look at him, I see my fiancé and remember how he was supposed to be my husband by now. All the memories of our hard times and fights don't matter. I want him to be my Rionn, and he is an entirely different person.

The best option seems like talking with my dad. He has never been the best dad, but he was also not the worst one. I knew he would always protect me from everything. I always tried to make him proud, and he tried to make me happy in return.

But now, I am not making him proud.

Woe in Total Darkness

So, I am not worthy of being happy in his eyes. I lost all my value.

From what I heard from the maids, he has been in his room since he came to see me that first time. He looked at me with so much disappointment before leaving angrily. He never came again. He left me on my own.

I feel like everybody gave up on me, and it is so easy to give up on yourself when that happens. So, I watch the view and let the chambermaids prepare me however they like daily. I let them put me in hideous dresses. No one is ever going to see me anyway. I am going to pass away sitting on this windowsill.

Between the familiar wind and bird noises, suddenly, I hear a knock. My first instinct is to look down to see if it is coming from outside, but then I hear it again. Someone is knocking on my door. It feels so foreign, so weird. No one has ever knocked on my door since I woke up in this horrible reality. Chambermaids just come in whenever they need. They probably think I am mute.

Thus o have no idea who is knocking, but after the third time, I clear my throat and say, "Come in." Even speaking feels weird after sitting here for days like a plant. At least my vocal cords are still intact.

The door slowly opens, and the large form appearing in the archway makes my heart jump. Rionn is here looking a little shy. I don't like how hesitant he looks to step inside my room, but he looks cute when he is shy. I let myself enjoy his sight for a minute before realitt barges I my mind. It is impossible to escape from it.

"Can I come in?" he asks with a sweet voice.

"I said, 'come in,'" I answer. My body is rigid, but I try to conceal it. I know he is not my Rionn, and it doesn't matter, but I still don't want to give a bad impression to him. I still care what he thinks of me.

He steps inside the room. I let my eyes take him in. His dark hair is short, just like I remember, he is wearing head-to-toe black, his skin is the perfect golden color, there is a charming light in his dark eyes, and his lips are almost curled in a smile. I want that smile more than anything. I want to know he is here with me and that I am not alone.

Rionn's eyes subtly take on my appearance, and for the first time, I feel bad for wearing an ugly blue dress. It looks like something I would wear when I was twelve with all the overflowing tulle and lace.

He doesn't seem amused by my hideous dress, though. Instead, his lips pull a bit, and he says, "Nice braids."

"Chambermaids did it." Everything about my looks is their work. I actually liked it when they washed my hair and braided it for me, even though the braids are much thinner than I am used to. No one knows what I am actually used to. This is the hairstyle I used when I was little; that is all they know about me.

Rionn easily walks near me and sits on the other end of the windowsill. There is some distance between us, but we are still close. I want to be even closer. He seems relaxed and easygoing. It almost feels normal.

Only it is not. I need to remember that so my heart won't break even more than it already is.

"Didn't you want it?" he asks, a little worried. "They should have asked you."

I don't tell him the maids think I am mute. I don't want him to know how depressed I am. So, I shrug and answer, "It is okay."

"It looks good on you."

Familiar warmth blooms in my chest. "Thanks." I see him smiling, and my heart beats faster. It feels like the times when we flirted for the first time.

But that thought quickly shatters me. Deep down, I know it shouldn't be like this. He is supposed to be my husband, not a random flirt. My heart shouldn't jump up for this.

My bottom lip wobbles, and I dig my teeth into it to stop it. "Why are you here, Rionn?" I don't call him Alpha like I should. I cannot get myself to do that.

Thankfully Rionn doesn't seem bothered by my use of his first name, but he looks hesitant again. He is always so hesitant around me

I see him swallow before speaking. "I just..." he stops and looks out the window for a second. The next moment those dark irises are again on me. "I just cannot stop thinking about you. I cannot stop feeling guilty for not knowing everything we have lived together."

My eyes sting at his words. The thought of him thinking of me makes me want to smile. For a second, I fill with hope, but I know it is a mistake. "We didn't live anything, Rionn. Only I believed we did."

"Still, I wonder," he pushes. "I wonder what happened between us. I wonder how you felt and how I felt. I mostly wonder if the me you knew is the same as the real me."

"I like to think he is," I say quietly.

"Me too." Rionn smiles. "From the way you hold onto me, it seems like he is a great guy. I hope I am as great as him."

Tears fill my eyes because the Rionn I know really is a great guy and... "I miss him so much." I feel so alone in here.

"Maybe I can be him," he says in a low voice, and my chest tightens. He looks so genuine. He looks just like my Rionn. "I don't know him but don't you want to give it a chance? I am here, and I can be a friend."

Only I want him to be more than just a friend. I want him to be the Rionn I know. His suggestion is so perfect, so charming. I want to say yes. I want to spend all my time with him instead of on this windowsill, but I know it is unfair to him. I cannot lead him on just because he looks like my fiancé. I cannot use his kindness like this.

"I can't do it. It'll hurt me so much."

"I will never hurt you," he says like he means it. He talks like he really cares for me, and I want to cry.

"No," I manage to say. "I cannot do this to you, and I cannot do this to myself."

"Just give me a chance, Zuraya."

My name on his lips almost makes me cry. I want to hear it more, but I know it is so wrong. He is not my Rionn. My Rionn was just a dream, and this is a real person I shouldn't hurt. "Please don't push me," I beg because if he does, I will cave.

Sem Thornwood

He understands my struggle and nods. Then reaches for my hand and presses his lips to my skin. "I'll be around," he whispers. "And I don't plan to give up."

Why does he sound so much like my Rionn?

16

Lenora

I look at the white shirt in my hand. "I don't think I have anything fitting for the Northern weather."

"Because it is awful weather," Andy says from my bed and giggles. She was supposed to help me pack but instead, she is just lying in my bed. I knew I should have got one of my odalisque to help me.

I shrug. "It is cold."

Andy shakes her head and spreads her dark hair on my white linens even more. "I still cannot believe you accepted to stay there. You know it will be like torture, right?"

I fucking know how it is going to be. Spending months with Zuraya Haliyes in the Moon Kingdom is the last thing I want in life. This mission is associated with everything I despise. It will give me pain being there.

Fortunately, I am used to enduring pain. "You know why I am doing it, Andy. Those moon spheres will be helpful."

She raises on her elbow and rests her head on her palm. She looks so pretty without even trying. "You think you'll be able to do it? I mean, you are the best fighter out there, and you also nicely manage the political manners. You are a skillful individual, but I don't think helping someone out of depression is one of your expertise."

I want to groan at her words because I know that too. It is definitely out of my field. However, crying about it is not going to fix anything. I'll have to find a way somehow. So, instead of showing my frustration, I smile and ask mockingly, "Don't you think I can be a good friend, Qassandra?"

"To me? Yes." Andy says. "To Princess Zuraya? Not so sure."

"You know, a little faith would be helpful."

Andy rolls her eyes at me. "I have faith in you. I always have faith in you. I am just warning you, Len. I know you'll do anything for the good of the Folk, but this is a strange request. I don't want you to waste your time."

I don't want that too. I am aware of all of Andy's concerns. I just prefer to kind of ignore it. I want to believe I can do this. If I can do this, I can create a dynamic I have been working on for years. With King Lunar's help, this war against the Darkness can be easier.

Another reason I am hopeful is that I can get more intel about the Curser while I am there. Being close to Princess Zuraya can be more beneficial than I can imagine. If I can catch the Curser and ruin his fucked up cult, I can win this war.

Though that is a secret reason. I am not even going to tell Andy. Instead, I again give a runaway answer, "Well, I believe I can do it. Also, Rionn offered his help as well. Princess has a weird thing about him, so maybe I can use that."

It is not a lie. Rionn really wanted to help, and he even seemed enthusiastic. Sometimes his will to help me beyond reason scares me. I am afraid he has developed feelings for me that I cannot deal with, but I didn't mind this time. I can very well use his help.

I don't think Andy agrees, though, because her face turns cold as soon as I say Rionn's name. She sits up. Her spine is all straight. "Len, I know I made jokes about your relationship with the Alpha, but you should be careful around him."

Maybe I should be weirded out by the fact that she talks like she actually knows Rionn, but at this point, I don't. I am only confused because I thought she was getting over her hate for the Shifters.

"Why do you say that? I thought you were okay with Rionn. He is not like the ones before him, Andy."

"I know," she murmurs. "That's what you keep telling me."

"And I am telling the truth." If I had any doubt about that, I would never let him get this close to me. What happened to Andy when she was back in the Moon Kingdom is unforgivable. And I know Andy is not the only one who endured the pain inflicted by those Shifters.

"Len, I am happy you are getting some dick, but this is different. I know I was always relaxed about this, but that was because I thought it was nothing more than just some fun. Don't let him trick you into you are friends or possibly something more."

I go tense. "I am not stupid, Andy."

"Well, you are ready to accept his help," she argues. "He might seem innocent, but you can never know what is going on inside his head. He can be handsome and charming, but at the end of the day, he is still a Shifter."

My blood boils in my veins, but I manage to keep my cool on the surface. Being treated like I am dumb is the last thing I need in life. My mother is doing it enough. I don't need it from my best friend. Still, I don't lash out. I simply say, "I'll keep in mind. Now help me pack."

———— (————

It didn't take long for me to return to the Moon Kingdom. I needed to deal with some things back home. I can still go back from time to time, but I made sure to leave enough sun spheres and appoint the right people for the right jobs. They just need to keep on track with the Dark Patches until I can finish here.

A small problem emerged with the Giants before I left, but I believe I can deal with that here too. Thanks to ancient Seelie magic, we have cauldrons that help us communicate with people far away. I can still have meetings and inform my soldiers quickly when something is needed or get the information without delay.

Sem Thornwood

The talk I had with Andy didn't leave my mind since. I acted distant towards her after her words but also couldn't stop thinking about them. At first, using Zuraya's feelings towards Rionn made sense, but I am not sure if I can trust him with this.

I didn't write it off completely, but I will be careful with him.

Also, it gave me a bad feeling to play Zuraya like that. She clearly has deep feelings for him, and I don't want to use them just for my benefit. If I am going to do this, I want to do this for real. I don't want to trick her but rather really heal her.

Unfortunately, I have no fucking idea how to do that.

I only came up with the first step. I need to see how her condition is. When I left, it was not promising at all, but I hope maybe she got better when I was away. Maybe my help is not even needed.

I feel like Zuraya Haliyes is a strong individual. I wish she is strong enough to heal herself without my help. I am not too hopeful, though.

I just need to see it for myself. That is the reason I am walking towards her room only minutes after I landed at this palace. I haven't even seen my room. Zuraya is much more important at the moment and every moment for the next four months.

There is one guard at her door, and when I step inside the antechamber, I see her three chambermaids sit and talk together. No one is inside with her. It makes me a little angry, but I can manage that later. Instead, I go and knock on her bedroom door. Just a second later, a kind voice answers, "Yes?"

I open the pretty door and step inside the room. I give her a huge smile after closing the door. "It is me."

Zuraya looks at me with a tired expression. She is cleaned up, and her hair is braided, which is a big step up from the time I last saw her. She is as beautiful as I remember from our childhood, but her skin is still a little ashen, her body thin, and there are bags under her eyes. She looks so empty.

My hopes crush, but I don't focus on that. I only focus on Zuraya and her fluffy purple dress. It is hideous.

"Who keeps sending you?" she asks, visibly fed up.

Woe in Total Darkness

My forehead wrinkles, but I still walk toward the windowsill she is sitting. "This is the first time I came."

She looks away, almost closing me off. "Rionn came the other day."

Warning bells ring inside my head. For a second, I feel bad for acting so cold toward Andy. She might actually be right about Rionn. But it is not the time to make assumptions. I don't need more enemies.

"I didn't know that," I answer truthfully and sit on the windowsill. She is sideways with her knees pulled close to her chest. She is leaning her back onto the stone behind her. It is a hard position with my wings, so I sit normally and let my legs fall free off the side. For a second, I feel bad for sitting so comfortably because Zuraya is not, and it might be because of the fact that she cannot fly off if she ever falls.

She doesn't look bothered, though. She only looks at the view with dead eyes. I let her break the silence, and she really takes her time. I don't mind, actually. She is my only duty at the moment.

Zuraya side-eyes me only for a second before speaking. "I heard you were gone. Why did you come back?"

"Where did you hear it?" I ask, trying to contain my excitement. Maybe she does get out of her room and talk to people. Maybe her empty act is only because she doesn't like me.

Unfortunately, her next words make my hopes crumble. "Maids like to gossip."

"But you didn't hear about me coming back?"

She is silent for a second, but then I swear I see her lips curl at the sides a little, not a real smile but good enough for me. "I guess they need to work on their gossip."

"Seems so." I give her a full-blown smile.

"So, why are you back?"

I don't want to play her, but I already decided not to answer this question honestly. I cannot tell her I am here to fix her in return for the moon spheres. I want to tell her the truth, the deal I made with her father. But definitely not now. I am not into sabotaging myself. "Intel about the Curser. I want to catch him."

Zuraya shakes her head, and her face wrinkles. "It is so weird," she mumbles.

"What's weird?"

Finally, her eyes come to me even though her head is still hanging between her shoulders. "You being like this. A soldier... No, a General. You are just like Davon Archard, and it is weird."

I have never found being a soldier weird. I have been trained in fighting from a very young age, like every heir. I was already into it by the time Qyron died, but his death really pushed me to become the General of the Sun Army. After failing him, I never wanted to fail someone again.

Still, I guess it is normal for Zuraya not to know these. "Was I not a General in..."

I don't know what to call it, so Zuraya fills it for me, "In my dream?"

"I guess we can call it that," I say, but that doesn't sound exactly right.

She shakes her head at my question. "You were not. You were just a princess like me."

"How was I?" I ask and am surprised at the fact that I am actually curious about the answer. Talking about this can help me find exactly how they managed to trick Zuraya's brain.

She stays silent for a minute, and her eyebrows come together. "I actually never saw you. Obviously, I knew of you. You were the perfect princess. Your people loved you, and you made it look so easy. I wished I was like you, but I never saw you. You never visited the Moon Kingdom."

I am actually a little surprised at her confession. I would never guess Moon Princess to tell me how jealous she was of me while I was the one jealous during our entire childhood.

Her confession is not good, though. It means she doesn't care. She accepted her whole life was a lie, and it doesn't matter. It is bad. It is what makes her look so empty, alongside one other thing.

"It doesn't make sense," I say, and interest sparks her dim blue eyes. "I really haven't visited here for seven years. But I would

Woe in Total Darkness

have visited if..." I don't have to finish it. I don't have to say Qyron's name to hurt both of us even more.

Zuraya nods knowingly. "I thought you should have too. He loved you so much."

I try to imagine an older Qyron. I want to know how my life would have been different if my brother had been alive. I still don't know what the source of Zuraya's dream is. I need to ask questions to figure that out. I need to ask her questions about the Curser. But all I want to do is ask her about Qyron.

I want the same dream if it is going to mean seeing Qyron one more time.

I don't even realize I am silent until Zuraya speaks again. I am ashamed of myself for losing my target when she says, "So, you will be here for a while?" She is clearly trying to get my mind off of Qyron.

That was supposed to be my job. I really suck when the subject comes to my dead twin.

I shake the pain away. I need to focus on Zuraya. "Yes," I answer.

"It must be horrible for you," Zuraya says. "You Sunfolk have a weird obsession with your homeland."

I chuckle a little and again see the smallest smile on Zuraya's face. *She likes talking to me,* I realize. *She leaves that emptiness in her head for a second for me.* I can work with that. "It is not an obsession. It is the calling of the Desert." I miss it even now. The weather here is just too moist. My skin feels oily and sweaty all the time.

Zuraya shakes her head like it amuses her, but her eyes have an added layer of sadness. I can only guess what she is remembering. I can only guess why the Sunfolk talk is making her smile.

"It is not so bad," I say. This time I am the one trying to change the subject. "I'll probably get to see Maha give birth."

It is just an honest thought. I say to distract her, but it does something more. Zuraya's head pop up, and her eyes round. "The Seelie Princess?" she asks. "She is here and pregnant?"

I nod softly. I understand it might be surprising for her.

"Why is she here?" Zuraya asks before letting me say anything.

139

"Well, it might be an interesting story. She is married to Davon Archard."

With every word, I watch Zuraya's eyes go even wider. "And she is pregnant with his child and almost ready to give birth?"

"Can pop any minute," I confirm. But I am confused. "Did you hear about it from the maids?"

She looks away and shakes her head. "No, they don't talk about Maha at all. Some Moonfolk has the tendency to ignore Seelies at all costs."

"I know," I say, but I am not ready to leave the Maha subject. "Are you surprised to learn she is married to Archard? It was quite the eventful union."

"No," Zuraya shakes her head. "I am not surprised at all. Maha was sent here five years ago for the bonds between the two countries. She met Davon back then, and they fell in love. They had to hide their love for years. But they were so desperate for each other that Maha told her sister at the end. Queen Mav was furious, but their love conquered it all. They got married, and then Maha got pregnant."

My jaw drops. Maha actually came to the Moon Palace for protection from the Darkness but other than that it happened exactly like she described. It was a big scandal, an unexpected event. It also all happened while Zuraya was kidnapped. There is no way for her to know unless someone told her. "Who?" I ask. "Who told you the story."

She looks at me, amazed. "No one. No one had to tell me because I lived through it. I was here when it happened. Maha told me, and Qyron before anyone knew. I attended their wedding."

"Zuraya," I say softly. "That is impossible."

A single tear leaves her eye. "I know. But I was there for all of it."

It is strange in so many ways. I want to dive deep. I want to know what kind of spell they used on her. But more than that, I want to make her feel good. That is my goal, after all.

"She is here for real, though," I say. "You can actually see her." *She is not dead.*

Woe in Total Darkness

Her eyes fill with hope like she didn't even consider that option. "I can see her," she murmurs to herself, weighing the idea. But just a moment later, tears fill her eyes, and she shakes her head. "I cannot do it."

"Why?"

She keeps shaking her head. "I can't."

"Maha is the nicest," I reach out and, without thinking, cup her hands in mine. "You don't have to worry about her. She can be a good friend to you just like she was before."

Zuraya looks down at our clasped hands like she cannot believe I actually dared to touch her. "I can't," she says again, sternly. "She was my friend, but she is not here. She doesn't know me."

"You can change that. You can befriend Maha again. I am sure she will be happy."

"No!" she pulls back her hands. "I cannot go through that, Lenora. I cannot stand one of my best friends looking at me with unrecognition in her eyes. It hurts too much."

I understand her point, but I am also angry because she doesn't even want to try. "You cannot spend the rest of your days on this windowsill Zuraya."

"I can," she says with a sad smile. "Don't push me, Lenora. Maha is no different than Rionn. Both hurt me, and I cannot do it. I am not strong enough."

"You can do it," I encourage.

Zuraya looks at me with hatred. "I cannot get over my pain so easily, Lenora. I am not *you.*"

With that punch to my gut, I just leave.

17

Lenora

I look at the intricate designs on the ceiling as I try to regulate my breathing. My whole body is covered in sweat. I am only now getting down from my high, but I am still somewhat tense. The sweet ache between my legs cannot stop my mind from working.

When I left Zuraya's room, I was too hurt. I knew it was stupid. I shouldn't be hurt because of words from a girl I don't even care. Unfortunately, I cannot control my feelings. Someone so close to Qyron blaming me like that was awful.

The only solution I could think about was sex, so I found myself in Rionn's room. We didn't even talk. He just said, "You're back," and then I kissed him. I thought fucking him would empty my mind.

It didn't. As I lay in his bed buck naked I still feel hurt. I can't stop thinking about Zuraya for even a second.

I need to do something, but I have no idea how I can when she doesn't want to heal and hates me. I have nothing I can use against her.

Next to me, Rionn chuckles and turns his head in my direction. "Well, that was a good way to announce you're here." His muscular body is also sweaty, and he does look extremely hot, but

Woe in Total Darkness

I cannot make my mind focus just on that. I cannot shut the world out for a quick fuck. I usually don't have a problem with that.

It is annoying.

I try not to show it to Rionn, though. "I was actually surprised you are still here."

He gets up on his elbow and pushes a sweaty strand of hair off my forehead. "I didn't want to leave before you came back. I told you I want to help with Zuraya."

"You don't have to. I know you have things to deal with back at home."

His fingers start a journey on my cheek and slowly descent to my neck. I normally would like a little teasing, but I am too tense. "Nonsense," Rionn says. "I'll be glad to help. I am actually sad for the girl."

I am not sure if he is really sad or he is doing it for me, or there is a whole other reason. "I heard you talked to her. You know it might be actually bad for her. She thinks you are her fiancé. Don't give her hope."

A sinister smile fills his face, and he pinches my nipple. "Are you jealous, Lenora?"

I laugh loudly. "Yeah, definitely," I mock, and for a second, Rionn looks annoyed by my reaction. He should know better.

Honestly, I am a little jealous, but it is not like he thinks. I am not jealous because there is a gorgeous princess who wants to take Rionn from me. I don't have any ownership over Rionn, and I never plan on declaring one. Instead, I am jealous because he has a way of reaching her. He can actually manage to use her emotions against her.

And that is the last thing I want him to do.

"I just want to be her friend," Rionn says. His fingers are now dancing on my abs, and his eyes are focused there too. I am not sure if he is just mesmerized by my body or if he is trying to hide his eyes from me.

I am not sure about his intentions, but I am sure about Zuraya. She told me Maha would not be any different from Rionn. I want to test the waters. "Does she want that too?"

He looks at me just for a second. "Yeah." He leans down to kiss my stomach. "She might have other hopes for our relationship, but I told her I just want to be friends. I *really* feel bad for her."

The only thing keeping me from grunting at his words are his kisses that move closer and closer to my center. "You shouldn't lead her." *You should leave this to me.*

"I am not," he argues, lifting one of my legs to get between them. Now he is kissing the inside of my thighs. For some reason, I know this is not just his desire for me. He wants to distract me.

Maybe I am being delusional, but Andy's words swim around inside my head. I know Rionn is lying to me. I know Zuraya did not accept his friendship. Rionn has no plans of leaving soon, and whatever he wants, it is more than just helping me.

The next second, his tongue meets my heated flesh, and I grant him my silence. I don't ask more questions. But I know I have to be careful with him now.

I won't let him play with her emotions. Nothing can come between me and Raya's well-being.

18

Zuraya

I try not to flinch from my maid's touch as her fingers move along the scars on my back. Those are old wounds. The salve she applies is not for the pain. They are healed. It is probably for the look. Like missing scars can fool anyone. I am missing my wings.

However, I say nothing. I just let them go by their routine. I don't care. I let them pamper me and listen to their gossip quietly.

They usually repeat things I know. They also talk about Rionn and Lenora. Thanks to them, I know both of them are still here. Rionn came to see me twice, even though I always turned him down. His presence only hurts me. He is giving me hope, and that is the last thing I need. I only need silence and alone time, so I can mourn not just my best friend but my whole life.

However, I am a little disappointed Lenora didn't bother to come again. I know she did what I wanted, but I can't help but feel guilty. I feel like she doesn't come back because I hurt her.

I shouldn't care.

But I do.

I am not even sure if it is because I see her as the only thing connected to Qyron or because I thought she was not the type of person to give up so easily. I am surprised. I cannot help but entertain the thought of her once or twice when I am sitting on that windowsill. They are not always positive thoughts. Sometimes I find ways to hate her. Either way, I cannot get her out of my head.

At one point, my maids talked about her and Rionn. Apparently, some members of the court keep seeing them in each other's rooms. They say Rionn and Lenora are a little too close. My maids think there is a secret forbidden love going on. Honestly, it sounds more like they are just sleeping together.

Although I even doubt that.

The idea of them together is ridiculous to me. Of course, I hardly know them, and I might be wrong, but I still don't believe it. The reason is not that I am jealous. Of course, I don't like to think of Rionn with somebody else, but he is not my Rionn, and I have no right over him. He can be with whoever he wants.

The reason I don't believe they are together is my source. The chambermaid gossip is not always true. They are just exaggerating to make everything more scandalous and fun.

Right now, they are rubbing oils on my body before putting on my ugly pink nightgown. Something to sleep in shouldn't have that much tulle.

"Did General's kid born?" one maid asks the other. At first, the word "General" makes me think of Lenora, but I quickly realize they are talking about Davon Archard. Involuntarily I peak up and listen more carefully. I am lucky my maids pay no attention to me even though their hands are on my skin. At least they are no longer putting salve on my scars. Right now, the oils are just for the smell and the dry skin. I can endure that.

"No, not yet," answers the maid taking out my nightgown from the dresser.

The hands on my shoulders stop. "I heard the Seelie went into labor yesterday." She is Princess Maha K'rra, and they can use hundreds of names and titles to talk about her, but they use the word "Seelie" and say it like a curse.

I hate it, but I don't react. I try hard to soften my muscles and lift my arms to let them put the nightgown on me. Just when the fabric covers my eyes, I hear them again. "Turns out it was false labor. If you ask me, she faked it."

Woe in Total Darkness

Another maid laughs while I try to keep my expression blank. "She is such an attention seeker. I bet she'll fake it a few more times just to make people talk about her. She just cannot accept no one cares about her in this court."

They all nod, and one smooths down the dress on my body. I grit my teeth, and the one right in front of me murmurs, "Savage."

My blood runs cold. All I want is silence, but I cannot stay silent against this. I bury my nails into my palms just to stop myself from slapping the maid and hiss under my breath, "Shut. Your. Mouth."

Her back straightens, and she eyes me with shock mingled with distress. "Princess?"

This time I directly look at her and speak for real. "I said shut your mouth. Are you aware that you are talking about a *princess*? If you have no respect for her, then you have no respect for me. What names do you call me behind *my* back?"

The maid's eyes fill with horror, and I can swear her hands are shaking. "Of course not, your Highness. She is different than you. She is..."

"Also a princess," I cut her off. Nothing else matters. "What do you think General would think if he heard you talk about his wife like that?"

With the mention of Archard, she looks even more scared. The Archard I knew, would rip off the spine out of anyone who dared to insult Maha and the look on my maid's face confirms the real Archard would do the same. "Please forgive me, Your Highness."

"I won't do to you anything for this once," I declare. "But you will never speak about Maha again, not in my presence and not when you are out of my sight. Never! Do you understand me?"

A few tears slide down her cheeks from my harsh tone, and she nods quickly. "Yes, Your Highness."

I look around me. "It is the same for all of you." They repeat the other maid's words. "Now, all of you leave. I'm going to sleep."

All of my maids nod and move to leave. I am still angry from their words, but there is something else inside me. I am refreshed or excited. I don't know exactly what it is, but somehow, I feel powerful. Before I can think more and sink back into my shelf,

147

"Also," I say to stop them. "I don't want to wear these ugly clothes anymore. I also don't want clothes without backs."

"But Your Highness," someone starts.

I cut them off with my hand. It feels so natural. "I don't care where you find it. Bring a Shifter tailor or an Earthling from the Sun Khanate. Just make it happen." They stay silent for a second before I send them again.

Afterward, I take off the ugly dress and, without thinking, get under my covers naked. For the first time, I actually fall asleep on my bed instead of the windowsill.

——— ᴄ ———

I look at the stone structure without taking a breath. There has been a knot in my throat since the moment I left my room. After speaking to my maids, the idea of leaving filled my head. It took me almost a week to decide where I would go and then another three days just to gather my courage. I am still not sure if it is the right choice. My windowsill was definitely safer.

But I cannot stay there forever. I understand that slowly.

I didn't really talk to Rionn, and Lenora never came back. Actually, my maids were the ones that gave me the courage to leave the room. After badmouthing Maha, they turned out pretty decent. They listened to me, and that made me speak even more. They also brought me lovely dresses with their backs covered. The fabric over my back made me more comfortable about leaving the room.

Not too comfortable, though. That's why I came here a little after midnight when everyone else was sleeping. This place seemed like the only place worth enough to risk leaving my room.

A maid suggested I might want to visit here when I mentioned my search for ideas. It is a place that didn't exist in my dreams. It is a tomb. Qyron's tomb.

I force my lungs to accept the air and breathe in deeply. I will need it. I can already feel tears ready at the back of my eyes, and my pulse is speeding like crazy despite my efforts to be calm. This place will show me he is really gone. It is a physical symbol of his death.

It might seem too melancholic, but I do need a reality check. I need to accept what is happening to me even though I don't want to.

Slowly I step towards the tomb and reach the archway. I can see the inside from here. In the middle, there is a big rectangle-shaped stone. It is the same warm color as the rest, but the inside is much more extra than the outside. Outside it looks like a simple tomb with cute flowers surrounding it. The inside looks like the Sun Khanate treasury vomit all around. It probably would have been raided if it was not inside the palace walls.

The thought makes me sick.

Instead, I focus on the décor. There are golden plates everywhere, and so many valuable gems are buried in the stone's surface. The ceiling is not fully closed, and I can see some hidden small mirrors around the tomb. I can tell they are there to shape sunshine when it is daytime. I would like to see that.

I like the tomb. I know this is here because my friend died, and I want to cry, but a voice in my head tells me he would actually like this tomb.

I wish I could share it with him. My heart burns with longing.

This time I am not longing for everything I lost. I only long for Qyron. I know I could have done this much better if he had been here. I could have dealt with everything else somehow.

But he had to go out and die on me.

He was my breath, and now I am choking.

Softly I brush my fingers over the stone. My maid told me it was not known if his body was really here or in the tomb back at the Sun Khanate, but I want to think it is here. I still want him close.

"You know it is hard to believe," I whisper. I don't feel even a little ashamed for talking to a stone. I deserve to be unreasonable. "I cannot believe you are here. This space is too small for you, Qyron. You were thin but tall. You cannot fit inside here comfortably."

My fingers flex over the stone, and I am not touching it anymore. I am holding onto it. "But then I remember you can actually fit." I cannot stop crying as I whisper, "Because you never grew into the height I remember you in."

It was all a lie. I cannot bring myself to voice that out loud.

I picture the Qyron I have known for the last seven years. I try to imagine if anything about him changed after the attack. If the real Qyron and the one in my dreams were any different. I want to know who that Qyron was because even if he was not real, he was still my best friend.

Rionn mentioned whatever I have lived for the last seven years could just be a dream. Someone must have used a spell and caged me in an oblivion. It was all my imagination.

I don't believe that. I cannot believe that.

Even looking at this tomb, I don't have any urge for revenge inside me. I am too tired for that. Yet I want to know. I want to know more than anything.

How did they do it?

I want to know who made up the Qyron in my head. I know it cannot be me because I could not make up Rionn as well. I could not create someone I have never seen in my head, and Rionn looks exactly as I remember. My father looks the same as well. All the changes he endured while I was gone, I was aware. He didn't look strange at all.

And I am sure if I said yes to Lenora and met with Maha, she would look the same as well.

I didn't miss as much as they thought, and I want to know how. I don't know if it would hurt less if things were different. I don't think any reality without Qyron can hurt less.

A little part of me still stupidly hopes that they actually sent me to an alternative reality and they can actually send me there again. I prefer anything over this.

I sniff loudly and decide to sit on the floor. There is no other place to sit, but Qyron would enjoy sitting on the floor. A smile pulls my lips, but I also feel tired of that. I just want to stay here for a while. I am hopelessly waiting for Qyron to send me something. Anything.

He will help me even beyond the grave.

I wait.

And wait.

And wait even more.

My limbs feel cold from the stone and the wind. Dread fills my bones more and more every second. I keep thinking if it was a mistake to come here and I should have just stayed in my room. I cannot decide what is best for me. I cannot decide how much I can take.

And just when I am ready to leave, I hear footsteps, and before I can open my eyes, a voice calls, "Hey."

For a second, I think Qyron sent me help, but when I open my eyes, I understand it is not that. It is just Lenora Mitharaus.

I haven't seen her for a very long time, and despite my annoyance, I am not too upset to see her. I won't voice it in a million years, though.

She makes me forget the things I lost because she was never a part of it.

I know I am the reason she never came back after her first visit. I broke her heart. Afterward, I did regret saying those words to her, but if I could just go back in time, I am not sure if I would hold back despite knowing the consequences. She might be charming, but she is still Lenora.

I quickly rub my face clean off of tears and snot. "Are you here for a visit?" I ask, looking at her head because her body is hidden behind the walls. I don't know if she comes here often. I actually thought I would be here alone at this hour.

I hoped for some peace, but I guess not.

"Yes," answers Lenora. She still doesn't step forward. "But not to Qyron. I came to visit you."

I don't know if I should feel happy or upset over the fact that I didn't hurt her enough to keep her away. But mostly, I am surprised. "Why after this much time?" It only has been a little over two weeks, but at this point, it is a long time for me.

Lenora shrugs. "I wanted to give you time."

"And you chose now?" I make an effort to show my irritation. I wanted her to come back, but I also wanted some alone time with Qyron. I might be the problematic one, but I don't care.

"Yes, it was on purpose."

"You wanted to see me here instead of all the times I was at my room completely available?"

"Exactly." There is a smile on her face. It feels too weird because the smile is genuine and way too sweet. It doesn't fit any version of Lenora Mitharaus I know. "I wanted you to be ready."

"For what?"

"For my gift." She finally steps to the side, away from the wall. I cannot see her clearly until she takes a few more steps inside, but when I finally can, my mouth goes dry. There is a big furball in her arms. I know many foxes have the same orange-colored fur, but deep down, I know this specific fox.

Lenora carefully sits down next to me while the fox licks her chin. "You didn't want to see Maha, but I thought Sury was a safe zone."

"Of course he is." Without even realizing my lips upturn, and I reach for my best friend's other best friend. A part of Qyron I am very familiar with.

Sury happily settles in my arms. He has always been very calm, unlike his owner. He would never leave Qyron's side, never run away. He was always there wherever he went. And now he is all alone.

Just like me.

"I gathered a search celebration for him after the attack. He was walking around the palace looking for Qyron." Lenora keeps her voice very stable, but I can sense the slight shake on Qyron's name. It almost always happens when she says his name.

"You searched for him?" I am actually surprised the rough-mannered General decided to search for a pet.

Lenora looks offended by my question, though. "Of course I did. I knew how important he was to Qyron. I searched for both Sury and Mona."

Now I am even more surprised. The little white-furred fox was native to the South, but she was mine. Mona was a gift to me from

Woe in Total Darkness

the Sun Khan back when Qyron just started living here. She gifted us those foxes. Even their colors matched our aesthetic. We loved them so much. Both of them were so cute, but still, Mona was *mine*.

I wasn't expecting Lenora to care about her.

"Why would you search for my fox?"

She shrugs like it is the most normal thing. "They are living things. They deserve to be cared for as well. Also, I knew how much Sury meant to Qyron, and I guessed Mona should mean the same to you."

Her words make sense, but they don't suppress my shock. Nothing about her matches the Lenora in my head. I squeeze Sury in my arms, rubbing my cheek into his soft fur. With the comfort he gives me, I prepare myself for the answer to my next question. "Where is Mona?"

"I found her in your room. She was hurt badly. She probably tried to fight whoever came to take you."

My throat hurts. Mona was a predator by nature, but she grew up pampered. She didn't stand a chance but still tried. "She didn't make it," I say.

Lenora shakes her head and touches Sury's head with her fingertips like she is afraid of scaring me off with her closeness. "I am sorry. I took her to a healer, but her injuries were bad."

I don't answer. Instead, I kiss Sury's head. The fox stays calm in my arms. For a moment, I almost feel like everything is okay, back to normal. I didn't realize I needed something so small to feel hopeful. The fox is exactly the same as I remember, and he doesn't give me that unrecognizing look. He curls up to my chest like we are back in my dreams.

Maybe I can actually do this. I just need some hope. I need something that feels familiar without hurting me.

And funnily, the only person I feel like won't hurt me is Lenora. She cannot break my heart because she means nothing to me. I don't really like her but she is safe, and I want that more around me.

Sunshine always made me feel safe.

I nibble my bottom lip nervously before looking back at her. Lenora's eyes are transfixed on the stone in the middle. I cannot figure out what she is thinking. "Can I want something?"

"Of course," she looks at me so genuine, and my chest tightens a bit.

"There was a thing we did with Qyron." My cheeks heat a little under her gaze, and I look away before the last part. "Can we do that together?"

"Yes," she says without a stop. "What is it?"

I am getting disturbed. Why is she so good to me? Why does she act like it doesn't matter what I want; she will give it to me anyway?

I swallow hard before explaining it. "We would touch each other and free our powers. The feeling of them crashing was different. Maybe it is stupid, but it was our thing."

"It is not stupid." She holds out her hand for me. "We can do it."

Even now, I can see her skin slightly glowing golden. It is so familiar but also so foreign. I have never done this with anyone but Qyron. I never guessed I would do this with Lenora.

After a few seconds of hesitation, I lift my hand. Nervously I put my hand over Lenora's. She easily twines our fingers, pressing our palms together. A buzz fills my skin from the contact. It feels different than Qyron. Not better or worse, but just different. I can tell this power is Lenora's, even in my sleep.

I close my eyes to reach my own light. Since I woke up, I never actually tried to do it. For once, I never needed it, but it was more than that. I was scared. I am scared now, but I still want to try.

And I feel safe.

Lenora's power gets stronger on my skin. I know she can burn me with it, but instead, it is just warm and comforting. It helps me focus. I try to feel the power in my heart. I reach into the darkness inside me for the light of the moon. I call for the power my ancestors stole from Goddess Tisasa.

I reach the light I am destined for.

But I can't find it.

Woe in Total Darkness

I know my skin is not glowing at all. I cannot feel it in my veins or even in my heart. There is not an ounce of light inside of me. I am all empty.

"Shouldn't you also shine?" Lenora asks with genuine wonder in her tone.

I don't answer and instead focus on the feeling of her power over me. I want mine to answer her. I want mine to mash with hers.

I can't do it.

"Zuraya?" For the first time, she actually sounds concerned.

My eyes burn, and I grit my teeth. "I can't," I whisper. I don't want her to know I am broken, but I don't think I can tell it to anyone but her. I open my eyes and see her shining. She keeps the light around me to keep me safe. "I can't reach my power."

She doesn't look at me with pity or mockery. Instead, she looks thoughtful. "Since when?"

I don't pull my hand away. I like her Sunshine over my skin. It makes her a little more bearable. "Since you brought me here. This is the first time I tried."

Lenora nods like it makes sense. It doesn't. It is horrible. I am the sole heir of Moonshine.

Now I am *actually* useless to my father.

"It might be because you didn't use it for years," Lenora murmurs. It doesn't make sense to me, but it seems like it does to her. "We can fix that."

I try not to get hopeful. "How?"

"You should train like it is the first time. I can actually train you. Our powers might be opposites, but they are also the same."

Both of our light is coming from Tisasa, but I don't know if it feels the same. I actually never asked Qyron how he reached his power. I have no knowledge if Lenora can really teach me, but her words still give me hope.

I don't want to be disappointed. "Are you sure you can do it?"

She lifts an eyebrow. "Do you have a better idea?"

I really don't. I am scared of failure. I am already broken enough. I cannot handle it if this doesn't work.

But I also cannot run away from all my problems.

I am torn. "Do I have to answer now?"

Lenora looks heartbroken for a second, but she hides it fast enough. "Of course not. Take your time. I am here for a while anyway."

"Then I'll think about it."

"Okay," she murmurs, nodding her head. She looks really eager to help me, and I don't know if I should be bothered or happy about it. This Lenora is better than I imagined, which is not exactly a good thing.

After a moment of silence, she asks, "Do you want to go back?"

I am actually ready to return to my room, but I am not sure if I want to be with Lenora right now. I still don't know how I should feel about her. It makes me uneasy. "I want to stay a bit longer. You go."

She doesn't argue but instead nods and stands up. She rubs some of the dust away from her body and walks to the entrance. After two steps, she stops and looks at me. "I hope you say yes, Zuraya," she says, almost like a confession. "Qyron died, but we are still here. The pain never goes away. Yet we have to keep living despite of it."

Silver lines my eyes, and I feel more awful for my words to her. I hate that I acted like she didn't get hurt by his death.

She hurt as much as I did. And she got to live. All she is trying to do is show me how.

Only I am not sure if I am as strong as her.

It is just another thing I hate about Lenora Mitharaus.

Thankfully she doesn't push for an answer. She looks understanding. Before she leaves for real, a playful smile appears on her face, and she says, "I liked the dress."

19

Zuraya

I adjust the neckline of my dress nervously, even though it looks pretty good. It is a blue silk dress. The skirt is flowy like I prefer, and there is a deep cleavage at the front. Most importantly, the back is completely covered. It looks like a dress I would actually wear. I still don't look like myself. My face is clear from any metal, my braids are too tight, and one of my horns is broken.

I don't have my wings.

It even makes walking a little harder, but I am getting used to the new balance of my body. I am not getting used to being broken, though. I might be better than I first came here, but I will always feel broken without my wings.

At least I don't spend all my time on the windowsill anymore. It has been a week since I left my room to see Qyron's tomb, and since then, I have left every night. I don't do anything exciting. I just walk around the palace when everyone's inside sleeping.

I am just trying to keep living despite the pain. Just like Lenora said.

I still haven't given her an answer. I am not ready. A part of me wants to do it, but I am too anxious. I don't have the courage to say yes. My mind is filled with all the horrible things the training can entail. I am worried about leaving my room during the day; I am worried about the court seeing me without wings and with a broken horn.

I am worried Lenora will see how horrible I am and give up on me.

I am so scared of failing.

Still, I think about her every night, just like now. I stay in front of my mirror, looking at my specially designed dress. I know no one is going to see me, and I don't want anyone to see me, yet I still try to look good. I put on a nice dress and remember Lenora's words.

One night I even caught myself smiling at the memory. It was awful.

Annoyed with myself, I take Sury in my arms and make my way to the doors. My maids don't follow. I told them I wanted to be alone. I also told them to keep this a secret from absolutely anyone. If the court starts gossiping about me walking around late at night, I won't be alone anymore. They will sacrifice their sleep for a chance to see me up close seven years later.

I don't want to be seen. I know probably everyone knows I lost my wings but letting them see is another thing.

Alone walks are good. Still, I cannot help but wonder if Lenora will find me again. I don't know if I want her to, but it is always on my mind when I stroll in the dark.

I bring Sury to make myself believe I am not alone and don't need Lenora to find me.

I clear my throat like it can help clean my head from the thoughts of the Sun Princess and open the doors of my room. Just as I do, I come across a familiar face. Rionn looks surprised that the door opened without him knocking.

Breath leaves my lungs at the sight of him. He looks so much like my fiancé. "Rionn," I say, trying to smile.

He, on the other hand, smiles for real. "Your Highness, I'm glad I caught you."

My skin itches. "You can just call me Zuraya."

He doesn't look uncomfortable. He only nods. "Okay, Zuraya." He is still smiling. "Were you going for a walk?"

Woe in Total Darkness

I was, but he isn't supposed to know that. I nervously put Sury down. "Well, I can stay here if you want to talk about something."

"No. I actually came to ask if I can join you on your walk."

My eyes bulge out. "How do you know about my walks?" Inwardly I curse my chambermaids. I specifically asked them to keep it a secret. Was it so hard?

Now Rionn looks a little worried. "I am sorry if I disturbed you. I have seen you from my window for the last two days. I thought you might want some company." With the next words, his neck turns red. "I also wanted to spend time with you."

I can feel flutters in my heart, but they are not like before. My feelings are not so strong for this Rionn, yet I am not completely blank. At first, I felt uncomfortable because he looked at me like a stranger, but it doesn't hurt me so much anymore.

I have other things to hurt over.

Right now, I only see him as a courtier who is eager to spend time with me. His intentions can be one way or another, but he is clearly insistent. The princess, who needs approval from everyone around her, would feel bad for rejecting him.

Only because of that reason, I smile softly and answer, "I would like to walk with you."

Rionn grins like I granted him a great gift and holds out his arm. I hold onto it and let him lead me. I know with him by my side, the walk will not give me the peace I crave every night while I leave. This will not help me clear my head.

But it might help me in another way. I try to be optimistic.

I fight the pain.

We stay silent until we step out of the palace. Rionn seems to understand my want for discretion since he doesn't say anything and keeps pace with my quick steps. Now I am actually a little worried about being outside since he said he saw me from his window, but I try not to focus on that. There is always a risk of being seen. If I consider everything, I won't be able to leave my room ever again.

When we put some distance between us and the palace, Rionn is the first to speak, "I have to admit I am so happy seeing you leave your room."

I shrug. "I am just trying it out."

"It takes a lot of courage, Zuraya. You are really strong for being able to do that."

I don't feel strong, but I still appreciate his words. "Thank you."

He nods, and we again stay silent for a while. I actually like it. I imagine he is not here, and I am free to enjoy the forest. I don't remember a time when I strolled around alone. I was always with Rionn or Qyron, but now that I know how it feels, I kind of like it. Being alone is easier than being with Rionn, and I tend to prefer easy these days.

But then Rionn speaks, and ruins it. "Have you thought about my question? You know about being friends."

"I never said I was going to think about it." I just rejected him. Perhaps it was too harsh.

Rionn doesn't look offended. Instead, he gives me a charming smile. "Yet you said yes to the walk."

"Maybe I am changing my mind," I say, a little shy. We reach the woods, and I feel a little more protected by the long trees. I actually look up at him. "So much is happening in my mind. I am sorry if I hurt your feelings."

Rionn shakes his head. "Nonsense. You don't have to worry about me, Zuraya. I don't want to be a burden but a help instead."

"I don't know how you can do that." Lenora did it perfectly, and I was still too afraid to accept.

"I can be a friend," Rionn says confidently. "I can make you get to know me for real. Maybe you like this version of me too."

I feel overwhelmed. He is too persistent, and it doesn't make sense at all. I stop in the middle of the woods and look up at him. "Why are you flirting with me, Rionn?"

He keeps his posture, but vulnerability touches his dark eyes. "The Rionn you knew, didn't he fall for you so fast? Wasn't he enchanted by you? Maybe I am the same."

I am sure I have never told him how my Rionn and I met. I know he is just guessing, but it is kind of true. I had a crush on him, and we flirted for a while, but he was persistent back then too. From the moment we met, he always looked at me like I was something magnificent.

But it still doesn't make sense. Not in the way Rionn wants, at least.

"He fell for another version of me. I was not this wreck back then."

Rionn shakes his head and takes a step towards me, making my pulse pick up. "You are still that, Zuraya. You are still magnificent. Maybe you cannot see it, but I can."

I shake my head. "You are not telling the truth." I am not who I was. "I appreciate you trying to help me, but this is crazy. I mean, isn't there someone in your life anyway?"

"No," Rionn answers fast.

Too fast.

I guessed he must be already engaged or in a relationship with a nice Shifter, but the way he answers awakens something else in my head. I remember my chambermaids gossiping. I remember that one gossip I didn't believe. Maybe I was wrong.

I lift an eyebrow skeptically and ask, "Really? No one?"

His jaw flexes with nerves. "No one serious."

"Lenora?" I ask. My heart is in my throat as I ask. I don't know why. I am not jealous over Rionn. I don't even want him like that. Not even a bit.

Rionn looks away, suddenly looking uncomfortable for the first time. "Lenora and I are not together. It would be way too complicated."

"You have no kind of relationship?"

"We have sex. It is hardly a relationship."

His admittance makes me uncomfortable. I only had sex with Rionn all my life, but I know it doesn't mean the same to everyone. Qyron had sex all the time and never had someone special. Rionn and Lenora can have meaningless sex.

Still, I am uncomfortable because I don't like the idea of Lenora spending her time with Rionn all those days when she didn't visit me. It is stupid, but I want to be her priority. It makes me feel special.

And I realize I *can* be her priority. All I need to do is say yes to her offer. I can let her train me, and then she will spend her time with me instead of Rionn. She will put *me* first.

All my fears leave me for a while, and I feel stupid for not saying yes straight away. I feel confident at this moment. I feel strong.

My eyes lift to Rionn. Maybe his presence does empower me. I don't know if it is because I really do need a friend to talk to, or is it because he really is like my Rionn. Do I feel more like myself as I act like old Zuraya?

The dresses sure helped.

Maybe Rionn does too. Maybe I do need him.

I am not sure, but I want to try.

"So you are not exclusive?" I ask. My shyness is long gone. I just need answers. I need to remember who I was and if I can still be her.

Rionn shakes his head. "No, not at all."

"Can I want something then?"

"Anything," he says, and he sounds genuine, but I cannot stop comparing him to Lenora. She did it better.

It is not about her, though. It is about me and who I was and who I am.

My chest tightens before asking because I realize how hard it is going to be. I tried to accept this reality so much that I kept telling myself Rionn was not real. Now I feel like I am trying to prove the opposite even though I am not.

I just want to *know.*

"Can I kiss you?" I blurt out, and Rionn's eyes bulge. "Just to see how it feels. It means nothing."

"It won't mean nothing to me."

Those words make me pause for a second. I don't want to break his heart but I need to see the differences between here and there.

Woe in Total Darkness

"It might," I say. "Or it might mean everything. I just want to try, but it doesn't mean I am ready for you to pursue me. This is an experiment."

Rionn looks away and thinks. It takes so long that I am worried I actually hurt his feelings. But then his dark eyes turn to me. "Okay," he says. "I'll kiss you."

I nod, feeling nervous, but Rionn seems confident. He steps closer and wraps an arm around my waist. It feels so familiar that my hands automatically go to his chest. He cups my cheek and leans down. I close my eyes, and the next moment I feel his lips on mine.

He starts slow, kissing and nibbling my lips softly. I let him set the pace. When he licks the seam of my lips, I let him in. I let him deepen the kiss. I let him press my body to him to make me feel how much more he is feeling from the kiss.

It is a normal kiss. Nice I guess. I have never been blown away by kissing anyway. Still my eyes sting. It makes my heart ache.

This kiss makes me sad.

Because it is so familiar. It is precisely how Rionn always kissed me.

So, when he pulls back and looks at my wet eyes and cheeks with worry, I don't say anything. I only bury my face into his chest and cry. I let him hold me. I want to believe he is not my Rionn, but the kiss proves otherwise. The more I cry I also feel proud of myself.

I took action. I did something even if it hurt me.

I can do more.

I can be strong.

When my tears dry, I pull back but don't let Rionn speak. I don't let him kiss me again or walk me back to the palace. If my Rionn can exist in this world, the old Zuraya can too. And I know just who to talk to bring her back.

———— ⸱ ————

I leave Rionn alone and run. My shoes are making it uncomfortable, and my plan is probably very stupid. Lenora is most likely in her room sleeping deeply right now. I should go to her tomorrow. I should send a maid.

I don't want to wait, though.

So, I just run.

I feel like she always knows where I am. I also feel like she will always be where I need her to be.

It doesn't make sense at all.

I keep running.

When I reach Qyron's tomb, it is drizzling. I don't care about getting wet, but the clouds make the night even darker. The moon is nowhere to be seen. If I had my power, I could have shone like the moon.

I will get my powers back.

I take slow steps towards the tomb, and just when I think the darkness is all emptiness, a flash of lightning goes off somewhere far away. It lights up the night. It gives me enough to see enormous golden wings inside. She is really here.

"Lenora," I call out.

Something shifts in the darkness, and she steps out of the tomb. Now I can kind of see her. "Zuraya," she greets me. "I was not expecting to see you. It is late."

I don't care about that. I am not here for small talk. So, I just get into the topic, "I want you to train me."

Lenora's wings tighten on her back, and she takes a few more steps toward me. Her skin is very dimly lit with an orange shine, and I can see her face's pretty features. Her eyes are wide, but she looks happy. "You are accepting my offer?" she asks.

I nod.

She grins. "Sure?"

I nod again.

"Good," she murmurs. "I'll come to take you before midnight tomorrow." Then she moves to leave.

My pulse picks up. I feel like it was so short. I want more of her. I want to feel more proud of myself. But I also know she will never praise me for anything. She will not treat me like I am broken.

Woe in Total Darkness

That's what I like about her.

Suppressing my smile, I turn her way. "Are we meeting at night? Wouldn't that be tiring?" I actually don't mean myself. I do nothing all day anyway.

Lenora looks at me, shrugs, and very calmly says, "Tough luck." Before she turns back, I see a slight smile on her face. "Wear something comfortable."

I don't answer. I just stay there and watch her leave.

I am smiling for real, maybe for the first time since I came here. I smile for the first time since I lost my best friend.

I would never have guessed Rionn's kiss to make me cry, but Sun Princess's moodiness to make me smile. Although I know, it would amuse Qyron very much.

20

Lenora

I try to suppress a yawn. Thanks to years and years of heavy schedules, I am actually good at this. It hasn't been any different these last weeks.

After Zuraya deliberately tried to hurt me, I understood I was doing something wrong. I was angry and sad for a while, but I didn't have the luxury of giving up. I had a mission.

I realized it was not even about how depressed she was. It was about me. She didn't like *me*.

So, I decided to work on her without her knowing.

In the end, she agreed to train with me. I don't know what exactly pushed her after our talk at the tomb, but I was the one who pushed her to the tomb. I had more influence in Zuraya's life these past weeks than she realized.

I need to go back home, and I need to find the Curser. Yet my mind is all filled with making the Moon Princess smile. She consumed most of my time.

I try to look at the bright side, though. Getting moons spheres will help more than a trip back home, and Zuraya can actually help me find the Curser.

I am doing this for the good of these lands. Nothing more.

Woe in Total Darkness

Now I walk to her room with a wooden box in my hands. I normally do my own training very early in the morning with the first light of the sun. That is not going to work well for Zuraya, though. Her power is going to be stronger at night when the moon is up.

Actually, it has been dark for a while now, but I wanted to do it close to midnight. We need to go somewhere fitting for the training, and I know Zuraya wouldn't feel comfortable leaving the palace when most of the court was awake. They stay up late here compared to my home, but still, it is safer at this hour. For the last few days, when she has been taking a stroll, I watched her and made sure no one came her way.

Now that she is going to be with me, it is going to be harder to do that.

It is the best plan, even though it means I have to go to bed very late, catch a few hours of sleep, and then wake up for my own training with my soldiers. It is an important occasion. Every morning at least a few Moonfolk comes out to watch the legendary warriors who keep them safe train.

Or they just view us as entertainment.

I don't mind either way. Their opinion is the last thing I worry about.

When I reach Zuraya's room, I just go inside. If she is not ready yet, that is her problem. Her maids don't stop me; I am a little annoyed. They might be on my payroll, but they shouldn't make that obvious.

When I get inside, Zuraya is waiting for me. Her little braids are in a big braid at the back of her head. She is wearing tight black pants and a black shirt that looks too big for her. She probably didn't have any clothes for this occasion. I am sure her newly hired Earthling tailor will solve that problem soon.

I actually know he will. He is just another who answers to me. He is Sunfolk.

Despite everything, her outfit looks more fitting for the weather than mine. I put on boots, but I am wearing an armless white top and a brown shalwar. I must look ridiculous because Zuraya looks at me with a stunned expression.

The way her eyes bulge and her lips part makes me a little nervous. I don't feel cold, but I am anxious that I look weird. She is just speechless.

"Is there a problem?" I ask trying to hide my nerves.

Zuraya's throat moves, and she looks away, mumbling, "No, of course not." She rubs the back of her neck before turning back to me. "Are we leaving?"

I look at her blushed cheeks and try so hard not to smile. All my worry disappears when her eyes quickly scan me once again. I feel so stupid. I don't look weird at all. Or at least that is not the reason Raya was looking at me so shocked.

I just look really, really good.

Good enough to make her blush.

It is so difficult not to grin at the situation, but I manage. Only a small smile peeks out. "Yes," I say and clear my throat. "But before, I have a gift for you. In case we come across someone on our way there."

Her sweet shy expression turns into one of worry. "Our way where? I thought we could do it in my room. It is large enough."

It is, in fact, large, but there is no way we are doing it here. "We are trying to free your power Zuraya. That includes freeing your mind and your body. You have been inside this room all the time. Nothing is getting free inside these walls."

Raya's shoulders slump, but she nods. "You are right." She eyes the little box in my hands. "I hope you have a pair of wings inside that."

When I see the side of her lips tip up, I let myself smile at the joke. "Close enough. Come."

She does without protest and I open the box for her see. "I have it made specifically for you. These things are common in Sun Khanate, but we usually use gold. This one is silver. I had it for a while but was waiting for you to be ready."

Zuraya reaches inside, but her eyes go to the little fox sleeping on her bed. "Do you have a stock of gifts for me that you keep for specific times?"

Woe in Total Darkness

A sinister smile fills my face. "You would like to know, don't you?"

Instead of answering, Zuraya just takes out the silver horn from the box and goes to the mirror. I cannot give her wings, but we cover our missing limbs in the Desert. Sunfolk is traditionally more fighter spirited, so we have more Feyadas who need these. The gold sometimes even look better than the original body part.

But I know Raya doesn't like gold. She is the Moon Princess, so all of her jewelry is silver. The horn tip I gifted her is now included.

Even though she tries to hold it in her head, wondering if it will fit, I know it will fit perfectly like a glove. I didn't send off guessed measurements. One of the maids specifically measured her good horn, and this new one is made to reflect that one. The perfection of the Moon Princess is going to be maintained.

I see Zuraya's finger tremble a little, but she looks excited as she asks me, "How do I put it on?"

"We can glue it down, but that won't be very durable. I suggest implanting the silver at the front. I can do it, but I'll need to do some filing."

"It is okay. Let's implant it."

I can hear the excitement in her tone even though she tries to hide it. She is so damn desperate to be a little more normal. Getting rid of a reminder of her imprisonment means so much to her.

Suddenly I am filled with pride just because I made her happy like this.

I like that she is going back to her real style with the dresses, but she doesn't need to replicate her missing parts for an audience. She is underweight, and there is hollowness on her face. Yet she is still so beautiful. I don't think anyone who sees Raya can think about missing wings or a broken horn. They would be too busy losing their breath over her beauty.

But it doesn't matter what I think. If she is going to feel more confident with the silver horn, I am happy I am the one who gifts it to her.

I move over and make her sit on a chair. I have seen many golden implants, but that doesn't mean I knew how to put one on. I specifically studied it so I can put the horn in for Zuraya.

I thought it might strengthen our bond since she is not very fond of me.

Or just wanted to do it myself. No particular reason.

I ask the maids for the specific tools I need, and like magic, they find them very quickly. Probably the best way I used my money is these maids. I can reach Zuraya so easily, thanks to them.

I am pretty sure she would have figured out what I did if she didn't have the illusion of me not caring about her at all. She has no idea how much I care.

Even my previous dislike towards her disappeared these last days when I followed her like a shadow. There is nothing to dislike about her.

Absently I arrange her head in the right position so I can fit the silver tip onto her broken horn. I am fixated on my work until I hear her sharp intake of breath. When my eyes move to her face, I find her looking at me and realize I have never been this close to her while she was conscious. I carried her in my arms when I rescued her, but she doesn't remember it.

Now I can see her eyes so clearly. It is not just a vibrant light blue. There are violets, pinks, and greens in there.

It is like aurora in her irises.

My mouth goes dry. It is stunning.

Suddenly I feel a surge of satisfaction from what happened earlier. She is so fucking pretty, and I made her blush. I can affect her so easily.

Maybe she doesn't hate me as much as she thinks.

The thought makes me want to smile, but when Zuraya clears her throat and looks away, I get a reality check. She tries to turn her head too, but my hand on her horn stops her. Just like that, I realize the position makes her face way too close to my chest. It is indecent. And I know it makes her throat go dry, just like mine.

However, it does not matter. She might be so beautiful, and there might be tension between us. She is not a Feyada I am courting. I am not trying to fuck the depression out of her.

She is Zuraya Haliyes.

She is my duty. My way to get moon spheres from King Luran. I am just helping her for a reason.

But maybe I can still be her friend.

I ignore the sudden heat she caused me. She is just attractive. It is normal for my body to react. I don't mind. I just rearrange myself so I don't push my breasts onto her face and get to work. I don't look down at her eyes again. I just focus on implanting the silver. I feel her body stay tense the whole time, but I ignore that too. She has been a prisoner for so long. It is only natural for her to feel flustered being so close to someone. I can't hold it against her.

When the silver tip is perfectly secured in place, I swallow to hydrate my throat and step back. "All done. Let's go."

21

Zuraya

Kissing Rionn must have turned on something inside me that has been off for a while. It sounds very unreasonable but I have no other explanation for what happened.

I am not sure if now I am going to go around getting aroused by anyone who gets too close. A side of me stupidly finds that thought comforting because I don't want it to be something exclusive to Lenora.

It doesn't make any sense.

Unfortunately, I know it is not true. My maids got closer than she did while preparing me, they gave me a bath while I was stark naked, and their touch did nothing. Lenora's shouldn't do as well.

I hate that she totally understood it. I couldn't hide any of my reactions. She saw my blush, and then she saw me looking at her like a starved little kitten. I could tell it amused her. She probably tried so hard not to laugh at me. She must think I am so stupid.

It is her fault, though. It is late at night and very chilly. No one needs to wear clothes that show off their arms, especially if they have really nice arms.

I don't think I have ever looked at anyone's arms before. I mean, it is a fact that Lenora is beautiful, but it never mattered to me. It

Woe in Total Darkness

shouldn't make me blush. Rionn is attractive, and I didn't blush even when he tried to kiss me.

Maybe that's because I am used to him.

I don't know and don't want to think about it. I just want to forget. I need to focus on the training and not on how Lenora's blonde hair looks shiny even in the dark.

Damn me.

"Climb starts," she chirps when we reach the side of a cliff. I thought we were going to the beach to avoid prying eyes. I was actually excited. I love the beach.

Now I'm not sure where we are actually going. I mean, the steps leading up to the cliff's peak gives me an idea, but I want to ignore that. "Where are we going?"

"To the top, of course." Lenora smiles brightly at me. "Closer to the moon."

"That doesn't make any sense."

"I don't like my methods questioned. Come on, it will be a nice warm-up."

Warm-up? That is a full-blown workout and one that I am not ready for. Also, one I didn't ask for. "I wanted you to help me train so I can reach my power. I was thinking of more of a spiritual training than a physical one."

Lenora's eyebrows furrow. She looks at me like I am stupid, and I am back to hating her once again. Not that I really stopped. "Your power is both tied to your soul and your body. You cannot reach your goal without either of them, so now stop crying and follow me up. You know I also need to train with my soldiers at sunrise, and you are taking too long."

My eyes widen. She is going to train once more after me. Surely she must be mad. And just because I don't want to deal with a mad General, I follow her up the steps. Though my complaining continues. At least it does until I am out of breath.

Lenora makes it look too easy. She climbs like it is nothing while I sweat and cry right behind her. I want to snap her head off. How can she have so much stamina? I look at the tightly clasped wings and repeat the same words over and over again as she keeps looking perfect.

I hate you.

I hate you.

I hate you.

"So, what made you finally say yes?"

"Huh?" I startle by her question.

Lenora looks back at me, and I want to keep repeating how much I hate her. She didn't even break a sweat. She looks as if we are taking a stroll around the garden. And she repeats her question with a very non-shaky voice, "What made you say yes to training with me?"

I try to regulate my breathing for the answer. Actually, I don't even know what the exact answer is. "I guess Rionn helped." I had the realization right after kissing him.

"Rionn?" she asks, surprised. "I didn't know you two were spending time together."

I shrug even though she cannot see me. "Well, he was very insistent, so I accepted at last. I wanted to see what being old Zuraya would feel like. So, I kissed him, and I decided I wanted my powers back. It is kind of stupid." I don't even know why I am giving her all the details.

Lenora's wings twitch slightly, and her spine gets straighter. "You kissed him?"

Now I am also tense. The climb feels harder than before. I remember how Rionn accepted the gossip about him and Lenora. I didn't let it annoy me back then, so I can do it again. "It was just an experiment. You don't have to worry."

"Why would I worry?" her voice is hard like steel.

"I know you two are sleeping together, and it is okay. I am not trying to steal him or anything. He just saw me walking alone at night and wanted to accompany me. I kissed him just to see how it felt. Nothing is happening between us."

Lenora's wings flex annoyingly. I am so focused on her that I realize we have reached the top only when she stops and turns to me. "I don't care if you steal him, Zuraya. It is really not that important to me."

For some reason, that bothers me. "You want me to be with him?"

She looks uncomfortable but doesn't change the subject. "Honestly, I don't, Zuraya, because it is complicated, and I don't know how it is going to affect you. I don't want you to get hurt. But you are an adult, and you are the one who can decide what will happen. So, if you do decide to be with him, I just want you to know I will not be a problem. Does that make sense?"

I stay speechless and just nod. I want to go back to hating her, but it is difficult when she is being really considered. Everybody in the palace worries for me, and I am sure everybody wants the best for me. The difference between them and Lenora is that she doesn't try to force me into what's best. She doesn't treat me like a broken princess, but like I am just Zuraya.

I like that more than I should.

"Good," Lenora exhales. "Now we can start our meditation."

As she walks toward the edge, a silly smile fills my face, and I start complaining again. Our banter is good. It is easy, fun, and, most importantly, safe.

———c———

The meditation part of our training is easier on me. Because of the climbing, I actually feel sleepy, but I don't let it consume me. I had a lot of spiritual training before. That was always the route I took to reach my power. I never needed the physical workout part. Despite my complaints, I don't plan on ending this. I trust Lenora. Besides my father, she is the only person who can understand my power, and I know my father does not want to see my face.

I remind him of his failure, how he no longer has an heir. I am actually surprised that he didn't remarry after my kidnapping to have another child. It seems stupid since his trust in me is not very strong.

It was always hard to understand my father. I had a good relationship with him by being the perfect princess. I made him proud of me because that was the best thing I could get from him. He is a frigid male.

Maybe that is why I am not very broken over his disinterest in me. I never had any parental love. My mother, who my father only married for political reasons, died while giving birth to me. I heard she was lovely and would love me very much if she was alive.

Only she wasn't.

My father was only there to make sure his heir was up to his standards. And I was.

Until I wasn't.

Honestly, losing Qyron hurts me more than losing a mother who I never knew or losing the love of my father, which never really existed. Maybe it is a blessing. One less thing to cry over.

"You are not focusing," Lenora murmurs, and I open one eye to look at her. Her form is perfect, and she looks to be in total bliss. Her skin shines dimly with Sunshine. She looks magnificent.

I close my eyes immediately.

"Sorry," I apologize. "My mind is somewhere else."

I should be good at this, but it feels different. I try to follow Lenora's lead, but then I see her shimmering. My instinct is to reach my power. Unfortunately, it is not there.

I don't know what to focus on if my Moonshine doesn't exist.

A few minutes ago, Lenora told me I was focusing too much. I was forcing my power. Apparently, now I am not forcing it enough. I should let my mind empty. I should not think, but I cannot help.

Lenora exhales deeply. "This is not working. Your mind is too full."

I flinch. "Sorry."

When I open my eyes, she is no longer shining, and her eyes are open too. But she is still sitting on the floor. Her body is turned towards me. "Don't apologize. I am your teacher now. It is my duty to find the way that works."

It makes me feel a little better even though I know I am the problem here. "Do you have any ideas?"

Woe in Total Darkness

"I have a few," she murmurs, looking away. "What was your main choice of weapon?"

"Weapon?" my eyes widen.

Lenora looks at me like I am stupid. "Yes. I know you are not a soldier, but you are a princess. You are obligated to train in certain topics. Surely you got war training. What did you choose as your main weapon."

I cringe inward because I know everything she says is true. Only we don't always follow the ancient rules here in the North. "Qyron and I didn't really like those classes." Maybe the mention of her brother will take her mind off of it.

Fat chance because Lenora answers easily, "Qyron was an archer. He trained in archery since he was four years old."

Well, he didn't train much here. I roll my eyes. "Okay, I didn't like those classes very much, and I was already good at other things. My father thought they were unimportant anyway, so I bailed on them early."

She tilts her head sideways and gives me a disappointed look. "Oh, Raya."

My breath hitches. I cannot even focus on her expression. "Raya?" No one calls me that. I am not sure if I even like it.

I probably don't.

Lenora looks away and gets on her feet. I get the feeling that was a slip. Though her tone is playful when she speaks. "Is there a problem? I thought we were becoming friends."

"We are?"

She nods. "We are."

"So, you won't get angry at your friends for skipping war lessons?"

"I won't get angry," she says. A sinister smile forms on her face. "But I'll make sure you'll get them this time."

I groan. I just want my light back. I don't need to fight someone to do that.

"Are we gonna do it today?" I ask.

She shakes her head while flexing her wings. "No, it is getting late. I want to sleep a little before my morning training. I'll think of something new for tomorrow."

"Okay," I say. I am weirdly disappointed. I was not expecting to reach my power from day one, but I thought I would make some progress. The only thing I did was climb a damn high peak.

I feel like nothing has changed.

I realize I am frozen in my tracks when Lenora stops at the top of the stairs and looks back at me. "Is everything okay, Raya?"

Something flutters in my stomach, and despite my failure, I smile. "It is," I answer and follow Lenora down the stairs.

Maybe something did change tonight.

22

Lenora

Tonight I am walking to a chamber I haven't visited in the Moon Palace yet. It is for a reason. Last night made me realize I need to be more focused.

Normally at this hour, I go to Rionn or let him come to my room. We brainstorm about things and have sex. It is an easy routine. It helps me scratch my itch so it won't be a distraction between all my duties.

But I realized Rionn is a bigger problem than not getting any sex.

What Raya told me still annoys me. I shouldn't mind who she kisses, but I don't want her to get hurt. I don't trust Rionn with her at all.

He doesn't deserve her.

The second she told me they kissed, I decided to end whatever I had with Rionn. Not because I want her to have him all to herself. That is not at all. I just realized sleeping with him made me too relaxed around him. I became careless.

It is clear that he has other intentions with Raya. This is no longer about helping me.

The worst of all, he is using me for it. Rionn told her he saw her from his window. No shit. I knew that was a lie the second I heard

Sem Thornwood

it. I always stalk Raya when she is out at night. I know she was never visible from his window. I know he usually falls deep asleep after we have sex.

I also know how he got that information. He was in my damn bed. One of Raya's chambermaids came to give me a report. We mentioned the night walks.

He was fucking listening.

Not anymore.

I roll my shoulders and shake my wings in an attempt to get rid of my rigidness. I am not going to lie about why I came here, but I still want to look casual. This visit carries the need for my duty, but it is also a friendly visit. I want them to know it.

Before reaching the door, I smile and face the Moon Army soldiers waiting at the door. This is the only room guarded by them. There are royal guards all around, but they are not enough for this one. It is always either moon soldiers or Seelie guards.

"Please let the General and the Princess know I am here," I say sweetly.

The soldier nods and goes inside. Just a short while later, he is out and letting me in. I find them in the antechamber. Maha is sitting on a big chair that looks more like a throne. She is wearing a yellow dress, her white hair is up in a bun, there is a smile on her face, and both of her hands are on her huge belly.

"I can't believe you still haven't given birth."

She just pouts her bottom lip in mock sadness. "I know! It is all this one's fault. Seelie pregnancies take six months, but apparently, Feyadas carry their young for fourteen months."

"Torture," I say with a smile.

Davon Archard comes from the little bar on the corner with two drinks in his hands. Even inside his own chamber, he looks like a soldier. His spine is straight, and his wings are tucked tightly. He hands me one of the drinks with a cold expression and then perches on the handle of Maha's chair. When he gives her the other drink, his eyes turn impossibly soft. It is hard to believe how fast he changes for the Seelie Princess.

Woe in Total Darkness

"Do you come to talk about pregnancies, Your Excellency?" Archard asks, looking pissed for interrupting his private time with his wife. Honestly, I don't care about his sharp words, but I really don't like that he calls me Your Excellency.

Thankfully Maha elbows him on the side. "Don't be rude." Then she gives me a warm smile. "Len is always welcomed."

"Thank you," I chirp and take a sip of my drink. It is an awful Northern wine. I am sure Maha is drinking something without alcohol, and I would prefer hers right now. This tastes like piss.

Literally. It is warm.

"I actually came here to discuss some matters."

"See," Archard says, looking down at Maha, and she only rolls her eyes.

"Would you prefer I just came here because I missed you?"

Archard looks horrified at the thought. "No."

"Good then," I say with a grin. "I am here for a reason. We need to talk."

General puts a hand on his wife's shoulder protectively. "Maha will stay. I will share whatever we discuss with her anyway."

That is definitely a security hazard but also cute, I guess. To me, a General should put their duties above anything, but Archard puts Maha there. It is a relationship not fit for people in our positions, but Archard looks extremely happy with her.

I am just a bit envious.

That doesn't mean I am going to go out there looking for a significant other. Falling in love would be a disaster for me.

I shake the thought away and shrug. "I want her to stay anyway. She should be a part of this."

Maha actually looks happy and a bit proud. "Oh, I should?"

"Yes. Your input will be important for my questions."

She nods, determined. "Of course, it will." Archard just grins down at her. Honestly, it is even weird seeing him smile.

My first question is to Archard. "Why is Rionn Ay Ujk still here?"

His expression turns blank instantly, and he looks at me with those muddy eyes. "Why are you still here?" That gets him another elbow in the gut from Maha. He only puts his hand on her belly lovingly in return.

"I have an agreement with the King. I am here for a reason."

Maha's eyebrows come together, and she looks up at her husband. He explains, "Moon spheres in exchange for fixing the Princess."

I don't like his wording. I know Raya is broken from everything she went through, but I am not fixing her. I am just helping her to gather herself back up. I am just the little push she needs in her life.

"You are doing a good thing, Len," Maha says cheerfully. I really do love her.

"Thanks," I say with a smile, and my eyes go back to the General. "Ay Ujk is getting in my way. I am worried he will hurt Zuraya."

Archard looks uncomfortable due to my use of the Princess's first name. He rubs the back of his head. "He is Moonfolk."

"Oh, and I suppose you are a guy who has great distaste towards anyone who is not Moonfolk."

He growls low, and Maha looks a bit worried. His arms tighten around her. "Don't bring Maha into this. Rionn Ay Ujk is a ruler in his own right. I cannot order him to go. He is here to help us get the Curser."

I want to groan. I know Rionn is above me to them. He is not only Moonfolk but also a monarch, not an heir. I am risking my life every day to keep these lands safe, and I am still lowly to them. Moonfolk Feyadas are not very fond of Shifters, too, but I guess Sunfolk is even worse than them.

I decide not to push. "Are there any developments about the Curser?"

They both tense. It is a delicate subject for everyone. "Still tracking," he says. It means they don't have anything.

I don't blame him for this one.

"I actually have an idea about it. We should focus on Zuraya. I cannot stop thinking about her condition. They made her believe

Woe in Total Darkness

she was still at this palace, living her best life for seven years. I want to know what kind of spell they used. It might be helpful."

Archard looks indecisive, but Maha speaks before he can fill the room with negativity, "Are we sure she is not just traumatized? It can be a way to deal with what happened to her. Poor thing might have created a whole life in her head to not get hurt."

I know Maha has no bad intentions, but I don't like her words. I want to believe Raya would have fought them even without a choice of weapon.

That reminds me, we have training in a few hours, and I am in a good mood again.

"I don't think that is the case," I say casually. "It could be something similar to mind manipulation which means it is a holy power. I was wondering if you have ever heard such a thing, Maha? Seelies have more stories about Tisasa."

She thinks for a minute and then shakes her head. "I don't think so. The powers we have in our stories are the powers you have. It is all about light."

"Are you sure?"

Archard again looks protective. "Don't push her!"

I try so hard not to roll my eyes, but I fail. "I don't push her. We are merely talking."

"This is not Maha's concern. She is stressed enough as it is."

Maha looks at him with soft eyes. "I am not stressed, love. It is okay." Her hands move over her swollen belly, and she gets thoughtful. "There might be a book," she mumbles under her breath.

Archard looks a little pissed, but I don't care. "What is it, Maha?" I ask. She is a fucking Seelie. She is my best hope.

She pulls the neck of her dress nervously. "There is a book about the powers. It has historical stories, so I am not sure if it is reliable about the powers, but it tells the story of Tisasa's powers getting stolen away. Maybe there is something."

It sounds like nothing, but if the book refers to the event as "powers getting stolen," then it is definitely a Seelie book. It might include something. Maha wouldn't tell me if it was nothing.

183

"What is the name?"

She cringes just a bit like she doesn't want to tell me. "Theft of Faith. I have it in my personal library. You probably cannot find it anywhere else if you are not willing to visit the Seelie Kingdom."

"I would love to visit, but I don't. I can't leave Zuraya. Also, your sister is never too happy to see me there."

Maha throws her hand. "You go there to help. She is just grumpy."

That and she blames us Feyadas for every bad thing. I still cannot believe she let Maha marry one of us instead of just killing Archard. She is still not fond of him, but he got what he wanted anyway.

When Maha tries to get up to retrieve the book, Archard stops her with a hand on her shoulder. "Sit, My Flower. I'll get the book." He leaves for another room after kissing her forehead.

Maha's cheeks are a darker shade of green when she looks at me again. "He is pampering me a lot."

"As he should."

She giggles, but then her eyes look a little more serious. "Do you really have problems with my sister? We haven't talked a lot since I got pregnant. She is mad because my half-Feyada child is going to be an heir, and she has to have a kid to stop that."

I am not surprised. When it comes to Queen Mav, everything is about her. She probably thinks Archard got her sister pregnant just to force her to have a child when she doesn't want to. She is a little suspicious when it comes to Feyadas. Most Seelies are.

I avoid commenting on their family problems, though. "She actually hates me more than she used to. I think it is because I am here instead of fighting off the Patches. If she could, she would just take me to the Seelie Kingdom so I can fight the Patches there all the time."

Maha's face falls. "It is hard back there."

"I know. Hopefully, the moon spheres will help, and hopefully, my country won't get into a war while I try to get them."

She goes rigid. "What do you mean war? Is Mav threatening you?"

Woe in Total Darkness

That would be something to get me away from my current mission. "No, it is the Giants. There are Patches in their lands. They are fighting the creatures, but they don't have the resource to close the Patch, and they don't know how to either. My soldiers are trying to help but the Giant King says he prefers to be swallowed by the darkness than to let Sun Army into his lands."

Maha winces. "Oh, that's bad."

I nod. "It is. I mean, if they want to die by the curse, it is their choice, but if their whole land is filled with the curse, I am afraid it is going to be so damn hard to close that Patch."

"King won't listen to you."

"I don't think he will listen to anyone who is not a native of these lands." I give her an expectant look. I won't ask it straight away, but I need her. First, I let my soldiers deal with the Giant King, but he is becoming too much of a problem. I need to fix it without leaving Raya alone.

Maha gives me an understanding look and says, "I'll talk to Mav."

I just hope she can convince her sister so I can give all my attention to Raya. It is definitely much more entertaining than dealing with Giants.

23

Lenora

Feyadas came across the water. They left their lands. They flew for days to get free from the Fairy regime. When they reached the shores of the Isle of Ae, they were sick and tired. They lost many on their journey. They were refugees in these lands.

The first one to accept them into the Isle was the young Queen Mirrina K'rra. She was determined the land was going to provide anything we needed. Tisasa sent these creatures here, and Tisasa was going to give them what they deserved. They were welcomed.

Shifter Alpha and the Giant King were hesitant, but Queen K'rra insisted that Feyadas were to be the children of the Isle, just like the natives. They were not the enemy. They were friends.

Queen Mirrina wanted to decide on their fate with their leader, but Feyadas seemed to have two leaders. Half of the group was loyal to Lady Obana Haliyes, and the other half was loyal to Lord Ruen Mitharaus. It was making things harder and harder. They were in need of a home, but the negotiations were not going well.

To make things easier, Queen Mirrina suggested a marriage between the two but Lord and Lady were absolute rivals. They refused to marry, and they kept refusing to work together. In the end, it pushed Queen Mirrina so much. She was a faithful Seelie *who believed these newcomers were going to be good news. She believed it was going to work out in the end, but the hate between the two leaders was making things too hard for her.*

In the end, Queen gave up and told them they could claim any land that was unclaimed along with their followers. The Seelie Kingdom was going to help both of them to build their own civilization. They were going to have support. They just needed to let the Seelies have peace from their bickering.

Lord Ruen decided to claim the frightening Desert. He was determined he and his followers would be able to adapt to the deadly conditions of these lands and be more powerful than ever.

Lady Obana claimed the rocky Northern lands where the waves were too close for anyone's comfort. The ground was either too soft or too harsh and not much grew. She said it would be okay if she could just get some livestock. If the wild animals close to Shifter Territory were able to live, surely her animals would also live.

Queen Mirrina was true to her word. She helped them get started. When Lord Ruen managed to conquer the Desert and become too powerful, she didn't feel threatened. She helped him with his spices. She let him build a trading lane and many caravanserais.

When Lady Obana managed to become a provider of meat for other regions, she only felt proud. Queen even defended her against the Alpha when he complained about how she was threatening his borders. She wanted everyone to be friendly.

Everything was going okay despite the bumps. Queen's help was very valued by the Feyadas. They were loyal to the Seelies. Mitharaus family of the desert were very sympathetic towards the customs of the natives. They become closer to the Seelies. Haliyes family of the North became important for everyone's meat needs. They were not on the best terms with the Shifters, but everything was working out smoothly.

Unfortunately, Queen Mirrina was not aware of the evil she had created. She accepted those creatures for her Goddess. She saw them as the gift of Tisasa. But despite everything, Feyadas did not accept the faith. They never respected Tisasa as much as the Queen did.

The heirs of the two Feyada families wanted to end the rivalry between their parents, and they wanted to learn more about the culture of the lands. Vaughn Mitharaus and Carin Haliyes gave the now old Queen Mirrina K'rra sweet words. They showed friendly faces. They made her let them visit the Sacred Lands in the South. She let them go to the small islands, and she let them discover the Ancient Temple of Tisasa.

Queen Mirrina K'rra was expecting their return with a strong faith from the sacred lands. Instead, they returned with Tisasa's powers. These newcomers stole the powers of the Goddess and caused the Queen to take her own life as a result.

Only then the rise of the Feyadas began on the Isle of Ae.

———ᴄ———

I climb the steps as Zuraya follows me. I whistle a low tune. I know she is irritated when I act so easygoing. Spending time with Zuraya is actually not bad. I don't have to worry about the Giants, the Curser, or the Patches. I can just come up to this hill and have fun annoying Raya.

My job is to help her find her power, but that won't stop me from having fun. I can be a friend and a teacher at the same time.

Honestly, this is the first training I am allowed to have fun. I like it.

The soft breeze turns a little harsher, and I can feel the cold even on my feather-covered wings. That is my least favorite thing about the North. It is always cold.

"I see you covered your arms this time," Zuraya says from behind me.

My lips curl in a smile. "Did that upset you, Raya?" I like teasing her. It is just my nature, and I don't have to hide it from her. I mean, what is she going to cost me if I act a little casual?

I hear her huff behind me. "I am just making an observation."

Woe in Total Darkness

"Oh, yeah, I'm sure." I laugh. "You know I can train topless if you like my arms so much." I am not as squeamish as the Moonfolk. Also, I have really nice tattoos I can show her if I take this horrible top off.

"I don't want my teacher to freeze to death."

I am a little touched. "You know it is okay to like my arms. I train hard for them." I turn around, and she is forced to stop and come face to face with me. I smile teasingly. "Since my weapon of choice is a sword." Then I turn back and keep climbing.

Raya groans behind me. "You are impossible. I never needed a weapon. In my dream, everything was peaceful. The Curser was dead."

I wish I lived in her dream.

When I reach the top, I see everything I demanded is already here. Two big chests contain props for our training. I don't focus on them just now, though. Instead, I again turn toward Raya, a bit more serious this time. "I started researching about our powers. Physical training was a big part of my journey, so we will try that, but I will also look for other ways. Just give me time and some trust."

She looks stunned just for a second but then nods. "Thanks."

My main goal is to find out how they put her inside a dream for seven years, but I am sure that book will also help me figure out the light powers a bit more. I really want to be able to help Raya.

For the moon spheres, of course.

Otherwise, I wouldn't care. Not even a bit.

Zuraya looks around. Her breathing is still a little fast. "Oh, what are those?"

"I made my soldiers fly those here. Their time will come later, though."

"What are we going to do first, then? Meditation?" Thankfully her voice is not mocking or disinterested. The spiritual side of the training is an essential part of the process, even if it feels like nothing at the beginning. It always helps me feel more connected to my power, and I hope it will do the same for her.

But there is another thing before that. "I want to try something else first."

"What is it?"

"I know you cannot reach your light yet," I say carefully. "I was wondering if you can reach your other power."

"My other power?"

"Body manipulation," I say helpfully. My mind manipulation always feels different than my light, so I am hoping it can be the same for her.

Raya thinks for a second. "I don't think I tried. It was not something I used a lot anyway. Most of my duties included being social in the palace and looking pretty. I didn't need it much."

It does sound like a peaceful world. Although it also sounds a little boring. I would never want Raya to waste her potential like that. Looking pretty shouldn't be her priority.

But again, it is not my life. It is hers.

"How you used it when you did, though? We can give it a go."

"I did some healing. I was not a healer or anything, but I helped around the court and used it on myself for little things. It helped with the looking pretty part."

I smile. "Well, that means you didn't need it a lot."

For a second, she looks at me confused, and then her cheeks heat. I cannot help it. I love making her blush. It is almost like no one ever dared to say such things to her. I actually doubt that because even in her dreams, I know Qyron would be playful. She must have heard playful flattery before.

Maybe it not the words but just me.

Without forcing her to answer, I pull out my sword from my belt. The moon is almost full, and the light dances along the glass sword. "Pretty," Zuraya mumbles. It is also deadly. With a quick move, I swing it and cut my lower arm. Not very deep but enough to draw blood. I am actually stupid because I also cut the arm of my cozy grey top.

Raya eyes my cut, and she looks worried. That's why her next words surprise me, "Trying to show off your arms after all."

Woe in Total Darkness

I see her smile, and my expression mirrors hers. "Can't help my need for attention."

She laughs, but then her laughter dies, and she winces. I realize she is looking at the dripping blood. She gets closer and holds my arm in her hands. "A smaller cut would have worked too."

"Like I said. I love attention."

Her lips press together, and she pushes the clothing away so she can actually focus. The cut is bloody, but it really is not bad as it looks. With my constant pain, I don't even feel a thing. Of course, Raya doesn't know that. Almost no one knows.

She is holding my arm with one hand, and the fingers of her other hand move gently over the cut. She closes her eyes and takes a deep breath. Her fingers flex over the wound but never push hard against my skin. It is apparent this is not her first time.

I hope to see my cut stitch itself back together by her touch. I even hope to see her shine.

But nothing is ever this easy.

I feel a tingling over my skin. The spots her fingertips are touching feel cold and a bit itchy. I can actually feel my skin on the opposite sides of the cut wanting to reunite. Only it never happens.

Zuraya tries and tries hard. Her breathing gets fast, and her body trembles. Her face looks like she is about to cry. I cannot take it.

"Stop."

She goes on. Tingling continues, but nothing else happens.

"Raya, stop!"

That works. Her eyes open, and the tingling disappears. She looks at the cut that is still there. One single tear slides to her cheek. Her bottom lip trembles. "I am useless."

My chest hurts, and I hate it. I am used to seeing pain. I am used to seeing desperation. At this point, I have a hard shell around my heart so I can endure the agony that is always around me. I don't let it get to me.

Raya's tear gets to me.

I reach and brush it away with my thumb. Her pale eyes lift to mine. "It is okay," I soothe. "You will succeed."

"Do you really believe that?"

She looks so sad. I don't want her to look sad. I want her to be annoyed by me and make jokes. I want her to complain about my methods. I want her to look away as she blushes. I would take anything but her sadness at this point.

It makes me feel like shit.

I say, "Of course." And I really do believe it. This was better than when she tried to use her light. "Your power is still there, Raya. I can feel it. We just need to work."

She looks away and then nods. Her hands leave my arms, and she brushes away the wetness from her eyes. She inhales deeply and turns back to me with a smile. "Then let's meditate."

I can't help but smile back. *That's the spirit.*

———— ᴄ ————

"Do I really have to try all of them?" Raya asks when I show her what is inside the chests. There are all kinds of weapons. I want her to choose her main one, and since she didn't train with these things, she cannot make a reasonable decision until she knows how all of them feel.

I nod, determined. She might not like this, but it will help her reach her power. Being one with a weapon will be helpful. If she can see a weapon as an extra limb of hers, she can most likely see her power as one too. It is all about mentality, but to train it, we have to get physical.

"You really want to see me fail over and over again, don't you?" she asks mockingly.

"Wrong," I say, all serious. "I want to see you succeed with one of these. You just need to see which one calls to you."

"What if none of them does?"

"One will. Trust me."

She huffs but doesn't complain more. I know I keep asking her to trust me, and I didn't actually do anything to gain it, but I don't have any other choice. I cannot help her if she doesn't trust me.

Luckily, I feel like she really does.

"Which one do you want to start with?"

Woe in Total Darkness

Zuraya eyes all the weapons inside the chests. There are probably a few she doesn't know the names of. I brought everything I could think of. A few of them are traditional weapons of the ancients. In Sun Khanate, we are open to using them, but I know North is a little bit stiffer when it comes to that.

It is almost like they don't want to accept the traditions of the natives, and they also want to erase their own history as well. Even the weather shows that. Our ancestors came from a warm forest in the Mainlands. We are not fit for cold.

The Moon Kingdom lives like witches. They are also adapting their racist ways. Even on the Isle of Ae, there is no escape from the superior race.

"Arrow and bow," Zuraya says, and I shake off the history lesson from my mind. I guessed she was probably going to choose that. It was Qyron's weapon of choice, after all.

I don't point that out. "Very well." Let's start with that.

Thankfully unlike Raya, I am trained in all of these weapons. I am not professional on all of them. Not at all. But I am good enough to show her the basics. I can handle it until she chooses which one to go with.

I take the arrow and bow and hand them to her. "I'll show you and guide you for a bit with all of them, but when you set your choice, we will carry our training to my regular training with the Sun Soldiers."

Raya almost drops the bow. "What?"

I know the idea of other people makes her uncomfortable, but I try to act like it is the most normal thing. "It makes me sad to admit it, but I am not an expert in everything. If you choose a weapon, I am not the best at, one of my soldiers will train you under my guidance."

She shakes her head. "Then I'll choose something you can teach me. I am not ready to train with others."

"You should choose the weapon that calls to you. We are not going to start training with them tomorrow anyways. You'll have time to prepare yourself."

She doesn't look even a tiny bit convinced. "No, I'll still choose something you are good at. I don't want to see anyone else."

"I won't tell you what I am good at then." Although I doubt it will be too hard to tell when I start showing her the basics. "You cannot hide forever, Raya."

With those words, she gives me an angry look. I can see how broken she is under that fire, though. "Maybe I want to."

I can very easily tell that is not the case. She is just afraid.

I reach and take her free hand in mine. That startles her, but I don't care because she doesn't pull back. "I know it is scary," I say. "But you won't be training with them alone. I will be there. I will always be there for you."

Her eyes flutter, and her throat moves with a swallow. She looks at me with so much trust that I feel like I am going to drown. She seems so fragile. I just want to keep her safe from everything. I want to crush all her sadness.

"Promise?" she asks with a whisper.

I nod, "Promise."

Her eyes briefly go to my lips and then come back to my eyes. A blush fills her cheeks, and this time she looks away. Her hand remains on mine, though. "I am not accepting it yet, but I will think about it. We'll talk when the time comes."

I smile. "Deal."

24

Zuraya

"A little higher," Lenora instructs, and I aim the bow higher. My arms are so skinny and weak that I have difficulty holding them. But I promised myself I was going to try anything. I complain, but I still do what Lenora tells me.

She is the only one I can trust with this.

"Stop," she says, and I lower my weapons with a sigh. Lenora comes close while shaking her head. "You still hold it like it is a stranger. You have to act like it is a part of you."

"I know," I murmur. I know because she keeps saying that. I understand what she means, actually. I remember watching Qyron train with his bow and arrow. He wouldn't move them, but his body would move around the bow. He would adapt to the weapon instead of making it adapt to him. I actually try to mimic him but apparently, it doesn't work. Lenora is disappointed in me.

It makes me uneasy.

It is so stupid, but I do crave her approval. I want someone to be actually proud of me.

I like spending time with her. I like how she banters with me. I even like her flirting, even if it makes me blush. I don't have to think about everything I have lost when I am with her. I can be my old self and my new self simultaneously. I am glad for the distraction.

So I try my best. If not for me, for her.

"Hold on," she says and moves to my back. "I guess we can do it like that." In the next moment, her arms go around me, and I try hard not to shiver. Okay, I like spending time with her, but I don't like it when she is physically too close to me because it makes me feel weird.

I don't like it because I like it too much.

I shouldn't feel so aroused in the arms of the Sun Princess.

I should feel this for Rionn, but even when he kissed me, it was not this good. I cannot see the logic there, and it drives me crazy. My body is betraying me.

Lenora's hands curl around my hands, and her arms line up with mine, all the while, her skin is shining dimly. She does have great arms, but soon I realize her whole body is amazing. She looks hard with muscle all over, but I can feel her soft breasts when she presses her front to my back. Her hands are callused from working with a sword, but they are so pretty. The skin of her face and neck looks so soft even though she spent all her life in a damn desert.

I hate how perfect and warm and beautiful she is. It makes it so hard to hold onto my control.

"Let me show you," she says like we do this every day and adjust the bow and arrow into the position they are meant to be. She acts like we do this every day while I try not to squirm because of her breath on my neck.

Her touch always makes me feel so weird. It is almost like something is bubbling inside me. Inside my belly. Around my heart. In all my veins.

I focus on the weapon as much as I can. I focus on Lenora's words. She is explaining how I should hold it. She is showing me. Unfortunately, all I can think about is maybe my lack of wings can be a good thing if it lets her hug me like this.

"Understood?" she asks, but I cannot answer for a few seconds because my throat is dry. That makes her say, "Raya?"

Woe in Total Darkness

That nickname makes it even worse. I say I hate it, but it also does terrible things to my insides.

"Understood," I say as quickly as I can because if she keeps staying close any longer, I will start rubbing my thighs together, and that is the last thing I should do. I should focus on the bow, arrow, and target in front of me.

Thankfully Lenora entangles herself from me, and I take a relaxed breath. She stays a few feet away, and from my peripheral, I can see her put her hands on her hips. "When you are ready."

I nod because I just don't trust my voice. I gather all my focus. I do my best to ignore Lenora. I need to do this. I need to find my weapon. It is much more important. I keep repeating that in my head and focus on the target. I aim and finally let the arrow go.

At the first moment, I am so proud of myself because I actually managed to send out an arrow even after Lenora's closeness. Unfortunately, everything crumbles the next moment because my arrow flies a few feet away from the target and onto nothingness.

Now I am annoyed. Maybe it is better than being aroused.

"It is okay," Lenora soothes immediately. "This just means we have to try another weapon. I never said it is going to be fast."

"I guess I am not very patient."

She shrugs and starts to put the weapons inside the chest. "Try to look from the good side. As long as we keep trying, it will only be the two of us. After you choose your weapon, we will start training with my soldiers. This just gives you more time to get ready for that."

"I still haven't said yes," I say stubbornly, and Lenora gives me a devilish smirk like she knows she can convince me into anything.

I am sure she can, but she doesn't know the way. It is not with her words.

Despite her flirting and her closeness, I know Lenora will never actually try anything. It is absolutely absurd, and even if it wasn't, it is not allowed. She is the Sun Heir, and I am the Moon Heir. It is forbidden by ancient rules that there would be anything romantic or sexual between us.

Not that I would want it if it was allowed. We are just playing.

I am pretty sure my attraction to her is nothing but my body being confused. I have never been with anyone but Rionn. I wouldn't even know what to do with Lenora. I am just reacting to her warmth. I just have been really alone, and she is always around.

That is one of the reasons I am considering accepting her offer to train with her soldiers. I am absolutely horrified by the idea of letting others see me up close but not being alone with her all the time might be helpful. Surely I won't feel this aroused during training.

I will probably be just anxious, and at this point, I might take that over desiring Lenora.

I am not completely sure, though. It is a big step. Lenora doesn't care about my broken horn or my lack of wings. She understands my inability to reach my power too. I don't know how others will react.

"I was actually going to ask you something about that," I blurt out.

Lenora straightens after closing the chest. "Ask away."

"Can I maybe come and watch your training from afar. I am not ready for them to see me, but I want to see it. Maybe if I see it as something familiar, I won't be very afraid."

She doesn't even think. She just nods. "That is a great idea. I think I know where you can watch."

"Really?" I ask, suddenly anxious but also excited.

"Really. Do you want to watch it this morning?"

"Yes." Now I am also excited to see Lenora in her natural surroundings. I hope she looks hideous training.

———⟡———

Lenora and her Sun Soldiers are training in the small courtyard. No one really comes here, so it makes sense. And if it is reserved for them, no one is going to bother them.

She took me to one of the high bridges in the palace that had a perfect view of the training. It is not a private place. Anybody can just walk here, but thankfully it is not a very common lane. I am actually surprised Lenora already discovered it here. It does

Woe in Total Darkness

connect one part of the palace to the other, but it is the highest bridge. It is easier to take lower levels. No one comes up here just to change locations. They must come here for the sole purpose of coming here, and there are better places to spend time in the palace.

I am still kind of anxious about being in the open while it is very light outside. I am afraid someone is going to walk in and see me. My nails hurt from being buried into the stone railing.

I keep repeating facts in my head, saying there is no reason for anyone to come. I know it is true. I still can't relax fully.

Watching them helps, though.

They are a small group, seven people, Lenore included. I want to know what kind of relationship she has with them. If they are her most trusted soldiers. Though I doubt that because she must have left someone she trusts behind. There must be much to do back in the Khanate. I never actually asked her how bad things were. I never asked about the Curser. I kind of act like it doesn't exist.

Though I remember. I was here for some of it. I remember how bad it was. Patches of Darkness kept appearing in random places, and horrible creatures came with them. It was possible to fight the monsters and destroy the Darkness with our powers, but it was not enough. The Darkness ruined the land it touched. It ruined the farms in the Seelie Kingdom and the trading lanes in the Sun Khanate.

I can't imagine how bad it must be now.

Still, I don't ask. It is safer this way.

I try to build a new life. I don't want the reminder of the person who kidnapped me and killed my best friend. I just want to get my power back and be the princess I was. I just want to spend time with Lenora.

I watch her as she spars with a soldier after her warm-up. It is a very intense warm-up, and she looks amazing. All my hopes of her looking like a doofus fly out of the window. All of her body flexes and reminds me of how strong she is.

She is using the sword she always carries on her belt, but this is the first time I actually see it in action. It is a peculiar sword. I knew it looked like crystal. I didn't think too much of it since it might just be a rich design. I don't know much about swords anyway. Though I know, I have never seen a sword like that.

The crystal-like design looks so pretty. When she fights, the sword shines brightly with her sunshine. It is not just a weapon. It is also her power. It is amazing and unlike anything, I have ever seen before. I wonder if I would have gotten a similar weapon if I had continued my training.

I wonder if I'll get one this time.

Even though I sucked at anything I tried, and the weight I lost during my captivity made me very weak, I still dream about it. I like the idea of having such a unique weapon. I like the idea of being able to spar with a Sun Soldier.

Lenora doesn't free her power over her skin like she does when she is with me, but she shines so brightly under the sun that I want to be bright just like her. I want to be able to gather attention even without my power.

Maybe in every reality, I envy Lenora Mitharaus.

Only this time, it doesn't exactly feel like envy but more like fascination. I cannot take my eyes off her. I am enchanted.

That is until I hear someone speak right next to me. "Aren't they amazing?"

I jump. I haven't even heard footsteps. I look at the source with a hand over my heart, and the sight makes my eyes bulge even further.

"I am so sorry," Maha says, reaching a hand to pat my shoulder. Her other hand is supporting her big belly, and she really does look worried. "I didn't mean to startle you. I thought you heard me come."

My throat tightens, and I shake my head. "I didn't."

She smiles, looking at the courtyard. "You really must be so focused. I cannot blame you, though. Their training always looks so good, very graceful."

I look down for a second, but I am still dazzled by Maha's presence. I knew someone could have walked in while I was here, but I never thought Maha would. If I did, maybe I would not have

Woe in Total Darkness

come. I was very nervous to see her. I didn't want her to look at me like Rionn did. I didn't want to see her not recognizing me.

Although it doesn't feel like it right now. Yes, she is not a close friend right now, but she still acts like Maha. It feels too weird. Almost like I had never left my dream.

She is just Maha.

I don't want to burst the happy bubble and smile back. "Yes," I say. "They are very graceful." It is not a lie. Especially Lenora looks very delicate despite her apparent strength.

But I am not that interested in them right now. I am surprised someone actually managed to get my attention away from Lenora, but this is Maha. This is one of my best friends. She is the sweetest. I want her to be just that here as well. I cannot lose Qyron and then also Maha.

She watches the soldiers with a small smile on her face, and she looks just like I remember. Her skin is deep green, and her silky hair is white. She is wearing colorful flowers in her hair that I always find adorable. Her horns are different from mine, and they are decorated with fragile chains and more flowers. She looks like she is spring herself. Even her pink dress is absolutely in disagreement with the weather. It covers her arms, and it has a long skirt, but her swollen belly is all naked. She is very proud of her baby.

She is my Maha.

Her grey eyes move to me, and she giggles as her cheeks turn a darker green. "Oh, I am so sorry. I forgot to introduce myself. I am Princess Maha K'rra."

Of course, she is introducing herself to me because we are strangers. But for some reason, her introduction doesn't bother me much. She might not know me, but she doesn't look at me like I am a stranger. She is warm and sweet.

"I know all that," I say with a smile. I reach out a hand because meeting her all over again doesn't feel weird at all. It feels good. Like I am getting a friend back after painful weeks locked inside my room. "I am..."

Before I can even say my name, Maha jumps a little and gives a squeak. "Zuraya Haliyes. Of course, I know who you are."

My heart stops for a second. I feel like I am back. I feel like all the pain I went through was just a joke. It was all a nightmare, and now I am awake. But, of course, it only lasts for a second. I know it is not so hard to recognize me.

I look down, ashamed because of my silent thoughts. "Because of the eyes?" I don't have the heart to ask if it is because of the lack of wings and the broken horn.

"I mean, it does make it very obvious," she giggles again, almost oblivious to my worsening mood. "But I think I would recognize you even without seeing the eyes."

I feel a little sick but I still ask, "How?"

Maha doesn't look affected even a bit. She has no care for the world, as she explains. "Well, you may not remember, but I met you when you were really young. You haven't changed a lot. I can still tell you are that little girl sitting at the dinner table like an adult. A proper princess."

I chuckle, but it is a bit sad. I know I was that type of kid, but I don't think I am still the same. "I have changed a lot," I say. *I have lost a lot.*

Maha thinks for a second and shakes her head. "Well, I don't think so. You look the same, just older."

A smile forms on my face. I want to tell her I am not a proper princess anymore. I am not even a proper Feyada.

But I don't. I don't want to be miserable.

"I must admit, though, I am surprised to see you outside," says Maha. "I thought you didn't leave your room."

I squirm a little. "I do leave my room, but I am careful."

She nods and smiles. "You must be. You are a mystery to the court."

"I don't think it is a big mystery." Everybody must be aware of how much of a failure I am. They must know I had been rescued, but my heart and mind didn't.

However, Maha shakes her head. She doesn't look at me with pity. "They really don't know much. There is a lot of gossip, of course. Some of them are real." She winces at that. "But most of them are lies. The court doesn't know what to believe, so it is not

Woe in Total Darkness

as bad as you think. They obviously know something is going on since you haven't made an appearance, but they are just curious."

Her words surprise me. I was here thinking everybody knew my condition. I thought they were disgusted by me, just like my father. I was terrified of their looks. But what Maha says is actually comforting.

Still not enough for me to let everyone see me and verify their gossip, but it does make me feel a little better.

I look at her with skepticism, though. "You don't seem surprised. Are you just good at picking the right gossip?"

She giggles and shakes her head. "I wish that was it," she says, and I can hear the familiar amusement in her tone. "I am just married to the General, and he knows things."

Yeah right. I guess my question was stupid, but I cannot stop being a little skeptical of people after what I have been through. I am not very trusting. I only trust Lenora because I have no other choice. Now I also want to trust Maha just because she acts and looks exactly like my Maha.

Before I can speak, she starts mumbling to herself, "I mean, most don't approve of this, but he shares everything with me. There are no secrets between us. It annoys some people a lot. They think it is dangerous because I am a Seelie."

I am angry at anyone who made Maha feel bad for what she is. I hate it. My friend deserves happiness.

"He is your husband. I think it is normal for him to tell you everything." I don't just say that to make her feel good.

"Well, most think he should be a General before my husband."

That makes me laugh. "Davon Archard will never be anything before being your husband."

She giggles with me, but then her expression turns somewhat serious. She looks at me with interest. "You know him," she murmurs. "Were we married back where you used to be?"

Back where I used to be. I like her wording. "Yes. You were the greatest love story."

Maha gets a dreamy look like she is amazed at how their love is epic in every reality. "Oh, isn't that wonderful?" She looks at me sweetly. "Did you know me back there? Were we close?"

"Yes."

"Oh," she says. She doesn't look surprised or disappointed. She looks excited. "If Davon and I are the same here, maybe our friendship can be the same as well. Would you like to come to my chamber for tea sometime?"

And I smile at my friend. "I'd love to."

25

Lenora

Vaughn Mitharaus was insistent the Seelies now worshipped him and Carin since they stole the powers of Tisasa. However, after the Queen's death, he realized it was for nothing. They went back to their countries and claimed their thrones.

Vaughn married very soon in the hopes of creating an heir to his powers. He also got to work on controlling them. He stole the Sunshine from Tisasa. He was training hard to make his power useful. Even his land was now called the Sun Khanate. Unlike his father, he made peace with the Northern Feyadas, who now called their lands the Moon Kingdom. Together they were planning to conquer the whole Isle.

They were no longer refugees but invaders of the land. Luckily Queen Mirrina's daughter Queen Myra was not ready to bow.

Vaughn's biggest mission was to train his power, but he still poked the Seelie Lands. He didn't only steal Tisasa's powers but also started sending spies and thieves to the South. He was now after knowledge about the power. He stole many books and personal belongings from the palace. With good faith, he shared his possessions with Carin so they could start training against the natives of the Isle.

Sem Thornwood

———c———

I close the book Maha gave me. At this point, I haven't seen anything I didn't know. It is the history of my people, but it is told from a different perspective. The language is very anti-Feyada, but I cannot exactly blame them. Nothing in the book is a lie. It just tells it a little differently.

I am only hoping for it to talk more about the powers. I actually wish I had the books Vaughn stole from the Seelies, even though it is wrong.

I got too many history lessons though none of them was from a Seelie teacher. Their knowledge might be different, and it might be helpful. They obviously know more about Tisasa and the powers my ancestors acquired – or stole, depending on the perspective.

When I took a look at the book, I realized there were some pretty damaged pages. I actually have to skip a part about Vaughn and Carin's relationship because it was unreadable, but I don't think it is that important. They were just the best of friends despite their families' rivalry. Some dramatic historians also like to say they were brothers because Lady Obana slept with Lord Ruen. They say the kids knew the truth, so they wanted to have their solid brotherly connection.

Personally, I don't care what they were. I am sure it will help nothing. The part I am sad about that was unreadable was their journey to the Sacred Lands. I am sure it doesn't tell the real story. No one knows how they actually acquired the powers. No one knows what happened there. When Vaughn and Carin died, the secret died with them.

Still, I would like to read it. I am sad this book is in bad condition. It makes things very hard for me. I really wonder how it became like this. Seelies value knowledge and books way too much but this book was not taken care of properly.

Unfortunately, I cannot ask Maha because it would be rude.

At least, it means the book is very old. I need ancient knowledge anyway. I need to go into the root of Tisasa's powers. It will help me solve all these shitty problems.

At least, I hope so.

Woe in Total Darkness

This is a different route than I tried before. I just hope these are not just little stories to spread hate toward Feyadas. I doubt Maha would give it to me if it was all useless though. Hopefully, I can find something helpful that just escaped her clever mind.

I rub my eyes and open the book again to do some more reading, but the moment I do, someone starts hammering my door. I don't let any guards on my door; I just lock it down. I know whoever comes to see me has to knock, but they can do that gently.

Annoyed, I get up. They keep knocking aggressively, and I get madder and madder with every step I take.

When I open the door, I see the red face of Rionn Ay Ujk. "Relax, buddy, I am the twin with the good hearing," I say dryly.

"We need to talk," he says and steps inside my room.

I follow him as he goes to my bedroom. "That is all we can do. I hope you remember I ended our little bed activities. Also, I am not into angry fucking." Not with him, at least.

"Don't worry, I remember," he grits out. I ended things after I found out he snooped on me for information. He took it well, but I could tell it annoyed him. He suggested to fuck one last time, but I refused. No more Shifters for me.

I am not particularly interested in sex these days, anyway. My full concentration is on Raya. I don't have time for anyone else.

"I came here because we need to talk about Zuraya."

My hands flex at my sides. I don't want Rionn to have anything to talk about Zuraya. I want him far away from her. Just for her safety, of course.

I shrug and turn away so I can hide my emotions better. "I don't think I have anything to talk to you about, Zuraya. She is none of your concern."

My eyes are not on him, but I can see him go rigid with anger. Shifters get tense easily. "You have to stop those stupid trainings. She is just rescued. She is not well. The last thing she needs is to hurt herself while trying to learn how to fight. We have to show her she doesn't have anything she needs to fight. She needs friends, not weapons."

Well, I am her friend. This training made me her friend. And I am not sure if I am better than Qyron or Maha, but I am sure as hell better than Rionn. He is just trying to seduce her for his own good.

I actually enjoy her company. Maybe far too much.

I don't say those, though. Rionn doesn't get to know my relationship with Zuraya. I don't want him touching what we have. So, I just say, "Weapons can be friends."

"Are you trying to annoy me, Len?"

I giggle and turn back. "Well, it is quite fun, isn't it?"

He shakes his head like I am too much to handle. "Are you jealous?" he asks. "I mean, you were the one who wanted to stop fucking me. You put distance between us, and now I see bruises on Zuraya that she got from training with you. Are you jealous I am interested in her? What we have and what I am trying to have with Zuraya are different things. You have to know."

I look at him, eyes wide and mouth open. He really does think highly of himself. He really thinks I hurt Zuraya because she stole him from me.

Does he think I am in love with him or something when I was merely using him to relieve some tension? If someone's in love, it is him. He was the one who kept sending me those letters.

I am furious. But I know if I show him how furious I am, he is just going to be more convinced that I am fascinated by him.

It is best to keep my cool. "You should not try anything with Zuraya. I am trying to help her, and you are going to ruin it."

"Me?" he looks offended. "She needs me to get better. Me and Maha, we are what she remembers, what she knows. I am sure she likes our company more than yours."

I try so hard not to grit my teeth. "Have you asked her?"

That throws him off. He looks at me without saying anything for a few moments. I am unsure if Zuraya likes me more than him, but I know he never asked her. He doesn't care about her. There is something else he cares about, although I haven't figured that out yet.

Rionn lifts his chin and says, "The King is happy about our union."

Damn this guy. I thought he was sweet. "What union Rionn? Did Zuraya say she wanted to be with you?" I am almost sure she didn't, but still, my pulse picks up as I wait for the answer.

"No," he says to my relief. "But I am courting her. It is good when we spend time together. It would be much easier if you stopped this training nonsense. She is usually too tired to see me. She doesn't need training. She needs me."

He is getting way too cocky. A part of me wants to ask how good it is when they spend time together. What do they do together? Did they have sex yet? Is she happy with him? I am dying to know, but I am also afraid to know.

I also think if Rionn knows Zuraya cannot reach her powers. I wonder if he still is this angry, knowing her struggles. Does he really think he is more important than Moonshine?

I can't tell that to him, though. That is Zuraya's secret, and I won't betray her.

"I am sorry, Rionn, but I cannot stop. I have a deal with the King, and this is the way I am helping Zuraya. I hate it when my methods are questioned." I hate it even more, when it is Rionn doing it instead of Raya.

"He wants her fixed, and you are not doing that," he argues. "She doesn't need to know how to fight. She needs love, and I intend to give that to her."

I almost choke at the word love. Rionn doesn't love her. He shouldn't be the one to give her love.

Or at least I don't want him to be.

"She doesn't need fixing," I say harshly. "She just needs help, and I am providing it. Honestly, I would prefer you out of her life, but Zuraya is an adult, and that is her decision. Training with me or not is also her decision. If you have a problem with me, talk to Zuraya because I am not backing down."

He might be the Alpha, but he doesn't know who he is dealing with yet.

26

Zuraya

I have to admit letting Maha into my life really helped me. Lenora is still the one helping me with my powers. She is the one who gave me the courage to take some steps, but Maha made me realize I could be the old me. Despite the lack of wings, I am still Zuraya.

I liked my life back where I used to be, and spending time with Maha made me think I could maybe retrieve that life. The most important part was Qyron. He will be absent no matter what, but I can still do my best.

That was the reason I let Rionn see me a lot more. I could tell he was not so different from my Rionn. This time I was not as excited to flirt with him as I was the first time. Still, I wanted to try. I wanted to get the same happiness he used to give me. I always accepted when he came to my room to take me out on walks. We sometimes visited each other's rooms to have more private talks too.

I also let him kiss me a lot. Even when I am not that into it.

My body is weird. Maybe it is about my power or about my trauma, but a side of me believes I can fix it with Rionn. He is the only one I have had sex with in the past. So, I should be more comfortable with him.

Woe in Total Darkness

It is not very pleasureable but it has never been.

Obviously, I cannot trust my feelings right now. My body is only blossoming when I am with Lenora, and that is just wrong. I should train my body to be turned on by Rionn.

Also, I need to get rid of all the pent-up arousal from my sessions with Lenora. The safest way to do that is by myself, but when I tried that indecent thoughts about strong tattooed arms and soft skin filled my mind. I cannot let that happen so my next choice is Rionn.

That is the reason I am in my bed with him right now. He is on top of me, between my thighs. We have our clothes, but I can still feel the hardness of his cock rubbing against me. I wonder if it ever excited me.

Now I cannot focus. My mind drifts to different places, and I do my best to ignore it. I try to focus on his lips, his body, his touches.

Rionn's lips move toward my neck, and he whispers, "You feel so good, Zuraya."

I don't answer. I just close my eyes and try to focus on the moment. I let him put his hand under my skirt. He strokes my folds gently, and I feel ashamed because I am absolutely dry as sand. Thankfully Rionn doesn't point it out. He just tries to work me out softly without hurting me.

It is sweet, I guess, but I remain dry. I don't feel an ounce of arousal.

"Are you tense?" Rionn asks. I am glad he is trying to be understanding.

I am not sure if it is because I am tense, but I don't have any other idea. I don't want to make him feel bad just because my body is broken. "A little bit."

Rionn pulls back and gives me a charming smile. "Let me relax you a bit then."

I don't know how he is going to do that. Before I can even guess, his body moves down the bed, and he pushes his head under my skirt. Oh, okay. Now, this should feel good.

Hopefully.

When his tongue darts out to lick me and spread some wetness, I close my eyes even though he is all covered under my skirt. It actually makes me feel a little better. And now I feel even more guilty. I want to get wet for him. When he was kissing me, I gave him some fake moans just to not crush his ego.

My body is a traitorous thing. Why do I get slick between my thighs while training but cannot do that while having sex with my fiancé?

And now, the thought of Lenora fills my mind. I am really awful, but I cannot help it. As Rionn's mouth keeps working between my legs, I remember the times Lenora was too close to me. I remember the warmth of her soft skin and her breath on my neck when she was trying to show me how to use the bow and arrow.

I remember how she tended the wounds I managed to create when we were training with a hammer. I still have bruises. I imagine those were different bruises.

I imagine Lenora between my legs instead of Rionn. Her tongue parts my folds as those orange eyes look up at me. She wraps those magnificent arms around my thighs, and her fingertips press onto my flesh. I can feel her Sunshine all over me.

She licks and sucks just the way I need. Only when I start begging she fills me with her fingers. "You taste so good," she murmurs against my heated flesh.

My thighs tense, and my toes curl. I am so close.

I want to come all over Sun Princess's mouth.

"You like that, huh?" Rionn says with a chuckle and almost ruins everything.

I cannot feel guilty only because I am too close to climax. I just want to come. So, I push his head back down. "Please keep going."

I want to beg her like this. I want her to tease me until it is too much. I want to wrap her pretty blonde hair around my hand and guide her mouth all over me. I want to see her go crazy for me.

The thought is so nice that I soon tense. My sex squeezes around Lenora's fingers, and I trap her head between my thighs. I look into her hungry eyes. I come shaking and crying.

Woe in Total Darkness

This feels amazing.

Only when I come down from my peak, lips press one last kiss to my folds, and Rionn emerges from under my skirt with a red face and a smirk. I remember he was the one licking me. Only then the guilt and disgust fill me.

Rionn comes back up and kisses me. I only kiss him back because I feel awful for what have I done to him. He tastes like me, but deep down, I know he was not the one who made me come. He was not on this bed with me, which is a great problem.

Fuck.

———❦———

After my release, I kindly thanked Rionn and told him I was not ready for more. I didn't want to hurt him, but I couldn't let him touch me more when I imagined someone else. It was not fair to both of us.

Also, when I remembered he was the one touching me, I felt horrible. I realized I didn't want his touch. Maybe I never did.

When he left, I was freaking out. My body felt great from my release, but my mind was frantic. It was a huge mistake thinking about Lenora in bed.

I didn't even know how I was going to look at her face at our training tonight.

I was ashamed, and I am still so ashamed.

To clear my head, I went to Maha's room, and luckily my friend was always ready to spend time with me.

I know I cannot tell her what happened, but I am sure talking with her will still help me. I just need to think about anything but Lenora.

"So, how is your training with Lenora going?" Maha asks.

I try so hard not to groan. "Good," I cut off. "You know I started spending time with Rionn again."

Maha's eyes widen. "Oh, that's nice. Davon told me something about him, I guess. Was he your lover where you used to be?"

I nod. "He was my fiancé, actually. We were going to get married the day I was rescued. Interestingly this Rionn is also interested. I am having a hard time separating where I used to be and here. It is giving me a headache."

"If Davon and I can work in both places, maybe you and Rionn can too."

That is why I keep trying. That is why I let him kiss me and touch me even though I don't like it. I am hoping I will eventually.

Even though I never really did even where I used to be.

But thinking like this also makes me sad. If everything is the same, why is Qyron not here? It doesn't sound fair. Getting my old life back without Qyron in it also doesn't sound realistic, but I still try.

After all, I tried hanging onto the new things. It lead me to imagine Lenora while coming. It was no good.

I am not sure how Rionn and I are going to work, though. I clearly cannot let him touch me when my mind is filled with another. However, that is not the only problem. Even if Lenora was not in the picture, I still feel uncomfortable when he touches me. I was with him because he was my perfect match, because I cared about what everyone thought so much.

I don't anymore.

Is it so bad if Rionn and I won't work this time? Can I still be happy without him?

I already lost Qyron.

The thought depresses me a lot. I want to ask Maha. I want her to tell me it is okay if I cannot fall for Rionn this time and that it is okay to be a different Zuraya. I can still be happy.

Unfortunately, I cannot because Maha winces, and her hand goes to her belly. She looks in pain, and all my thoughts leave my head. "Are you okay?"

Maha takes a deep breath and gives me a forced smile. "Yes, yes, don't worry. I sometimes get these contractions. I think the baby is telling me, 'Please, mama let me out.'" She giggles, but I still see another wince.

Woe in Total Darkness

I am worried despite her words. "Do you need to rest? I can leave if you want. Don't be afraid to be rude. I don't mind."

Maha laughs. "You are sweet. Don't worry, I am good. I cannot move a lot anymore, so it is nice to have you here, actually." She gives a pause. "But if you want to leave, you can. I know you have training at night, and then you watch the other training early in the morning. You need sleep."

How the conversations always turn back to Lenora?

I actually feel like everything in my life keeps turning back to Lenora. It is annoying.

"It is okay," I shrug. "I usually sleep a lot during the day." Since I added watching Sun Soldiers in the morning to my routine, I also changed my sleeping habits. I just sleep whenever I can. I am not very busy anyway.

"How is the training going?" Maha asks. "I feel like Lenora is really determined to push you." She eyes the bruises on my arms.

I chuckle and look at them. Turns out that choosing your weapon was not so easy. I hurt myself occasionally. The worst was when I tried to use a hammer. I hit my legs a few times accidentally.

Every time I did, Lenora got worried. She kept her cool, but I could see it in her eyes and in her body language. She scolded me but also tended to my wounds very gently. Even now, it brings butterflies inside me.

It is awful.

"She is great," I answer. I cannot tell Maha how Lenora turns me on, but I don't want to hide my emotions. I enjoy her company, and I am not ashamed to accept it anymore.

"She really is," Maha agrees. "I don't think I have ever met anyone so selfless. For years she has been working hard for the good of the people. She almost dedicated her life to fighting the Curser. Every day she is hunting Patches and fighting creatures. Honestly, I still cannot believe she stayed in the North this long. It must be killing her."

Well, I never thought of it like that. I like Lenora, and I do know she is a great person. I envied her where I used to be because she was the perfect princess, accepted by her people. Here she is both that and an ideal General accepted by everyone. I heard that she is the shield of our lands against the Darkness.

I heard my chambermaids call her Lightbringer, and that was a title that belonged to my family. I am sure not all Moonfolk accepts her as that, but it is clear that she deserves it.

She is dedicated to her cause.

But she really has been here for quite some time. She is not fighting the Darkness or closing Patches, but instead, she is helping me pathetically try to reach my power.

I never realized I was holding her back. I never realized she sacrificed things to be with me.

A side of me is devastated because I am getting between her and the cause of her life. However, another part of me is jumping up and down with excitement because she lets me get in the way. She values me more than I thought.

It shouldn't mean anything. Even if we both feel the same, it *cannot* mean anything. Yet my heart doesn't understand logic.

"I am lucky to have her. It is almost unbelievable she took time off for me."

"Of course, she would want to help you." Maha smiles. "Also, she is still helping the Folk while training with you."

I don't really understand what she means by that. "Do you think my power can be beneficial against the Darkness Curse?" I know my dad is not doing anything, just like Khan Güne. "Is that how she is still helping?"

She pauses for a second, thinking. "Honestly, now that you said it, I do think your power can be beneficial. Your training means more than you think. Although I was not talking about that. I was talking about the moon spheres."

I am confused. "Moon spheres?"

"The deal your father and Lenora have," Maha explains. "It was over moon spheres."

"I really don't understand, Maha. What deal?" I get a bad feeling, but I need to know.

To my horror, Maha gets an uncomfortable look. She only now realizes I have no idea what is going on. "You really don't know?"

Woe in Total Darkness

"I wouldn't ask if I did."

She puts her hands on her belly like she is trying to protect her baby from my grumpiness. Her eyes also focus there, but she still explains. "King Luran was not very pleased with your condition when you returned. He asked Lenora for help. In exchange for helping you, she is going to get moon spheres that she can use to close Darkness Patches."

I look at her dumbfounded. I never thought Lenora had any benefit from this. I thought she wanted to help *me.*

I thought we had something between us even though it was forbidden.

Lenora Mitharaus doesn't want to help me. She doesn't care for me. She doesn't even care for herself or her own good. She only cares about the Folk of the Isle.

And I am just another burden in her duty-filled world.

27

Lenora

Vaughn Mitharaus was the first one to start a family among them two. He had a wife and two known concubines. Two years after stealing the powers from Tisasa, he had his first son from his concubine. This was also another experiment for him. He wanted to know if the power was going to end with him or if it was going to continue with his bloodline.

Unfortunately, Vaughn's son showed signs of Sunshine power in him. After that, Vaughn started trying to have more children. It was at that time he took another concubine and married. He wanted more of this power. He wanted an army.

Vaughn also pressured Carin to start a family. It was important for Feyadas. He needed heirs to take over his power and continue his legacy. Vaughn was hoping they could create an army of sun and moon together to start a war against the natives.

Carin was reluctant. He didn't listen to Vaughn but instead waited for a good union. Five years later he decided he found someone he wanted to marry, he was ready to start a family. Carin had a daughter. He was not into the idea of creating an army, so he just declared the daughter his heir and said she might be the only child he'll ever have.

Vaughn was not happy. Their bond was getting weaker. He was afraid of the Moon Kingdom turning against him. Since he was no longer very close to Carin, his advisors had another idea. In order to create a Feyada alliance, they wanted kids to be engaged.

To this, Carin agreed, and the Sun Prince and Moon Princess became engaged to be married when they were old enough.

During this time, Vaughn kept having children to grow his army. But things didn't go as he planned. With every child, powers seemed to be less effective. His heir was almost as powerful as him, but his youngest kid only barely shined.

This discovery made Vaughn realize something else. The marriage between the heirs was really risky. He was not sure if his younger children were even able to pass the powers to their own children in the future. His only hope was his oldest son. He knew it was the same for Carin. If the heirs married, the child they'll have might have been useless or even dangerous.

Neither Vaughn nor Carin wanted to take their chances. The engagement was canceled, but it was not enough. They wanted to ensure their bloodline would remain strong even years after their death. This led to them making an agreement, so no Mitharaus and Haliyes ever got married. The two nations were going to have an alliance at all the times, and the heirs were going to have a close relationship, but it was going to be strictly political.

This way, they created the first ancient rule. It was also the one that was never forgotten despite the years.

It was forbidden for a Mitharaus and a Haliyes to fall in love.

———c———

I whistle a simple tune as I walk toward Zuraya's room. At this point, I think she is brave enough to meet me outside the palace, but I like going to her room every night to retrieve her. I like it way more than I should, just like every other thing about Zuraya.

I am not sure which weapon we are going to use tonight, actually. I don't want to treat her like she is breakable. I know she is strong. But still, the last time we used a hammer, she hurt herself. I don't want it to happen again.

I spent my life in training. I have been with soldiers for so many years. I hurt myself bad too many times to count, and I saw people I care about get hurt too.

It never bothered me as much as when I saw Raya get hurt.

She had so many bruises on her when I found her chained to that fucking cave. I never want to see bruises on her again. I want to show her how strong she is, but at the same time, I want to protect her with everything I have.

I am so annoyed that no one can see how strong she is – how passionate.

I am not even sure if she sees it. Maybe if she did, she would be less scared of everything. However, I understand. The trauma she went through was not an easy one. I wish I could just erase it all.

My whole life, I wished I was here seven years ago when the Curser's men came to the palace. I wished I was here to stop them. I would even give up my life to stop them. I always wished to be able to save Qyron. Now I wish I was here even more. I wish I was here for both Qyron and Raya.

They deserved to be protected that night.

As I come closer to her chamber, I shake the bad thoughts out of my mind. I don't want to ruin my time spent with Raya. We might see each other in the dead of night, but our training is always the highlight of my days.

When I step inside, Raya is not waiting for me like usual. One chambermaid is there tidying up the antechamber, but there is no one else. That is weird.

"Where is the Princess?" I ask.

The maid looks uncomfortable but then moves to fix up some pillows. "She is in her bedroom."

Oh, she is still getting dressed, then. That explains the lack of chambermaids too. I sit down on the couch, thinking about how I'm going to tease her about being late. Because I know I am not early. I am very punctual.

"I'll wait here then." I actually want to close my eyes. I'm a little tired, but I don't want Raya to know that. I can't risk her seeing me taking a nap.

The maid looks up from the pillows, and she really does look uncomfortable.

"Is there a problem?"

She tangles and detangles her fingers in a nervous gesture. "You shouldn't wait, General. The Princess is not coming. She wanted me to tell you she doesn't want to train anymore."

What? "I am sorry?"

"That is what she said. She said she was done with the training and with..." she pauses nervously. "You."

Yeah, well, she is not. At least not like this. I immediately get on my feet and go to her bedroom door. I reach for the doorknob. I don't care if she is presentable or not. This is fucking stupid, and it doesn't fucking make sense.

The door is locked. She knew I was going to burst inside. And she thought a lock was going to keep me out. I can so easily break this door. It won't even take much effort. However, I don't. I don't want to scare her off.

Instead, I punch. "Raya, open the door!"

No answer.

So, I punch some more.

And more.

"Go away," she says at last. "I don't want to train."

Honestly, that is okay, but it is not what her maid said. Maybe I am going about this all wrong, but hearing she was done with me kind of got into my head. I cannot leave without seeing her.

This time I knock gently. "Let's talk, Raya."

"Please leave."

"Raya," I growl. I shouldn't be this grumpy, but unfortunately, I am a little intense when it comes to her. "You know I can break this door, right?"

She doesn't say anything for a few seconds, and I start losing all my hope. Maybe talking about door-breaking was a bad idea. But then I hear her footsteps on the other side, and the door opens. "You can leave," she says to her maid and then goes back to her bed. I hear the maid leave with quick steps.

I get inside her room and close the door behind me. We might be alone, but I want more privacy. I want to understand why she is doing this.

Raya sits on her bed and doesn't look at me. "You really have anger issues."

I might when it comes to her. "I don't."

She rolls her eyes. "I only let you in so you won't break my door. I am not coming to training."

"Today?" I ask hopefully.

This time she looks at me, and her eyes almost murder me with their intensity. "Ever."

And she didn't even think to talk to me about it? My jaw flexes, but I try to be calm. "Is this about Rionn?" maybe telling him to talk to Raya was a mistake. Maybe he really convinced her to stop seeing me.

Zuraya looks at me like my words offend her. "Rionn?" she asks with an unbelieving voice. "Why would it be about Rionn?"

"I happen to know he doesn't want you to train with me."

"And why would I care what he thinks?"

So, it is not him. I really don't understand. What the fuck happened?

"It is not about Rionn," she repeats with gritted teeth. "It is about you, Lenora."

Fuck, that's even worse. What did I do? I never want to hurt Raya. I do my best to control myself around her. I try to be kind, and I even keep my attraction hidden. I want to make her feel safe.

Did I somehow slip?

My chest tightens. "What did I do?"

Raya shakes her head like she cannot believe me. "You lied to me, Lenora. You tricked me for your *honorable* duties."

Now I know I really fucked up because she is right. I lied to Raya. Honestly, I lied to her so much that I don't know which one she is referring to. It was all for her own good. I did it to help her.

But after all, I lied.

Woe in Total Darkness

"I did," I accept way too quickly. "I lied to you about a lot of things, but I did it to help you."

A joyless laugh escapes her. "To help me? No, Lenora, you did it for the moon spheres. You never told me you had a deal with my father. I thought you cared for me. I thought you wanted to help me. But you were just trying to be the hero. Have you done anything in your life that was not for a duty?"

I hate her words because I do care about her. If I knew her like I know her now, I would still want to train her. Even if King Luran decides not to give me moon spheres, I will still want to help her.

But it didn't start like that. It started because Seelie Lands needed more light power to fight the Patches, and I made it my mission to get it for them. I did it because I wanted to fight the Curse.

But maybe I can come clean now. Maybe she'll believe I deserve a second chance because things have changed.

I take a deep breath and confess. "I lied to you about more than that."

Raya looks so disappointed that my stomach flips upside down. "You did?"

"I did," I say, forcing myself to look into her beautiful eyes. "I lied to you because I needed those moon spheres, and you hated me. You didn't even want to talk to me. I had to find a way to reach you, so you would let me help you. I paid your maids for information, and I paid them to talk about Maha so I could get a reaction out of you. I learned everything you did. I followed you at night. I showed myself at the tomb. I told Maha to show up when you came to watch me train. I manipulated you, but I did it to help you. I needed to do those things, so you will let me reach you, Raya. But the time we spent together was all true. I never acted like someone I was not. I just created the right opportunities."

Zuraya looks at me with huge eyes. She looks shocked and betrayed, and sad. I hate seeing her like this. But I cannot keep lying. I need to face her wrath.

Her blue eyes fill with tears, but she keeps them back. "You had no right!" she hisses.

"I know."

"You played me."

"No," I say harshly. I won't accept *that*. "I just needed opportunities. So, I created them. I did it to help you, Raya. I know my methods were unethical, but they worked. I got to help you."

One tear escapes, but she doesn't brush it away. She just kept looking at me with disappointment in her eyes. "You didn't do it for me, Lenora. You didn't even do it for yourself. I cannot even call you selfish because everything you do, you do it for a reason. You have a mission, and I understand that, but it has blinded you."

Blinded me? Doesn't she understand I have to do this? "And what should I do, Raya? Do you have any idea how much pressure I am under? No one fucking does anything to save these lands. Someone *has* to do it, and I am that person."

"You don't have to be the hero all the time. You are so focused on this that you don't even care that you play with people's emotions to reach your goal."

My throat burns. "I didn't play with your emotions." I never wanted to do that. Not even in the beginning of things.

"But it felt like it," Raya says with a broken voice and gets to her feet.

"I didn't want that. I am not blinded, Raya."

She steps closer to me. "Prove it to me," she says. She looks sad but also hopeful. Maybe she will really give me another chance. "If you are not blinded, tell me something you did for yourself. Give me something that is not a duty. Prove to me that is not all you care about."

My hopes slowly shatter. I look at her pretty face and pleading eyes, but I cannot think of anything. In my whole fucking life, I cannot think of anything I did for Lenora. It was all for the Sun Princess or for the General. I never did anything just for myself. I never said fuck it to my duties.

I cannot.

More tears gather in Raya's eyes. "Please," she whispers.

I understand why she needs this. I know if I cannot give her anything, this will end. I won't be able to get the moon spheres, but more importantly, Raya will hate me again.

Woe in Total Darkness

I don't want her to hate me. I want her to know I care more about her than those fucking spheres. I want her to know I am genuine.

An idea forms in my head, and my breath catches in my throat. "I'll show you," I say. "I'll show you something that is only for me. I'll let go of all my damn responsibilities for it."

"Then show me," she says hopefully.

I am very, very dumb because the next moment, I cup the back of her head and press my lips to hers.

28

Zuraya

Oh, sweet Tisasa.

I was not expecting this.

Lenora's lips are very soft against mine. Her grip on the back of my neck is solid, but her kiss is hesitant like she is waiting for my consent. I don't even need to think about it. I wrap my arms around her waist and kiss her back.

She makes a soft noise in her throat, and her free hand comes to my waist. She is taller than me, so I have to tilt my face. Her hand guides my head nicely. Her lips now move around mine expertly. My short nails bury into her waist over the fabric of her top. I want her closer to me. She makes my whole body vibrate.

And I thought I didn't like kissing.

Her tongue softly touches my lips. I open up for her and reach with my own. Lenora is leading the kiss, and I don't mind it even a bit. I like it when she takes control. I just let her make me feel good.

My fingers itch to move. I want to touch her everywhere. I want to do everything with her. Lenora rubs my back sweetly, but she doesn't touch anywhere inappropriate. I remember how she was hesitant at the beginning and think she might be letting me make a decision again.

Woe in Total Darkness

I like that about her.

I like everything about her.

With one hand, I reach to her neck so I can hold onto her better, but my other hand moves down from her waist. I go slowly, letting her have enough time to stop me. Instead, Lenora kisses me harder, and I put my hand over her tight backside. I can't help myself and squeeze. Everything about her body is amazing.

Lenora moans, and she nudges my legs with her knee. I am instantly more needy than I have ever been in my whole life. "Yes," I whisper between kisses and feel her smile.

I can feel her kiss all over me. I can feel the buzz of it on my skin, and I can feel it bubbling my blood. I can feel it deep inside my chest.

She nibbles my bottom lip when her leg settles between mine. I want to rub myself all over her shamelessly. I feel too good. I have never felt this good, and this is just a kiss.

"Raya," Lenora says breathlessly and tries to pull back. Almost instinctively, I pull her back down. She smiles and kisses me, but a few seconds later, she again pulls back. That hand at the back of my neck moves to my cheek, and I feel her thumb brush it. "Raya," she whispers again. She looks at me with a shining glow around her skin and adoration in her eyes. I can so easily lose myself in her.

"Yes?" I breathe out. I want to kiss her some more, but I also don't mind watching her face this close. She is so beautiful, and she looks at me like I am the most beautiful thing in the room.

She beams. "You are glowing."

I mean, it was a fantastic kiss. It can have that effect. "Thank you."

Lenora chuckles, but she doesn't lose that enchanted look. She presses one soft kiss onto my lips. "No, Raya. You are really glowing."

My brows furrow, and I bring my hand up. Then I see. My skin is all shining with Moonlight. I glow so brightly. Now everything makes even more sense. I felt her kiss all over my body because I was shining.

I felt her warmth over my chill. She made me reach my power. She made me shine.

Funny how she tried so hard to help me with lies, and the second she let go of her control, she helped me the most. She made me happy. She gave me hope.

And she gave me my power.

I laugh. Can't help it. This time I look at her with tears of happiness lining my eyes. "If I am only going to be able to reach my power when you kiss me, we have a problem."

Lenora presses herself to me. "I'll have no complaints."

And now I really want to rub myself all over her. My sex is aching. I still cannot believe she kissed me. It happened too fast.

"Damn," I murmur, but I can't find the strength to detangle myself from her.

"What?" she asks, worried.

"I was supposed to be mad at you," I pout.

Lenora winces but doesn't let me go. "You can be mad at me," she says, pressing another kiss on my lips. "Just don't hate me."

"Never," I answer quickly. "I can never hate you." She lied to me and manipulated me, but I still cannot hate her. What she did was so wrong, but I also know why she did it. I know she didn't mean to hurt me. I know she is the Lenora that gave me the will to live again.

Before she can speak, I again look at my glowing skin. I can feel the power flowing in my veins. I try to control it, and it is so easy. It is so damn easy that I want to cry. "Maybe we need a new approach for the training."

Lenora chuckles. "So, you think all that meditation didn't help?"

I giggle too, but I actually wonder. All it took was really just a kiss. "Do you think it was all for nothing? All I needed to do was kiss a Princess? It sounds cheap."

Lenora gets a serious look and slowly pulls back. She is still close, but we are not tangled together. Now I don't have a blinding light around me, but I keep it there anyway. A dim moonshine coating my skin. I am not ready to leave it just yet.

Woe in Total Darkness

"It is about reconnecting with your body," Lenora says. "With weapons training, I was trying to make you connect with a weapon. If you could feel a weapon as another limb, you could do the same with your power." She gets a sad look. "I never thought you needed to connect with your body before you connect with a weapon."

I think about it. I never had a problem with using my power, but it is clear that Lenora knows more about the technicalities.

A little teasing smile forms on my face. "If I knew kissing you was going to help me reconnect, I would do it sooner."

She lifts a finger. "*I* kissed *you.*"

"Well, I pushed you."

Now we both smile, and I want her to kiss me again. I don't want to be lost in a conversation about my power. I want to talk about us. I want to know if this means we will kiss again in the future because I really hope it does.

I never knew kissing could feel this good. I thought I was not into it, but maybe I just needed to have the right kiss. Now nothing else is going to compare.

"Did you look the same?" Lenora asks, throwing me off. I realize she already got her serious face back. She means business. I wonder if I always have to push her to kiss me.

"Where I used to be?" I ask. I want to end this conversation, but I also want to know what she is thinking. I still want my power back, and I know she is still my best chance. Only she is now even more than that.

"Yes. Was your appearance the same?"

"Kind of," I say and try not to look down at my too-thin body. I gained a little weight in the last few weeks, but I am still far away from how I used to be. "I was way thicker. My hair was a little different. I had some alterations too."

She looks down, lost in thought. "Maybe you should look like that again. You need to feel comfortable in your body. You need to feel like yourself. That will be helpful for you to use your power."

"You are saying I felt like myself when we kissed? It doesn't make sense I never kissed you before."

Lenora nods to herself and smirks. "Well, you must have felt very comfortable in your body. I thought the training would do that too, but I guess I was doing everything wrong."

I don't want her to think that. "I do feel comfortable when we train. Not with every weapon, but I mostly do. I am just a little too tense."

"Do I make you tense?" She looks sad.

"Yes," I answer and look down because I know my cheeks are heating. "You distract me. My mind goes very far from training when you are too close."

Lenora groans. "Raya, now I won't be able to focus at all when we train."

"You were able to focus before?" I cannot be alone in this. She is the one who kissed me after all.

Lenora gives me a heated look. I am surprised despite all of her flirting, she never looked at me like that. She usually makes me blush, but right now, I am not blushing on my cheeks. "You distract me too. I was just holding onto my control because I was scared of making you uncomfortable. I never thought you felt the same."

My heart hammers in my chest. "So what does it mean? The kiss."

Lenora gets close to me again. She doesn't touch me, but I can feel her warm light embracing my cool one. "What would you want it to mean?"

"I asked first." I feel a little uneasy. "It doesn't have to mean anything. I know I pushed you..."

Lenora cuts me off with another kiss, and I feel like I am on top of clouds. Her hands on my cheeks and her lips on mine feel just so right. I know it is supposed to be wrong, but no one can make me believe this is wrong.

When she pulls back, she presses her forehead to mine. "I don't want to stop kissing you," she says, and my heart flutters.

"I don't want to stop kissing you as well."

"But no one can know," she says like it is giving her pain.

It doesn't hurt me. I already knew that. I don't want to announce to the world what I feel for Lenora. I just want her to myself for a little while. I know that is the most we can have. "They don't need to know," I say. "I mean, you are helping me after all, aren't you? I cannot reconnect with my body when I am sexually frustrated."

"Yes," Lenora breathes out. "You need to release some tension."

I nod, brushing our foreheads. "And I don't want to sleep with Rionn." Especially after my kiss with Lenora, I cannot even stomach the thought.

Lenora's fingers on my cheeks tense, and she makes a choked sound. "I don't want you to sleep with Rionn. I don't want you to touch anyone but me."

"Deal." I don't desire anyone else. "And you too."

"Deal," she giggles. For a few moments, she just holds me close. Then she whispers, "Do you want to continue training?"

I know I can say no this time, and she won't break my door, but I also know training is good for me. Lenora is helping me. I need the training, and I think it does make it easier for Lenora to stay here, and I am not ready for her to leave just yet.

I nod again. "We can go to the hill."

To my surprise, Lenora shakes her head and lets go of me. She steps back. "No, not tonight. I think we should start training with my soldiers from now on."

I knew it was going to happen at one point, but still, anxiety gets a hold of me. I know Lenora is going to be there for me, but I am still scared. "Why?"

The heated look from before again appears on her face. "Because if it is just the two of us, I don't think we will do much training."

Oh. I think she is right. Though is it really so bad? "I don't think that is a problem."

"No," she says quickly. She reaches out and holds my hand. The look she gives me is very intense. "I want to take my time with you, Raya. I want to tease you. Also, I want to help you. I am going to fuck you, but we will not stop our training for that."

Ah Tisasa. Now I am really wet.

I know I will regret it later, but I cannot help it. She completely has me at this moment. So, I say. "Okay. We can start training the day after tomorrow." Because after everything, I need some time to gather myself.

I need some time before Lenora completely destroys me.

29

Lenora

Vaughn did share his findings from the stolen books with Carin. He wanted both of them to get stronger. Carin was less power-hungry when it came to himself. Because of this, Carin is usually said to be good at heart, but he was actually just the lesser evil.

Carin learned how to use his light mostly from Vaughn's knowledge. After that, he focused on his body manipulation power. He was not very enthusiastic about it but tried to learn about healing. It was much different than Vaughn's power, so he had to figure it out on his own, but he didn't complain. He just dedicated his life to getting better at healing spells.

Unfortunately, he was much different when it came to his daughter, his heir. Carin made it his mission to train his daughter much better than himself. He only ever had one daughter and wanted her to perfect her powers. He wanted her to be more powerful than Vaughn's children. Some say it was because he was angry at Vaughn and wanted to beat him at his own game, and some say it was just because she could have a safe life.

In the end, her powers lead up to her starting a war with the Shifters and becoming the Queen who ruled over the native *creatures of the Isle. She enslaved the Shifter Territory with her stolen powers.*

Carin was not more ethical than Vaughn when it came to his daughter's training. He never stole knowledge because he didn't need to, but he would use brutal ways to train the Princess. To teach her healing, he would wound his own soldiers and staff so she could practice. When they realized she could make anyone feel pain with her body manipulation power, her father gave her people she could torture. Princess grew up torturing various helpless creatures just so she could perfect her craft.

———ᑯ———

"You are holding it like you want to let it go, Raya. That is not the way."

She breathes through her nose, looking mad. "That's because it's too heavy."

Actually, the sword she carries is light, but she doesn't have much muscle in her body. She is gaining some, but it is a process. And despite her weak arms, she does her best. I know that. I just like to push her. I know she needs to be challenged.

Today is a big challenge on its own. This is the first time Raya and I are not alone in our training. We are surrounded by my soldiers in the small courtyard. It is bright with morning sun. Soldiers don't look our way that much, but Raya is still tense.

I hate seeing her like this. Making her mad is a good strategy for me at this moment. I prefer her madness to her fear. When I took her to the training grounds this morning, she was shaking with fear. No one looked at her weirdly or commented on her presence rudely, but she was still tense.

Even though I knew it was scary for her, I never imagined her to look so terrified. I thought today was going to be flirty or maybe a little weird because of our kiss. I thought the effects might distract her a bit, but apparently, it was not enough.

Being seen is still terrifying for Raya. I hate that she is so self-conscious. I understand why but I still hate it.

Woe in Total Darkness

When she couldn't relax when we were warming up, I even suggested going back. I liked challenging her, but I didn't want to traumatize her further. I never want to treat her like she is made of glass, but I also need to move at her pace. I shouldn't rush her. We have time.

I gave her a choice, and she chose to stay.

She made me too fucking proud.

What I felt at that moment could be even better than the kiss. Or maybe a close second because the kiss was just magnificent. It was wrong, but I know I would do it again, given the chance. I couldn't even care what a big rule I broke by kissing her. I couldn't care how much I liked it. Instead, when I went back to my room last night, I touched myself shamelessly over a memory of a fucking kiss.

It was just that good.

Still, we need to talk about it. I know Zuraya said she wanted more, but it could mean nothing. It was an intense moment, and I don't want to hold her to a promise she made when the emotions were flying high. I want to decide on our boundaries. I hope she still wants me, but I'll just have to accept it if she doesn't. I am a big girl, after all.

I am going to talk to her about it after training because this is important. I don't want us to pass out on training just because I am not thinking with my head. Being surrounded by others helps, at least. Also, the urge to help Raya stops me from teasing her intentionally. Still, when I get too close to her, I can feel her breath hitch, but I am not doing it on purpose.

I am completely innocent.

Now I watch Raya fumble with the sword in her hand. I remembered she wanted to train in something I am good at so she wouldn't need to spar with someone else. Honestly, that will make me happy, but I am not going to manipulate her to like my weapon. I just wanted to give her a sword today because this is her first day of training surrounded by strangers. I wanted to give her something safe.

"Want me to show you again how to hold it?" I ask with a smirk.

Raya looks away like she does when she blushes. "No," she murmurs and turns back to me with a pleading look. "I really don't think this is for me. It is too long for me to use properly, and I cannot even carry it."

Oh, well, there is an idea. "Do you think it would be easier if it was shorter and lighter?"

"Yes! But it won't be a sword then."

"There are all kinds of swords." But that is not what I am thinking of. "Do you think you can use both of your hands?"

Her eyebrows rise, and something like relief fills her features. "I actually will feel more in control if I can use both of my hands," I told her to hold the sword with one hand, and she was not a big fan.

"That's what I thought," I murmur and take the sword from her. I go to the chests full of weapons. I made my soldiers carry them here from the hill. I reach deep into one until I come across what I am looking for. These are simple ones, but if she likes them, we will upgrade them.

I hold them in my hands and turn to Zuraya with a grin. "Daggers." It is just what she needs. I don't use it very much, but I have the glass dagger on my hip. It is sister to my sword, and even though I don't usually prefer it, the dagger has its moments too.

Raya giggles. "Isn't that something you use to kill your cheating husband in his sleep?"

I am taken aback momentarily. "Your mind is much darker than I anticipated."

She shrugs and gives me a sweet smile. I want to kiss her so badly. Before I can act on impulse, I give her the daggers, and she holds them like I showed her. For the first time, she actually looks confident with her weapons.

My old sword instructor would say it is like magic when a warrior finds their weapon. You can tell it is a perfect match, and now Zuraya looks like she has found hers.

"Attack me," I say. It is always the first thing we do. Of course, I am going to teach her the basics, but I first want to see how her instincts match with the weapon.

Woe in Total Darkness

Raya looks a little hesitant, but her hold on the daggers is strong. "I don't want to hurt you."

My eyebrows climb to my hairline. "You are very confident."

She smiles. "This just feels right."

"Come on. Attack me."

Until now, I was always able to stop her bare-handed. It was not the hardest thing I have ever done, but I never told her that. I don't want her to be offended.

Raya takes a deep breath and then jumps on me with her two daggers. Her stance and her movements are sloppy, but they are not the worst. She just needs to be taught. My hands immediately rise to stop her attack and bind her wrists so she can't touch me. She successfully avoids one of my hands on the first try, but on the second, I manage to bind her. She loses one dagger because of my hold on her wrist, but she holds onto the other one. It might seem like Raya sucked to an outsider, but she didn't at all. It was her best work. I just know daggers are made for her.

"That was great, Raya," I say with a grin.

She mirrors my expression. "It was, right? I really felt confident with these."

"That is the most important part." I half-heartedly let go of her hands and bent down to take her fallen dagger. I give it back to her. "If you want, we can add a chain between the two of them. That way, you won't lose a dagger, but it might cause some other problems. We need to practice."

Zuraya nods, but then her face turns terrified. She lets go of the daggers and reaches for my arm. "Oh my Goddess, I cut you."

She did? I look down and see blood spilling from between Raya's fingers. Her skin glows with Moonshine as she tries to patch me back together. I haven't even felt the cut, but I guess this is good practice for her. Maybe I should knowingly let her cut me from time to time. Too many cuts can mess up my tattoos a bit, but she is more important than those.

I inwardly kick myself because if other Sun Soldiers heard that thought, they would precisely do that to me.

Zuraya pulls back her bloodied hand over my cut. Her eyes fill with so much anxiety when she sees the cut is not healed. Though I can tell, there is some improvement. It is not bleeding anymore, and I can see the skin is kind of coming back together. It is still a cut, but it is somewhat healed.

She still looks sad, though. I hate that.

"You did it," I say with a smile. I really don't care about the wound. I never cared about any wound.

Zuraya looks at me like I am stupid. "I cannot heal you, Len. I am so sorry."

Oh, she is sorry. I just cannot focus on that immediately because this is the first time she called me Len. It is a moment to cherish.

I reach out and cup her cheek. "It is okay. You made it better, Raya. You are getting your power back. It is slow, but it is happening." I am so thunderstruck by her. "You are doing amazing."

"Don't lie to me," she says. She still looks a little sad, but her magnificent eyes have a shine to them.

"Never again."

She looks down, and then her eyes go to my soldiers.

I don't want to make her feel uncomfortable, so I pull my hand back after saying, "We will talk after this, okay?"

She nods. "Okay."

I take a few steps back. "Now, train with your daggers a bit. I have something I want to try afterward. It is kind of like what you just did."

She looks worried. "Please don't cut yourself again."

I chuckle. "Don't worry, I won't. It is just something I read in the book Maha gave me." It still entails me getting hurt but only if Zuraya is successful. I don't care about pain anyway.

Zuraya accepts, and after I wrap my arm up, we spend some time with daggers. I show her the right stance, and it again results in us getting too close. The tension between us is extreme, but I do my best to ignore it. It is not the time. From the tension of Raya's shoulders and a few times her breath hitches, I can tell she is doing

Woe in Total Darkness

the same. Maybe kissing should have let us get it out of our systems, but it seems like it made everything worse.

Now that I know how she tastes, I want her even more.

I show Raya some moves, and her posture is much better. It is almost like she was waiting for these daggers. I know when she learns some more moves from me, she can spar with Hashim, whose weapon of choice is daggers.

"I think that's enough for today," I say after we train for a while with the weapons.

Raya beams up at me holding her daggers like a little kid. "It was good training! I like these a lot."

"We will work on them more. I want to try the other thing now."

"Okay," Raya answers and lets go of her daggers half-heartedly. She looks ready to pout; it is the cutest thing I have ever seen. "What is it?"

"I was reading the book Maha gave me," I say. "There, it talked about how Carin Haliyes trained his daughter for her body manipulation powers. One thing he did was to wound his soldiers or staff so she could work on them."

Zuraya's eyes go wide. "I am not letting you cut anyone, so I can train."

"Of course not," I smirk. "You cut me enough for us to train."

She looks a little tortured again, and I feel bad. "I am really sorry."

My hand itch to reach out and touch her again, but this time I hold onto my control. I wave my hand instead. "It is okay, really," I say. "We are not going to do that right now anyway."

"Thank Tisasa."

I chuckle. "The other thing Carin Haliyes did was to give her people to torture. She would use her power to give them pain, and she would use real subjects. I thought it might be a good way to practice for you. You don't have to worry a lot, though, since you probably won't be able to really hurt me in the beginning. We can just build it up from there."

To my surprise, she doesn't look very alarmed but instead looks skeptical. "You want me to train in pain instead of healing?"

Oh yeah, that must sound weird. "I have two reasons for that," I confess. I only want to tell her one of them, but I don't want to lie to her again. I don't want to hide things. "I have to mentor you in using your powers. I will be the one to feel the effects after all. I feel like I will be able to guide you better when you are training in giving pain instead of healing."

She nods like it makes sense. "What is the other reason?"

That makes me go uneasy. I look away, but I still answer. "If anyone ever comes for you again, I want you to be able to defend yourself."

Suddenly I am the one that is tense and anxious. I don't want her to feel scared.

With so many worries, I look up at her face. I expect her to look angry or frightened, but that is not the case. She looks sympathetic. She looks fucking thankful. "I would like that."

———ᴄ———

We leave our pain training to later because Raya says she doesn't want to hurt me twice in one day. I respect her wish mostly because she has been more than brave enough today. She deserves a break from the training.

Unfortunately, that break includes some serious talk, but we have to do it. We cannot continue ignoring this or trying to act like nothing is happening. We need to decide what we want and what we are going to do.

So, after our training, I suggest we take a walk. At this point, I know which places are the most deserted on the palace grounds. Most people prefer to stay indoors this early in the day anyway.

"Are you taking me to a private place?" Raya asks as we walk.

"Yes," I answer. "We need privacy." No one else should hear about our talk.

She gets a teasing smile. "So you can kiss me again?"

A groan sticks to my throat. She knows how to push me, but this is not the time. I should be the strong one here. "So we can talk about if we should kiss again."

Woe in Total Darkness

"I thought we agreed we would last night." She sounds genuinely confused.

I turn to her. I don't want her to think I do this because I am having second thoughts. I have no regrets, even though what we did was almost a crime. "We did, and I have no problem with that, but we still have to talk. I don't want to feel like I pushed you while we were under the influence of intense emotions. Talking and deciding things with a clear head will be good for both of us."

"So this talk doesn't mean you are never going to kiss me again?"

I smile. "Not unless you don't want me to."

"Oh, I definitely want you to kiss me."

My muscles tense with arousal. I don't want her to catch the scent of it. We cannot afford distractions. "Then we should quickly get somewhere private and have this talk."

"I think we should run," she says, almost too seriously.

I cannot help my grin but still reach for her hand and start running to the location I had in mind. "Come on." Raya follows me while giggling too loudly.

When we reach a clearing between two towers, I stop. It is a tight space, but it is private. Zuraya eyes our surroundings for a moment, but then her glowing blue eyes turn to me. "We really should use this place in a good way."

"I know a lot of other places like this." I cannot help flirting, but we are not here for that. I shake my head. "We have to decide on some boundaries, Raya."

She shrugs. "I don't want any boundaries with you."

Fuck. I almost groan. "You shouldn't say things like that while we are alone."

"But that is the whole point," she beams.

I love making her blush, but I also love this daring side of her. I love that she is comfortable with me. "We need boundaries because what we did last night was very wrong, Raya."

Her face falls. "Oh."

"But I don't want to stop just because it was wrong and forbidden and all that shit," I say quickly.

She gathers herself with my words and looks hopeful. "Me too."

241

"But you understand why we need boundaries, right? We cannot treat this more than what it is. We cannot let anyone know, and we cannot let emotions into this."

Raya nods, looking serious. "Of course. It is not different than you helping me, right? We cannot train with so much tension between us, so we have to relieve it somehow. I don't know if you are currently sleeping with someone, but I..."

"I am not," I cut in. I want her to know.

"Okay, that's good," she murmurs, looking relieved. "So, this is just us helping each other. It is just sex."

Hearing it from her lips causes heat between my thighs. I have only kissed her yet, but she wants more. I want more too. I just want to make her go crazy with pleasure.

I wonder if she is ever fucked properly.

I swallow the lump in my throat. I am not going to fuck her today. I want to make it good.

"Okay," I say. "If we agree, we can have this. Just sex until I leave."

Something like sadness passes her eyes just for a second. I am not even sure if I saw it correctly, but the next moment she smiles. "Just sex," she repeats. "Now, can you please kiss me again?"

So, I do.

30

Zuraya

"Your Highness, are you sure you want to get them all at once?" The Feyada asks as he is pulling my bottom lip out. I don't think this is the best time for the question. He had already pierced the bridge of my nose and my septum. Now it is time for my bottom lip. He is going from top to bottom.

I try not to pull my lip away and answer, "Yes." I want it all at once. I need them all back.

I close my eyes when I see him bring the needle close. I think happy thoughts like how Lenora kissed me again the other day. I think it was a nice way to seal the deal. I was stupid for thinking I didn't like kissing. I am addicted to her kisses. They were soft but intense. I lost myself in her again. I wanted to do much more, but unfortunately, Lenora stopped before things could escalate. Our hands did some discovering but not much. She said she wanted to make it really good for me, so we should go slow and learn each other's bodies.

Honestly, I don't care. I would let her do anything she wanted to me. I never really liked sex either but I bet she could change my mind about that.

Ugh.

My thought gets interrupted by the pain when the needle pierces my bottom lip. My eyes heat with the pain, but I try my best not to cry. I cried a bit on the previous one and felt a little ashamed. I am used to my maids seeing me every day, but the Feyada who pierces me is a new person. He is the royal jeweler, apparently. I don't remember him from where I used to be, but back there, I got all my piercings when I was much younger. He might be a new one.

I feel him put the silver ring into my lip. "It is all done, Your Highness."

I finally open my eyes and take the mirror from him. I look at my reflection. My face is throbbing with pain, but I can try to heal my wounds a little faster later. It's worth a shot.

Thankfully I am not regretful at all. I know I could have gotten them one by one, but I am impatient. It made sense when Lenora said I shine because I feel comfortable with her. I do feel relaxed when I am in her arms. I don't think about all the horrible things that happened to me. Being with her just feels right to me despite everything.

However, I know it is not forever. Lenora is going to leave at one point. I need more permanent solutions. I need to feel comfortable in my body. I need to look like I did before.

Of course, I cannot bring back my wings, but I can get back my piercings, and I can get my hair fixed. I want to see *me*, when I look into the mirror. I also need to gain some weight, but that is more of a long-term decision. I cannot gain weight in one day, but I can get pierced in five places in a few hours.

As I look into the mirror, I understand it was the right idea. I look so much like myself that I can cry. I can still be myself even after my trauma. I don't have to let them steal me from me.

A smile forms on my face, and I look at the jeweler. "It looks great. Now let's do my nipples."

———— ɩ ————

"I'm here, I'm here." I stumble into my antechamber while still trying to button the cuffs on my shirt. Lenora is here at her regular time. At this point, I kind of feel brave enough to go to the training

Woe in Total Darkness

grounds by myself, but I don't have the heart to tell her that. I like when she comes to get me.

And now, since we train in the morning, I like to start my day with her.

Unfortunately, this morning I am a little late. Yesterday was exhausting. After I got my piercings, I wanted to get my old braids back. Undoing all those tiny braids and then giving me my regular thick braids took some time. I also wanted to choose an outfit I was going to feel like myself. It was a success. I am wearing a white shirt with designs on its cuffs and neckline. My pants are blue and very comfortable. My braids are tied at my neck, and even though I am not wearing a pretty dress like I mostly do, I feel like myself.

All of this meant going to bed a little late and, as a result, getting up a little later, but I feel like it is worth it.

I even feel it more when I look up at Lenora's face. Her pupils are dilated, and her lips are slightly parted. She looks speechless.

I know it is because of me, but I still ask, "Everything okay?"

She openly looks up and down, appreciating me. A small smirk appears. "You got piercings."

I beam up at her. "I did. I used to have them, but when I came here, only my ears were still pierced." Probably because I got them when I was a toddler. "I got all five of them."

Lenora looks at my face with adoration, but then her eyebrows come together. "I only see three."

Oh, this is working great. "I'll show you the other two later."

For a moment, she looks confused but then her eyes fall to my body. She is trying to guess where I have them. Her throat moves with a swallow. Her whole body looks tense, and I try to take deep breaths without making it obvious just so I can smell if she is aroused.

But when she says, "I can't wait," with a heated look, I know I don't need to try. I don't need to doubt Lenora's attraction to me. She likes me, and nothing is stopping her from showing it.

I know we need to keep whatever is going on between us a secret, but even before we kissed, we were flirty. We bantered a lot. Also, now I know my maids are under the payroll of Lenora. If she is not worried about them, I am not, either.

I trust her judgment.

It is hard to hide my smile when she doesn't move from her spot and doesn't stop looking at me. I look at the door and then back at her. "Should we leave?"

Lenora blinks a few times. "Of course. Sorry. I guess I got distracted."

My smile turns into a full grin as we move towards the door. "You sure did."

She stops before we can leave my chambers and turns to me with a lifted eyebrow. "Don't get cocky, Raya. I am still your teacher, and I can really take revenge."

That only makes me more excited.

Something like vulnerability touches her eyes, and she gets serious. She reaches for my hands, and I put them in hers immediately. Her thumb brushes my palm. "You look magnificent, Raya," she says with a sweet tone. "But it is not because, apparently, I am very attracted to piercings."

I giggle, but my heart is hammering.

"It is because you look too real," Lenora continues. "Even your smile is more genuine. You look happy to look like this, and I love seeing you be yourself."

My vision gets a little blurry with tears, but I hold them back. "Thank you." I don't know what else I can say.

"Let's go to training," she says, bringing my hands to her mouth for a kiss. "We need to work on these skinny arms."

We both chuckle as we make our way to training, and even though I know she is going to be very hard on me, I cannot stop smiling.

31

Lenora

Only after having six kids did Vaughn realize his plans to create a big army of Sun Soldiers were impossible. He was expecting all of his kids to have the sun power he possessed, but that was not the case. The truth came out when the kids started growing older and started training. Every new child had fewer powers than the one before.

The differences in powers of the Mitharaus children were very unique to their own. It was not very obviously less power but more of a different gift. The oldest child was able to perfect his skills in every aspect of the sun power, but the others usually took other roots. The second child was very skilled in the Sunshine, but they were not able to use mind manipulation very well. With every child, a new and bigger weakness was there. In the end, Vaughn realized the power was getting weak with every new child, so he stopped having more. His hopes for a great army were crushed. Instead, he started to train his Feyadas. He managed to create a very strong army, only they didn't carry the power of a Goddess.

Vaughn made his oldest the General of the Sun Army. He was skilled at his powers but not so much with ruling over a great army. He died during the first war against the Giants. Vaughn was devastated because he died before having any children, and that *meant he was now left with less powerful heirs. Only in a few months, he realized he was wrong again because his second oldest child was now as powerful as their late brother. The death of the oldest heir meant the powers were going to pass on to the next in line. Because of that, Vaughn decided when he died, his powers must be passed on to his heir since he was also stronger than all of his children.*

Because he was the most powerful at the time, he decided to lead the army himself with a new Feyada General and defeated the Giants. They claimed their lands as part of the Sun Khanate, but Giants never actually accepted this. It has led to many disturbances throughout history. Feyadas kept fighting with the natives of Ae for many years. They managed to win almost every time just because of the power they stole from the natives' Goddess.

———᚜———

Even just a day after Raya is terrific. She almost gets better by the second. It makes me wonder if she practiced or if it was just because of her new look.

And, oh, her new look. I couldn't even stop myself from going speechless at the sight of her. Her thicker braids fit her face a lot better, and all the metal on her face brings out her features more. Even her clothing is more fitting. She definitely looks more attractive, but more than that, she looks happy.

She looks how she looks seconds after I kiss her. That gets me going more than ever.

When I gave her the double daggers, even her stance was better. I started the day by showing her a few simple attack moves. She practiced them over and over again on a dummy. She needs to work on that before she is ready to spar with me and then after, with Hashim. I told Zuraya the dummy was going to stay here, and I gifted her the daggers. She can come and train even when we are not here. I know she feels more comfortable during the night, so that might help.

After the dagger practice, I want to work on her powers again. It seems like she doesn't have a lot of problems with her light anymore. She can shine, and as she does, all my soldiers look at her with awe, and I feel proud even though this was all her.

She looks beautiful, surrounded by that colorful white light.

Unfortunately, she is still not her best at body manipulation. I try to coach her using my knowledge of giving people pain with my mind manipulation, but apparently, they are not very similar. Getting inside the mind and making people think they are in pain is entirely different than actually putting pressure around their muscles and veins to hurt them for real.

Raya is actually better at coaching herself. She uses her past knowledge and continues with some trial and error. She does her best to give me pain. I really focus when she does that so I can tell apart my usual pain and the one she is inflicting on me. I stand there completely motionless, and I can tell it kind of bothers her. She doesn't want to hurt me, but she also doesn't like when I am not affected at all.

I need to focus on seeing how good she is, though.

And honestly, she is not terrible. I feel her power sneaking inside my skin and spreading pain along my muscles. She can't go deep into my internal organs, but she is good. It wouldn't overpower anyone in a fight, but it would give her an advantage. She has to be able to do it while fighting with her daggers, though.

It is our next step. She needs to learn how to mix her powers and physical fighting skills. That is the best part, but she has to learn both of them separately first.

Overall it is good training. I know Raya might not feel like it because she is kind of impatient, but it is good. Even after the training, when I need to have a meeting with my Commander back home, I think about what we can do the next day.

"Hey," Raya approaches me while I am lost in thought.

I grin down at her. "Hey. You were great today."

"Thanks," she says, a little shyly. "I wanted to ask something."

"Ask away."

"Can we go somewhere?" she says and then looks around to see if anyone heard it. "I mean, there is a place I want to visit. Will you come with me?"

I falter with an answer for a second because I do have things I need to do. I might be away from home, but I don't let go of my heavy schedule. Especially because Mav refused to help me with the Giants.

Raya takes a step away at my hesitation. "Sorry. You must be busy."

"I am not," I say quickly, and even to my ears, it sounds like a lie. I shake my head. No more lies. "I mean, I am, but it is okay. I can reschedule for you."

"Sure?" she asks.

"Sure," I answer, and the smile on her face is worth all the pain and lack of sleep rescheduling are going to cost me. At these moments, I understand why everybody called her the pretties face on the Isle. She has breathtaking beauty. Even looking at her smile makes you feel special.

It is dangerous, but I am not ready for withdrawal. First, I need a real taste of her. Not just a taste of her skin, her sex. I need the full Zuraya Haliyes experience. I need something I can look back at when I am no longer here.

Doesn't sound like "just sex" to my ears, but she doesn't need to know. I am the only one who is going to get hurt, and I don't mind it that much. This is a pain I will welcome.

After I give one of my soldiers instructions to reach my contacts for rescheduling, I follow Raya to wherever she wants to take me. I told her maybe we should change since we both were sweaty, but she told me we were going to get wet again anyway.

Those words don't help my dirty mind to ease down.

Only when we reach our destination, I get her real meaning. We are on a beach close to the palace. There are a few nice ones, but this one looks way too small and secluded for anyone to enjoy. There is muddy white sand on the floor that is so much different than the sand in the desert, but there are also pebbles. Everything is rocky in the Moon Kingdom.

The water looks angry and way too cold, but the sight of it makes Raya smile so wide that I find myself smiling as well.

She takes a deep breath of ocean air. "I always loved coming here," she says. Her eyes are close, and there is a peaceful

Woe in Total Darkness

expression on her face. "I love the wind and the waves. I used to come here so much that the ocean smell was always all over me. It disgusted the Court. Someone even told me I smelled like Mermaids. I was so ashamed back then. Now I don't even care."

Moon Court is truly weird. I take a step and get close to Raya. We are not touching, but I know she can feel the heat of my body on her arm. "You don't have to care. Ocean smell won't scare me away."

Her smile broadens, and she turns toward me. "Then I should scare off everyone else with it so we can have some privacy."

"Great idea."

She reaches for my hand, and her fingers intertwine with mine. Even that small touch electrifies my whole body. "Come on," Raya says cocking her head. "Since you are not scared, we can dip our toes in."

My eyebrows climb to my forehead. "You got to be kidding me."

She looks worried. "What? Why?"

I look at the freezing ocean. "Do you want to kill me? This looks brutal. Why are we even doing this?

Raya giggles and closes her hand over her mouth. "Oh, Tisasa, General Lenora Mitharaus is afraid of the water."

"No, that is not true. I just don't like the cold."

She keeps giggling, and her hand leaves mine. She walks back to the water. Her eyes are on me, but her hands are busy untying her boots. "Come on, it is not so cold."

I just stand there. "I am from the Desert."

Raya rolls her eyes, and when her feet are free, she rolls up her pant legs. "You are just scared. Admit it." Then she turns back and runs to the water laughing.

I usually don't care what anyone says about me. I am confident enough in myself to not care about stupid allegations. I know I am not scared. Sunshine keeps me warm so the cold is not a big problem. I can handle it. I just don't enjoy it. It is stupid to enjoy it.

Raya saying I am scared doesn't mean shit. Or at least it shouldn't.

Unfortunately, it does. I cannot be the one to lose in our banter, so I reach down and take off my sandals. I mean, how can I be scared? I am wearing sandals while she was in boots. She is not making sense. I should show her that.

I hear her squeak and clap of her hands. "Are you coming?"

"I have a reputation I need to protect." Apparently, only when it comes to her.

I can see her slurry looks when I am pulling up my shalwar to my calves. "Come show me what a big bad general you are."

I can't help my smirk. I walk into the water towards her. "You shouldn't rile me up," I say confidently, but it is all ruined when I wince against the cold. I immediately send my Sunshine toward my feet. It is wet and freezing, and I am sure I felt something brush up the side of my foot. Who in their right mind would enjoy this?

Raya apparently.

She laughs again, but this time doesn't tease me. Instead, she reaches for my hand again, and for some stupid reason, I am happy to hold her hand. "Come on, I'll warm you up."

"You are crazy," I say, strolling right next to her. "Is this really the most fun you can have around here?"

She shrugs with a small smile on her face. "I mean, there are other things too."

My body heats at her hidden meaning. "I think I will prefer them," I mumble, and again something weird touches my foot, and I shriek. "What is in this water, for fuck's sake?"

Raya cannot stop her laughter. "Oh my, you really cannot stand this. It is so cute."

I try to shake off whatever is around my ankle. "Something touched my foot, and I am not cute." No one ever called me cute. It doesn't really go well with being a soldier.

"Oh, but you are," Raya laughs even harder. "It is just seaweed, Len. If it really scares you, we can leave."

Okay, that is enough. "Don't push me, Raya."

She keps laughing at me. "Just accept that you are scared of the water."

Woe in Total Darkness

"I am not," I say harshly and reach for her. I easily lift her from under her bottom and get down. The sand and the water help with our fall, but I am still careful with her as I put her down on her back with my body covering hers. I am between her thighs, and her body is mostly underwater. My legs are also in the water, and more seaweed touches my skin. This time I don't care, though.

Raya looks at me with huge eyes, and her breathing gets fast. I cannot help but press myself into her, right between her legs. "You are not laughing anymore."

She shakes her head. "I am not."

I look at her face. The metal all lined up in the middle of her face shines under the sunlight. There are droplets of salt water on her dark skin from the splash I caused while getting us into this position. Her eyes are huge, and they carry all the colors of the aurora.

She is so exquisite that my breath hitches. "You look so good like this," I say with a husky voice.

Her throat moves. "With my piercings?"

"No," I shake my head even though that is also true. "Like *this*. All wet and breathless under me."

She bites down her bottom lip as a smile blooms, and I want to have that. She looks away for a second like it is too much for her. "Well, hopefully, the next time I am like this, we won't be in the ocean."

"Because it is cold?" I tease.

"No, because you made my braids get wet. It is going to be hard to clean them now."

I wince. "Shit. Sorry."

"It is okay," she shrugs. "But you can give me a better apology." Then her eyes go to my lips, and my body is burning despite the cold water. She loves kissing so much, or maybe she just likes it when I kiss her.

My hands wrap around her thighs to make sure I am settled between her legs perfectly. I lower my head and press my lips to hers. Raya immediately puts her hands on my neck. She kisses me like she is starving. Her body curls under me softly, and I can almost feel the heat of her sex against my lower abdomen through our wet clothes. I might be imagining, though.

I squeeze her thighs, and Raya dips her tongue into my mouth. I can feel the ring on her bottom lip, and weirdly it fuels me more. Even though I am the one on top, she takes the reins. She kisses me desperately. Every time her tongue moves playfully into my mouth, I fill with the urge to sit on top of her face and feel that tongue between my legs. The thought makes me even more aroused.

Raya rolls her hips into me, and I cannot stop thinking how wet she must be. I want to roll down her pants and taste her. I won't even mind the cold water we are in. I just want her.

She wraps her legs around my waist. Her back arches and our breasts press together, rubbing as we kiss. I love the feeling of that, but before I can enjoy it, Raya winces under me, "Ah!"

That didn't sound very pleasure-like. I immediately pull back, confused. "Are you okay? Did I hurt you?" Maybe I was too lost and didn't realize it.

"No," she says, and then, "Yes." My body tenses, and she shakes her head. "Not like that." Her cheeks heat and she covers her face with her hands.

"Hey," I murmur, reaching out and prying her hands out of her face. "Tell me what happened."

Raya teeth her lip-ring. "It hurt when we touched but not because of you."

"You have to explain it better."

She groans softly. "You know I just got these piercings. They take some time to heal. When I realized if my lip was sore I couldn't kiss you, I healed the wound." She looks away sadly. "I couldn't manage to heal the others, though."

I nudge her chin so she will look at me. I am beaming down at her. "Raya, you healed yourself? That is amazing."

Her lips upturn, but her insecurity doesn't leave her eyes. "I couldn't heal all of them, though. And now I cannot even rub myself all over you because my breasts hurt."

Woe in Total Darkness

My attention goes to her chest with those words like a hellhound. My eyes bulge. I guessed before but having her confirmation made it more real. I just cannot look away from her chest. Her shirt is wet, and I can faintly see her dark nipples and the outline of the ladders in them.

I lick my lips because they are dry now and whisper, "Can I see them?"

I hear Raya suck in a breath and her thighs flex around my waist. "Yes," she breathes out.

Without needing anything more, my hand flies to her buttons. I am so hungry for her. I know I cannot fuck her today. I can do things without touching her breasts, but I want to give her everything in our first time.

Later.

Still, I want to see her, though. If I don't see those two little piercings now, I might go mad imagining them.

My hands work her buttons fast, and her soft skin comes into view. I push the fabric aside and let her breasts free. Raya is thin from her days as a captive, but her chest is much bigger than mine, anyway. Her breasts are full, and I can't help but cup one with my hand. Raya hisses, but I cannot look up at her. Both her nipples are pierced, and the metal ladder provokes me.

Without thinking, I lean down and lick her nipple softly. Her skin smells like chamomile and tastes like berries. A drunken groan leaves me.

Raya whimpers.

I press a kiss to the same nipple and look up at her flushed face. "Did I hurt you?" I ask.

She shakes her head, and I go to lick her other nipple. The little bud is hard and swollen against my tongue. I cannot wait to be able to really suck on them. I'll gladly suffocate and die right here, but only after I thoroughly ravished her.

I keep my kisses and touches soft. Raya's legs tighten around my waist, and she arches her back, pressing her chest into my mouth. "At the end of this, I will be ruined," she breathes.

Oh, Tisasa, I really don't think so. I lick my way back up to her neck and suck softly. Then I reach up to press a short kiss onto her lips. "Raya," I say, all my amazement apparent in my tone. "Look at you. I will be the one that is going to be ruined."

She moans and throws her head back so her lips will tease mine as she speaks. "More," she says.

It kills me, but I have already decided on my answer. "No."

She doesn't ask me why. She just says, "Please, Len."

"No," I say again, even if it hurts. "You are in pain."

Raya shakes her head. "You don't have to touch me there. I need more."

I bury my face into her neck and breathe in her scent. "No," I say for the last time. "When I fuck you, I am not going to hold back, Raya."

Her eyes open, and she bites down her bottom lip. I expect more of a fight, but instead, she just says, "Okay." She trusts me to make it good for her.

I whisper over her lips. "We can just have fun in the ocean without sex. Apparently, you think that is possible."

She giggles and brushes her nose to mine. "Not while we are wet."

"Ah, don't worry about that."

Then I help her out of the water, and when we sit on the beach, I use my Sunshine to dry us off. She looks so amazed by it that I kiss her again. But we mostly just talk. We don't talk about anything important, but we just sit and spend time together without sex. It is uncalled for since this was not part of our agreement, but I cannot find it in me to care.

32

Zuraya

"Any day now," Maha says with an eye roll. "This is what they keep telling me for the last month."

Lenora shakes her head next to me. Her disapproval is so apparent. "It is all because of the Northern medics. They don't know shit about most things." Her orange eyes come to me, and she looks apologetic. "Sorry."

"I am sure they know what they are doing," I answer, but it is not because I am actually offended. It is because I don't want to worry Maha more than she already is.

Thankfully she just looks annoyed. "I have a Seelie healer with me."

Lenora lifts a perfect blonde eyebrow. "Are they the Royal Healer?"

Maha shakes her head. "Of course not Mav would never let me take her."

I see Lenora shake her head again. She is really not good at hiding her annoyance towards this. She is typically very neutral, but I guess it is different when it is about someone she cares about.

Back where I used to be, I would never guess Lenora Mitharaus to be so fond of Maha. In my mind, they always seemed so different to me, but I can see how much she likes her.

After our training today, we realized she was watching us. It actually surprised me since I now knew the first time I saw her watching the training, she was just sent by Lenora.

When we realized she was there, Lenora was the one who suggested finishing early and sitting with Maha. We are in her chamber since she has a great terrace with a view of the ocean. I like it here.

I kind of feel a little weird being here with Lenora, but I also love it. We do spend time in others' presence now since her soldiers are always around when we train, but this is different. Right now, we are not obligated to be together. We are just here with someone else around.

I know I shouldn't enjoy it as much as I do.

Thankfully the tense topic keeps me from constantly looking at her with a dumb smile. After our little trip to the beach, I am even worse. The longer we keep delaying the sex more frustrated I get. I cannot stop thinking about her and how her mouth felt on my skin or how her body felt between my legs. I just want her to take me.

To be perfectly honest, I am not sure how to go about it. I have only ever been with Rionn and learned everything I know from him. Now that I think about it, most of those things revolved around his cock. I am not sure how sex is supposed to go when there is none. I don't have any doubts about wanting Lenora. I know I will like having sex with her, and my imagination does work. I have pictures in my head of us doing filthy things.

I am just nervous. I don't want to mess it up, and I don't know what I should do.

I get even more nervous as we wait. I am both sexually frustrated and anxious. It is a horrible combination. I just hope both will go away after the first time. I can learn what I should do, and finally, having Lenora can just get her out of my system.

Not so sure about the latter, though.

"You should have gone to the Sun Khanate." Lenora's words bring me back from my thoughts. Now I can go back to looking at her and thinking how attractive she is when she is angry.

Oh, Tisasa, help me.

"I wouldn't have been accepted."

Lenora looks murderous. "Of course, you would have been, Maha. I would make sure of it. Desert is at the top of the medical field. Healers back there also know a lot about interspecies pregnancies. You would have been taken care of. They probably had that baby out of you already."

Maha doesn't look convinced. She looks a little sad, too, and that breaks my heart. "I am a Seelie princess married to the Moon General. I know I wouldn't be welcomed. Also, I wanted to be close to Davon. I need him during this time."

"You need a good healer more than you need, Davon."

Maha gives her a small smile. "I always need him more than anyone."

Well, my logical side knows Lenora is right, and Maha needs good medical care. I still swoon over her words. Maha and Davon's love always astonished me. I feel like nothing can hurt when you have a love like that.

Once I believed maybe Rionn and I were like them. Now it only sounds amusing.

"Maybe you can go now," I suggest trying to find some middle ground. I know Sun Khanate has the best healers. They are in the middle of the Trade Road, so that also means they are the perfect spot for gathering knowledge from both Nort and South. They could help Maha better, but I also understand how she wouldn't want to be there all alone.

She needs Davon as much as he needs her. It feels like the world would be corrupt if they were ever separated. It is that kind of love.

"My body cannot take the journey now," Maha says, waving her hand like she is bored with the conversation. "Please talk about something other than my pregnancy. I need some distractions. Just tell me how the training is going."

Lenora doesn't seem very happy with the change of topic, but I understand. All of us can need some distraction sometimes, and Maha deserves it.

I give her a big smile. "It is going great. I am learning how to use daggers. I kind of nipped Lenora today, so I am getting better."

To that, Lenora actually smiles. "True," she says, showing the almost invisible nip on her elbow. It was nothing, but I know she never goes soft on me. She always pushes me to do my best, so even the smallest accomplishment feels amazing. It feels even better when I see the pride in Lenora's eyes. I care about her opinion above anyone else's.

Maha is smiling, but she looks more surprised. "I thought you were only training for your powers. What is up with the daggers?"

"It is all part of the process," Len answers before I can. She looks at me and her fingers softly brush mine. "I want to challenge her a bit. She is good at handling all of them."

Her praise makes me blush. Lenora does tell me when I am doing good, but it is different when she says those things in the presence of another. I like how she sees me as someone strong when I have been broken so badly.

"That is great," Maha claps. "I am sure you will be at your best by the time of your name-day."

"My name-day?"

Maha looks at a very uncomfortable-looking Lenora. "Isn't that the deadline King Luran gave you? He wants everyone to see you as the perfect princess by then."

"Oh," I say. That thing. I don't like being reminded of Lenora's deal with my father. I am still angry that she lied to me, but there is more than that. She did come clean, and I trust that she didn't lie to me again after my confrontation. It still bugs me, though. I don't like that she is only helping me because of a deal she made. Whatever we have feels real, but the last seven years of my life felt real too. I just cannot believe her so easily.

Mostly, I try to ignore why she is helping me, but it is always at the back of my head. Lenora has to train me so I can be the Princess my father wants.

But she definitely shouldn't kiss me. That part is not for a deal.

Unfortunately, I cannot stop but question those too. I know she is only doing it for her, but I worry if she is playing me. After she refused to go further on the beach despite my pleas, I got suspicious. I am afraid she is doing it only to keep me close.

I don't want to believe it. I want to think Lenora is with me because she wants me, but it is hard to get rid of my doubts.

Woe in Total Darkness

I don't want Lenora to just see me as a duty.

Before things can get even weirder, Lenora stands up. She looks really uncomfortable. "I really should leave," she mumbles. "I have a meeting."

"Oh, I don't want to hold you," says Maha sweetly.

I don't want Maha to see, but my eyes still look at her with so much hope. "I'll see you later?"

Her lips upturn a bit. "Of course." Then she looks at me a beat longer like she wants to kiss me and leaves the room. I wish she could have kissed me. I wish she could give me something assuring.

"Okay, so what is happening there?" Maha asks with an excited tone.

I look back at her, a little distracted. I just cannot stop thinking about Lenora. "What?"

"Zuraya, I am not a kid. I am also not a part of the stiff-necked Moon Court. I can tell when there is sexual tension in the room, and we were drowning in it until a minute ago."

My pulse picks up with fear. I don't know how she can even tell. Lenora and I do have tension, but we were doing good. We were discreet. We did nothing to tip her off. How can she even see it?

Her eyes widen when she sees my fear. "Oh, Moonshine, don't worry, I won't tell anyone. It is not a big deal."

It is forbidden by ancient law. It would put us in so much trouble. "This is a big accusation Maha. You shouldn't say this to others. Lenora is merely helping me get better. We are just friends."

Maha rolls her eyes at me, bile I am making no sense at all. "This is not an accusation, Zuraya. I am a Seelie. We don't care about the little rules you made up. I can see there is something between you, and if there isn't, it is going to happen soon. I don't care what it means; I am actually happy for you."

"Are you?" I ask carefully. I am not fully convinced, but her words do make sense. Ancient rules are made by Feyadas, and Seelies hardly care for them.

She nods with a smile. "I really like both of you and want you to be happy. Just make sure no one gets hurt."

Okay, now she is really messing with my head. I could have understood if she was against it because it was forbidden, but this is weird. "Why would someone get hurt?"

Maha shrugs and looks away for a moment. When she turns back, her voice is rather hushed, like she is keeping secrets from the walls of her own chamber. "Look, I really love Lenora, and I come to love you. I think you will be good together, but you must remember that Len is not just a soldier. She is a princess, a politician. I just don't want you to be on a different page than she is, intentional or unintentional."

My stomach turns. "You think she would use me?"

"No, definitely not," Maha shakes her head immediately. Then she reaches for my hands and takes them in hers. "I just don't want you to assume more than she gives you."

It is good advice. I know it is. Still, my throat goes dry because Lenora didn't give me anything yet. Not more than to satisfy the deal, at least.

33

Zuraya

I fix the neckline of my teal dress. It is slightly different from my usual attire, but I wanted to look tempting. It is an armless dress and shows way too much cleavage. It is not skin tight, but it does cling to my curves. It looks more like a Seelie dress, but it is what I need tonight. I am also wearing a black cloak over it because of the weather, but I think it still works. My braids are not tied back or up in a turban like I usually do in training. I want to look natural but also breathtaking.

Tonight is my best chance to get rid of my doubts. I am not sure if Lenora sleeping with me actually proves anything, but it will to me. I just want her to take risks for me. I want to know it is real.

She made no deal to kiss me, and that was purely for us, but the longer I think, the less sure I get. She knew if she didn't kiss me, I was going to stop my training. I cannot stop but wonder if that is the only reason she did it.

When I am in Lenora's arms, I have no doubts. I lose my mind when my skin touches hers, but I know it can be dangerous. I need to be vary.

My goal tonight is to get what I have been craving for so long. If Lenora turns me down again, I will keep my distance from her. I will just take the goodwill she grants me because of a deal she

Sem Thornwood

struck. And if she actually accepts me... I will decide what I'll do later.

Now all my piercings are healed, so she doesn't have any excuses. Because I invited her for a late-night walk, I am pretty sure she knows what I have in mind. I just need to keep a close eye on how she acts and pray I am interpreting everything right.

I jump a little when a soft knock comes on my door. I look at the mirror one last time. I have never been self-conscious about how I look, but it is hard not to when you are a half Feyada now. I don't have big proud wings anymore. But I still look good. I also know I will feel better about myself when I see how Lenora looks at me. She always looks at me like I am perfect.

"Come in," I call out, and the face of one of my maids appears. She informs me that Lenora is here, and my heart starts jackhammering inside my chest. I take a deep breath closing my eyes to gather myself, and when I am somewhat calm, I step out of my room.

The second I see her, all the calm leaves me. Lenora fills out the room like always, even though her wings are tucked on her back. She is wearing a red tunic I have seen for the first time. It is tight, and the flowy material on the arms almost leaves them bare, showing off her many tattoos. The tunic seems to be more for the appeal than practicality. The black pants she is wearing are also tighter than her usual ones. Her hair is not in a braid but instead flowing down her shoulders like pure sunshine. I am not even sure if I have ever seen her with her hair down.

It feels good knowing she also dressed up for our little late-night walk. I like that this is all for me. No one gets to have her like this but me.

Before I can even finish admiring her looks, she sucks in a breath. I look up at her face, and she seems flustered. She looks at the maids briefly. "You sure you won't be cold in this?"

I want to giggle. I can tell this is not what she wanted to say. I shake my head and step closer so only she can hear me. "You'll warm me up."

Woe in Total Darkness

Lenora leans down, making our faces get closer. When she whispers, I can feel her breath on my lips. "I am going to lose my mind, Raya."

I like this. I like that she cannot stop herself even though my maids are still around. I peek a little at them to see if they are looking and when I see it is all clear, I lick Lenora's lips. "Good."

She looks like she is holding back a growl. I stifle a smile and reach for her warm hand. "Let's go for our walk," I say, and before we leave, I look back at my maids. "You are free for the night."

I feel giddy when we leave my room. I just let Lenora lead me while I smile stupidly. As soon as she is close, all my doubts and headaches just disappear. I again look up and down at her strong and graceful figure. "I didn't know you owned anything other than fighting attire."

"You are in for a surprise then." She chuckles. "This is nothing. I actually own a ton of dresses. Just like a real princess."

I giggle, but the thought is too enticing. "I would love to see you in a dress."

She side-eyes me, and I can see flames in her orange eyes. "One day, you will."

It is crazy how even that makes me excited.

I cannot stop my beating heart around her. She knows what I want for tonight, and I really hope she will give it to me.

I mean, I even cleared out my room.

"Where are we going?" I ask when we leave the palace and not go towards the woods. I really don't want to go somewhere crowded. I don't want Moon Court around me, not just because I am not ready to let everyone know how thin and wingless I look but also because I want to be in a place where I can touch Lenora freely.

I am actually a little disappointed because she is manipulating the situation, so I cannot get close to her. But then she answers with a smile, "To the greenhouse. I crave some strawberry."

My brows furrow. The strawberry garden is actually around the greenhouse. "Do you mean we are going towards there? We cannot get into the greenhouse. It is closed most of the time."

There are special days and nights when the Court can visit it, but it gets really crowded at those times. I hope that is not the case.

Lenora smirks and squeezes my hand. "You see, it is really easy to get things done around here with bribery. I spoke with the gardener, and he is going to leave the doors open for us."

A beam up at her. This is perfect. She is really making this special for me.

"It is a little dark," Lenora mumbles. Then she looks at me with a grin almost as big as mine. "But I think we can manage a little light."

I nod. "We definitely can." It is easier to glow when she is around anyway.

For the next while, we just walk toward the gardens. We come across a few shadows in the darkness, but whenever we do, I realize Lenora moving her wings to keep me out of eyesight. She also never lets go of my hand. She is the only one who knows not to treat me like glass, but she also knows when she needs to protect me.

Never in my wildest dreams would I think Lenora Mitharaus to be this good to me.

For me.

"I really cannot believe anything grows in this climate," Lenora says when we reach the garden. For the first time, she lets go of my hand so she can crouch and pick up a strawberry.

I laugh at her words. "And this is coming from someone living in a desert?"

She turns back to me with an insulting expression. The stem of a strawberry on the side of her mouth makes it kind of comical, though. "I am offended," she says with a high-pitched voice. "You may think it is only sand in there, but shit grows in the desert."

"Only shit?" I joke.

For some reason, her look turns heated, but she is smiling. "I would tackle you for that, but you are lucky I am curious about the greenhouse."

Woe in Total Darkness

I roll my eyes and push my braids over my shoulder as I start walking toward the giant greenhouse in the middle of the field. "It is okay. You can tackle me later."

The next moment I hear her shuffle to her feet and feel her arms around my waist. She holds me with strength, and one of her hands pushes a strawberry to my lips. I part them willingly to accept. I don't know what it is about Lenora, but I like her embrace more than I probably should. Rionn was very strong, too, but he never felt like Lenora did around me.

She buries her face into the crook of my neck playfully, and I can smell the sweet fruit on her breath when she speaks. "You are very bratty tonight."

I put my hand over hers as we keep walking and shrug. "Maybe I was always bratty and just starting now to be myself again." I know it is mostly true. I always had a shy side but being an adored princess since birth also made me a little brat. Losing my wings kind of ruined that for me, but maybe I can get it back. When I am around Lenora, I feel like I can get back everything I once was.

Lenora loosens the arm she has around me so we can walk side by side. "That makes sense. You are getting your real self back."

I throw my head back so I can look at her. "So, me being bratty doesn't bother you?" I know it would bother most.

"Not at all." She smirks. "I know I can handle it."

Okay, now I am getting so hot that I feel like I don't even need the cloak anymore. Lenora can make me feel good about myself while making me extremely wet. It must be a gift.

I look away, so she won't see me being flustered. "Are you usually into brats, then?"

"Not really, but I like *you* bratty." She leans down and nibbles my ear briefly. "I think it suits you. I hated seeing you be self-conscious when you didn't need to be. I know I'll enjoy seeing you acknowledge just how amazing you are."

My feet stop with my heart and turn to her. We are just at the front of the greenhouse. "Do you think I am amazing?"

Lenora chuckles, but her forehead is wrinkled. "You seem surprised."

"You just never told me that."

"I tell you every day at practice."

I try so hard not to roll my eyes. "Telling me I am doing amazing because I didn't drop the dagger is different than... *this*."

"Well, it is good that you are not dropping your daggers," she says. "But even if you did, I would still think you are amazing. When we were little, I always thought you were kind of annoying. I saw you as the girl who stole my brother." With the mention of Qyron, her eyes shine a little brighter, and her voice drops lower. "But we are not little anymore. I can really see you for what you are now."

My throat burns from everything, but I am not going to ruin this with questions or tears. I just reach to cup her cheek and smile. "I do too."

Lenora turns her head to kiss my palm and whispers onto my skin. "Let's go inside."

And only then I realize how much in the open we were. It is late at night, but the moon is bright, and the strawberry field does not have much of a cover. I realize how close she was to me for the whole walk and how she didn't care if we were accidentally seen.

My smile grows, and I step inside the greenhouse with her.

This has never been a place I visited too often, mostly because of its unavailability, but I cannot deny its beauty. It houses flowers from all around the world. I can only name a few of them, and most I have never seen anywhere but here. I know most of the flowers come from the Seelie Lands, but some of them don't grow on the Isle at all. I remember my father telling me some of the flowers are from the Mainlands or even from the Continent. I have no idea how they got them, but they are pretty.

I do my best to focus on their beauty, so I won't get distracted by Lenora. If she chose to come here, she is probably curious about the flowers. I don't want to ruin that for her.

When we stop in front of a little yellow flower Lenora gets a weird look on her face. I examine the small plant. It looks like a sunflower but is way too small. I don't get the significance.

"This is the latest addition as far as I know. It is called 'Morning Sun,'" says Lenora. "It came from the Sun Khanate."

Woe in Total Darkness

My brows furrow; I cannot imagine such a lively flower in that dry climate. "This grows in the Desert?"

Lenora shakes her head. "That is the weird part. It shouldn't have grown in a desert, but it did. A strong little flower despite all the hardship that has been thrown over her. It always fascinated me."

I look at the flower again, but this time differently. "Who wouldn't be fascinated with it?"

Lenora smiles like what I said is too funny. "It was my mother's gift to King Luran," she says before I can ask anything. Then she starts walking again, but my mind stays with the Morning Sun that bloomed even in the worst situation.

For a while, we stay silent. I don't want to disturb Lenora, but she looks thoughtful, and her focus is not entirely on the flowers. Still, I don't want to ruin her greenhouse visit. I only stop when she does. We are in front of a purple flower with big dotted leaves. I think it might have significance too, but Lenora doesn't even look at the flower. Her eyes are on me.

"You know," she mumbles. "We never did that thing you wanted to try."

All I could think are dirty thoughts. I actually try to remember which one of my fantasies I shared with Lenora. I am sure my face is beat red from imagining her in various positions. I decide to give up and just ask. "What thing?"

Lenora sees my expression and giggles a little. "I am talking about touching our powers. You weren't able to reach your power when we tried the first time. I know we have touched while glowing before, but we never did with all of our might. It may feel different."

It may. I am happy she remembered it. I know she was glowing a little against me when we kissed for the first time, and I remember it felt good. Still, I won't say no to trying again. It always felt so comforting when I did it with Qyron.

I hold my hands to her, my palms up. "Let's try," I smile.

Lenora starts glowing almost instantly, and I close my eyes so I can focus and catch up with her. I reach into the depths of my

Sem Thornwood

heart to get my Moonshine and direct it over my skin. Chill breaks out, and my hairs stand to attention.

I can feel Lenora's power against mine on my palm. It is warm and sweet. It is so familiar that my power wants to embrace it. Actually, it wants to more than embrace it. My pulse picks up because I can feel my power kissing hers and wanting to be together. I can feel the effects all over my body but mostly on my chest and between my legs. This has my nipples hard as nails.

I open my eyes and see Lenora breathless. She looks so pretty surrounded by the golden light, but more importantly, her pupils are huge, and she looks almost as aroused as I am. This power touching does more than I anticipated.

"Should it feel like that?" Lenora asks, and between all that arousal, I see some fear in her orange eyes. "You said you did it with Qyron a lot. Did it feel like this?"

"Absolutely no," I say, breathless. "It did feel like a sweet embrace, and there was some electric when we did it, the satisfying kind. Although it was never satisfying like this."

"That's a relief," she says under her breath. "So it feels the same to you?"

"It feels like I'll die if I don't kiss you."

Lenora breathes out and shakes her head. "Well, it doesn't feel the same then because to me it feels like I'll die if I don't fuck you."

Oh. Good thing I am already wet, then. I briefly look around. Everybody knows the greenhouse is closed, but they can visit the strawberry field anytime they want. We are inside, but the walls are all glass. If someone decides to have a late-night field trip and comes close to here, we are sure to be caught, especially with the way we are lighting up the place.

But I don't think I can actually wait until we get back to my room. So with hopeful eyes, I ask, "Here?"

Lenora's hands leave mine and come to my waist. She pulls me close to her and whispers onto my lips before kissing me, "Right here."

I wrap my arms around her neck and let her make me lose myself in the kiss. When her hands come to the backs of my thighs

Woe in Total Darkness

and lift me, I wrap my legs around her waist. She sits down on the floor with me on her lap.

She feels like shockwaves on my skin, and my blood boils with every touch of her tongue.

When Lenora's hands slide to my bottom and she squeezes, I cannot help but moan. We are doing this in a glass box. Nothing matters.

I feel like my mind is going blank. I cannot think of anything but Lenora. I just want to get close to her. I want to see her come. I want to know how she sounds when she is drowning in pleasure.

I *need* it.

Frantically Lenora reaches for my cloak first, and when that is out of the way, she presses a kiss to my shoulder and pulls down the straps of my dress. My hands are in her hair, keeping her face close to my skin, and she doesn't fight it at all. When my naked breasts come into view, she groans and licks the valley between them, making me whimper. "Are you healed, Raya?"

Even her voice fuels the electric dancing along my skin. I nod but then realize she is not looking at my face. "Yes," I answer, waiting for her warm, willing mouth.

She doesn't make me wait too long. Her lips close around my nipple, all the while, hands move between my naked back and my fabric-covered bottom. With her other hand, she is working my other nipple. The piercings are healed now, but they still make things more sensitive. I cannot help my moans and my grinding on her lap. I want to come so bad.

Lenora bites down my nipple hard, and I cry out with pain and pleasure both. She only chuckles to my skin and soothes the sting with her tongue before doing it again. I realize she might be obsessed with my breasts just like I am obsessed with her arms.

Her hand on my rear taunts me because of the barrier there. I also don't like that I have to try hard to find naked skin on her so I can touch it. I touch her neck, her head, and her arms, but I want more. This is not enough.

"Skin," I breathe. My sex is throbbing harder with want the longer she plays with me. "I need more skin."

"Oh, Goddess," she says under her breath and reaches under my dress. She lifts the fabric until it bunches on my waist, and suddenly I am almost naked in her lap. I am all hers. She keeps kissing and nibbling my breasts, but a hand sneaks between my legs from behind. She traces two fingers between my folds, and her moan vibrates against my skin. "You are all wet, Raya."

"I am," I confirm. "I need you." I look down at her, desperate. I cannot stand her teasing. I roll my hips on her fingers, but they are not pressing as hard as I want. In my mind, I always wanted Lenora to take the lead because I had no idea how to have sex with her. I was nervous.

Right now, I really don't care. I don't want to wait for her to tease me into oblivion. I want to take what I want instead. For the first time in my life I am so desperate to have sex.

So, I reach for her buttons, first taking off her tunic and laying all her naked perfectness out in the open. I push her shoulders, so she is on her back. Her wings sprawled on the floor, and her pale tattoo-covered skin is visible. She doesn't fight me at all, but her eyes have a daring look.

She makes my mouth water, and I lean over her for more kisses. Our breasts press together. I rub my chest over hers, making her go crazy as much as she made me. I love the sound of her whimpers. I love how perfect she feels against me.

I lick her soft neck as my hands roam all over her. Lenora throws her head back, giving me more access. She has so many freckles all down to her breasts, and almost every inch of her is covered in golden-colored tattoos. I would never think they work together, but at this moment, I want to kiss every freckle and trace every golden line with my tongue.

I suck on the side of her neck, just the tip of a ray of light coming from the sun on the front of her neck. I nibble the skin, not caring how it might look tomorrow. I just want to consume her.

My mind is not my mind anymore.

My body is not my body.

At this moment, I belong to her.

I move down with the help of her hand in my braids. I lick the valley between her breasts just like she did to me earlier. Then I

Woe in Total Darkness

take a nipple into my mouth, nibbling the way I know I like. I just hope I can make her feel as good as she makes me.

Lenora whimpers around my name when I suck on her swollen bud, and I get more courageous. I lick my way down. My hands roam over her hard stomach. She feels like she is built from stone, but despite it, her skin is always so soft. I lick the skin above the waistband of her tight pants. "I need this off," I say.

Lenora nods frantically. "Yes, yes, please." She reaches for her buttons and helps me take them off of her. Just a few seconds later, she is completely naked under me, and having her like this makes me feel powerful.

I look at the many tattoos on her legs that I never got to see. I can smell her arousal in the air. Her skin is covered with a light layer of sweat, but the moisture I am more interested in is between her legs.

I want to do many things for her. I want to give her pleasure, but my inexperience rises. I feel self-conscious all over again. I don't know what to do.

Then I look at Lenora's face and see her eyes are half-lidded. She looks happy to be here with me. She looks like she is glad it is me who is doing this to her. I also can tell she knows how I feel because she reaches for my face the next moment. "Kiss me," she whispers. "All will be well when we kiss."

I do as she says because she is right. Everything becomes better when we kiss. I can forget about all my worries when her lips are against mine.

I kiss her hard and tangle our legs. I cannot stop myself. "I just want you too much," I say between breathless kisses.

Lenora squeezes my bottom, helping my movements, and only then do I realize I am grinding on her thigh. "You already have me, Raya," she says and kisses me again. I can feel her moan against my mouth as much as I am.

The more I roll my hips, the more pleasure builds inside of me. I have never climaxed during sex. I thought I would be worried because of it but my mind is empty. I just want to reach my high with her.

When I move faster against her thighs, Lenora moans even louder, her legs twitching between mine. I look down and see that my leg is also pressing against her sex, and every time she moves me by my hips, she rubs me against her.

The realization makes everything even better. I don't know if we should really do it like this, but I cannot stop. I am throbbing for release. I keep kissing and touching Lenora everywhere.

"Harder," she moans desperately, and her fingers on my backside flex. "Fuck me harder, Raya."

Oh, Tisasa, help me.

I move faster, building pleasure for both of us. I can feel her wetness against my thigh, and I never want to wash it again. I want her scent over me forever. I shine more with pleasure, and Lenora does the same. Electric dances over every part of my skin where she is touching me. The sensitive nub between my legs is begging for release.

I know I am close, but I don't want to have this alone. I want to see her.

I nibble her ear. "Come with me, Len." I let her push me down as hard as she wants. I let her decide on the pace. "Please."

"Fuck," Len curses, throwing her head back. Her hips roll up, rubbing harder, and I feel her body tense under me. I immediately know I cannot hold any longer as well.

Our moans fill the glass greenhouse. I don't know which is my voice and which is hers as we reach our peak together. We come all over each other, and I fill with so many primal thoughts. I have never felt like this. I have never felt satisfied because I marked someone.

My hips move as we both come down from it, and then my body collapses. We are both breathless. I lay on top of Lenora for a while, trying to find my strength again. Her chest moves fast under my ear, and she is rubbing my back with one hand. Even exhausted, she manages to make me feel special.

I love that.

When I somewhat gather my breath, I look up at her face. Lenora gives me a drunken smile, and I smile too. I press a soft kiss onto her lips, but some of my anxiety comes back despite her happy expression. "I didn't do it wrong, right?" I ask. Her eyebrows come together, so I keep rambling, "I have only ever been with one person before, and he was a... well he. I didn't know how to go about this. I just did what felt good. Was it okay?"

Lenora shakes her head with a smile like I am being silly and kisses me. "Raya, if it feels good for both of us, it cannot be wrong."

I swallow. "So, it was good for you too?"

"Absolutely. I came really hard."

I look away, blushing. "Yeah, I kind of felt that." When I look back at her, she has a smug smile on her face. "I was just a little nervous. I never came during sex before."

"Really?" she ask surprised and a satisfied grin captures her face. "Now I have to make up for every shitty sex you had."

I giggle. I know she can do it.

Then seriousness touches her fatures and she cups my cheek. " But about the other part, do I make you nervous?"

I laugh. It is cute that she is concerned. "Ah, Tisasa, no. Actually, you make me the opposite of nervous. Every time I worried over anything, I just reminded myself it was you who were with me."

She smiles so beautifully. "Good," she touches her nose to mine. "I always want you to feel comfortable with me. You have nothing to worry about anyway."

"I don't?" This time I am the one that is smug. I have always liked compliments, but I like them even more, when they are from Lenora.

"Of course, you don't. You were perfect. I mean, I had my fair share of lovers, but..." she pulls back, and her eyes roam all over my body appreciatively. "You are just something else, Raya."

I shrug. "I didn't have my fair share, but I don't think I could get one better than you." I don't think anyone can have this much of an effect on me.

Lenora buries her face into the crook of my neck. "Such flattery."

I bite down my bottom lip to keep a moan in as Lenora sucks on my neck. "I actually cannot wait until we do it again."

This time she actually throws her head back and laughs out loud. When she looks back at my confused face, her eyes turn heated. "Oh, Raya," she says with a husky voice and pushes my braids out of my face, pulling them in the process. The slight pain in my scalp actually feels good. "You think I am done with you?"

That makes me a little confused. "We both came," I say. I mean, I am not very tired, but I guess this is just learned behavior. After both parties find the release, you can just go to sleep.

Lenora shakes her head and gives me a look that causes a fresh wave of wetness between my thighs. "There is no way we are leaving before I find out how sweet your cunt is." Then she taps my bottom with her free hand. "Come on, sit on my face."

My eyes widen. "What?"

"I want to lick you. I mean, of course, if you want that too."

My skin glows a little lighter with arousal. "Oh, I want that. I definitely want that."

"What is the problem then?" she asks, all confused. "Have you never done it? I can be gentle, don't worry."

That is not the problem at all. On the contrary, I don't want her to be gentle. "I did it before, many times." Rionn went down on me a lot even though I had to fake my recations. "I just never done it like you suggest."

She looks at me with empty eyes for a second, but then realization fills her firey irises. "Oh, the sitting on my face part." Her face wrinkles. "You really never done that? I mean, he never..." She looks away, annoyed. "Fool."

I can't help but giggle. I rub my chest against hers, dragging my piercings. "So you really want me to?"

"Definitely," she answers quickly. Her hand comes between my legs, and she cups my sex. "Now, please put this on my face, or I will go crazy."

I straighten so I can move up her body. I am very nervous, but I try hard to stop my legs from shaking. I am excited about her mouth, but the position feels too intense. I feel like I would prefer to be in her position, actually. Earlier I was so drunk that I took charge without even thinking but now that I can actually think a little more clearly, I don't like that. I want her to have control.

Woe in Total Darkness

Lenora grabs me by my thighs and pulls me over her face. I look down, and her hungry eyes make my body tremble. I sre as wont need to fake anything this time. I try to find the best height to stay on. I don't want her to hurt her neck trying to reach up, but I also don't want to crush her. Floating so close to the floor kind of hurts.

"Raya," she says with a warning tone. "You are hovering."

"Yes?" I don't understand the problem. My cheeks heat with embarrassment. "Am I doing it wrong? Staying very low hurts my thighs."

Her eyes soften a bit, and she kisses the inside of my thigh. "That is not it. I told you to sit on my face. You are not sitting."

"I'll crush you!" I say nervously.

Lenora doesn't answer me but instead wraps her arms around my thighs and pulls me down. I let out a little scream. My hand goes to Lenora's head for balance, and I hear her moan against me.

Oh, I can feel the vibration all the way inside me.

Pull connected her mouth with my center, and her tongue works me slowly. I look down again, seeing her licking me. I can feel her tongue lapping around my most sensitive spot. Her orange eyes are on me, and it feels way too intense. I cannot even form a thought looking down at her. She licks and sucks, almost playing with me as I whimper above her.

Lenora reaches my hand and places it on her jaw. I close my eyes and moan ever louder. I can feel how her mouth works with my fingers now. I can feel everything.

Her other hand goes to my bottom, and she sneaks a finger between my cheeks. The next moment I feel her at my entrance. She sucks on my nub and slowly circles my hole. When I am almost dying from her teasing, she pushes two fingers inside, and I fit tightly around them.

Lenora starts fucking me with her fingers, and when she touches my sensitive spots both outside and inside, I know I am a goner. I look at her beautiful face. I feel so special because this amazing creature is working all for my pleasure.

She doesn't even let me move my hips the way I want. Her fingers move inside, setting the pace. She has me whimpering and begging for release on top of her. Every time I say, "Please," she gets more intense.

I might be on top, but she is holding all the power. I am just hers to use as she sees fit, and I have no complaints at all.

Her pace quickens, and soon enough, I tighten around her fingers, coming onto her mouth. I look at her as soon as I can actually open my eyes and give her a tired smile. My body is completely useless, and before I really crush her, I let myself collapse next to her on the floor.

I watch Lenora as she licks the fingers that were inside me and rubs her mouth with the back of her hand. She turns to me with a smile, and I know she has ruined me for all else.

No one will ever be able to make me feel like Lenora just did.

34

Lenora

Haliyes Princess made a lot of reforms after she took over the throne. Her alliance with the Mitharaus family actually managed to handle the cruelty of their fathers. They decided to be more respectful towards the power that was stolen from Tisasa. Feyada history changed alongside their ruling. They wanted to bury some events, but most importantly, they wanted to bury some dangers.

It is interesting that the princess wanted to destroy evidence about abilities concerning their powers right after she conquered the Shifter Territory and stole the Lunar Stone. She declared herself the Ruler of Northern Feyadas and all Shifters. Yet she didn't want the next of her kin to know how she did it.

As far as known history goes, the Princess learned this strange method when visiting the Sun Khanate in her youth. Khan Vaughn wanted to see how good she was at using her powers since her father put so much effort into her training. After a little sparring session, the Khan was very impressed with the Princess that he wanted to share some of his knowledge with her. King Carin never accepted Vaughn's advice on their stolen powers, but the Princess was different. She wanted to know what kind of information Vaughn was holding.

Vaughn took the princess into the dungeons to show her how his power actually worked. First, he brought some of his soldiers, and in a few seconds, he managed to make all of them scream like they were dying. There was not even a mark on their skin, but their reaction seemed like they were being torn to shreds. It was Vaughn's mind manipulation. He could make them think they were in pain so well that they felt it all over their bodies.

Next, Vaughn called for a small feast into the dungeon, and they ate. He then told her he wanted to show her something more memorable. He read a lot about the Goddess and, more importantly, let his mind run free. He wanted to push his limits and see how much he could do with this power.

When the Princess said she wanted to see it, Vaughn pulled back the power he was using on her. The Princess found herself and Vaughn back at the training grounds they were in earlier that day. Vaughn told her everything they had done for the last few hours was just an illusion inside her head. He managed to make her see whatever he wanted while she couldn't even realize it.

Vaughn called this mind capturing and thought if he could work long enough with the Princess, she could manage to conquer body capturing. Princess was so mesmerized by the power and finally accepted.

At the end of their training, she held power too strong for any mortal to have. It was more brutal than mind-capturing because Vaughn's victims never knew what happened to them if Vaughn didn't feel like explaining. He was able to shape their minds in a way that could protect them from harm. Unfortunately, that was not the case for the Princess.

The Princess could capture the body of someone and make them dance to the tune she wanted. She could move the bodies like they were puppets. And while she did that, the minds of those people would be completely untouched. They would be conscious to know someone was controlling their body, and there was nothing they could do to stop it.

That was a brutal power and eventually led to her using it in the war and winning against the Shifters. The war gave her a lot of trauma, and she decided to not follow her father's legacy and make a better one. She agreed with the Khan of that time to keep these extreme powers under wraps so the ones after them could never know about them. They managed to create many new ancient rules in the hopes of keeping peace on Ae, but there were still things that weren't reversible.

I watch Raya finish up her training with Hashim. When she got good at things I could teach her, I decided to let her spar with him. At first, she was a little nervous about training with someone else but quickly got over it. Thankfully the person who is good at daggers is also happens to be my friendliest soldier. Everybody loves the big softy Hashim.

"You did great today, Princess," he tells her with a smile. At first, he called her "Your Highness," and Raya almost puked. She wanted to be more casual with him, but Hashim insisted on at least calling her Princess.

Raya beams up at him and then at me. "Hear that? I was great."

I stand up from where I was sitting and walk towards her. "Well, he is right." I look at Hashim and give him a nod. "Thank you, Hashim. You can continue with your own training."

He gives me a big smile. "No problem, General. I enjoy training with the Princess."

When they share a smile, something ugly blooms in my chest, but I quickly push it down. I remind myself Hashim is no more than a friend to Raya. I also remind myself it was my name she was screaming with pleasure just the other night. That gives me a strange sense of pride.

I knew having sex in the greenhouse was risky. It was not my plan, but when we touched our light, I just couldn't stop myself. I don't remember a time I was this desperate to have someone. Zuraya felt too good to resist.

Honestly, I couldn't even tell she was nervous until she told me. She just looked too consumed by her lust. I liked how she got on top of me and got what she wanted. I liked that she was not shy at all. But I also liked controlling her when her cunt was in my mouth. I especially liked being the first person to bring her release. When she confessed her worries, I just needed to give her something safe. I wanted to show her that even if she is on top, I can take the reins. I can dominate to make her feel more comfortable. She doesn't need to worry when she is with me.

After tasting her on my tongue, we were both a little tired. I would have fucked her until the sun came up, but it was not the best idea. I didn't want to overwhelm her, and our location was not very suitable.

Instead of continuing, I took her back to her room. She got into bed, looking all kinds of disappointed because I was leaving. It was sweet, actually. She really thought I was going to leave her after sex.

Obviously, it was risky for me to stay in her room. The maids were on my payroll, but if they could be bought by me, they could be bought by someone else as well. I didn't want to give them something to talk about. I got in bed with Zuraya, and after we kissed a bit more, I let her fall asleep in my arms. I told her I had to leave before morning, but there was no way I was letting her sleep alone. She seemed satisfied with my plan.

I had to leave her at the end, and it was too fucking hard. I promised myself that I was going to create a night where neither of us had to leave. That was my only consolation.

Despite leaving, I know it was a good night for both of us. I know I don't have anything to worry about regarding Hashim or any others.

She is all mine.

At least until I leave.

I watch Zuraya as Hashim gets away. Her skin has a dim layer of light around it, just like every time she trains. I get a devilish smile and touch her arm with a glowing hand of my own. "You fight well when you are in a good mood. Did something happen to make you happy?"

Raya looks at me with fire in her blue eyes, and the part of her arm where I am touching glows a little more. Now I can feel electrics all over my skin, and it makes me even more aware of my lust for her. I know she can feel it too.

Woe in Total Darkness

I exhale with pain. "If you do this, we won't be able to finish today's training."

Raya chuckles. "You know you think those words are gonna stop me, but they do the exact opposite."

"I'll have to be the responsible one then." I pull back my hand and can even feel my blood-flow slowing. It is insane how much her touch affects me.

She mock groans. "I hate when you are responsible."

We smile at each other, and I feel better than I have for most of my life. At this moment, all the shit I have to deal with doesn't matter. Only Raya does, and I am going to put all my effort into her. I much prefer to put in those efforts when we are both naked, but I don't have too much time left here, and I want to make sure she gets the best training until I leave. I want to fulfill my part, not because of moon spheres but for Zuraya.

"You know you always glow a little when you are fighting."

"Is it bad?"

I shake my head quickly. "Not at all." It just gave me an idea. "Why do you do it?"

Raya shrugs. "No reason, actually. I guess it is like an instinct. Maybe I feel like it can protect me like a defense shield even though I know it isn't."

"It is not a defense shield," I explain, even though she already knows. "But it can enhance your attack. I use it when I fight with my sword. Combining your moon power with your physical strength is a great move."

"How am I supposed to do that?"

I look down for a second considering what I am about to do. "There are different ways as far as I know, but I use my Sunshine with a glass sword."

Zuraya looks at me expectedly. "I don't have a glass dagger or anything. How I should do it?"

Maybe the great sex really got into my head, but I don't stop. I reach into my belt and take out the glass dagger I have there. I don't use it a lot anyway. Or maybe that is just how I fool myself.

Whatever it is, the next moment, I hold out the priceless ancient weapon towards her. "You can take this one."

She looks down at the dagger, and I actually hope she doesn't know the significance of it. "It is yours," Zuraya says.

Well, there are more critical things about it than being mine, but anyway. This just confirms she has no idea what this dagger is. I guess I can thank her lack of education for the first time.

I nudge the dagger toward her. "I have many others back home," I lie.

She still looks skeptical. "You sure?"

This time I go as far as putting the dagger into her hand and closing her fingers around it. "I am sure. I only use my sword anyway." That is also not true. I mainly use my sword, but the dagger comes in handy sometimes.

Maybe I should feel bad about lying to her again, but this is not like the other times. Also, it is not exactly a lie but more of a wordplay. I just know she won't accept the gift if she knows exactly what it is.

I want her to have it more than I want to keep it.

"Okay," she smiles down at her new weapon. "I use double daggers, but I suppose I can use this with my regular one. Maybe you can send me a matching one when you are back at home."

Well, good luck to me finding that. Although her smile is so beautiful that I think maybe I can recreate this ancient weapon just so I can make her smile like this again. "Maybe."

"So, should we start?"

I shake my head. I don't like to change my schedule. "You can train with it yourself to get used to the feeling and the weight after we have your body manipulation training." I feel a little uneasy saying the next part, "But I have something I need to talk to you about first."

"Of course. What is it?" Zuraya says, but her eyes are still mostly on the dagger. I would keep smiling like a fool for giving her such a nice gift if my mind was not full of things I wanted to share with her.

Woe in Total Darkness

Unfortunately, I have to. I read that little part of the book just last night, and I cannot stop thinking about it since. I know it can be very well connected to Zuraya, and she has a right to know. I don't want to keep it from her. "Do you know anything about body capturing?" That is the best start I can use.

Zuraya thinks for a moment, like she is searching for an answer. "I don't think so. What is it?"

"It is about your power."

She smiles, but it is not a joyful one. "I figured as much. It is about my body manipulation, right?"

"Yes," I nod. "You know how you manipulate my body to hurt when we train or when you manipulate it to heal?"

"Yeah."

My voice lowers instinctively. There is a reason this shit has been under wraps for years, and I should know why. "What if you were able to do more?"

Her body goes rigid. "I don't like what I think you are saying."

"You shouldn't," I say, not knowing if it is a threat or a reassurance to her. "I am saying that what if you were so good at using your power that you were able to have full control over someone's body. What if you were so good that they have nothing they could do to stop it?"

"It would be horrible," she says without a pause. I can both see and feel her unease, but I need her to understand. "Why are you telling me this?"

She looks scared like she is expecting me to ask her to train in this forbidden skill. "Training together, we have seen any power you have has an equivalent in me. What would be the equivalent of this?"

She looks away nervously and swallows. I can actually see the exact moment she finds the answer. There is no victory in her eyes at all. She doesn't shine with the happiness of getting the right answer. She looks absolutely terrified. "Total control over someone's mind."

"Mind capturing," I say with a whisper and see her shiver visibly. I want to hug her close to my chest. I know that she knows what it means. I don't want to hurt her with this, but I need her help. I don't want to hide things from her.

At least I don't want to hide *this* from her.

Raya looks at me with sad eyes. "Do you think this is what happened to me?"

"It makes more sense than anything else."

This time she looks a little scared. "But this is a sun power, isn't it? Only a Mitharaus can do it."

That is the part that makes me nervous. This is my power. I want her to have answers about what they did to her, but I also don't want her to fear me. I don't want her to doubt me. This is the reason I actually wanted to tell her more than anything. "It is. That is the weird part."

"Who could it be?" she mumbles more to herself.

I wish I had answers for her. "I don't know." I reach for her hand, and she looks up at me. I expect to see fear or distrust in her, but all I can see is hope. Those eyes put more burden on my back than a thousand moon spheres ever can. "I promise I will find who that is, Raya. I am working on it."

"How can the Curser have sun powers, Lenora?"

"I don't know," I say truthfully. "It might be an ancestory thing or something else, but whatever this is, it will be helpful in my investigation. I promise I will find whoever did this to you."

This time Raya nods and looks around before pressing a kiss to my knuckles. "I trust you."

My heart burns, and I vow to myself that I will not betray that trust. I truly hope I am telling the truth.

"Do you want to stop our training for today? We can go to the beach."

She looks intrigued, and I think she is going to say yes, but then she shakes her head. "No, I need to train. I cannot let them get to me again."

"I won't let them ever get to you again," I say, but we both know I will not be here forever. At one point in time, I will leave Zuraya all alone.

Woe in Total Darkness

Sadness lingers in the air between us. "If it is okay, I want to train on my own now."

"It is okay," I only say. The more I am close to her, the sadder she is going to get. We just need to clear our heads up.

Then I leave her to train. She keeps working on her glow and her daggers.

I leave the grounds, and she is still there training.

When I come to see her before dinner, she is still sparring, and when the moon gets high in the sky, she is still training.

Zuraya Haliyes never wants to be dependent on anyone else, and I don't know if I should be sad or proud.

35

Lenora

"I still think this is sheer torture," I say, watching Zuraya dip her toes into the horrible ocean water. This time I just remain on the beach, sitting on my nice blanket. No muddy sand on my clothes, please.

Raya throws her head back and laughs. Her hair is in a blue turban, and she is wearing matching robes. The fabric is flowing around her ankles and flying all around her because of the wind. This place might not be my favorite, but I like watching her like this. She looks so beautiful when her smile is so big, and I can count every perfect white tooth.

She shrugs, looking towards the depths of the ocean. "I really don't understand how this can bother you. I mean, you have Sunshine. You can warm yourself up."

"It is not about the cold. It is the waves and the muddy sand and the seaweed." I groan. "Oh, Tisasa, it is mostly the seaweed." I visibly shiver, thinking about how it felt wrapped around my ankle the last time.

"Oh, my poor baby," Raya says mockingly. "And I forced you into this seaweed-filled water. So you say the last time we were in it together was awful?"

Woe in Total Darkness

I look at her expression. She has one eyebrow up, and her lips are itching for a smile. We both know it was further from awful. "Is that why you agreed to take a break from your training?" I make my voice drop an octave because I know it makes her flustered. "You hoping for a repeat performance, Raya?"

"You know that is the only thing that can make me stop training."

I smile, but it makes me a little uneasy that she is right. It has been three days since I told her about mind capturing, and Raya hasn't stopped training. It is almost like she is preparing to kill the Curser herself. She wants to get her revenge. I am a little concerned about how much she pushes herself, but I cannot tell her to stop. I understand why she does this.

I would have done the same.

So instead of making her stop, I use other tactics. I have come to realize the idea of some alone time with me intrigues her more than training. It flatters me, especially because I like spending time with her more than training too. And there aren't many things I enjoy more than training.

"It seems like the sloshy ocean water is more intriguing than I am, though."

Zuraya shakes her head with a smile and walks towards me, bare feet. "That is not true at all." She comes close, almost ready to jump on me.

"Raya," I whisper with a warning tone, even if it hurts to stop her.

Her smile doesn't disappear, but she looks a little confused. "Len."

"Don't kiss me."

Now she looks hurt. She stops just above me. "Why?"

I know she would be over me right now if I hadn't said anything, but we cannot have that right now. I hate that we cannot touch anytime we want, but we both knew what we were getting into. "We have prying eyes."

Her shoulders tense, and she looks around without moving her head. "Where?"

"Above," I say. I spotted that person while I was lying down on my blanket, and I know they have not moved since then. They might be a good spy, but I am better. I have trained my mind manipulation power to recognize when there is a mind in reach. I cannot exactly read anyone's thoughts, but I can understand the main thing on their head at the moment, and they are sure as hell spying.

"Shifter," I explain. "I mean, probably Shifter since you have no Earthlings here." I would have recognized wings or green skin.

"Should we leave?" Raya asks. She lost all the brightness from seconds ago, and I want to strangle our spy just for that.

I shake my head and shift a little on my blanket. "Come sit next to me. We are allowed to spend time together. We just shouldn't kiss. The sex part of our relationship is out for today."

I expect her to look a little disappointed, but her anxiety covers it all up. She sits next to me, and I can hear her breathing. She is trying to calm herself. It is admirable she is now able to do that by herself. She has come a long way, and despite all my current irritation, I feel pleased.

Still, I ask, "Are you okay?"

"Why are they spying on us? Did we do something suspicious, or are they just want to see the freak princess?"

"Don't call yourself that," I said, gritting my teeth. I hate when she insults herself like this. I want bratty Raya. "They are not here because they are so curious about how you look. There are easier ways to learn that." We both know she has been seen by some people at this point. She always keeps a distance and does not interact, but they do see her. And those people gossip.

Almost everyone knows she doesn't have wings now.

This Shifter is not curious and definitely not here to mock Zuraya.

They are here to spy on her. I fill with so much anger because I know Rionn sent them. I know he is still not stepping away. He has no other reason to be still here other than Zuraya.

I know I have no right to push him away. He has more chances with her than me. He can actually be with her if they both want, but I cannot let him get close to her. I cannot help my jealousy. This thing between us might be doomed from the start, but until I leave, she is mine, and I won't let anyone take her away from me.

Woe in Total Darkness

It is me that she looks up with trust.

It is me that she reaches for comfort.

And it is me that is in her mind when she gets wet between her thighs.

Rionn Ay Ujk is not getting my girl. Not while I am here to keep her. He can send as many spies as he wants. Zuraya wants me and not him.

I actually want to kiss her. I want to fuck her right here on this beach. Make her scream so loud that the spy can hear every bit of begging she gives me. I want them to tell it all to Rionn. I want to show him my claim. But my logical side knows that is a terrible idea. I cannot give him such important information. What we are doing is wrong, and I cannot risk him using it against Raya or against me.

"Then why are they here, Len?" Zuraya asks again. She looks shaken.

"Hey," I say, turning my body towards her. "Don't think about them. This is our time. Just focus on me. Tell me something."

"Like what?"

I think for a second, looking around. "Like what you used to enjoy doing, so the next time I want to take you somewhere, this hellhole won't be my only option." I actually want to know more about her despite knowing it might be dangerous for my heart.

This makes Raya smile. "Well, now I also like the greenhouse."

I look down at her body, remembering our time there. "I cannot kiss you. Please don't make this harder on me."

She laughs. "Okay, okay, let me think. My life was actually not very fun. I cannot think of a lot of things."

"For some reason, I don't believe that."

"Okay, it was not boring," she giggles like she has got caught. "But it was not because of what I have been doing. Honestly, training is much more exciting than everything I used to do there. What made things fun was the company." Her eyes drop with sadness. "Mostly Qyron."

I don't want her to get sad. I refuse to talk about my brother in a woeful manner. I know he would never want that. He always

291

brought joy around him, and I don't want his death to change that. "Tell me," I say. "How was he like?"

She looks down. "You know what he was like."

"Only up until the attack. You got to have him after that too."

A single tear rolls down her cheek, and my heart breaks into a million pieces. She reaches out and holds my hand. "It was all a lie."

I look down at our clasped hands. Zuraya Haliyes is so fucking strong, but still, when she needs it, I want to be her rock. I loathe the idea of her reaching to anyone like she reached for me.

Though she gets my silence wrong. "Sorry," she mumbles and pulls away her hand. She tries to quickly brush away her tears. "Crying about things that never even happened while holding hands was not part of our 'just sex' agreement."

It is almost like she stabbed me right in the chest with a dagger. "Zuraya, our decision didn't mean we cannot be friends." I hold her hand again. Calling it "just sex" never meant I didn't care about her. I just wanted us to be realistic, but maybe I got it wrong. "Are you not happy with the boundaries we decided on?"

Raya looks up at me with glossy eyes. So many emotions pass her face. She looks like she cannot decide what to say or cannot dare what she really wants to say. Her delicate throat moves with a nervous swallow. I hold my breath waiting for her answer. I don't even know what answer I am hoping for. But at the end, she says, "No. This is the best for both of us."

I nod, trying to get rid of the unnecessary disappointment in my gut. "Good," I murmur. "I want us to be in the same chapter."

"We are," she says almost too fast. Again she brushes away her tears and gives me a smile. "So you really want to listen? Even though none of it was real."

"I always want to listen," I assure her. "Just because it happened in your head doesn't mean it was not real. It was real to you, and that's all I care about."

"I cannot tell you about real Qyron, though."

Woe in Total Darkness

I know that, but whatever version she had must be better than not having him at all. "Did he feel real? Did he change after the attack, or was he like the same person?"

She gets teary again. "He felt too real."

"Then tell me. Let me feel like he was really there too."

Raya looks at me again and smiles for real this time. Her eyes go down at our intertwined fingers like she is a little shy. "We spent almost every day together. He always managed to make every day enjoyable. He would always gossip about the court and make me laugh. And he was always too dramatic."

I laugh. "Yeah, that sounds like my brother."

She joins my laughter. "He was also always by my side. When I was sad, he would bring me a roasted pinebird for us to devour. It was our favorite meal. When I had nightmares, he would come and hold me. He couldn't hold me for the whole night though he was a terrible sleeper. We would wake up like we came from war." She gets a longing look. "He just always knew how to make me feel good."

I wish I could be as good at that as Qyron was, even though what I want from her is very different than Qyron. Or at least, I think. "Were you always just friends?" When she gives me a weird look, I get defensive. "I am just curious."

Zuraya looks at me like I am silly, and I actually like that look more than I should. "It was always platonic between Qyron and me. We kissed once just to test it but you know there was nothing. We were strictly friends." She gives me a small smile. "You are the only Mitharaus I have been interested in seeing naked."

I sigh with relief mockingly. "Thank Goddess, we can pass the question about my mom then."

Zuraya punches my arm, and we both laugh. "I think if he was here and knew what was happening between us, he would approve of it. And that would be a first."

I think about it for a moment. If Qyron was here, everything would be so different. I think about how he would react to me sleeping with his best friend. I know it can be hard, and what we are doing is not something to approve of, but I know Qyron would. He never cared much for the rules, and he loved both of us. He would be happy.

But then something else hits me. *Why would it be a first?*

I spin so fast that my neck hurts. "He didn't approve of Rionn?"

"No," she snorts with a shake of her head. "They hated each other."

Good job, brother. I am strangely too happy that Zuraya's best friend would approve of me but not Rionn. It doesn't mean anything, but sometimes I just let myself feel silly. I do it mainly around Zuraya. She makes me want to let go.

"I never understood back then," she says with a lower voice. "I thought he must accept Rionn since I was happy with him. He was always there for me when I was planning the wedding. He made me feel better when I felt overwhelmed and helped me with things, but he always made it apparent he was not fond of Rionn. I didn't understand then, but I do now. I know he is not fitting for me."

I try not to get too happy about her words. "Why do you think that??"

She looks puzzled now, like she doesn't really understand as well. I don't like seeing her like this. "I am not sure yet," she says. "Maybe it is just a feeling."

"It is okay to rely on your feelings."

"Oh, you say that?" she asks, amused. "I always thought you must be a facts kind of person. Rules must be defining your life."

"Some things are worth breaking the rules for."

I can see her blush even though she tries to hide it by looking away. "Now you are just trying to make me embarrassed."

"I need to fill up my quota before I leave."

"What do you mean?"

Fuck I forgot to tell her. "I am leaving tomorrow morning."

Her hand leaves mine, and she looks ready to cry. "Back to the Sun Khanate? You are telling me now?"

"No, no," I try to assure her. "I am sorry I worded it wrong. I am leaving for a day, maybe two. I got some intel today. They caught a Seelie at the border that can be connected to the Curser. I need to go check it out. I was going to ask you if you would be okay

Woe in Total Darkness

training by yourself and Hashim until I am back. If you want to take a break, that is okay too."

"Len," she growls. "Do you want to give me a heart attack?"

"I am sorry. I just didn't realize you could have taken it the wrong way. I mean, I would never leave for good like that. I won't surprise you. I will be here until your name-day ends. I just need to take a look at this."

"Okay," she murmurs more to herself. I can see how nervous I made her, and I feel horrible. "It is good that you are making progress. I'll be okay for a day or two. Just please don't do this again."

I cup her cheek despite knowing the Shifter is still watching us. Right now, making Zuraya feel better is more important. "I'll never do such a thing to you, Raya. I'll never leave like this."

Her bottom lip trembles. "Sometimes I wish you never have to leave at all."

"Sometimes I wish that too."

36

Zuraya

"Princess, you have a visitor."

I lift my head from the book I was not reading and look at my maid. I am actually trying to heal the little cuts I make on my hand. The book is only there to fool my maids because I know they'll inform Len about almost everything. I know she would not approve of my way of practicing, but she left this morning, so I am free to be naughty for a bit.

The reason my eyebrows come together is also the fact that Lenora is away. It is nighttime, but I don't think she returned before it was even a day. I also know Maha is too big and tired to leave her room at the moment. There is no way for me to have a visitor.

I ask, "Who is it?"

"Alpha Rionn Ay Ujk."

My heart drops even though I knew it could not be Len. I was still hoping a little. Also, I am a little surprised that Rionn is here. We haven't seen each other much lately. I don't know what to think about his arrival, and I don't know how to feel about him, but there is no way I am sending him away. That would be rude. "Let him in."

Woe in Total Darkness

My maid gives a curt and then leaves. I quickly heal the wound in my hand and lick away the drop of blood that is left behind. In the next moment, the tall form of Rionn fills up my room. His clothing is far from Shifter and more fitting for the Moon Palace. He also has a warm, charming smile on his face. That smile does nothing for me.

Rionn is still a very attractive guy, but he doesn't affect me anymore. I am not even sure if having Lenora in my life is the only reason. I am not even sure if he ever really did.

"Hello, Rionn. I was not expecting you."

"Maybe I wanted to surprise you," he says playfully. "I haven't been able to see you recently. You are busy."

I am not sure if you can call it that. Other than my mornings and nights, I am mostly in my room or with Maha, but since I am worried about being seen, there is not much time for Rionn to actually come and see me. I have not been very available for him.

And honestly, it didn't bother me much.

I still say, "I am sorry. I started training so I could reach my power."

"I heard," he says, and I don't even know where he heard. "Are you going to train tonight?"

The look on his face says he already knows I won't. I only train in the mornings now. "No," I shake my head. "I am free."

"Then maybe you will honor me with a walk. I positioned my soldiers specifically around the gardens so you won't be seen."

"Of course," I smile and let Rionn take my hand, but it feels off. Even the way he is being thoughtful rubs me the wrong way. Lenora does keep people away from me, too, because I am not comfortable, but she never goes beyond her way to make her soldiers stand guard. Sometimes a few wandering eyes catch me from far away, and it actually helps me. I get the strength to make myself seen since they will gossip to the whole court anyway.

Lenora gets me better than Rionn, but I cannot blame him for it. He is just trying to do his best. He is good. He has always been good. He just doesn't make me feel like Lenora does.

Maybe my Rionn and this Rionn are different. Although the only difference I can find is my reactions to him. I try my best not to feel guilty about it. I did nothing wrong after all.

"I am glad you accepted my invitation," Rionn says as we walk down the isolated hallways of the palace. "After our time in your bedroom, we have not seen much of each other. I was worried I did something you didn't want."

Instantly the guilt I try to ignore fills me. I almost forgot all about that. I can't help but cringe when I look at him. "It was not like that at all. I am sorry for making you feel that way. It was my fault."

Rionn shows me his easy-going smile. He is so good at acting like he doesn't care about anything but the Rionn I knew could lose his temper so easily despite it. "There was no fault, Zuraya. It was just a little punch to my pride."

His words don't match his expression. Still, I cannot blame him. I was the one who let him taste me and then completely ignored him afterward. I didn't plan on it. I thought it would help me, but all I could think about was Lenora's face.

But my attraction to her doesn't make what I did right.

"I am truly sorry, Rionn," I apologize again even though I can tell he is not very fond of that. "I shouldn't have used you like that. I was just not sure how to heal. I didn't know how to cope." *It was a mistake.*

He looks away and shrugs. "I wouldn't mind being used by you, Princess."

This is going to somewhere I am not happy with. His flirting makes me feel uncomfortable, and just like when he was between my thighs, I cannot think about anything but Lenora. I don't want her to feel betrayed. We only agreed on not sleeping with others but even accepting Rionn's offer to walk feels like cheating now.

"I would mind," I say, a little harsher than necessary. I just want him to understand, so I don't keep feeling so guilty. Although I soften my tone when Rionn flinches. "I am a lot better now, Rionn, and I am more aware of myself. I just don't want to give you hope."

He is silent for a second. "So, back to friends?"

Woe in Total Darkness

"I would like that." He is someone I would like to keep in my life, but the thought of being romantic with anyone but Lenora sickens me, which is concerning because I shouldn't be romantic with Lenora either.

Too many worries for one day.

When we reach outdoors, Rionn smiles at me, but it is not completely real. "Where do you want to go? Maybe the beach? I heard you like it there."

I lift an eyebrow judgingly. I know how he knows that. I am not stupid. I know the Shifter watching us from above yesterday was his spy. I try not to get mad at him after breaking his heart, but I am not taking him to a place I took Lenora to.

"We can just stroll around the gardens. I am not in the mood for the beach."

"Very well," he says, and I can see understanding in his eyes like he is putting the pieces of a puzzle together. I am not sure if it is worse to make him think I like him or let him understand something is going on between Lenora and me.

Rionn doesn't look at me as we walk in the gardens. I can sometimes see the silhouette of his soldiers around us, but I try not to mind. I came to adapt to the Sun Soldiers being around. I can do it for others too.

"You know I realized something the other day," Rionn says, still not looking at me. He seems a little tense.

I act like I don't realize his rigidness, like everything is normal with our walk. "What is it?"

"You told me we were together in your... dream."

That is not my favorite way to describe the last seven years of my life anymore, but I don't correct him. If I try to correct everyone about this, it will be a long miserable life for me. "I did."

This time he actually looks at me. "But I never asked if we were fated mates."

Oh, maybe this will be the thing that'll stop him from chasing me. "We were not," I say truthfully. "You haven't found your mate where I used to be. You had to settle."

He chuckles. "You say it like it is a bad thing."

Sem Thornwood

"Isn't it? You Shifters are always looking for you fated mates."

"Not me," he shakes his head. "I am smart enough to know I won't find my fated mate. That would be a miracle considering the curse on my family."

"Miracles exist."

"Yeah," he says and then sighs. He looks a little sad. "That's why I asked. Everything would be very easy and convenient if you were my fated mate."

I smile only because I can tell he is joking. "Unfortunately, life is not always easy and convenient. A new thing is always out there to get you." I should know.

Rionn nods, and then his eyes fall to my belt, where I carry my dagger. "I think that makes your point," he says. I always carry it with me. Even with one of the realm's strongest warriors by my side and his soldiers surrounding us, I don't feel entirely safe.

I need to rely on my own power too. I don't trust anyone to keep me safe but me or Lenora.

"The handle looks very intricate," Rionn says. "Can I see the whole thing?"

I feel a little uneasy about pulling out my weapon just like that, but I still do because it is ridiculous. I hold the dagger to him, but my hands are still close to my body, so he won't try to take it from me. I don't want to hand my dagger to him.

Rionn's eyebrows fly up at the sight of my glass dagger. He reaches to touch, but his fingertips stop just an inch away from the blade. He looks astonished. "This is a gift from Lenora," he says. It is not even a question.

"It is," I confirm. "How did you know?" I ask, even though it is very apparent. The craftsmanship looks nothing like I have ever seen. The glass weaponry must be something unique to the Sun Khanate.

"It is the Glass Dagger," he says like I am stupid. "How did she give this to you?"

I shrug, feeling a little weirded out by his reaction. "I picked a dagger as my main weapon. She said this might be helpful since I can also use my Moonshine. I am not very good at it yet, though."

300

Woe in Total Darkness

"So she just handed it to you? Just like that?"

"Yes? She said she had many more. I don't understand why it is a big deal. Is it like a very expensive dagger or anything?" I am not even sure why that would matter. Lenora is rich beyond words.

"Expensive?" Rionn throws his head back and laughs. He looks way too amused by my question. "Oh, Zuraya expensive doesn't even begin to describe it. This dagger is priceless. The Glass Sword and the Glass Dagger are ancient weapons of these lands. They were under the protection of Seelie Queen. They were kept in a sanctuary for hundreds, maybe thousands of years, until they were stolen by the Mitharaus family. Since then, they have been carried by the Khans. Her mother gifted those to Lenora when she became the General of the Sun Army. They are not things to be handed over easily."

His words shock me. I look down at the dagger in my hands with huge eyes. I knew this was a fine weapon, but I never considered it could be this precious. "She never told me that," I murmur. "She just gifted it to me like it was the simplest thing."

"We can never know what is going inside Lenora's head," Rionn says.

I don't care about the biting tone he uses. I don't care about his words. I just focus on my heart that is hammering inside my chest. I cannot think of anything but her.

Nothing is more precious to her than me. Maybe she is not aware yet, but I can see it. She will too. Her heart already knows. Her mind will catch up soon enough. And when that happens, everything will become even more dangerous.

I am ready for all of it as long as she is with me.

"Zuraya," Rionn calls, taking me away from my trans. "Do you understand what this means?"

"It means that she cares for me," I say without even thinking. "This is the kind of gift you give to someone you care about."

"Or someone you are trying to manipulate."

My brows come together. I know Rionn is annoyed with Lenora because she spends so much time with me, and they have some bad blood, but that does not mean he should talk badly about her. He is straight up trying to accuse her.

I won't stand for that.

"Lenora is not trying to manipulate me."

"She is only around you because she made a deal with your father. She only wants the moon spheres."

"I already know all this, Rionn. Lenora told me."

"And you still trust her?" he asks, stunned.

"I do," I say without hesitation. I trust her more than I trust anyone else. "I know you see me as a weak little princess, but I am not. I am not stupid, Rionn. I am perfectly capable of deciding my relationships."

He shakes his head with a sad expression. He seems helpless. "You don't know Lenora like I do, Zuraya. I can imagine what kind of thing is going on between you two and I know you are aware of the dangers it brings. I know you both know what you are pursuing is dangerous. However, you don't know Lenora. You think rules are the only thing in your way, but it is not. Lenora never cares about anyone more than she cares about her status. She only loves power. And I worry that it is going to break your heart in the end. She will never see your relationship the way you see it. It is always going to be about a quick release for her."

My heart drops, and I fight so hard to keep my breathing even. Rionn's words hurt me. I know he wants to attack us, but his words, mixed with the uncertainty of our relationship, affect me too much.

He has been with her the way I am with her. What is he is right?

It hurts my heart because that is where I carry Lenora, and I believe she does the same. Only I am not entirely sure.

Yet I also know there is a bigger threat. I cannot let Rionn know what is going on between Lenora and me. I also know him enough that denying will not work. "What are you going to do?" I ask. "Are you going to tell someone?"

He looks taken aback for a second by the question. He looks at me like that is the stupidest thing I can ask. Then says, "No."

"Then what are you going to do, Rionn? Are you going to blackmail me with this?" We both know he wants me, and if he threatens to hurt Len, he can so easily have me.

Woe in Total Darkness

Rionn looks at me with shock. "What kind of person do you think I am, Zuraya?" His eyes are full of hurt, but I cannot even care at this moment. When I look at him, expectedly, he shakes his head. "I won't ever hurt you, Zuraya, but I believe Lenora will. So the only thing I am going to do is wait. I will wait for all this to end, and when she leaves you broken, I will be ready to piece you back together. I will always be here for you."

I don't even know what to say to those words. He is trying to be good but only manages to make me uncomfortable. I don't want to be with him anymore, so I go back to my room and go to bed without saying anything.

I don't want to think about his words.

I don't want to think about anything.

37

Lenora

Shifters were natives to the Island just like Seelies. They lived peacefully together until the Feyadas arrived. When the Seelie Queen agreed to give the Northern Lands to the Haliyes family, Shifters disagreed. They didn't want strangers so close to their lands, their forest.

Seelie Queen played peacemaker between the two nations and mades Shifters accept the Feyadas. The Moon Kingdom didn't attack Shifter Lands for a long time. They coexisted very close together. That was until Carin Haliyes died and his daughter took over his throne.

The young queen was hungry for power. Khan Vaughn was sick, and his lands were getting weaker against the Seelies. She was worried the borders could come change. She was also hesitant about how the Sun Khanate was going to act after Vaughn's death. She was scared, and wanted to prove herself with her powers.

Shifters had different beliefs than Seelies. Not just about trusting the newcomers but also about religion. They believed in Tisasa, but they believed in the Moon more. They mostly disregarded Tisasa's other features. They lived around the Moon. When the Haliyes family stole the moon powers, some said they should be *worshipping them now, but the Alpha refused. He knew the power was stolen, and a mere Feyada could never be the same as their precious Moon. They didn't accept the Haliyes family held the full moon power because a part of it belonged to them.*

Shifters had the Lunar stone that they believed carried Moonshine. As long as they had the Stone, the Haliyes family could not rule over Moonshine.

Young Queen saw this belief as an opportunity. It was a great way to prove her strength and create fear. She used the power she later forbade and got into a war with the Shifters.

At the end of the war, Shifters lost their autonomy. Their land has become "Shifter Territory," and even if the Alpha family kept their rule over the Shifters, they were now part of the Moon Kingdom.

To ensure they would not rise against the Kingdom, the Young Queen decided to take their Lunar Stone into Haliyes' possession. This broke the Shifters too much. Their Alpha committed suicide. He couldn't take losing his wife, his Luna, in the war only to lose the Lunar Stone as well.

The oldest son of the Alpha, Darga Ay Ujk, took his place, but despite his mature age, he was not yet able to find his fated mate. He waited years and years until he took a wife just to have heirs. Darga was a great Alpha despite the condition his lands were in. He has always been loved by his people and remembered well, but he is also known as the Alpha, who announced the Curse.

Darga couldn't find his fated mate until he died, and in his late years, he decided that there was a curse on his family. Because Feyadas took the previous Luna and the Lunar Stone, Ay Ujk family had been cursed with never finding their fated mates.

He also left a prophecy on his deathbed. He said one day, an Ay Ujk is going to find his equal, his fated mate, his Luna. She is going to be the "Alpha that has been promised." His people also called her "Luna that has been promised," too. The idea of her gave Shifters strength for so many years. Even with every Alpha dying without a mate, they didn't lose hope because her arrival was going to mean their independence.

Because before dying, Darga promised that when an Ay Ujk found his fated mate, the Shifters would take back the Lunar Stone.

———ɕ———

I lean back at the wall, my arms crossed, and watch the Seelie just a few inches away from my feet cry and puke. Her green skin looks ashen, and her hair is so dirty that it looks more black than blonde. When she looks up, her mouth is also dirty from puking so much, and her cheeks are wet from her many tears. Her eyes are dark and beautiful, but at this moment, she looks horrible. She has a few cuts on her face, but those must have happened when she was first captured. My torture does not harm her body. It only harms her mind, and that is more than enough.

"This can go on forever, Loralei," I say. "I don't have to worry if your body is intact. I can torture you without a pause." I mean, it will tire me at one point, but the soldiers say they suspect Lorelei is very high ranking in the Curser's cult. I will push my limits for that.

Lorelei gives me an ugly smile that is full of spit. "Even with a Goddess' power, you still have to eat sometime, Princess."

She thinks she can push me. The only thing she does is annoy me. I will get answers from her, but I want them fast so I can go back to Zuraya sooner. It is unfortunate that she seems to be stronger than most.

"I can eat and still manipulate that little mind of yours. It will be easier for the both of us if you speak now."

She laughs like I said something funny. "You really think you can break me?"

"I can break anyone."

"But the Curser is breaking you."

I don't even flinch. The Curser has been my biggest problem since I can recall, but her words don't affect me much. I have questioned so many before her. I know how to keep my cool. I have heard worse.

Woe in Total Darkness

I had questioned a Feyada that said he was in the room when my brother died. I listened to him describe how they ripped out his heart out of his chest and didn't even flinch.

Loralei really doesn't know who she is up against.

"I actually like my odds," I say coolly. I also like giving her some time to gather herself. It hurts them most when I fill their head with pain when they are not expecting it. "I stole one of the Curser's biggest treasures."

She growls low in her throat. "Princess," she murmurs or spits. It is hard to say when her mouth and face are covered in snot. I don't even touch her, but the pain she thinks she has is enough to mess her up this badly.

I cannot stay too mad, though, because the visions of Zuraya fill my head. I have come to realize it is hard to keep her away from there. Since I left the Moon Palace, I have not been able to stop thinking about her. I keep remembering memories and imagine everything I am going to do to her when I go back.

I don't even want to think how hard it is going to be when I leave her for good. I act like our fates are not doomed.

Annoyance fills me. I cannot stand Lorelei wasting my precious time. "She is safe and sound now. I will ensure no one will ever touch a hair on her head. You are losing. Accept it."

"Do you tell yourself that so you can sleep at night?"

I usually sleep thinking of Raya's kisses and touches, but she doesn't need to know that.

I crouch down so I can look at her face. "What do you tell yourself at night, Loralei? How do you comfort yourself knowing you support someone who supposedly created Patches all over our map. Patches that kill thousands of innocent lives, Seelies, Feyadas, Earthlings, Giants, and Shifters. They kill families, Loralei. Children. Babies."

She looks at me with so much hatred in her eyes, like I am the villain here. "Every night, I pray before I go to bed. I sleep peacefully, knowing they are in a better place now. They are with Tisasa in the sky, in the earth, and deep in the ocean. I sleep proudly, knowing I am fighting so their sacrifice won't be for nothing. And every night before I fall asleep, I repeat the same words, Princess, 'For something to reborn, it has to die first.'"

Honestly, I was okay with letting her speak to get out of the torture longer, but she doesn't get to utter those words in front of me.

Anyone who speaks the motto of the Cult deserves my wrath.

I let my power free around me. I cannot help my skin to glow warmly. I can feel her mind like it is in the palm of my hand. After years of training, I can easily find the pressure points. I can easily snap their minds. So I press onto her pain. I make her feel like all of her muscles are spasming. She can feel the burn and the ache. Her sudden screams are proof enough.

I keep the constant pain for a while and watch her body writhe on the floor. More tears fall down her cheeks. I don't want her to puke again, though. We were in the middle of talking, after all. I stop before she loses consciousness.

Loralei trembles on the floor even when I stop. She looks like a wreck, but the hatred doesn't leave her eyes. "You whore!" she says, spitting.

I only smile. "Sorry, I really hate when someone says those words." Cultists believe when the Darkness swallows up the whole Isle, the healing will actually start. They somehow believe it will not kill the pure ones, the believers of Tisasa. The Goddess is going to get her power back and let the Isle be reborn from the Darkness with all the good creatures in it.

A crazy person's tale. I have no idea how someone can be so dumb to believe this shit, but they do.

"Your Curser is not a savior, Loralei. They are a murderer. And you will help me find them."

She laughs maniacally. "Why do you think I have the knowledge to help you?"

I wish she could just stop this charade and give me a location. It would be so very convenient. "You are an important part of the Cult, Loralei. I know you are very high ranking."

"That doesn't mean I know where they are. The Cult is good at hiding, Princess. Look how long it took you to find the Moonshine

Stealer. At this rate, you will be dead before you can even learn who the Curser really is."

She is pushing me again. It is not very effective. Only I don't like her calling Zuraya 'Moonshine Stealer." We have stolen nothing. Our ancestors did.

They don't see they are the ones hurting these lands. I have no idea how the Curser brainwashes them this well.

"I think they must be a Feyada," I say, changing the topic. I don't want her to talk about Zuraya. "The Curser must be a Feyada living in Seelie Lands. I mean, they mostly attack those lands. It fits the profile of a racist Feyada."

Loralei gets offended at that. "You don't know what you are talking about, Princess."

I also really fucking hate when she calls me Princess. "I think I do. I mean, if they hate Mitharaus and Haliyes families so much, they are attacking the wrong place. I stop many Patches in the Desert, but the South still has the worst. And look at the Moon Kingdom. No Patches have ever been created there. I think the Curser kind of likes them."

"That is a lie!"

I almost got her. "Do you have any other theories why the North never gets a Patch then, Loralei?"

She looks at me for a few seconds like I am a puzzle, and then the side of her lip tips up. When she smiles, I really want to hurt her. "It is because of the Princess," she says.

"Zuraya?"

She nods. "Darkness started with Tisasa, from the sacred lands. The reason it never reached the North is Princess's sacrifice. Tisasa gives forgiveness but takes something in return, and the Curser only works for Tisasa."

My blood turns cold. I don't want her to even think about Zuraya. They hurt her enough. However, I know this can lead somewhere. So, I ask, "What sacrifice?"

"You must already know," Loralei says with a smile. "Weren't you the one who rescued her? Haven't you seen her condition? Haven't you seen what we did to her, what we took?"

309

They took too much from Zuraya, but I know what she is talking about. It is Zuraya's biggest insecurity. It is something so valuable. "Her wings."

"Yes," Loralei hisses like a snake. "She stole from Tisasa, so we stole from her."

"She stole nothing. You have tortured an innocent."

"None of you are innocent!" she shouts but then gets back her calm, psychotic expression back. "I was waiting for them to bring her. They gave her in my care, and I gave her the chance to pay back to our Goddess."

The realization dawns on me, and I can feel the Sunshine trying to escape from my pores. I can hardly contain myself. "You were the one who did it?"

"They told me to keep her safe, undead. We needed her alive until she inherited her father's powers so we could take away the moon power entirely. I hated I couldn't kill her. I prayed and prayed to Tisasa, and she spoke to me in the end. She told me to give her a sacrifice. Zuraya had debt too big to handle."

My body gets warmer, and Sunshine pours into my hands. My logic tries to stop me, but it is hard to hear it over my pounding heart. I want to destroy this Seelie. I want to destroy anyone that has hurt Zuraya.

Loralei gives me an ugly smile. "I hope she still remembers the screams she let out when I was cutting her," she murmurs. "I have never seen so much blood."

I know she might know the Curser's identity. I know I need to interrogate more. I know I should keep my cool.

Yet I can't. Her words manage to push me enough, and I free the Sunshine in my palms. I send the light all over her body and listen to her screams as she burns. I don't stop. I can only see her hurting my Zuraya.

She deserves the burn.

Loralei screams and writhes on the floor as I ignite her down to the bone. And when I am done, I leave the room with every intention of turning back to the Moon Kingdom. I just try not to think about how this is the first time I killed someone during questioning.

Woe in Total Darkness

38

Zuraya

    I don't have nightmares anymore, but I always get a little scared before dozing off. The bad part is I don't even have dreams. I sometimes go to sleep thinking of Qyron, hoping I will dream of him. I just want a little piece of my best friend, but it never happens. I just sleep like the dead, and every morning I wake up to the sound of my maids.

    I usually don't wake up during the night, but since this is the third night Lenora has been away, I am not sleeping very deeply. Last night I woke up like five times because I was excited. Unfortunately, she has been gone for longer than she said. I just hope it is worth it.

    Tonight I also fell asleep a little on edge. I am just waiting for one of my maids to come and wake me up. My body is alert.

    So I easily feel the warm hand on my thigh and the covers over me moving. My eyes slowly open to the dark room. I can only see the bumpy silhouette of my covers, but I can feel much more. A soft breath over my bare sex and fingers all over my legs.

    Maybe I should be alarmed, but I am not. I can feel that it is her. No one can match her energy.

    No one feels like her on my skin.

Woe in Total Darkness

I pull the covers over my head and look down between my legs. Her skin is softly glowing in the dark, so I can see her. She presses a kiss to the inside of my thigh and smiles. "Hey."

I smile back. "You are here."

She nods and softly blows on my swollen flesh. "I came to make up for the lost time."

My hips roll on their own, trying to reach her mouth. "I missed you," I say truthfully. "So much."

"Me too," she murmurs, and then her tongue darts out to lick me thoroughly. "I especially missed this sweet cunt."

Her words make me go hot. Her tongue is working between my legs. My mind is filled with pleasure, but my stomach still rolls. I like what she is doing to me, but somehow I am annoyed that she went directly for my body. I want her to want all of me.

Maybe Rionn's words are messing with my head.

Just when I can think further, two fingers sink inside me, and I moan against the stretching feeling. I shouldn't question anything right now. I feel too good, especially when Lenora hits that sensitive spot inside me repeatedly.

"Len," I groan, feeling so close. My legs spasm around her head as she keeps fucking me with her fingers and licking me at the same time. I cannot help her effect on my body. "I am coming."

Then I do. My legs squeeze her head, but Lenora doesn't seem to care. She lets me ride it out, and even when I come down from my high feeling sensitive, she keeps her fingers buried inside me. Her body moves over mine. She moves her hand, fucking me again, and her body presses me down to the bed. Her other hand roams over my body. "You are so beautiful," she breathes into my neck.

"I am a little sensitive," I answer. I do feel good, but she is going a little hard on me.

"You taste so good on my tongue," she says, sucking on my neck. "No one fucks as good as you."

Now I really feel uncomfortable. "Lenora, please stop. Can we talk?"

Sem Thornwood

"Talk," she says mockingly and laughs. "Why would I want to talk to you? I only want to fuck you, Princess. That is all you are good to me."

Her fingers between my legs start to hurt, but her words hurt more. "Please, Lenora," I cry. I want her to stop. I want this to stop.

But Lenora keeps going. She keeps hurting me. As I cry under her, she whispers into my ear with a smile, "This is always going to be about fucking for me."

Then I scream.

And my eyes open.

I can hardly breathe, and I am still crying. But Lenora is not here. I am all alone in my room in the dark. Lenora is not tormenting me. She would never torment me.

And even though I know the only evil thing here is Rionn's words from the other day, I keep crying. I cannot breathe, thinking Lenora not caring for me.

I know it is still early from the noises outside. I hope I can sleep after I cry it out. I am not sure if the hollow feeling in my chest will let me, though. I try to compose myself. I wash my face and change out of my sweat-drenched nightgown. For a moment, I even consider going to the training grounds on my own, but I don't feel safe in the dark without Lenora.

I just wish she would come back soon.

After a while, I just go back to sleep and once again sleep like the dead. I don't wake up until my chambermaids come into my room in the morning. I stretch under my covers, trying to not think about last night. When I look out the window, it looks a little earlier than when I usually wake up for training.

"What is the time?" I ask my many maids now inside the room.

The one who actually woke me up looks at me nervously. "Your Highness, it is early, but you told me to wake you up when General Mitharaus came back to the palace."

I jump out of bed. "Lenora's back?"

"Yes."

Woe in Total Darkness

My heart is so fast I can feel it in my throat. "I need a dress fast. I need to go welcome her."

For some annoying reason, they don't run around my room to get me a dress. Instead, the one who just informed me keeps looking nervous. "I don't think you'll be able to, Your Highness. Your father called her for a meeting immediately. She will probably go there before even stepping inside her own room."

Disappointment fills me. I understand I am not the only thing in her life. I understand her duties. I just wish I could have seen her for at least a few seconds before she disappeared into a meeting. I just wish I could have hugged her once.

I try to keep my head up. I don't want to be weak. I will see her after the meeting. It is not a big deal. I should get used to being without her anyhow. I have lived twenty years without her. I can do it again.

I don't need her.

Just when I try my hardest to make myself believe that, a loud noise from outside takes my attention. The door to my chambers opens and closes harshly. My maids get into panic mode, but just a few seconds later, the door to my bedroom door also opens, and the mystery solves itself as we all see Lenora in the doorway.

Her golden braid looks messy like she didn't have time to rebraid it after flying for hours. There are faint circles under her eyes. She is still wearing her light flying armour. She looks tired and a little beaten, but when she looks at me, those orange eyes gleam.

Lenora doesn't even take a breather before starting to walk toward me. Her eyes are locked on mine, but she talks to my maids, "You can all leave."

I cannot look away from her, but I can feel many eyes on me. "Whatever she said," I say, and the maids quickly move out of the room. Neither of us pays any attention to them. We are too lost, too mesmerized.

I don't understand how my heart can beat this fast. I don't understand how just the sight of her can create chills all over my body.

It is almost like I look into her eyes and see her soul. And I know she can see mine as well.

When the door closes and Lenora's lips close over mine, I know this is more than what Rionn predicts. She kisses me softly like she is afraid of breaking me, but her hands hold me tightly like she is afraid of losing me. I know this is even more than what we agreed.

I kiss Lenora Mitharaus with everything in my body, in my soul, and I know I can never love anyone as much as I love her.

I cannot exist without her.

Our kiss turns desperate. We kiss for all the lost time. I bury my nails into the back of her neck and press my body to hers. I cannot get enough. As our tongues tangle, Lenora moans into my mouth, and her hands go to my bottom. She grabs and lifts me easily. I give a little squeak of surprise but then wrap my legs around her waist. Her hands massage my flesh, and I grab her jaw to control the kiss better. My whole body is aware of her presence, and I want more.

I will always want more of her.

When we are both out of breath, I pull back and touch my forehead to hers. For a few moments, we just stand like that trying to regulate our breathing. Then Lenora laughs. It is a small cute sound. I pull back to look at her face, and she bites her bottom lip. "Sorry," she says, smiling. "I didn't want to just barge in and kiss you, but I thought about this all the way here."

I press a quick kiss to her swollen lips. "You can always barge in and kiss me."

She raises an eyebrow. "Don't tempt me."

This time I laugh. Sweet Tisasa, how much I missed her.

"I missed you," she says with a soft voice like she had just read my mind. Her hands flex on my skin. "How are you? What have you done while I was gone? I want to know like I was here all along. Did you miss me?"

I can't help but grin wide at how silly she looks with all her questions. I love it when she is silly. I caress her cheek and answer her last question, "So much."

"I asked more questions. Come on. I want to know. I don't like that you were without me for three days." She pouts, but I can tell she is happy.

Woe in Total Darkness

All the worry my dream brought me disappeared with her arrival. I realize how stupid it was to doubt her. I realize she is everything I can ever want in life.

So, I kiss her once again. "I can tell you everything. We can have breakfast."

Her smile dims a little, and she groans. "Fuck, that sounds too good, but I can't."

I unwrap my legs, and she lets me on the floor. I don't move away, though. I want to touch her as long as I can. "Because of the meeting?"

She nods.

"You have to go right away?"

She nods again. "They tried to take me to the King's chambers right out of the gates, but there was no way I was going there before seeing you."

Butterflies set free in my stomach. I can't stop smiling. I am annoyed that she has to leave, but at least she is here now. She will come out of that meeting soon enough, and I will be ready for her. At least before she disappeared, she came to me.

She put me over her duty.

I wrap my hands around her glorious arms and pull her down. We kiss briefly again. "Go," I say softly. "When you are done, you won't be able to get rid of me."

"Raya," she says with a shake of her head. "I'll never ever want to get rid of you."

———⟨———

The meeting goes on for the whole day. When one of my maids tells me they are done, it is already dark. But I don't mind. I immediately leave my chambers to go to Lenora's. I am already in my pretty nightgown. It is blue silk, and the neckline is very low, so I am hoping Lenora will appreciate it the second I get rid of my heavy robes.

When I reach her chambers, I see Hashim guarding her door. He smiles at me and gives a curt nod, "Princess."

Sem Thornwood

"Hashim," I say, confused. "I thought Lenora didn't have door guards."

"Well, she doesn't," he says. "But she wanted to take a bath after the meeting and said she is too tired to leave the tub and stab someone if they dare to come inside with a threat to her life."

I can't help but laugh. "I mean, who wants that?"

"Certainly not me. I won't even leave the strange baths you have here."

I just shake my head, remembering how Qyron always complained about the baths too. I think they are okay. I like tubs, but I also love tubs that have Lenora in them. "So, can I go in?"

"I am ordered not to let anyone disturb her," he says, but then a little smirk appears on his face. "But I don't think she will consider you a disturbance."

I flush a little. "I hope not."

Hashim opens the door for me. I take very silent steps toward Lenora's bedroom. This is my first time inside her chambers, and I want to pry, but I also want to see her. Her bathroom is connected to her bedroom, and she is in the tub. Her face is turned kind of away from me, but I can tell her eyes are closed.

For a second, I smile at how sweet she is because I think she passed out from being tired. Then she speaks without opening her eyes, "If you are here to kill me, you have to know I can still fight when I am naked and wet."

My eyebrows climb to my hairline. "I would like to see that."

Lenora's eyes open, and she looks at me. "Raya," she whispers. "I was going to come for you. I just needed a bath. You deserve better than three days worth of sweat."

"That is very thoughtful of you."

She gets a sinister look. "Want to join me?"

I mock a shocked expression. "In your dirty tub? Never!"

"Your loss," she rolls her eyes and settles back in the tub. "I would have rocked your world."

I pull a stool and sit next to the tub. I look into her pretty face, and she does not look like she can do that. I wore my fancy nightgown, but I knew this was a possibility. Circles around

Woe in Total Darkness

Lenora's eyes look darker than a moonless night, and her skin looks too pale, like it has lost all the warm light inside her.

I caress her wet hair. "You are tired," I whisper.

She doesn't object. "I would still like to see what's under that robe."

Oh, she is going to see it even if we don't have sex. I have put effort into this look. I don't tell her that, though. I like to make her guess. "What if you finished your bath and I went back and called for some dinner? We can just eat, talk and maybe cuddle."

"Cuddle," she murmurs with a little smile, and I blush. "I'd love that."

I get a little more serious. I just want to spend time with Lenora, but I don't want to push her. I don't want to assume. "Are you sure?" I ask. "About me staying even though we probably won't do anything."

For a moment, her forehead wrinkles trying to understand my words. And when she does, she looks angry. "I missed *you*, Raya," she says. "Not just your body."

My throat tightens. I want to cry, but instead, I kiss her hard. She kisses me back without question. She doesn't need questions. She can see my soul through my eyes. When I pull back, I give her a huge smile. "I'll go get us food."

When I tell Hashim about finding food, he informs me that they hunted pinebirds on their way over here. He tells me to relax and that he will send some to the room. I cannot help my huge grin because it is definitely not the season for pinebird, and it is hard to catch them right now. Lenora just did it because she remembered I liked them.

She remembered I had them while I was sad and decided to fix my heart that was broken from not being able to see her for three days.

I don't bother her while bathing and just fix myself a bit until the food comes. When it does, I make them put it on the bed. Hashim informs me he is leaving so I lock the door after him.

When Lenora emerges from the bathroom completely naked my breath hitches at the sight. I realize I have never seen her naked under some good light.

She has scars and golden-colored tattoos all over her body. I realize her chest is free of any tattoo, though. I know Sunfolk tattoo themselves according to their life achievements, and every tattoo has a meaning, so I wonder why she is bare on the chest. Maybe because it is a glorious chest on its own. Lenora definitely has smaller breasts than me, but they are still full enough to grab. Her body is all muscles and curves. Her waist is small, and her backside is tight. Just like me, she doesn't have hair between her legs or anywhere else on her body except her head and her wings. Royals usually remove those with magic when they are way too young.

Her golden hair looks a darker color because it is wet, just like the blonde feathers on her wings. Her short horns shine with cleanness. Long horns are a symbol of pride for Feyada, but I like her shorter ones much better.

She is a masterpiece all over.

"Should I give a twirl?" Lenora asks with an amused tone.

Blood rushes to my cheeks, but I don't look away. I can't look away. "Sorry."

Lenora shrugs and moves to her closet. "I like you looking at me. I forgot to take clothes with me, but the next time I am doing it knowingly."

"I would like that very much."

Lenora giggles and pulls up a loose jumper. Wearing robes with wings is really hard. Personally, I don't have to worry about that anymore.

She looks at the food on the bed. "Mmhh, that looks delicious." Then she looks up, and her eyes dance around my curves that are apparent under the nightgown. "You look delicious too."

I smile and reach out a hand. "Come on, let's eat. It is pinebird."

"Your favorite," she smiles and lets herself fall to the bed on the other side of the trays, but her fingers still tangle with mine. Her smile dims a bit. "You look beautiful, Raya. I am sorry for not appreciating you enough. We can still have sex, you know."

I do get a little buzz between my legs from her words, but oh, Tisasa, she looks so sleepy. I just want her to have a rest. I want her to feel good. We can do all the other things tomorrow. So, I

Woe in Total Darkness

shake my head. "I want to see you eat and then sleep. Nothing more tonight."

She holds back a smile. "Okay," then reaches for the food. "But you tell me about what happened when I was gone."

"Okay," I accept, and then I do. Not many things happened in three days anyway, but I share every unimportant detail because Lenora listens to me with interest. She also eats a lot. I like seeing her like this. It is just so raw, so casual.

"So, nothing exciting happened?" Lenora asks when we are both done with eating. She moves the trays to the other room.

There is something I haven't told her, but I don't want to alarm her. I am also not very eager to talk about it myself. I move under the covers and she follows me. She has a sweet smile on her face.

I take a deep breath and say, "I talked to Rionn."

Her shoulders tense, but she hides it quickly. "Rionn? Why?"

"He wanted to spend time with me, and I didn't want to decline. It would be rude."

"Of course," Lenora says with a strained voice. I can't decide if I hate or love her jealousy. "What did you talk about?"

I don't even know where to start. I am also not sure if I should tell her all of it. In the end, I decide to go with the most important one. "He said he knows something is going on between us."

Lenora closes her eyes. "Fuck."

"But he said he won't tell anyone," I try to relax her immediately.

Her eyes open and she looks surprised. "Why? Keeping our secret doesn't serve him in any way."

I look away. "He said he will be waiting for me when whatever between us ends."

Lenora's hand hesitantly reaches for me under the covers. I feel her fingertips caressing the silk on my skin. I want her to really hold me, but she doesn't dare. "I just wish he goes back to his territory. I don't like him around you."

"Are you jealous?"

Her throat moves with a swallow, and she looks sad. "I don't have the right to be jealous."

Sem Thornwood

That is stupid. I wiggle a little closer, so her hand comes over my waist. "Of course, you have, Lenora. We said we would be exclusive." And we became even more. She has every right to be jealous. She has every right to be possessive over me. She is just too afraid to show it.

"I don't want to overstep, Raya. I never want to make you uncomfortable."

I shake my head vigorously. "You won't, I promise."

She looks at me for a moment. "Okay then," she closes her eyes. "I don't like Rionn around you. I get jealous, and I don't want you to see him again."

"Then I won't see him again." It is this easy.

"You sure?"

I nod and get closer to her. "I am. Come on, let's sleep. I have burdened you enough."

"You never burden me, Raya. I am the one who crushed your hopes for tonight. Are you sure you are okay?"

I roll my eyes with a smile. "Stop asking me if I am sure about things."

Lenora smiles too, but it is strained. "Well, are you, though?"

"I am," I assure her. "Just let me sleep with you. Don't send me away." That is all I want. I just want her. I don't care how.

"Never," Lenora murmurs, and finally, her arms wrap around my waist. She pulls me to her body, and her sweet warmth spreads over my skin. She holds me like I can slip away any second. She presses a kiss to my forehead and closes her eyes. "I'll never let you get away from me."

Maybe I should be alarmed by those words, or maybe I should be sad because they can never be real. But instead, they just make me smile. Lenora always manages to make me feel loved in her arms.

39

Zuraya

I wake up before Lenora in the morning. It is not surprising. She looked too tired, and I was very happy to let her hold me in her sleep. She fell pretty quickly, and I spent some time just watching her. My emotions were bubbling up too much. I know it can be dangerous, but I cannot help myself.

I cannot change the fact that I love Lenora.

Our reunion yesterday made me sure. There is no way I can exist without her on my side. That is a big problem for the near future, but I will try to focus on the positive. I can fix it when the time comes for her to leave.

At least, I hope I can fix it.

In the morning, I again just lay in her bed and watch her sleep for a while. I decide I want to spend all my mornings like this. I want to wake up next to her every day. Unfortunately, soon enough, the thought makes me sad. Believing it can be forever is not easy.

I eventually leave her bed. I still press a soft kiss on her cheek, though. She smiles a little in her sleep, and light fills my insides. I get the urge to pry into her room. I want to learn her secrets.

I want to find out all the consistency in her life, and I want to be one of them.

But I don't want to do those behind her back. I want her to show me. I want her to feel just like I feel and want everything I want.

That's why I leave without looking around in her room. I go to my own room to change and then make my way to the training grounds like I do every morning. I actually feel very safe here even though I am surrounded by people. The first few days, I caught some soldiers looking at me, but it was never in a weird way. They were just surprised to see me. No one made me feel ashamed of my lack of wings. The presence of Earthling soldiers also helped in that regard.

I feel like I am actually at home surrounded by them even though they are foreigners. When I come face to face with a particular soldier, I even think I made some friends because Hashim is definitely more than just my teacher or my sparring partner. He knows my favorite color and all the gossip I gather from my maids. I know he has a brother back home who is fascinated by him for being a soldier. I also know Hashim doesn't want him to be one because he can be much better with how smart he is.

Yeah, I guess I consider Hashim, a real friend. Maybe not as much as Lenora or Maha, but he is up there. I don't have many people around me anyway.

"Good morning Hashim," I call out.

He turns to me and smiles big. "Good morning Princess." He likes to call me that. I don't correct it anymore.

I look around and see that many soldiers are chatting with each other. "Why is no one training?"

He just smiles like a little kid. "They are gossiping. I mean, if you ask, they won't accept, but the ones who came back with the General tell about the mission, and the others listen, wishing they were there too."

"Isn't that a security threat?" I haven't asked Lenora about the mission because I thought it was wrong for me to know about it.

Hashim shrugs. "They are not telling them anything top secret. Just bragging."

I giggle. "Why are you not listening?"

"I listened yesterday in the meeting from the General. Later I'll brag about that. Now I just let them have their fun."

Woe in Total Darkness

I laugh at that. He is the sweetest. Hashim is Lenora's right hand, but he never treats the other soldiers differently because of that. He is just a very sincere person. I know that he is loved by others. I guess it is a good balance to Lenora's toughness. She is not a hard-ass, but she is not as friendly as Hashim.

"How was the meeting?" I ask while also shining my pretty glass dagger. Only one of them is glass, but I take much better care of it since I heard it was a precious weapon. It was already important to me because it was a gift from Lenora, but now it also represents how much she cares for me.

Hashim looks surprised by my questions. "Didn't General tell you?"

"I haven't asked. She was tired." Even if she wasn't, I wouldn't want to spend our first night together after three days discussing politics.

"That makes sense," he says. "She was tired enough when she came, and then she had to spend the whole day with the King."

For a second, he looks worried, like he said something wrong, but then I giggle, and he looks relaxed again. I would not want anyone to disrespect my father, but I also won't act like I don't know what kind of personality he has. So when I ask, "Was he hard on her?" I already know the answer is going to be yes.

Hashim nods. "He was mad because she didn't bring enough information back. It was very tense. He kept acting displeased with her even though she is the one fighting hard against the Curser for years. I have no idea how she remained calm. The Moon King is a little..."

"Intense," I finish for him. I know he has much worse words in his head. "My father is always on edge. Honestly, it is hard to please him with anything. I actually have only seen my father once after I was rescued. He hadn't called for me. He knows I struggle with my powers, so in his eyes, I am not even worthy of his audience. Someone who can be like that to his own child won't care about Lenora's feelings. He is just intense like that."

He looks downright sad at my admittance. "He really didn't want to see you? Not even when you were depressed?"

I shake my head. Honestly, the lack of my father doesn't bother me anymore. I learned to not require his presence when I am at my worst. I need to work and better myself for his acceptance. If I do everything to please him, I can earn his pride. Our relationship has always been like that. "The King won't give anything for free. I need to work to gain his affection."

He looks away, and I almost hear him curse under his breath. "And I thought the Khan was grumpy." It is normal for him to think like that. Hashim doesn't come from a royal family.

"My father is not grumpy," I say. "He just has very high expectations from everyone." That is the best way I can describe it.

Hashim looks at me with thin eyes. "You have a way with words, Princess. You are a politician as much as a warrior, aren't you?"

I smile at the compliment. I have grown up in a toxic palace. I am way better with words than a dagger. I just don't get to use it often because I am so scared of interacting with the court. I know I should let them see me soon, but until then, I can just have fun in my little safe bubble.

"Don't worry about my words. Would you like to spar before going over there to brag?"

Hashim nods and takes out his daggers. "This way, I can also brag about how I defeated the Moon Princess in training."

I roll my eyes. "Don't be so sure big guy. I have been stabbing that dummy pretty hard."

He puts a hand over his heart. "It truly hurts me when you compare me to a dummy."

"Would you prefer I compare you to Lenora?" I ask with a raised brow. Those are the only ones I have ever trained with.

"I guess I am good with the dummy."

<hr/>

Hashim trains with me for a very long time. Since the soldiers are not really training, they come to watch us. A few of them actually cheer for me too. It feels awfully nice. I still cannot really beat

Woe in Total Darkness

Hashim, but that is given since he has been training in this for years.

I do get better, though. I land more hits and block more advances. I feel like I tire him a little bit more. Hashim also informs me about the improvements in my stance. Maybe I am not fit to go to war with my dagger training, but I am good enough. Also, I usually don't use my moon power while training with Hashim. I am sure with that, I can hurt more. The touch of Lenora's sword burns her opponents. I am pretty sure I can freeze them.

Between the cheers of the soldiers, I hear someone speak. "Do you do bets? I'll like to put some money on the Princess."

Everybody stops to look in Lenora's direction. The soldiers look a little ashamed because they are not training, but their General only has eyes for me. I can't help but smile.

I answer, "Be ready to lose that money then."

Lenora doesn't say anything, but I can see her amusement all over her face. I realize she loves seeing me like this. It is either training or the fact that I am surrounded by her soldiers or both. But she looks at me like I am the embodiment of all her desires.

She looks around her soldiers briefly. "This is the end of the show, I am afraid. Everyone go back to training." When they start moving away, she looks at Hashim. "Thank you, Hashim. I'll train body manipulation with Zuraya now."

Hashim gives a curt nod and also moves away. With that, Lenora comes too close to me like the prying eyes don't matter. I smile at that and ask, "Slept well?"

"I did," she says, but there is a hardness in her features. "You were not in my bed when I woke up. I didn't like that."

"You sleep too much, General. I am afraid you are just a little lazy for me." I bite down my bottom lip to hold back my laughter.

Lenora raises an eyebrow and leans close to whisper in my ear. "I'll remember these words later when you are in my bed naked and vulnerable, Princess."

My breath hitches. I am way too excited for her to punish me for my joke. I know I'll love everything she'll do to me. Even when she says, "Let's start training," I don't complain. I am too happy at her side.

Lenora takes her stance a few feet away from me. "Hit me," she says like she always does.

This is my least favorite training, even though I do it with Lenora. I just really feel like I am failing every time. I won't stop trying my hardest, though. I close my eyes and reach into my heart. I feel my power buzzing over my body. Then I open my eyes and focus on Lenora. I can feel her body in the universe. I can feel every part of it. I can reach into every part of it. Slowly I wrap my power around her muscles, and I squeeze and scratch. I make them spasm. I tickle her bones and wrap around them, almost strong enough to snap them. I move over her skin. I pickle it all over and make her feel like she is stabbed by needles. I do my best to hurt her. I use all my energy and all my concentration.

And Lenora just remains motionless.

She has an assessing look in her eyes, and I can see some movement in her muscles, but that is probably my doing. She doesn't look pained. She doesn't look even a little bit hurt. She just looks cynical. I try to push harder, but nothing changes. My power doesn't affect her even a little bit.

So I stop, feeling like the biggest disappointment. All the confidence I gathered from my dagger training vanishes. All the happiness I felt moments ago disappears. I just want to go back to my room and cry myself to sleep.

I am a failure.

"Why did you stop?" Lenora asks, confused. Normally I should keep going until she tells me to stop.

"Because I can't do it."

Her eyebrows come together. "What do you mean? You were doing great. That prickling feeling over the skin is new. It hurts really bad. You are getting much better every time Zuraya. Soon you will actually break my bones."

She says those words with certainty, but they only make me feel worse because they are plain lies. I am not getting better at all. "Why do you lie to me?" I ask desperately.

Woe in Total Darkness

"I am not," she says, looking offended. "I promised no more lies."

And I trusted her word when she did that. Right now, I cannot trust her words over my own eyes. "You don't look even a little bit hurt, Lenora. I understand you are strong, but I have been working hard. I still cannot even make you flinch. It means I am not good. I am a failure."

She takes a step closer to me. Honestly, she looks more in pain right now. "You are not a failure at all. You are doing amazing. I am just good at hiding my pain. Can't you trust my word?"

I look away and pout like a little kid. "I can't over my own eyes."

I hear her sigh. She stays silent for a few seconds, watching the grass under her boots. Then she murmurs, "I am going to regret this," and looks up at her soldiers. "Hey! Everyone's attention is on me."

With so many eyes on us, I feel a little uneasy, but I am also curious about what she is going to do. I don't believe in my powers, but I am also full of hope for her to change my mind. I want her to make me believe I am actually worth something.

"Princess Zuraya has been training on her body manipulation for a while, but apparently, I am not the best person to try her powers on." Some soldiers chuckle at that. "Is there anyone who wants to volunteer to be her test subject? I have to warn you, it hurts."

Soldiers look uncertain, probably because of her warning. I want to tell them it probably doesn't even hurt a bit, but I don't. Before I can feel sad over the lack of volunteers, an Earthling soldier called Borran raises his hand. "I will do it, General."

Lenora looks worried. "You sure?"

He shrugs. "I am curious how it feels, actually."

"Well, take a stance," she says, showing him the place she just stayed, but she also looks at him like he is a fool. To me, his logic sounds pretty okay. It is not going to hurt a lot anyway, but it will be a different experiment for him.

Lenora stands next to the soldier and looks me right in the eye. "Do to him exactly what you did to me. This time you can stop when you feel uncomfortable."

I don't understand why I would be uncomfortable, but I also don't ask. I am too annoyed to speak anymore. Instead, I do what she asked me to do. I once again reach my power and make myself aware of the body I am attacking. I focus on his bones, muscles, and skin. I get ready to squeeze and spike. I focus entirely on the attack like I always do, even though I have no hope anymore. Then when I am ready, I just attack. I do what I did to Lenora just minutes ago.

But something different happens. Borran starts screaming.

I open my eyes in a startled state, but my power remains around the body. Borran is already on the ground, and he is writhing with pain. His pale face is all red, and his eyes are watery, so close to tears. He is crying and screaming, and I have no idea how I did that to him.

I immediately pull my power back when reality hits me and release Borran. He goes motionless at once. A few soldiers and Lenora run to his side.

"Are you okay, Borran?" Lenora asks.

Borran's eyes are open, but he only looks at her for a few moments, just breathing hard. Then he hardly nods. "I am." He is still trembling from the aftermath, but that doesn't stop him from looking at me with a tired smile. "I would never want to be your enemy, Princess."

A few laugh at the joke with Borran, but I stay frozen. I had never considered I could hurt someone this much. I never thought I was this powerful.

Then a thought hits me, and I look at Lenora. I never realized I hurt her this much every day.

How did she endure this?

Lenora takes a deep breath and starts walking toward me. "Take care of Borran. You can take the rest of the day off." When she reaches me, her hand closes around mine, and she pulls me away from the training area. It is time for some private conversation because I am way too confused.

40

Lenora

"So, you are strong and super resistant. Nice to know."

I turn to Raya after locking the door to my chamber. "We are getting into that straight away, huh?"

She doesn't answer. Instead, she sits at the edge of my bed, and looks way too sad. I want to punch myself for causing that. "Why haven't you told me I was hurting you that badly?"

I shake my head. That is an unnecessary concern. Not worthy enough for her woe. She didn't leave permanent damage to my body after all. I sit next to her and cup her hands. "It doesn't affect me as much as others, Raya. And I told you, you were getting better."

"And I tried even harder every time because I didn't believe you."

I try a smile. "Well, isn't it great that it fueled you?"

Turns out that is the wrong thing to say because Raya looks at me with horrified eyes and jumps up from the bed. "I agreed to train because I wanted to get my powers back, and after that, I was happy to learn how to defend myself. I never wanted to learn so I could hurt someone. I worked my power over you because I thought it was not doing anything." She looks at me again, and this time her eyes are glossy. "Don't you understand how much it hurts me to know I caused you pain?"

There are so many other ways for her to cause me pain. Physical pain is not the worst at all. I don't mind it. But I do mind anything that makes Raya this sad.

I hate seeing her sad.

I get out of bed and pull her into my arms. One hand cups her cheek so I can see her face better. "Darling, I promise it doesn't hurt me as bad as you think."

Her breath hitches for a second, but she doesn't soften on me. "How can you be so strong? Just because you can manage to hide your reaction doesn't change the fact that I gave you the same pain that made Borran cry on the ground."

"And I am proud of you for it."

"I am not proud of myself!"

I shake my head at her little outburst. It is not even precisely aimed at me. She is angry at herself for hurting me. My pain is really not worth that. It is too common.

"Raya," I whisper and kiss her cheek. Thank Tisasa, she lets me. "Pain doesn't bother me that much. I am always in pain."

"What do you mean?"

I swallow with a hint of hesitation. My strength is widely known, but my condition is not public knowledge at all. No one knows how I can resist pain so well.

The truth is a vulnerable thing to share for me.

But I will share it with Raya. Logically it is not very smart to let her know, but I want her to know. I want her to see the real Lenora and still look at me with those soft blue eyes.

I want to know I am worthy of it.

I reach for her hand and pull her to the bed so we can be fully seated when I tell her. Raya follows without a word. She remains silent but curious.

"My father is a Feyada, but he has Seelie ancestry. Since interspecies breeding might be a little problematic, my mother always blamed his genes for everything she didn't like about Qyron and me."

Woe in Total Darkness

Raya nods like she already knows that. Probably Qyron told her already. I don't think he told her about my condition, though.

"We were both born with some complications. It took some time for the healers to realize Qyron was deaf, but they immediately realized something was wrong with me. I was crying way too much, and my bones were weirdly shaped. They took me away as my mother gave birth to Qyron and handed only him to her since they were sure I was going to die. As far as I know, my father was the only one who came to check on me."

It always seemed too tragic to me. My mother hated me since I was born. She had another baby to hold and didn't care about the sick one.

Raya also looks sad, but I try not to focus on that. My story is not done. "Healers said that I had some problems with my joints. Apparently, they were almost non-existent, and my bones were standing together by chance. They told my father I would most likely be unable to move my whole life. One of them mentioned strong healing magic could work. My father took advantage of my mother's tiredness and her joy of having Qyron and stole a moon sphere from her. She had a few from King Luran as gifts. My dad gave it to the healers hoping it could help."

"And it did?" Raya asks with hope in her eyes, like my existence is not proof enough.

"Yes," I nod, assuring her. "They managed to make joints for me using the Moonshine and their own healing magic. I got to live, and I could move every inch of my body."

Raya smiles. "That is amazing. I cannot even imagine you dying so young. You not existing." She loses focus in her eyes.

I don't want her to get sad over things that didn't happen. I reach out and squeeze her hand. "It is an amazing miracle," I say. "But I am not fully healed from that. My body works fine but at the cost of pain. Every time I move, my joints feel like they have needles surrounding them; it even extends to my bones. Even when I am not moving, the makeshift joints put pressure on my bones and muscles. My body always aches, always hurts. There is not a second I am not in pain."

Raya gets a worried look. She looks down at my body like it has betrayed her trust. "How can that happen?"

I shrug. "It is not a Feyada thing, but over the years, I have learned many other species have illnesses that can cause chronic pain. Mine is a different cause, but the end result is the same. I am always hurting. That's why you don't have to worry. The outside pain doesn't bother me as much as it does to others. I am very used to it, so my tolerance got high over the years. When the pain is not caused by my body, I know it will pass, so I am better at handling it. The harder thing for me is the pain coming inside of me. So you don't have to worry about hurting me."

Unfortunately, my words fall on deaf ears. Raya doesn't look relieved. Instead, she looks more horrified. "Are you crazy?" she asks. "Is this supposed to make me feel better?"

"Yes?" I say, uncertain. "I am telling you the pain you caused me was unimportant. You don't have to be sad for hurting me. Isn't that good?"

"No!" she says harshly. She moves her body closer to mine in bed, and her hands cup my face. She holds me like I am a delicate thing. No one has ever done that to me. "You told me you are always in pain, Len. How can that make me happy? I don't want you to hurt. I want you to be happy. I want you to feel good."

I hold onto her hand and press a kiss to her palm. "I am happy, Raya." At least I am at this moment. I am always so happy when she is around. "And you do make me feel good."

"I make you feel good?" she asks, looking skeptical. "How? With sex? Does that work? Maybe it can take your mind off of the pain. Does it? Because if it does, we are fucking all day and all night."

I can't help but laugh. Only Raya can be so cute while talking about fucking me for days.

Honestly, I didn't mean sex when I said those words, but that is not wrong too. I was mostly talking about her presence. Even if she cannot take the pain away, she always makes me feel better. I care about my pain a little less when Raya is around.

But I quickly understand that answer is not going to satisfy her. She really wants to know how to reduce my pain. It is impossible to stop it, but there are actually things that help me cope with it better. One of them is the eyedrop drug but I don't mention that. It has more effects than just reducing pain.

"Your power," I say softly. "Your Moonshine on my skin usually helps. It is chilly and nice. It feels like putting ice all over me – which also makes the pain a little more bearable – but even better."

Raya instantly shines bright and wraps her arms around me. The chilly feeling soothes the pain in my muscles a little. "Does it really help?"

I nod, smiling, and press a kiss to her lips. "You know, sex *does* kind of take my mind off of it." Not fully, but still.

She doesn't laugh at my joke but instead straddles me. "Oh good, we are having sex then."

I let her press kisses all over my face, and my hands go to her bottom, but I also laugh out loud. She pushes me on my back, and I cannot help my amusement at her willingness to make me feel good. If I don't laugh this much, I sure will cry.

"Darling," I murmur and hear her breath hitch again. "I don't want you to fuck me just so I don't feel pain."

Raya looks offended, but there is a fire in her eyes. "Believe me, Len, I am not doing this to you just so you will stop hurting. I wanted to jump you since you have been back."

"Okay then," I accept easily. I shift our legs and put my knee to her sex over her pants. "I have no complaints." Then I put a hand on her neck and really kiss her.

Hard.

Desperate.

With so many emotions I am too scared to admit.

Raya presses her body to mine, and the dagger in her belt digs into my stomach. "Ouch." She pulls back with worried eyes, but I just smile. "We should get rid of the weapons."

"Oh yes," she giggles and sits up. Our legs are still tangled together, and she looks so fucking hot taking off her dagger belt. I take my sword off while still lying down because I don't want to miss out on this view.

Sem Thornwood

After we carefully put our weapons on the side table, Raya holds the hem of her blue tunic. She pulls it over her head, saying, "Maybe we should get rid of more than just the weapons."

"Fuck yes," I groan at the sight of her beautiful body. Her dark skin is so smooth and perfect. Her breasts are heavy, and two silver buds on both of her nipples tease me like nothing else.

Because I need to feel her skin on my tongue, I sit up. My hands go to her waist to keep her steady, and I lick down a road from her collarbone to the tip of one perfect breast. I suck on it, and the cool metal against my teeth actually feels good. Cool things always help with my pain.

Raya's body still shines with a faint Moonshine, and it feels like the best possible thing around me. It helps my pain, but since I am also shining, touching our powers just turns me on more. I want to consume her into my pores, into my soul.

I am the Sun, but I feel like I can never exist without Moonshine.

I switch to her other breast and nibble the tip as my hands roam over he body. I will never be able to get enough of her. "You make me so wet," I whisper into her skin, and my hips roll almost instinctively, making my thigh brush her between the legs.

Raya moans, and her hands dip into my braid. She undoes it while I keep licking and sucking her body. She kisses the side of my head. When I try to roll her onto her back, she resists. "No," she says.

I stop and pull back, my hands turning hesitant over her waist. "Something wrong? Do you want to stop?"

She shakes her head. "No, no, not at all." Slowly she brushes away my golden locks and looks at me with those soft eyes. Her cheeks blush in the way I like so much. It is not too easy to catch, but she can never hide it from me. I am too aware of her body.

"What is it?" I ask. I am dying to know what made her blush.

Raya bites down her bottom lip and looks down at my body. "I want to taste you like you did to me." My lungs squeeze with anticipation when her eyes move back to my face. "I have never done it before, but I really want to."

"It is okay," I assure her, breathless. Then I kiss her hard. "Fuck. It is better than okay."

Woe in Total Darkness

She giggles onto my mouth and then pushes me on my back again. Her body presses me down, and her mouth takes dominance over my own. It is cute when she tries to dominate me. I let it happen. Surprisingly it turns me on even though I have never let anyone else do that.

I just trust her too much. I am open to trying anything.

Raya's mouth moves to my neck, and her hands grab the hem of my white top. She easily pushes it off as I arch my back for her. I hear a soft intake of breath before she ravishes me again. Her kisses move down and down until she reaches my chest. She licks the soft skin between my breasts and tweaks a nipple with her thumb.

"I love your freckles," she murmurs between kisses and licks. "I want to kiss every single one."

I chuckle. "All of them?" I have way too many.

Raya nods and kisses a freckle close to my nipple. "I want to know your body so well that I can tell how many of them you have."

That makes me smile. I do want her to know my body that well. I want her to never touch a living thing but me.

Forever.

Just me.

Her hands roam over my arms and my stomach. I flex a little for her, and she moans. Her kisses go south. She actually licks my abs like a hungry little thing. I love seeing her so turned on. I love how it drowns out her shyness too.

Raya hooks her fingers on the waistline of my pants without much delay and gets an exciting look. "I want this gone," she says.

"I want it gone too." It is a traitorous piece of cloth that is coming between her mouth and me. I lift my hips to help her and in seconds Raya leaves me bare for her eyes to see. She pushes my knees apart gently and settles between them. She licks her lips like she cannot wait to taste me, but I can also sense her nervousness.

I reach down and cup her cheek. "Darling," I murmur. "Whatever you'll do is going to feel good." I am not even lying.

Even her presence is enough to make me wet. I doubt any of her touches can feel bad.

"I don't want it to just feel good. I want to make you lose your mind."

Like she hasn't already. "I can tell you what feels good if you want. I can help you. Just remember there is nothing to be tense about. It is just you and me."

She smiles and presses her cheek to my thigh. "Just you and me."

This sight alone makes me close to coming, so when she starts leaving little kisses on the soft skin moving towards my center, I exhale a relieved breath. I just need to feel her against me. I am burning.

"Tell me how to make you feel good," she whispers against my heated flesh before finally licking me. I thought she would be hesitant there too. I expected her to start off slow and shy. But that is not true at all. Raya licks me from bottom to top with enthusiasm and then moans. "You taste so good." Then she does it again.

I don't tell her anything for a while because what she does feels good. She discovers me with her mouth. Her hands spread me apart, and from time to time, her fingers flex over the skin of my thighs. She licks my cunt hungrily.

I like everything she does, but it gets too much at one point because it is not enough. She is driving me crazy by not giving me exactly what I want. And I realize I can just get it. I reach and touch the bud at the hood of my sex. "Here," I say, breathless. Raya already knows I am sensitive there, but not everybody likes the same thing. "Suck here. I like it more than licking."

She doesn't answer, but I swear I can feel her smile against me before her lips close around the spot I just showed her. She sucks it into her mouth, and I writhe with pleasure. "Yes!"

"Do you like that, Len?" Raya says with a sinister voice. "Do you like my mouth on your needy cunt?"

Oh Goddess, who is this?

I can only answer with a moan. Her mouth feels so good, but it is still not enough. I roll my hips to her face and try to speak. "Raya."

"Mhmm?"

Woe in Total Darkness

"Please put your fingers inside me," I beg. "Please."

I swear she grunts. I have never seen Raya be so primal. In the next moment, I feel two fingers on my entrance. She circles it slowly, testing me, but she doesn't have to. I am embarrassingly wet. When she sees that, she pushes those fingers inside me, and I stretch tight around them. "Fuck."

Raya pushes them deep, watching her own fingers like it is a miracle. "You feel so warm," she mumbles. Then her mouth again closes over my sex. She thrusts into me and sucks me at the same time.

It feels divine.

I can feel the release building on my lower belly. I watch Raya between my legs, working so hard for my pleasure. I grind onto her face more. Just when the peak is getting close, Raya's wandering fingers inside me curl toward a sensitive spot, and I scream.

"Yes! Don't stop!" I am too close. Raya, thankfully just keeps going with the same rhythm, and the pleasure builds until it snaps.

I tighten around her fingers, and my whole body trembles violently on the bed. I come into her mouth moaning and screaming. She keeps going, lets me ride it out, and doesn't stop until I am all spent under her.

When my body goes motionless, Zuraya looks up, rubs all the wetness from her mouth and chin, and smiles at me. "I liked that more than I thought I would."

I smile, too, and pull her up so I can kiss her lips. I want to taste myself on her. I want to know I am all over her.

We kiss slowly but passionately. Only when we part do I answer her, "You did?"

"Yes," she nods. "I liked how much power I had over you."

You always have so much power over me, Raya.

I squeeze the back of her neck a little jokingly and say, "Be careful. I always take revenge."

"I promise I will not complain at all."

"Good," I murmur. I roll us over, taking place over her on the bed. She gives out a little scream, but her eyes shine with anticipation. I reach for her belt. "I think we should get rid of these first."

"We really should," Raya says playfully. "They are all wet."

Oh, sweet Tisasa, help me. I pull down her pants, and the scent of her arousal fills the room. It is better than any drug I have ever tried. I can't help and bite down on her hip.

Raya yelps.

I grin.

I kiss up her body. She is magnificent. She is the prettiest thing I have ever seen, but I am sure most will agree with me. Only most won't be able to see her like this. She can lay with others. She can bear her naked body to them, but I will be the only one she ever bears her soul to.

I can't accept the opposite.

"I need to have you," I say desperately as I kiss her neck. *I need to have you forever.*

Raya wraps her naked legs around me and pulls me even closer. Her heat presses against my abs. "Then take me, Lenora."

I wish I could.

This time I kiss her lips hard. I am so mad. I am mad at her for being so perfect and mad at myself for falling for it. I am mad at the world for not letting me have her.

But I can have her for now. At this moment, in this bed, Zuraya Haliyes can be mine.

I grab her hips and ask between kisses, "Do you remember what we did at the greenhouse?"

"I can never forget."

Me too. "You asked me if what you did to me was right, and I said it could never be wrong if it feels good."

"Yes."

"Let me show you another way. It can also feel good."

Zuraya almost jumps with anticipation. She has a lustful smile on her face. She tries to reach for me when I sit up, but I stop her. She can touch me as much as she wants after I get us into position.

Woe in Total Darkness

I cross our legs and move my body closer to hers. Closer and closer until our centers meet, and I can feel her wetness against mine. The sight of her spread out for me to please fuels me. I roll my hips and rub myself onto her once to show her what we are doing.

"Oh," Raya moans. Then she experimentally mimics my movement. Her back arches and her hips move as she desperately tries to ride me. I also move and end her suffering. "You feel so good," she cries.

I pull one perfect leg over my shoulder to move better and keep rubbing her. I always liked this position, but with Zuraya, it feels even better. Her desperation, her voice, her want all work like a charm on me.

I want to cover her all over with my release.

I move harder, and our sensitive parts rub together. Raya moans so sweetly, and her body moves like she cannot get enough of me.

"Do you want to come, Darling?" I ask. "Do you want to come all over my cunt?"

A pained sound escapes her. "Len. You are killing me!"

"No, I am not." *I am just loving you.*

As our movements become more desperate, I ride her harder and faster. Her nails are digging into my legs. One of my hands is over her stomach controlling her movements, and the other is holding the leg on my shoulder. I kiss her ankle, and I bite down on her calf.

The room is filled with our moans and the wet sounds of skin rubbing against skin. I feel like even that can make me come. I don't even have to try hard when I am with Raya.

"I want you all over me," Raya says, her body trembling a little. I can tell she is way too close. "Len, please come with me."

"I am close, Darling," I inform.

We move like mindless animals, only focused on breeding. Raya's legs flex, and her body shakes. "Yes," she moans. "Fuck!"

She looks so fucking hot coming that it doesn't take long for me to follow. I throw my head back and scream her name. We come together. Our releases mix, and I cannot help but feel like she is always going to be mine.

I lean down over her and kiss her lips when I can breathe again. I never want to end this. "Raya, that was..." I don't even know what words can describe how good it felt.

"I know," Zuraya whispers. "I know."

I pull back to look at her, and she has tears in her eyes. She cups my face and looks straight into my soul. "Len, I think I..." she starts and swallows. "I..."

I don't let her continue. I kiss her lips. Slow but enough to make her stop.

"Don't," I whisper, even if it gives me so much pain because I know what she is going to say. I knew it was there when I came back from the border, but right now, as we lay in this bed with our naked bodies tangled together, I can feel it even more. I know exactly what she is going to say.

And I can't let her do that. The only thing worse than letting her say those words would be saying them back to her.

It doesn't matter if it is real or not.

We. Can. Not. Do. This.

I roll us over to our sides and kiss her slowly for a long time. I am almost trying to make her forget. But she doesn't. I pull back when I feel a tear reach our lips. She looks so sad that my heart breaks into a million pieces. I don't want to do this to her, but the alternative is worse. "I am sorry," is all I can utter.

Zuraya bushes away another tear and shakes her head. "It is okay." Only she doesn't look okay at all. "Just remember that you are not the braver one between us. You might be the General of the Sun Army, the Lightbringer. You might put your life at risk for others every day, but I am the brave one because I can say those words without fear. I can say them so easily. You are the one that is afraid."

My vision turns a little blurry with her words because it is all true. I am the one that is afraid. I am the reason for our end. "I am sorry," I say again. I kiss her briefly.

"It is okay," she assures me again and kisses me back. "It was only supposed to be sex after all."

But it became so much more than that.

I don't want to ever let her go, but I cannot hurt her further. "Do you want to leave?" I ask. "I won't blame you."

She looks hurt. "Do you want me to leave?"

I shake my head vigorously. "No. Never."

"Good," she smiles. It is a sad smile but a smile, after all. "Because I want to have you as long as I can. In this bed, we can act like we are free."

I smile back and kiss her. "Let's pretend we are free then."

41

Zuraya

I wait silently in the antechamber of my father's quarters. This is the first time he requested to see me after I have been rescued. I feel nervous as I can be.

I also feel weird because sitting here motionless makes me focus on how sore my body is from last night. The sensation makes me flustered, but I cannot blush.

This morning when my maids came into Lenora's room to ask for me because my father had called, I almost tripped over my own foot. I was not planning to leave her bed for a while but I had to. After kissing Lenora one last time, I returned to my chambers and found the most modest dress so no marks from last night would be visible to my dad. It would be difficult to explain, no doubt.

Thankfully the panic of being called by my father helped with the sad aftermath of yesterday. After Lenora stopped my confession, I didn't bring it up again. We just had sex, ate on the bed, and laughed all day and all night long. It was amazing.

So, knowing I cannot have it forever hurts more than anything.

I try not to think about it as I sit here. I focus on why my father might have wanted to see me. It causes a lot of stress, and stress suppresses my woe. Sounds pathetic but actually works nicely.

Woe in Total Darkness

When the door to my father's office opens, I immediately stand up. He looks as powerful as always. He is wearing a perfectly tailored blue tunic and pants. He has heavy necklaces full of stones, and just as I remember, he has only two piercings on his face, one on his right eyebrow and one on the left side of his nose. His braids are shorter than mine but still long enough for him to tie them on the back of his neck. His eyes are the same vibrant color as mine, and he has sharp features. Despite his age, he looks powerful. His expression is approachable but still holds a hardness.

I kneel to the floor as a courtesy. "Your Majesty."

"You can get up, Zuraya." He goes to the seat that almost resembles his throne. "And I am your father. You can address me as that."

I exhale and get up to sit on a seat facing him. "Thank you, dad," I say. His words relax some of my nerves, but I know my dad. I know his affection can disappear just as quickly. I know nothing is a guarantee when it comes to King Luran Haliyes.

"How have you been?" he says like it is the most normal thing. "I haven't been able to see you recently. I was very busy. I believe you'll understand."

He has always been so polite and encouraged me to be as well. He doesn't point out uncomfortable topics directly. People have to understand it on their own.

And I do understand. My father can act like there is nothing wrong with me, with us. He can talk about our relationship like it is perfect, and really, the only reason he hasn't seen me lately is because of work. However I still know it is because in his eyes I was not worthy yet.

Now I must be. "I understand, dad. I was actually surprised to hear from you today as well."

"I managed to find some time and really wanted to see you," he says simply. "Now tell me about yourself. I heard your training with Lenora Mitharaus has been going well."

I nod. Even hearing her name does something to my insides. "Yes. Lenora has been very helpful throughout everything. We really grew into friends. Her help has been very effective."

345

"It has?" my father asks.

"Yes."

But he doesn't accept my answer. Instead, he just keeps looking at me acceptedly. I know he will not spell it out because it will make him look like he does not trust me. Instead, he wants me to know he will never trust just words.

So, I do what he wants from me. I reach into my heart and spread my Moonshine all over my skin. I glow and glow and glow until the room is bright with my light. All the while my father doesn't move a muscle. He just sits and looks at me. Only when I pull my power back at the end of my show, he gives a small nod. "I am happy she has been helpful."

"She has been." For some reason, I want him to know she is more than that. She is not just someone who helped me in exchange for my father's payment. "She also has been a great friend to me. I also spend time with Princess Maha, but Lenora is very special to me. I believe we will be able to keep our bond strong for the rest of our lives."

Something passes in my father's normally unimpressed eyes. "Moonshine and Sunshine heirs are always expected to have a special bond. Years ago, I had the same with Khan Güne. A friendship between rulers is beneficial, but we should never forget our priorities, Zuraya."

Something gets stuck to my throat. I am not sure if my father went through what I am going through, but his words fit perfectly with my situation.

We could love each other, but that should not interfere with our duties. We should not openly go against the ancient rules.

Two princesses with light in their veins, and we can only love each other in darkness.

What a tragedy.

Before I can even leave my sad trance, my father speaks again, "Do you have any other friends apart from Maha and Lenora?"

I look up, a little shaken, and shake my head. "I have been a little closed off. I don't interact with many." I also consider Hashim a friend, but I don't think mentioning that is going to make my father very happy.

Woe in Total Darkness

"That is no problem," he says, surprising me. "We will do your reveal at your name-day celebration. The court will get to see you for real altogether. It will be a great affair."

"Dad," I say with a horrified whisper. I am getting better, but I am not sure if I am ready for what he planned. I don't want to be thrust into a room full of curious eyes before I am ready.

My father acts like he doesn't hear my whisper or see my terrified face. Instead, he asks me, "Don't you consider Rionn Ay Ujk, a friend? I heard that you two spent a lot of time together."

My surprise kind of gets in the way of my terror. I have no idea why my father talks to me about Rionn. "Not a lot of time," I answer him truthfully. I haven't seen him nearly as much as I see Lenora or even Maha. I can maybe call him a friend to entertain him despite my promise to Len, but first, I need to understand his intentions. Bringing him up is random.

"That doesn't sound right," he says, thinking to himself, but I know it is all a game. "I heard you two even spend some alone time in your chambers, more specifically in your bedroom."

What?

How can he know that?

I flush head to toe at his accusation because it is not even an accusation. I did spend alone time with Rionn. I let him into my bed. It doesn't matter if I had Lenora in my mind the whole time or if it was just one time. Whatever I'll say won't change the fact that my father thinks I am fucking Rionn on the regular.

The worst part is I have no idea what he thinks about it. He is very hard to read.

"It is not anything serious," I finally managed to say. I don't know what else I can say about that without telling my father how I am in love with Lenora Mitharaus.

His face remains calm. "Really? I thought it might be. I even hoped for it."

"Hoped?" I say with huge eyes. "So, you want me to be with Rionn?"

"As a father, it would please me to know my daughter has a happy marriage."

"Marriage?!" I think I am going to puke.

My father looks displeased with my outburst but doesn't answer me in an angry way. He is always calm but assertive. It makes it hard to argue, and his emotionless stance drives me even crazier if I ever argue with him.

"Zuraya," he starts calmly. "You have been gone for seven years, so I haven't been able to find you a good match for marriage. I couldn't fulfill my role as a father. Now that you are back and of marrying age, I need to do my best. I heard you were interested in Alpha Ay Ujk, and it gave me the idea. I believe he will be a great match for you, and he is also interested in this union."

"He is interested?" This shouldn't surprise me. I already know Rionn wants me, but I didn't think he would go as far as speaking to my father. I thought he wouldn't agree to a marriage, knowing my heart belongs to another.

Maybe I really don't know this, Rionn.

"Why did you speak to him before speaking to me?"

My father just shrugs. "I thought you were already interested."

"And if I am not?" *Please don't let me marry him. I don't love him.*

Maybe it is my imagination, but I see flames in my father's eyes. "I have chosen him to marry you, Zuraya," he says. "Are you saying no?"

I don't have a right to say no. I cannot go against him. I have to do everything to make him proud. I have to be his perfect little princess for the crumbs of his attention.

I cannot be happy and make my father proud at the same time.

I force a smile and answer my father, "Of course not. You know the best of everything."

"Splendid," he gives me a nod. A warm smile spread on his face. "I am only asking you to consider him. Maybe spend more time with him. People need to know we are looking for possible matches for you. If we don't get anyone better, we will announce an engagement between the two of you."

He has already made his decision, but he doesn't want it to look forced. He also wants to show everyone this great match.

Woe in Total Darkness

It is something to be proud of.

I have nothing to say but, "Surely."

This time he nods to himself and stands up from his seat. I follow. "I have some matters to attend to, Zuraya. You can go back to your training. Seeing you getting powerful really pleases me."

"Thank you, dad," I say, trying to sound cheery.

He comes close to me, presses a kiss to my forehead, and then disappears back into his office. Now it is time for me to leave with my broken heart and act like it doesn't hurt. I have to act like making my father proud is the most important thing in life. I have to act like whatever he says is always the right thing.

I have to act like my heart doesn't have a voice. I have to learn what it feels like to cry myself to sleep every night. I have to live a tragedy.

However I had enough tragedies for a lifetime.

I want Lenora as my priority, and King Luran cannot stop me.

42

Zuraya

I fumble with my fingers as I sit on my bed. I am sad and stressed, but I don't cry. It is hard to keep the tears back, but I manage. I need to be critical about this situation. I need to make a great plan.

Fortunately, I already did. I have sent word to Lenora about how I am not going to attend training today, and I am resting in my room. I know she is going to come here. She will be worried about me, or she will just want to scold me for missing training. She is going to come, though.

And when she does, I will tell her my plan. I know exactly what I want to do. I know what offer I will give her.

I don't know her answer, but I am trying to be hopeful. I cannot let us lose this.

I am not marrying Rionn or anybody else. If I ever marry, it is going to be with Lenora Mitharaus. I am ready to do anything for it. I have been to hell and back. Nothing scares me anymore but losing another person I love.

Just as I guessed, some while later, I hear voices outside my room, and my maid enters. "Your Highness, the General..." she only manages to say before I cut her off and say, "Let her in." I

Woe in Total Darkness

would tell them to always let Lenora enter my bedroom, but that might be suspicious.

If she says yes to my offer, we don't have to worry about that though.

Lenora comes into the room with a playful smirk and closes the door behind her. "I feel like a certain princess is trying to get into my head with great sex, so I won't make them train."

I smile back. "I hope it is not Maha."

"I don't want to be killed by Davon Archard."

I try to smile again, but I know I lack warmth. The haunted feeling around me doesn't let me fake being happy. I don't want to fake anything with Lenora anyway.

She sits next to me and cups my face. "Hey," she says and nudges my nose with hers. "What did he say?"

Because my father is the only thing that can sour my mood after the great night I shared with Len. I wish we could just go back. I wish we could stop the time so no one can interrupt us.

I wish Lenora and me were the only two people living on this earth.

"He said that he is proud of me for reaching my power. Now I am somewhat worthy in his eyes."

Lenora looks sad but doesn't let it consume her. "That is not bad."

"No," I shake my head. "It is not. But he also wants me to show myself to everyone at my name-day celebration."

She swallows hardly at the mention of my name-day. We both know that is the end of her agreement with my father. She doesn't need to stay after that.

I cannot let her leave.

"Are you ready for that?" she asks.

"I have to be." It could have been a big problem if I didn't have something much bigger.

"Darling," Lenora says affectionately and presses a kiss to my lips. "What is really bothering you? Let me help."

I take a deep breath. I cannot think of an easy way to say this. I just have to get over it. "My father decided I should marry soon."

"What?" she looks terrified.

"He even decided who my groom should be."

Lenora shakes her head. "It is too soon. You need time to gather yourself. You cannot marry. You have to tell him no. He cannot force you."

He can, but I don't point that out because Lenora knows it as well. She just doesn't want to accept it. Unfortunately, running away from reality never works. We need to take action if we want to be happy.

And I need to rile her up even more to consider my solution.

"Don't you want to know who it is?"

She pulls back and shakes her head. "I don't care who it is. I don't want to think of you marrying anyone. I knew it was bound to happen, but this is too soon. I don't know how to handle it."

"It is Rionn."

Lenora's eyes pop open, and she stands up in fury. All the jealousy I put away with assuring her I will not see him again comes back in full force. She really hates the thought of him with me. "He wants you to marry Rionn Ay Ujk?"

I nod. "I mean, he said he wants me to consider him as an option, but that means he already decided. I'll have to marry him."

She shakes her head. "You can't.

"I have to."

Lenora kneels at the end of the bed and holds my hands. She looks so desperate. I don't think I have ever seen her so helpless.

She looks into my eyes and whispers, "I can't breathe thinking of his hands all over you, Raya. You are mine."

Now tears sting my eyes. "I can never be anyone else's Len." I will forever belong to Lenora, body, mind, and soul.

"We can find a way around this," she murmurs, talking to herself. A moment later, her eyes come my way again. "He is just an option. If your father is so adamant about you marrying, we can find someone else. I'll help you. We can find someone who will be understanding. We can arrange a fake marriage for you. It will satisfy your father and the realm, but you won't be really married."

Woe in Total Darkness

All the hope inside me disappears. "Only I will be," I say. I don't want someone else. I want Lenora. "I don't want to be married to anyone."

"Maybe we can find a way to change your father's mind," she says, but her eyes make it apparent we both know that is not going to happen. If King Luran wants something, he will get it.

I look into Lenora's pretty face. Her golden eyes look sad and filled with tears, but she is still so beautiful. Her hair, her wings, her freckles, it is all perfect. I don't think I can stay alive if I don't ever touch her again. There are still too many things we haven't done, and I want all of them.

But we will never get them if we stay on Ae.

Without preparing her or myself, I blurt it out, "Leave with me."

Her eyebrows furrow in confusion. "What?"

"He cannot force me if I leave. We can leave together, Lenora. If we are not on the Isle, the ancient rules of this land won't affect us. We can escape from all of them. We can live the way we want." A tear escapes. "We can be free."

"Raya," she murmurs, looking lost for words. "Do you realize what you are asking of me?"

"I am asking you to be with me." *Isn't that what she wants? Why is she always so afraid to accept it?*

She stands up from the floor and starts pacing my room. "It is different than that, Raya," she mumbles. She looks more troubled than desperate now. She makes me feel like I had done something wrong when actually I just did what my heart desired.

Why is that so wrong?

"Where do we even go? This is our home."

I get a glimpse of hope at the question. I already thought about this. "We won't be accepted in the Mainlands as Feyadas, but we can go to the Continent. It is a place where different creatures can live together. We will be two nobodies. We can just build a life for ourselves."

Lenora doesn't look convinced at all. She shakes her head like nothing makes sense. "Leaving everything behind is much different than what we have been doing."

I shrug. "I don't care what I leave behind if I have you. I'll never love anyone or anything as much as I love you."

Lenora freezes on the spot. She looks up now, her eyes filled with plea. Her bottom lip trembles. "Don't say that," she whispers with a broken voice.

"Why?"

The question shatters all her composure. Lenora looks so broken, but her eyes remain on mine. A tear escapes and slides down her perfect cheek. "Because," she says, and her voice cracks. "Because I cannot leave with you."

Suddenly I can't breathe. "Why?"

This time she looks down like our connected gazes are too powerful for her to resist. "I have responsabilities, Raya. I have to stay here and fight back against the Darkness. I cannot let the people of Ae be consumed by the Curser. I cannot let them down."

"But you can let me down?" I ask angrily. "You cannot tell me that I am yours and then back off. You cannot be a coward anymore."

"I am not being a coward!" A vein on her neck looks ready to pop off.

I stand up, going nose to nose with her. She can say all she wants, but anything she cannot fight with her sword scares her. I know I want to push her. This is how everything started. Let this be the way everything ends as well.

"Tell me then," I force her. "Tell me you love me if you are not afraid."

"Don't do this to me, Raya."

"Okay," I accept. "Then tell me you don't love me. Tell me this was nothing more than just fucking for you so I can move on. Just tell me how worthless I was to you. Break my heart. Let me go."

She closes her eyes, and her facial muscles flex so forcefully. It is almost like she can make everything disappear if she doesn't see it long enough. But it is not enough. I know she can feel my body close; I know she can smell me.

Woe in Total Darkness

Lenora might not tell me the truth today, but I know she will never lie again.

And when she can't, I will know for sure that she loves me. She loves me, but she is not brave enough to go after it.

"I can't," she whispers after a long silence, and her eyes open. "I can't do it, Raya. I cannot leave while everybody counts on me. I can't give you what you want. I can't make this more complicated than it already is."

"I don't think that is possible." We are dreadfully tangled, and it cannot go farther than this. My head falls forward, and my throat burns. Her unwillingness punishes both of us.

"I am sorry," she says painfully.

I don't want to listen to that. "Leave," I say with a low voice. "Just leave me alone." *So I can live my pain in peace.*

Lenora doesn't fight me. She stays there for a moment, considering what to do, but then turns on her heels and leaves. She takes all my hopes and dreams with her.

I get into my bed, but I don't even cry; I just lay there motionless. I don't want to feel anything. I just want to disappear because a life without Lenora seems so dull.

43

Lenora

I can almost hear my joints squeak, even with the slightest movement. My bones ache painfully, and they stick to my muscles. It feels like I am bleeding inside my skin. Knives cut into me bone deep. I want to shred my skin. Same pain over and over every day.

It has nothing on the pain I feel in my chest, though.

Apparently, ripping off my own heart hurts more than any injury I have suffered. Since I left Raya's room, the ache hasn't decreased. I cannot take it.

This morning she came to the training, but she barely talked to me. She wanted to train with Hashim. The few times she spoke to me, she acted like I was a stranger. Like we were back at times we shared nothing.

She treated me like I was nothing to her. I know it is my fault, but it still hurts like hell.

"I can't leave," I whisper for the hundredth time. I press my forehead to my brother's cold tombstone. I wish he was here to help me. He is the only one here I can go to other than Raya, and she no longer wants me.

So the tomb was the only place I could come to. Maybe Qyron can help me with this mess. I need help. I stayed awake all night thinking about what I could do, but nothing came to my mind. I am just empty.

The logical solution would be to do nothing. I should just take the pain and let things stay as they are. Ending things with Raya was inevitable anyway. I should accept it. I should ignore the pain. I have been doing it my whole life.

But this time is fucking different. I cannot ignore the memories of her.

"Who is going to fight the darkness if I leave?" I ask Qyron. "Mom? King Luran? Who?" If I leave, it will mean leaving everybody on Ae to die. I cannot do that. I have always lived for others. I have been honest about my duties. I cannot change who I am just like that.

Would I still be the Lenora she fell in love with if I let everyone die at the end of the curse?

"Tell me what to do?" I plea to my non-existing brother. I even sign at the same time in case his ghost is here and unable to read my lips. I just need him.

I always need him.

Qyron's ghost doesn't send me a sign or anything, but I know my brother. I know what he would say if he was here. He would ask me why I was here with him instead of getting my girl back. I can only fix this by talking to Zuraya.

And honestly, I did try that. After the training, I spent some time hating myself but, in the end, decided to see her. I went to her room without knowing what I was going to say. I just wanted to talk to her. I wanted us to find a middle ground. I believed we could fix this if we had just talked.

But she was not in her room. Her chambermaids told me that she is out with Rionn. That's when my blood boiled with jealousy and anger, and I stormed into Qyron's grave. I didn't know where else I could go to.

I wish he was here.

If he was here, he would help me get her back. He would be happy about our relationship. He would do anything for us to be together. Maybe he would have talked mother into fighting the Darkness herself so I could actually go with Raya.

357

Oh, how much I want to go with her. Living somewhere we can be freely together, somewhere it is not forbidden to love her.

But I can't let people who believe in me down. I cannot let the Curser win.

She wants to know if I love her. She has no idea what will happen if I say those words. She has no idea what hearing them from her lips did to me.

She. Does. Not. Know.

And now she is with Rionn. She is going to fucking marry him.

Thinking about Rionn touching Raya makes my skin crawl. I don't want him near her. I don't want her to be with anyone but me. I cannot breathe, knowing she is going to kiss him, smile for him, and moan because of him.

It is going to kill me.

"Don't be a fool," Qyron's voice echo inside my head. "Go get your girl."

I know he is right. I know I cannot let Rionn win. I don't care that she is with him. She is going to come with me. She cannot treat me like nothing when I have learned her whole body with my lips. She cannot ignore me after telling me she loves me.

She is mine.

And she will never be anyone else's.

I storm out of the tomb and move to the gardens. I have no idea where they are, but I can walk until I find them. I don't think she is going to want to go somewhere too private with him, so they must be in the gardens. During midday, the palace is crowded everywhere, and Raya will also not like that. I can find them in a more secluded part of the gardens but not too secluded.

It shouldn't be too hard.

I do walk around a bit, but when I see a Shifter standing watch, I know I found them. I walk towards his direction, but he steps in front of me. "You cannot pass. Alpha has private company."

My hands turn into fists, but I force them to stay at my sides. "Do you know who I am?" I ask.

Shifter nods. "I do."

Woe in Total Darkness

I reach into my power and make his mind think he cannot move his limbs and walk, "Then you know you shouldn't say no to me." Paralyzing him works well because he doesn't stop me, and I don't need to beat the shit out of him.

After just a few more steps, I see them and freeze. My heart stops at the sight. They are sitting on a bench and smiling. I know that smile on Raya's face. It is not just a polite princess smile. He said something funny, made a joke, he made her laugh. This smile is just the remanent of that.

I should be happy that he made her laugh. I should be glad she is going to have a happy life with Rionn when I have to leave eventually.

But I can't.

Rionn looks at her with adoring eyes. He looks at her like she is the shiniest thing he has ever seen.

He looks at her like I look at her.

Like he loves her.

But no one can love Zuraya the way I do. No one deserves her more than I do. I cannot let anyone have her.

My heart defeats my logic, and I quickly make my way over there. "Zuraya," I call out.

They both turn to me, but I have only eyes for her. She looks surprised, but I don't miss her small, satisfied expression. "Len," she mumbles.

"Can we talk?"

Rionn interrupts, "We are kind of in the middle of a rendezvous."

Oh, I want to snap his neck so bad, but I keep my focus on Zuraya. "Come with me," I whisper. "Please."

She bites down her bottom lip and nods. Then turns to Rionn. "Thank you for this day, Rionn. It was lovely."

"Are you really leaving," he asks, not surprised but mad.

Raya nods. "I cannot let Lenora go."

Those words fill my chest with butterflies, and I want to peel her off of that bench. Thankfully she rises without letting Rionn say anything else. She holds my hand, and I immediately pull her after me.

I take her to one of the cracks I discovered in the palace's outer walls. It is small but almost entirely invisible to the outside. Someone can still walk too close from the right side and see us, but at this moment, I care about nothing. My brain doesn't work. My heart controls my body.

So, I slam Raya to the wall and kiss her.

She kisses me back. Our hands are everywhere. Our lips hard and angry. Intensity comes from the little time we lost. We are dying just because we could not touch each other for a day.

It makes it apparent that somehow Zuraya Haliyes became as essential to my life as the air I breathe. So, I breathe *her* in.

But then I push her back because I am sad and desperate and also mad. I press her to the wall with my body, but our faces remain apart. I look down at her with fire in my veins. I cannot take the image of her smiling at Rionn out of my mind.

Raya rises to kiss me again, but I pull back. I wrap her braids around my hand and position her head. "Why were you with him?"

A sinister smile appears. "I was getting to know my future husband."

"Don't," I pull her hair hard. "I can't fucking stand seeing you smile at him. Your smiles should be only for me. I want it all to myself."

"You're jealous," she says smugly.

I hate that she has so much power over me. She can manipulate me so easily. I hold her waist and turn her around. My body is still pressing onto her, but now her cheek is also flushed with the wall. "I am jealous, and I am angry," I say into her ear.

I want to kiss her, cuddle her, and love her, but I also hate her. I hate her for messing up with my head. I want to hurt her.

For making me obsessed with her.

For making me break the rules.

And most importantly, for smiling at Rionn.

"You are mine, Raya," I hiss. "Only mine."

Woe in Total Darkness

She arches her back against me. "I thought I was not anymore."

My hand tightens on her hair, and I bite down her naked shoulder. "You'll always be mine. I will always turn murderous when I see you with someone else. Especially after you promised to not see them."

Raya doesn't mention how everything about Rionn changed after our talk yesterday. She doesn't tell me I shouldn't touch her after our argument. Instead, she plays into what I want. "Do you want to punish me, Len?"

Fuck. "So much."

"Then do it," she taunts me arching more.

I clasp her neck with one hand and reach for her skirt with the other. It is a pretty glitter thing, and I hate that she wore this for Rionn. I gather the fabric up on her waist and secure it between our flushed bodies so her bottom is entirely bare to me.

I grab a fistful of that glorious backside. "Why were you with him?"

"I wanted to make you jealous," she says, and I slap her. Zuraya loses her breath with the impact. "Fuck."

She has to take one for everything she has done. "You love to push me, don't you?" I nibble her neck. "Why do you always have to push me, Raya?"

I can see a little smile on her face. "Because you need pushing." When I slap her taunting flesh again, her smile only grows. She is just full-on grinning.

"Fuck, Raya, this was supposed to be a punishment."

"And it is a good one."

I shake my head close to hers. "This just makes you wet, doesn't it?" I don't wait for an answer and instead reach between her legs and find her soaked. This time I slap her sex, and she shrieks. "So naughty, Raya."

"Everything you do makes me wet," she admits.

"Maybe I should leave you like this then," I say, but my hands again move between her legs. I start rubbing her softly. "I should leave you all wet and aching."

She moans when my fingers move to her entrance. "No," she begs. Her body tries to move against me, but I hold her steady.

"Why?" I fill her with two fingers. She is tight and warm around me. I almost moan too. "Tell me a reason why I shouldn't stop?" I ask and start fucking her, hitting that sweet spot inside her with every thrust.

Raya cries out against the wall. Sweat gathers on her neck and her back, and her sweet cunt gets slicker around my fingers. Maybe it is the situation or the position, but for some reason, she is dangerously close to her climax. More than she has ever been.

"Tell me!" I say again.

She moans and writhes but, this time, answers, "Because then I'll find someone else to finish it."

Fuck this.

I know she is only doing it to push me more. She just wants me jealous. Unfortunately, it fucking works. I don't want to imagine Rionn in my position. I don't want to think anyone seeing her like this.

She is mine.

"Who you'll find?" I ask angrily and start fucking her harder. Wet sounds of her sex fill the air. "Rionn?" I taunt her mockingly. "Do you think Rionn can touch you the way I do?"

She doesn't answer. Her legs tremble. I catch one leg under the knee so she can stay upright; in this position, my fingers can go even deeper. She presses her hands against the wall to steady herself.

"He cannot, Raya," I whisper against her skin. "He cannot kiss you like I do. He cannot fuck you like I do. He cannot make you come as hard as I can." Raya's cunt tightens around me, and I whisper one last sentence, "He cannot *love* you like I do."

And she comes all over me.

I let her ride it out. When she is breathless and shaky, I put her leg back down on the ground but wrap my arms around her waist to keep her upright. I kiss her shoulder, her neck, and her cheek.

Raya's eyes slowly open, and she looks at me with amazement. "You love me?"

"You already knew I did."

She shakes her head and turns in my arms. "Say it again," she says with a small voice.

I smile. "I love you, Raya."

She smiles back. "And again?"

"I love you."

"Again."

"I love you," I murmur against her lips. She kisses me. This time it is tender and emotional. It is loving.

When she breaks the kiss, the back of my eyes burn because this is all I can give her. I cannot tell her that I will leave with her. I cannot give her anything but my heart.

"I love you," I say again. "I can't act like I don't, but I don't know what to do, Raya."

She cups my cheek, silver lines her beautiful eyes. Her throat moves up and down, and finally, she whispers, "Take me to your room. That is enough for now."

So, I do just that. I want everything I can take.

44

Zuraya

I jump on the bed, looking excitedly at the tray Lenora is carrying. "Oh, food," I moan happily. I am so hungry.

After Lenora took me to her room, we had a few more sessions of love-making. I can proudly call it that now. It is not just sex anymore. We are making love. Lenora is in love with me.

Even the thought creates butterflies in my belly.

I know she didn't say anything about my offer. I know she is still not leaving with me. I am also aware I need to ask her about that. We should talk about the future, but when Lenora told me she didn't know what to do, I knew this was not the time.

There was no way for me to walk away from her after she confessed her love for me. I wanted it so much that I didn't want to ruin it.

I don't want to ruin it now. I just want a glimpse of peace.

I can live in her bed forever. She is taking good care of me, after all. I don't even know how many times I came today. I just know when I was a limbless mess, Lenora decided to stop, kissed my lips, and went to get us food. She also told me she was going to wash me when we were done, but I still have no idea when we will actually be done. I cannot get enough of her.

Woe in Total Darkness

Lenora sits down on the bed after putting the tray down. She is now wearing her pants and shirt again, and I hate it. I am also covered with an orange robe she handed me, so I don't feel weird next to her, but honestly, I would have preferred for both of us to be naked. I just love her body.

To distract myself from Lenora, I look down at the food. Oh, Tisasa, we have everything. My mouth waters. "We even have star-onion!"

Lenora smiles and reaches for a berry. "I had to make it princess worthy."

"They only grow in the Seelie Kingdom. We don't get them much in here." I reach for one and bite down the small fruit. Flavors pop inside my mouth instantly. I still think calling this fruit onion is a horrible idea. It is a sweet-savory fruit that is definitely delicious, but since it is also layered like onion and white, it is called star-onion. The star part comes from the star-shaped seed in the middle.

Lenora looks way too happy about my satisfied face. "Do you like it?" she asks with a smirk.

I nod while biting another piece. After I swallow it, the flavor still stays in my mouth. I lean over the tray towards Lenora. "Want a taste?"

Her joking nature changes into worry, and she pulls back. "No, no, don't kiss me like that."

My brows furrow. "You don't like it?" It is not possible this is the best fruit in the entire world.

She shakes her head. "I am allergic. If you kiss me with that in your mouth, I'll just go off," she makes a gesture to the floor with her hand.

My eyes bulge out. "You'll die?" Now I want to throw away all of them. I don't want something that can kill her so close to her. The thought that Lenora can die so easily is alarming.

To my relief, she shakes her head again. "I'll faint. I mean, I guess it is not exactly an allergy. It is special to star-onion. It can affect some people strongly and put them into a long sleep. I am one that can get affected."

That doesn't sound so horrible. "How long of a sleep?"

Lenora shrugs. "I don't know. Forever?"

I resist the urge to spit all the flavor out. Star-onion can be divine, but it has nothing on Lenora. "I am washing my mouth and never eating this again."

"You can eat it, Zuraya."

I shake my head vigorously. "I am not eating something that is going to stop me from kissing you." Kissing Lenora is more important than any food.

"Well, if you want to," she says. "I don't like things that stop me from kissing you too."

I smile naughtily. "Because you love me?"

She gets a heated look and leans over the tray to press a kiss against my collarbone. "Because I love you," she whispers into the skin.

I think I will never get tired of hearing her say that.

———— (————

After dinner, I am half lying on top of Lenora. We are too tired from our previous love-making and too stuffed from all the food we ate. It is okay, though. I like being lazy with her like this. I love talking to her, and I also love just staying silent.

I slowly peel open her shirt, just to look at her tattoos. Her naked breasts come into view, and my breath hitches a bit like it does every time. I touch the sun on her throat and slowly trace it. My fingers work all over the golden lines, going down and down.

She is mostly bare around the chest. There are no golden lines on her breasts. They continue from the skin under them. I drag my finger over the valley between her breasts. She takes a deep breath, and I smile at her reaction.

I look up without moving my finger away. "Tattoo on here would look good. Why is it empty?"

"All my tattoos have meanings, you know that, right? Both the placement and the design represent something about my life, about me. It is tradition."

Woe in Total Darkness

I nod. I know Sunfolk and their tattoos. I once thought it was kind of like our piercings, but piercings usually don't have very deep meanings. I know tattoos are almost sacred to Sunfolk. Not all of them have it. Qyron didn't have any. Although I realized all of the Sun Soldiers here do. It must be more common among them.

Still, I want to know why that spot is empty. "What a tattoo on here would mean?"

Lenora's eyes trace my face, and then she answers, "It is the heart spot. Most fill that out when they get married."

A lump gets stuck in my throat. If there is anything worse than imagining Lenora getting married, it is her getting a tattoo for a partner. Now I am jealous of a non-existent person. "Are you going to fill it when you get married, too?"

"No." She doesn't even hesitate. "It should represent love. I am actually thinking of filling it in the first chance I'll get. No need to wait."

My heart fills with warm light.

A grin stretches my lips. No matter what happens, I like the idea of her carrying me on her body. I don't think I can bear anyone filling that spot. It should be me.

Because she is mine as much as I am hers.

I pull myself up and attack her lips. "I love you," I murmur between aggressive licks. "You'll always be mine."

"Always," she answers and kisses me more gently. "Until my body dissolves into the mud and my soul is taken by Tisasa, I will belong to you, and after that, my soul will find yours so I can belong to you again."

Damn me. I am so in love with her.

———— (————

I sit on the bed with my back against the headboard, snacking on the leftover strawberries. Lenora is in my arms, her head is on my shoulder, her wings sprawled around us, and her naked body is covered in a sheen coat of sweat. She is taller than me, but when we lay down, she fits into my arms perfectly. I play with her golden locks with my free hand.

If I could stop time, this would be the perfect moment to do so.

I look around her room as she just relaxes. She might even be half asleep. I don't want to let her go, but I am also curious about her room. A fast look-out makes me think there are not many secrets here, though. It is not her real room anyway.

I should find a way to snoop into her room back in the desert.

Finally, my eyes fall onto a book at her bedside table. I reach with a hand and take it. It has a black cover, and it looks ancient. I cannot even read the name. It is both old and not very well taken care of.

"What is this book?" I ask.

Lenora moves her head, and I hold it to her so she can see. "The book Maha gave me," she says, sounding a little sleepy. "This is where I read about mind capturing and body capturing."

"Is this a forbidden book?" Those talents are definitely forbidden by the ancient rules.

She shakes her head and positions herself so she can look at me. "It is a history book, but it is pretty worn out. There are ripped pages and some other pages that are completely unreadable. I am trying to get the most I can, though. I was hoping it could help me find the Curser, actually."

"And did you?" I casually open the book and look at the pages. It really looks bad. There are pages that are still readable, but even they are not in perfect condition. If Maha has this version, though, this must be the only copy of this.

She tenses a bit, but I soothe her with a hand on her head. "Well, finding out about mind capturing kind of helped but not really. I also got to learn how crazy Vaughn Mitharaus was about having babies. It leads to some theories."

"Like what?" This is the first time I am hearing about it. I try not to get hurt since they are just theories, and she might not want to talk to me about the Curser for fear of triggering me.

Lenora really settles in my embrace. "Vaughn realized the sun power was decreasing with every child. He said that every child was

Woe in Total Darkness

weaker than the one before, but I also read it was not exactly a weaker situation but different. They would be good at fewer things, maybe, but they could be really good at that one thing. It is a bit different than what we have been taught. He also realized only the heir could pass the powers to their children, just like we know now, but I think he might have been wrong about that. He was the only one who had many children. Every Mitharaus or Haliyes after that has at most three children, and that is just one occasion. We don't have much knowledge about the lineage. I believe it could be passed, but maybe it stays hidden for years. Maybe it shows in a different way than we are used to. That makes me think the Curser must be coming from Mitharaus bloodline, and that's how he captured your mind. That could also be the reason for his Darkness power."

Now I am not sure if I was better off not knowing. "So you believe this is all made by one person. You don't believe this is a curse from Tisasa?"

She shrugs. "I am not sure of anything. That is just a theory. I am working on it."

I nod and absently keep playing with her hair. I can tell the topic makes her nervous. Her theory kind of makes sense, but it also has some blank spots. I don't know if I truly believe that. I also don't want to sour her mood.

I don't want to ruin our nice time together.

I ask, "Does it have anything else you didn't know already? Unrelated to the Curser."

Her body relaxes a bit. Then she easily nods. "It is actually a book about how we stole Tisasa's powers, but it also has information about what happened before and after that. The main story is the same, but the narration is different from our resources. It also has a lot of additional information." She pauses for a few seconds. "I even got to learn why there is an ancient rule against a Haliyes and a Mitharaus being together."

That gets my full attention. We grow up learning the ancient rules, but so very rarely do we actually learn the reason behind them. They expect us to just accept them without question. I did my whole life until there was a rule I could not abide by.

Sem Thornwood

"Tell me," I say excitedly. Maybe it will help us figure something out. If a rule has been made, it can certainly be changed under the right circumstances.

"Well, they were planning a wedding between the two heirs but then realized the power must go to the oldest child. Haliyes and Mitharaus child was recondite. They didn't want to mix the powers."

That doesn't make sense to me. "Wouldn't a kid like that would be just more powerful?"

She shrugs. "I guess they just didn't want to risk it. So they made the rule."

I straighten, and Lenora has to turn her head towards me. I feel so angry. "And now we have to pay for it because they didn't want to risk it? It doesn't make any sense. We cannot even have kids together."

Lenora sits up, and I instantly miss the warmth of her body, but she makes it up by holding my hands. "Well, we have to have heirs somehow."

My stomach turns thinking about that. I feel so jealous thinking of Lenora sleeping with someone else to have a child. I also feel disgusted by the thought of letting a guy put a child in me. I didn't find it so disgusting before I was rescued, but now I really do. I am even repulsed by the idea of them touching me.

I shake my head in denial. "I don't want that. I want you."

She stays silent for a second but then takes a deep breath. "My healer back in the Desert, Andy, is very interested in modern medicine magic. She once told me there are healers – mostly witches – who put babies inside females. They get pregnant without having sex with a male. She told me it was getting more common."

The thought appeals to me. I have never been a big fan of kids, but if I need an heir, I will birth a child that way. I will do anything as long as it will help me be with Lenora. Hope brings tears to my eyes. "Do you think it will be common enough to exist in the Isle?"

Lenora looks sad for a second but then smiles. "It is common in the Continent. I am sure if Andy can go there with a group for a while, they can learn how to do that. Maybe it can be real, Zuraya."

Woe in Total Darkness

"And we will end an ancient rule." I know it is no easy thing. I know it is not likely, but I want to hope. I deserve a little moment of hope.

Tears also fill Lenora's eyes. "Maybe we will," she says softly. "What we are doing is wrong, but maybe we can convince them it is not."

I get close and cup her face. Our faces are so close our noses almost touch. "When we first had sex, you told me if something feels good, it cannot be wrong," I say as a tear rolls down my cheek. "And loving you feels so good."

45

Lenora

"Your Majesty," I say with a nod once I am in King Luran's quarters. I hate that every time he asks for Zuraya or me, he manages to ruin our bliss. We are managing to be blindly happy about our current situation. We are trying to hope for the unthinkable.

King Luran never fails to remind us about our realities.

"Welcome, Lenora. How are you this morning?" He must be cheery since he is using my first name like we are old friends. Usually, he calls me General or Princess just to piss me off. Right now, he seems to be in a good mood, and for some reason, that makes me alert more than his anger.

Still, I give him a friendly smile. "I am very well, thank you. I hope you are doing okay as well. I was surprised that you requested me so early."

His eyebrows come together. "Really? I thought you would have pieced it together easily."

Well, now I feel stupid, but I keep my face calm. "I haven't," I answer.

Woe in Total Darkness

"Zuraya's name-day," the King says. "It is next week. I am considering a three-day affair. The whole court will be able to see their princess."

I get a little uneasy because I know it still makes Zuraya uncomfortable. She is not ready to face the whole court, but she will not say not to her father. "Did you call for me to talk about the name-day ball?"

"Of course not." Now he really looks confused. "Zuraya will finally show herself as the princess she is. She has physical shortcomings, but from what I heard, her power is extreme. She will be able to earn their loyalty that way, and that is all thanks to you, Lenora. You kept your side of the bargain. You made her the Moon Princess again from a useless limp body."

I hate how he talks about his daughter. I hate that he talks like I put a spell on Zuraya to be perfect. She was already perfect; she just needed time and someone to believe in her. I wish he could see her for her.

Not the Moon Princess but just Zuraya.

He speaks before I can even consider voicing those thoughts. "Now it is time for me to keep my end of the promise."

I stay straighter as the King goes to the other side of the room and opens a large chest. When I step closer, I can peek inside and see that it is filled with moon spheres. The reason why I did all this. The reason I agreed to help Zuraya. My great prize.

It doesn't feel great at all.

On the contrary, it feels sad because I know what they mean. They bring me to reality even better than King Luran's call. They remind me how I can never ever be with Raya.

I take a deep breath and wear a mask of myself I used to be before Zuraya. I act like moon spheres are the only thing I care about in life and ask, "Is this all?" all the while eyeing the other chest stacked together.

He opens another chest, and it is also filled to the brim. "I couldn't fit them all into my room, but I have made 200 moon spheres for you just like we agreed. You can take them now so you will have time to count."

Something sticks in my throat. "Now?"

"Yes," he nods. "I believe you will stay for the name-day to support Zuraya, but I cannot force you any longer after that. I also won't stop you if you want to leave before the celebration, but as the Moon Court, we will be happy to have you."

"I will stay for the name-day," I say quickly. I wish I can stay for much longer.

King Luran grins. "Perfect! You won't regret it. I am sure the celebration will be subject to many great moments."

That sounds like a weird way to put it. "What do you mean by that?" Surely he wants to make the celebration memorable, but he must have other plans too, if he said it like that.

Unsurprisingly his smile turns a little sinister, not much but enough for me to understand. "I mean, there might be new developments that will cause more celebrations in the near future. We would be happy to see you join us in those as well, General."

I cannot focus on his words. I cannot comprehend what celebrations he might be referring to. His words are not making sense.

Until they do.

My mouth goes dry, the back of my eyes burn, and my chest feels too tight for a deep breath. I want to disappear so I don't have to say those words. "You are really making her marry Rionn."

And he is planning it to be even earlier than I anticipated. He probably wants him to ask her during the name-day, and she is going to have to say yes. She cannot gather the courage to say no when she knows I can never leave with her.

Zuraya knows I have to obey my duties, and she is going to do the same.

I can't breathe.

"He is a great choice for her," he says easily.

I want to scream, *No, I am a great choice for her.* But all I can say is, "I don't think so."

The King looks offended, but I don't care. "Their union will be beneficial for both sides. Zuraya is the best bride Rionn Ay Ujk can ever find. The marriage will unite Feyadas and Shifters. We will be able to protect our land from the Shifter threat that has

Woe in Total Darkness

always been a problem. This way, Zuraya can still rule over them and be untouchable because of her husband."

Politics. He is only thinking about politics. I wouldn't have had a problem with this four months ago. I would think this was a fantastic idea if I had never met Raya.

But now it is different.

Marriage cannot be only about politics. It should be about love.

"Have you considered maybe she is not ready?" I ask, trying to control my fast-beating heart. I cannot let him see how my breath is shaking. "She is better with her powers and about social situations, but still, it has not been enough time since her rescue. She is still struggling. You cannot throw her into a marriage you decided."

Now he doesn't have his cheery expression. He looks petty. He looks ready to destroy me for daring to utter these words. He bends a little forward and asks, "Could the reason you are so against this marriage be your relationship with the Alpha?"

"I don't have a relationship with the Alpha," I answer quickly, but that is too quick and too stupid. I should have just acted clueless. Denial shows guilt. He is taking over me so easily and it is concerning.

"Lenora," he murmurs with disappointment. That is a tone I am very familiar with, thanks to my mom. "I might seem passive and behind the shadows, but I am still the King. This is my palace, and I know everything that is happening in it. I know how you and Rionn Ay Ujk frequently visited each other's rooms overnight."

"If you know everything so well, then you must know those visits ended a while ago. My opposition to this marriage has nothing to do with my own personal feelings towards Rionn."

His eyes turn into slits, and he looks like a snake ready to attack. "I also know who else has been visiting your room recently, General."

My blood turns cold. I have never considered him finding out about Zuraya staying in my room. I also thought if he ever found out, he wouldn't dare think what was really happening there.

I have been careless.

"She sometimes has nightmares. She doesn't like sleeping alone." It is a pathetic attempt at a lie. If Luran decides to bring this up, he already knows what is going on.

"You know, Lenora, some think just because we are royalty, we must be gods or monsters. They don't believe we can feel, but even royals have hearts," he says, looking terrifyingly sympathetic all of a sudden. "We can have desires of our own, but the difference between the commoners and us is that we should keep those desires hidden. They can only be fun little secrets. We live for our duties."

I don't want to hear these. I just want to storm off and act like he has never told me any of them. When I started sleeping with Zuraya, I thought if we were ever found out, it would be our downfall. I expected Luran to be angry. I thought I would get a punishment.

Instead, he wants me to just suppress it, and it hurts more.

I don't want Zuraya to be a fun little secret.

"Maybe things can be changed," I say almost in a whisper. I can feel the tears forming.

My love for her should count for something.

Our love should matter.

King Luran looks sad, and I already know I am not going to like his answer. "You have to be brave to change things, Lenora. It is a strength I have never possessed, but some might. Are you really willing to let your responsibilities go to have her? Can you choose love over duty?"

My vision turns blurry. My breaths are tight.

I know what he is trying to do. He is giving me a reality check, a wake-up call before it is too late.

"I don't know," I answer quickly. I can't breathe. I don't even wait for an answer; I just turn on my heels and get out of the room as quickly as I can.

I don't want his fucking reality check. I want to be delusional. I want to believe I can actually have Zuraya.

At least until I can no longer.

46

Zuraya

"Does it feel comfortable, Your Highness?" one of my chambermaids asks as she works fixing up my dress with two others. I think it looks good, and the skirt will mess up when I walk anyway, but they insist on making it perfect.

"Yes, it is okay," I answer. My seamstress put this dress together very quickly, just like the other two dresses I am assigned to wear during my name-day celebrations. Everything about today is making me nervous, but my father pressured me into acting like it doesn't.

Honestly, the dress is beautiful. It is white with a tight corset bodice and a huge skirt. My sleeves are also a little puffy, and I enjoy that too. The back is completely covered upon my request.

The dress shines with blue and pink hues when I move. I also have blue crystals all over. There are rings on all of my fingers, and I even changed the hoops on my face with ones that had blue crystals. Those also decorate the silver tiara positioned between my horns. One of my maids even shined the metal on the tip of one horn.

They made sure I look like the perfect princess.

I wish I could also feel like it.

I wanted Lenora to be here while I was getting ready. I wanted her to escort me to the ball. I requested this specifically from my father, but he declined. He said I should be alone so I could focus better. He said I should get into the ballroom alone so everyone could focus solely on me.

That is the last thing *I* want.

Lenora told me my father gave her the moon spheres. She didn't need to remind me she was going to leave after my name-day. We still decided to ignore all the facts. I didn't ask her anything, and she didn't reply. We just spend our precious time together. That's why I wanted her here today as well. I want her close to me as much as possible.

What we are doing might not be very smart, but I don't think the alternative is going to make any of us happy.

So, we go like this, and now that she is not here, I am more nervous than ever. I don't want to face the whole court all by myself. My only consolation is that she is going to be in that ballroom waiting for me.

"Look at me," she said when I told her how worried I was. "Just look at me and act like it is only the two of us."

I prep myself to do that, but I would have preferred if it could only be the two of us for real. I look magnificent in this dress, but the only one I care for to see me like this is Lenora. When I get too nervous, I try to focus on how she is going to strip me off of this dress at the end of the night.

It is good to focus on the positive.

"You are all done," a chambermaid says.

I take a deep breath, worry filling me all over again. "I suppose it is time to go."

She nods. "Everybody is waiting for you, Princess."

That doesn't help even a bit, but I mask it and move toward my door. I exit the room and cross the mostly empty hallways. Almost everybody is in the ballroom waiting for me. I encounter a few people, and they do look at me. Tonight is for everyone to look at me.

I manage to disregard their eyes. They are only a few people, after all. The problem starts when I come to the door of the ballroom. My body freezes over, and I cannot move. I can hear the music and people chatting. I know this ballroom. I know how many people are inside.

I don't want them to look at me. I don't want them to see how much I lost. The last thing I want to see is their pity, mixed with their disapproval.

I am an heir who is afraid of her own subjects. I wish I was like Lenora. She doesn't just look perfect, but she is actually perfect. Her people love and respect her. Everybody is aware of how much she is capable of.

That is not me.

"Princess," the guard closes to me, clears his throat, and my terrified eyes turn to him. "Everybody is expecting you. The King is already in attendance," he says, worrying me more. But then his voice lowers, and he looks a little worried, saying the next words, "Even the General Mitharaus is inside waiting for your attendance."

The horror I carried inside me slowly fades away. My heart beats a little slower, and I manage a relieved breath. A smile tugs my lips.

Lenora has the worst habit of bribing my subjects. She made my staff say whatever she wanted on multiple occasions. Most of them made me angry, but she is getting away with this one. She knew how horrified I was going to be, and without even being at my side, she found a solution.

I know she always believes in me, but she is also aware that I need her support sometimes, and she always provides it.

I take a deep breath and move toward the ballroom.

When I come to the head of the stairs, the first one to see me is the herald. He straightens, and before any eyes can fall on me, he announces my arrival. "Her Royal Highness Princess Zuraya Haliyes, Crown Princess of the Moon Kingdom and Heir of Moonshine."

Everybody looks in my direction, and as their gazes create uneasiness inside my chest, my eyes search for one person and one person only. The ballroom is full to the capacity, but I know it will be easy to find her in just a second because as they hear my name and see my form, everybody starts getting onto their knees out of respect.

It is going to be easy to see one person I know who never kneels as a courtesy.

As my eyes move over the kneeling figures, something else eases me. I see the wonder in people's eyes, but I also see something I am very familiar with from the life I led before. Fascination.

Wings or no wings. Even after seven years and one broken horn later, I am still Zuraya Haliyes. I am their princess and their future queen, and they respect me. They are fascinated by me.

I can feel tears of happiness threatening me just as my eyes collide with familiar orange ones. The sight of her takes my breath away. She is wearing a white uniform that is decorated with many gold chains. Her long hair is braided in both sides of her face She is also wearing a gold chain on her face. It circles her head, and a piece comes down on her forehead and turns into more pieces covering both cheeks.

Lenora's golden eyes burn with a familiar lust as she looks up at me, but she also looks so damn proud of me.

She looks so in love, and my heart beats faster.

I smile down at her, and she smiles up at me. In the next moment, her smile turns into a smirk, and she slowly moves without taking her eyes away from mine. Just like the rest of the ballroom, she gets into her knees.

Lenora Mitharaus is kneeling for me.

She only kneels for the people deserving. I have heard about it from Hashim and from other soldiers too. She doesn't kneel for her own mother. She has never knelt for my dad. But she kneels for me with ease.

Butterflies don't just fill my stomach, but they fill my whole body. My heart feels like it is going to explode. I let it happen. My power sets free, and moonshine glows over my dark skin. I hear impressed murmurs from the crowd, but I don't pay any attention to them. Instead, I keep my eyes on the only person I care about and finally descent the stairs.

Woe in Total Darkness

People get back on their feet when I make it all the way down. All I want is to get to Lenora, but she is a little far away, and everyone wants to tell me something.

"Happy name-day, Your Highness."

"It is great to see you here after so many years."

"Your power gives hope to all your subjects."

I kindly answer all of them and briefly touch their hands as a show of affection. I want to see Lenora, but the sea of people doesn't bother me as much as I feared. I am sure there are people who think badly about me. I am sure some are troubled by my current state. However, they keep silent, so everything thrown my way is highly positive.

I grew up getting used to being adored by everyone around me. I worked hard to make that happen. I sometimes pushed myself to a state I was not happy with. I did it all to make them love me.

And now they do. They murmur between them and smile happily toward me. And the best part is, this time it is really me. I am not in the headspace to act like someone I am not. I still have a side that is a bratty little princess, but I also have a side that is a girl who fought her nightmares.

And my people adore me.

I am something to be adored.

I want to tell it to Lenora. I want her to know how much she helped me. I want to tell her none of this would be possible without her. She brought me back to life.

Just as I start getting away from people a bit, someone gets into my path. He is standing between me and the road toward Lenora and looks way too happy about it.

"Would you grant me a dance, Your Highness?" Rionn says with a little amusement.

I smile for the sake of appearance, but I want to get away. I admit, I like it when Lenora is jealous, and the sex gets better when she wants to punish me, but right now, I don't want to do this to her. When Rionn is a real threat, I cannot push her like this.

I don't want to be seen with him. However, saying no would be extremely rude.

"I would love to, Alpha," I answer despite all my unease. "But first, I need a drink."

"I'll get it for you."

I hate him for pushing me while knowing very well I want to get away from him. He is aware of everything happening around him, but he just doesn't want to accept it.

Just when I open my mouth for an answer, someone else replies. "No need. I already have her drink here." Then Lenora hands me a wine glass.

My head snaps in her direction as my fingers close around the glass. From up close, she looks even more beautiful, and her eyes shine with possessiveness. That makes me wet between the thighs, and I hate her for it because we cannot do anything about it yet.

I don't even realize the hostile way Rionn is looking at Lenora, but I can hear it in his voice. "When you are done with that drink, I want my dance," he says to me, trying to be playful, but he cannot hide the edge in his tone.

I know he has his right to be mad at the situation, but I don't think too much about it. I don't want to think about Rionn. I just want to celebrate with Lenora.

With a huge smile, I look at her. "Now you have to dance with me all night, so he won't be able to get this turn."

She raises an eyebrow. "Wouldn't that be suspicious?"

I shrug. "Not enough to avoid it. I don't want anyone but you beside me tonight."

"Really?" she asks, looking smug. "Everybody is mesmerized by you, but look at that; you only have eyes for me."

I also only have my heart for her, but I keep that in.

Lenora's arms circle my waist, and she pulls me close to her body. At the same time, she takes the drink from my hand and puts it away. "Let's dance."

I can't help but chuckle. "I was going to drink that."

She rolls her eyes. "Ah, it tastes bad anyway. Also..." Her voice drops as her lips come close to my ear. "I have plans for tonight that won't work if you are intoxicated."

Woe in Total Darkness

That boils my blood. I subtly press my thighs together while she takes me toward the dance floor. "What kind of plans?" I tease.

Lenora smiles wickedly. We start dancing, and she holds me close and firm. Her lips again travel close to my ear. If someone hears her words, they might drop dead. "Well, you look way too delicious in this dress, so I think I am going to keep it on you for a bit. I am going to make you scream and sweat into your dress. When it is ruined, and I get too hungry for your naked skin, I will rip it off your body. I will leave you wearing only that crown, and then I will fuck you hard."

I barely suppress my shiver. I don't want people to see how flustered I get in Lenora's arms, but I also cannot help but stay away. I want to kiss her so badly in the middle of this ballroom. I know we look very inappropriate right now, but I cannot care. This can be the last moment I have her.

I want to make it good.

One of my hands is currently parked at her shoulder and moves up to touch the chains on her face. "I might want you to keep this. It looks hot."

"It is part of the formal uniform of Sun Soldiers. Hashim is wearing it too."

"I don't think it looks this hot on him."

She mocks a gasp. "That is very rude, Your Highness."

"No." I shake my head. "This is just me having only eyes for you."

Her fingers dig into my skin over the fabric. "Don't make me more possessive than I already am, Raya. I might just show all these people you belong to me."

Thought turns me on the way too much. I know it is just talking. I know it is never going to be more than playful flirting. Yet I fill with yearning. I want us to be cheery all night, but some sadness forms in my heart. I just wish I could show everyone Lenora is mine.

"I wish you could," I say and put my head on her chest.

Lenora's body tenses, but her hold on me softens. She is still holding me strong, but her touch is gentle. Her breath tickles my forehead like she stopped herself from kissing it. "I wish that too," she whispers and just holds me as we move to the rhythm.

While we dance slowly, my eyes collide with green skin on the dance floor. Maha is wearing a violet dress that doesn't cover much of her body. Her hair is decorated with lavenders. She looks as bright as always, but I can also see some distress in her eyes. It must be because she is still pregnant. She almost reached full-term of a Feyada pregnancy.

General Archard is with her. He is looking down at Maha with soft eyes that he reserves only for her. Maha's feet are atop his, and he makes them move to the music. He is carrying all her weight and bends his body well enough to make her comfortable.

Archard briefly kisses his wife, and I fill with jealousy. I wish that to be Len and me. I wish we could have everything they have.

"Look at them," I whisper.

Lenora's head moves right to left, searching for who I mean, and a few seconds later, a soft sound comes from her throat, and I understand she has seen them. I know she knows I was talking about them.

"Their love was not easy," I say. "They had many obstacles in their way. What they felt was forbidden too. Yet they managed to defeat it. They fought and got to have this at the end."

Lenora stays silent for a very long time, and her body goes rigid even as she keeps holding me. My words hit her hard. They remind her of her own cowardness. This is the last time I can push her.

I have no hope, though. I have accepted that I am going to lose Lenora.

"Their journey was no easy one," she agrees with me. Her chest moves with a ragged breath, and she whispers, "But it is different for us."

She is the one making it different. She is the one so afraid to fight for me. I want to yell at her for it. I want to hit her hard. I want to hate her.

But I can't. I know nothing will change her mind, and a fight will only ruin tonight. We are aware that my name-day is no joyous

Woe in Total Darkness

affair. This celebration marks our separation, but we need to smile for the sake of duty.

If nothing is going to change, I want to at least have her for tonight. I want a nice goodbye so I won't regret it later.

———ɔ———

For the rest of the night, I suppress my sour mood. I just cheer myself up because this is a precious time I get to spend with Lenora. I will understand the value of it better when she is gone, I am sure.

Lenora also goes along with my plan. She smiles and laughs all night long. It is just us as we have always been together. We flirt and laugh.

We are just happy because we are together.

And she is overly possessive tonight. I think she really doesn't want me to dance with Rionn, or maybe she doesn't want me to get uncomfortable with all the eyes on me. Throughout the whole night, she is always by my side and touching me one way or another.

I don't mind at all. I love her like this. I am sure there are people who mind our closeness, but that is something I can handle later. No one is going to make this a big deal anyway. A good relationship between Haliyes and Mitharaus families has always been seen as a good sign.

My father mostly leaves me alone too. He doesn't push me for anything. I feel like the plan for the first night was just for me to show up. I don't have to worry about my responsibilities yet. People are just happy to see me.

That's why I stay for way longer than I want to.

Only when it is late at night, I let Lenora pull me out of the ballroom. I can hardly contain myself at this point, and she seems to be the same. "Are we going to your chambers?" I ask.

Lenora stumbles a little and turns to me. Her eyes scan our surroundings before pulling me close to her body, and she whispers over my lips. "Tonight, I want to fuck you in your royal bed, Princess."

My thighs clamp together, and I quickly bite down her bottom lip. "Take me there then."

Something mischievous gleams in Lenora's eyes, and before I can ask, she reaches down and throws me over her shoulder. I yelp. My heart beats fast at the thought of someone seeing us like this. Being carried like this also feels a little degrading, and my stomach hurts a little.

But it also turns me on. I like it when she uses her strength on me. I like that she is too excited to go to my room.

I can just get lost in these feelings.

When we reach my room, she just barges in and commands my maids to leave. I hope they will be silent about our condition.

When the maids close the door behind them, Lenora puts me back on my feet. She doesn't even take me to my bed. She pushes me until my back is flushed with a wall and kisses me. It is a passionate, breathless kiss. She kisses me like she might never kiss me again.

Her hands are on my waist, and then they go to my bottom, and the next moment she is gathering up my skirts. She boldly cups me between the legs and hisses at how wet she finds me. "You really want me, don't you, Raya?"

"Always," I breathe and move to her neck. I kiss the soft skin and suck it into my mouth as she touches me the way she knows I like.

"You enjoyed yourself tonight, didn't you," she says, even though her eyes are closed from my kisses. I start unbuttoning her top, and she fills me with two fingers, stretching me. "You loved seeing them adore you."

I moan for her, but I don't refuse her words. I just push her top away to get more of her skin. Everything feels too intense. My hips move against her hand, and my mouth travels across her skin. I realize how good she is to me, and tonight is the proof of that.

They adored me because of her, because she adored me when no one did.

Woe in Total Darkness

"You did it," I breathe and suck her nipple into my mouth. I never want to leave her body. "You helped me be the princess they'll accept. You made them adore me."

"No!" Lenora's hand becomes rougher, and I throw my head back with a moan. "You did it yourself, Raya. I might have pushed you, but it was all you. They were amazed by you." Her lips come close to my ear as my sex starts spasming around her fingers. "You'll still be their precious princess long after I leave."

I bury my nails into her skin as I come. I feel drunk and dazed. The pleasure of the climax makes it hard for me to understand her words. For a moment, I cannot see beyond her praise. I just eat that up.

But she was saying something else.

Suddenly her extra possessiveness makes sense. Suddenly I understand why she kissed me so desperately. My eyes burn as I open them and look at her pretty face. I look at the girl I love, and I know what is in her mind.

This is a goodbye fuck.

This is the last time we get to kiss and touch. We won't have a future, and this is the only way we can say farewell.

Tears gather in my eyes, and Lenora shakes her head. "No, no, please don't. Let us have this last moment."

My throat feels tight. I don't want to ruin this, but I am sad. "Are you going to leave after fucking me?" I ask, feeling so hurt.

"No," she says, her voice desperate. "Of course not, Raya. I will stay for the night. I will hold you in your sleep for one last time."

I brush away tears, and Lenora helps me. "I wish it doesn't have to be that way." *I wish you would leave with me.*

"Me too."

I try to gather my posture. I swallow back the lump in my throat and cup Lenora's face. She still has her golden chains on her face, but they cannot hide anything. I can see the same sadness in her eyes, too, and I know our last night together deserves something better. "I want you to show me how much you love me, Len. Show me so I will never forget it."

"Raya," she murmurs, and her lips close over mine. She lifts me, and I wrap my legs around her waist. Lenora carries me to my bed. She slowly undresses me, paying close attention to every part of my body. Her own skin comes into view very soon as well. She gives me pleasure and lets me do the same to her. We reach peak again and again, that my body feels limp. Position after position, Lenora, shows me all the pleasure I can get in the world.

She almost gives me everything she has promised into my ear all through the night except one thing.

Tonight Lenora doesn't fuck me. She makes love to me.

When we are both too tired to keep an eye open, and the sun is ready to rise, she wraps me in her arms, in her wings. She keeps me close as we sleep like she can somehow keep me.

I let sleep take over me. I fall, knowing I will never drift in the arms of my one true love.

The sleep is peaceful, but after a few hours, when I wake up, Lenora is not there. I am all alone in an empty cold bed. I stare at the ceiling and try to convince myself everything I have experienced with Lenora, everything I have felt for her was a dream.

That makes me want to sleep forever.

47

Zuraya

I look up as my maid puts a series of products under my eyes. I have worn my pink dress as planned and let them tend to my hair and make-up like expected. I didn't fight back. I didn't complain.

Lenora broke me because of her duties, so I decided to focus on mine.

Still, they need to cover up all the puffiness around my eyes from crying.

I didn't want to cry. I really didn't. After everything I have been through, I wanted to hold it in for this one. I have lived a lie for seven years. I have lost my best friend. Those made me cry more than ever. I should have been out of tears already.

Turns out I was not. Tears just formed whenever I thought about never kissing Lenora again. I hate her for hurting me like this, but I also love her enough to never be able to hate her.

The door to my room opens harshly, and all my maids stop to look at the intruder. I also slowly bring my eyes to the large form in my doorway.

"Are you still not ready, Zuraya?" My father asks. He is wearing a white suit with green jewels. He looks powerful, like always. He also looks displeased with everything around him.

My maid answers before I can. "We wanted to make sure Her Royal Highness looks her best, Your Majesty."

His eyes travel along my face, and I don't know if he can tell my face is puffy and red under the makeup. I have no idea how well they hid my sorrow. My father's look also doesn't give me an idea. He just scans me and says, "She is decent enough. We have to go."

That surprises me. "We go together?"

"Yes. Tonight I will escort you to the ball."

"I thought it was better for me to attend alone. You said so when I suggested Lenora be by my side."

He shakes his head. "This is different. It was important for you to be alone yesterday. Today they already know you, and I want them to see us together. This is all a game, Zuraya."

"I wish I was informed about the game as well," I murmur.

He looks at the end of his patience. "Why am I still standing here, Zuraya? Come on."

I hold back a huff and get up. I want to care about how I look. I want to care about my father's games, but I really can't. I just want to be able to get through tonight without breaking. I take his arm and walk beside him. I don't have the strength to argue.

"Everybody was amazed by you yesterday, Zuraya. You did well."

So, now I have to speak. "Thank you."

"I am only telling the truth," he says without emotion. "Just make sure to grant time to our court as well. Yesterday people counted themselves lucky if they got a word with you, and none actually got a dance. Your sight is important, but they also should see you as someone real. Only then will they accept you as their queen. You cannot do that by being inappropriately close to the Sun Princess all night."

My throat goes dry with the accusation. My father has never been so harsh with me about Lenora. "I feel calmer when she is around," I say.

He doesn't soften at all. "You should learn to feel calm without her."

I hate that he is right, but I still whisper, "Maybe I don't want to."

Woe in Total Darkness

My father stops in his tracks and looks at me with fury. "You have to." This is the first time I have seen this much emotion on his face. "She is leaving after the celebration, Zuraya. You have much more important things to focus on. You better show the same affection you showed her to Rionn tonight."

Tears gather in my eyes at his hurtful words. "Rionn?"

"Yes, Rionn," he says, frustrated like he is talking to a stupid kid. "I don't care what you do in your private life as long as it doesn't affect your image. I will take last night as a fluke, but I don't want it to happen again. You will give your attention to the court and show affection to Rionn so people will not be so shocked about our surprise tomorrow."

I cannot even focus on his words. "Surprise tomorrow?"

He grits his teeth. "Stop repeating my words."

"I am sorry."

He looks at me with anger for a second, but then his posture softens a bit. He takes out a handkerchief and moves close to me. "Look up." I do what he says, and my father gently dabs away the tears gathering in my eyes. When he is done and my vision clears, he says, "No one needs to see you cry."

I use all my strength to keep more tears from appearing. I just want to be done with tonight. But I also still need answers. I want to know what is the façade my father had put me through. "What is the surprise, dad?"

He is mostly back to his cold demeanor, but I can still see his annoyance. "It shouldn't be too hard to guess."

"Just tell me."

He takes a deep breath, and his blue eyes meet mine. "Rionn is going to propose to you tomorrow."

I can't breathe.

"And you will say yes."

My bottom lip trembles. Maybe I didn't want to believe this was really happening, or maybe I didn't think it would happen so soon. Whatever it is, I feel so close to breaking.

I want to get into a ship and leave for good.

Only if Lenora was brave enough.

Now I have to be the brave one. I have to sacrifice my happiness so I can be a good queen. I swallow back my sorrow and reach for my father's arm, praying Tisasa to make me strong enough for this. "Let's go."

My father looks glad as he starts taking me toward the ballroom. This is what he wants from me. He wants me to be obedient and hold every real thing I feel inside, just like he had done his whole life.

So, I do it. If I cannot have love, at least I can have my father's approval. I can have his pride.

We step inside the ballroom, and I feel like I am underwater. My body is moving, but I don't have much control over it. Ocean salt burns my eyes. Everything is blurry, and every sound is unintelligible. This is the life I am destined for.

But then I see something clear. She is the only thing I can focus on underwater. She is the only light source.

Bright as the morning sun.

Lenora stands in a corner, leaning into a wall. She does not kneel today, but I know it is not a statement to me. She just doesn't want to kneel for my father.

She is wearing a simple white shirt and a white shalwar. She has gold chains on her face, but I can tell there is not much makeup under that. Her hair is also not in pretty double braids tonight. It is just tied on her neck.

When I focus more, I can tell that her eyes are a little red. She doesn't look like she has been crying all night, even though she looks drained. The redness in her eyes doesn't make sense, but it is undeniable.

Weird.

I look at her, and she looks at me. No words pass between our gazes. Nothing left to say anymore.

Still, I want to look at her forever. I want to go to her. I know nothing is going to change, and I know she is going to leave, but I still want to be next to her. I would even accept just staying next to her all night without saying a single word. I just want to know her body is next to mine and my mind is next to hers.

Woe in Total Darkness

But my father doesn't let me. He squeezes my arm hard enough to bruise, and I hold back a yelp. My head turns toward him instinctively, and I realize we have already stopped, and Rionn is already here.

"My apologies," I say, trying to sound sincere. I look at Rionn. "What were you saying?"

He gives me a smile that has the power to break so many hearts. Rionn Ay Ujk is called to be the most handsome man alive on Ae. I can see that. I can certainly say he is extremely attractive. He is also charming, and I know many will die to marry him.

He is just not who I want.

Maybe he has never been who I want. I feel like all the times I was in love with Rionn were an illusion. Whoever made me dream for seven years made me believe I loved him when I never did. I don't think I can ever.

And not just because my heart belongs to Lenora.

But when he says, "I was asking for a dance," I just smile and accept because royals are not meant to be happy. We just need to be perfect.

I smile my best smile. "I would love that, Alpha." Then I let him wrap his arms around me even though it burns my skin. I don't care if Lenora sees this. I just want to put on a show. That is my only obligation tonight.

Rionn takes me to the middle of the dance floor, and I can feel all the eyes on us. He looks at me with true affection. "You look breathtaking tonight, Zuraya."

"Thank you."

His eyes briefly move somewhere in the room before coming back to me again. "You also looked lovely yesterday, but I was not given a chance to show my appreciation. Only one lucky person was granted your interest."

"I apologize," I say because I really don't want to argue.

Rionn's smile turns a little fake, and his arms tighten around me as we sway to the music. "I believe the look on both of your faces means you have ended this craziness. It is truly the best for everybody."

"I suppose it is."

"I understand you might be sad over this, Zuraya. I just want you to know I will be here to help you through your heartbreak." His hot breath falls onto my ear when he leans closer. "I want to be good to you. I want to make you forget about her."

I almost laugh at his words. He actually sounds confident. He sounds like those words can attract me. I pull back so he can see my face when I speak. "Rionn, you can do everything in your power to have me. You can even be my husband, but you can never make me forget Lenora. You'll have to accept that if you want to be with me."

He chuckles. "You are underestimating me."

"And you are underestimating my love for her."

Now his eyes fill with anger, but he hides it quickly. He is much better at impressing a crowd than me. "If you want to believe that, then go ahead, Zuraya," he hisses and pulls me tighter to his body, pressing his mouth to my ear. "But you have to know that it will only make you miserable because even if you love her until the rest of your days, you will have to convince everybody that you are in love with me."

I keep my stand. "Then I'll be miserable." That was always meant to be my destiny, anyway.

Rionn pulls back, but his face is still close to mine. He smiles sweetly and murmurs, "Maybe it is a good time to start then." And he kisses me.

His lips are on mine, and I don't even have the chance to look surprised. I have to act like this is normal. I have to show people how much I love this. And he is right because it does make me miserable.

I do it, though. I kiss him back.

At first, I try to think he is Lenora, but that doesn't work. He feels so different in my body. He doesn't awaken any desire. I just want this to end.

So I try a different tactic. I focus on the fact that Lenora is watching. I think that I am only doing this to make her jealous. I want her to see him kiss me and get into action. I want her to

Woe in Total Darkness

punch Rionn and take me into her arms. I want her devastated and want her to change her mind.

I want her jealousy.

But my dreams don't come true. Rionn pulls back from our chaste kiss with a smile, and no one punches him. People around us gasp, and I am forced to smile back.

When he puts a small affectionate kiss on my lips, I do my best not to flinch, and when he whispers, "I will never stop trying to gain you," I just want to puke.

48

Lenora

When Zuraya Haliyes uses her body manipulation on someone, the pain is almost unbearable. It must hurt as much as mine, but the pain she gives is real. Your muscles knot and spasm. Your blood does not flow the way it should. Your skin feels like it is getting a thousand punches. She even leaves bruises sometimes.

It is almost as painful as when I was infected with the Darkness Curse.

Yet it doesn't come close to the pain I feel watching Rionn kiss Zuraya.

I hardly contained my rage. He was touching what was mine. He was kissing what was mine. I wanted to kill him. I probably would have done something to stop it if I was not so high.

I knew it was going to be a hard night. I needed something to keep me calm. I wanted to be in a state where I could show up and talk to people but feel everything less. I used the eyedrop drug Andy is so fond of. I never use it a lot because I don't want to be addicted like she is. I only use it when I am really stressed or when my pain gets too much.

Tonight was definitely an occasion that required it.

Woe in Total Darkness

Thankfully it is not very popular in the North, so people didn't understand I was high from my red eyes. Here they mostly use smoke that makes the skin prickly and the eyes black.

I also drank a lot. I convinced myself if I took too many sips, I wouldn't have to look around much. I didn't want to see her with him. I knew it was better for her. I knew it would be much easier if she could fall for him, but I still could not take it.

I never want to see anyone but me touch her.

As I sit on the ballroom stairs, I take another sip of my tasteless wine. I am the only one left here. I want to sleep. I have the worst headache. But I don't want to go back to my room. I cannot sleep in that bed without remembering how I shared it with Zuraya.

Her ghost will never leave my side if I lay there.

So I stay back. Maybe I will pass out somewhere, and someone will carry me to my room. That is the only way I can sleep there.

It is all dark now. Servants asked me if they should wait for me to leave, but I told them to do their jobs as if I was not there. So they cleaned and blew off all the candles. I remained on the steps with a bottle long after.

Dark doesn't bother me. It actually makes things less real. I can try to convince myself that I am in a dream, that Zuraya didn't really let Rionn kiss her.

I thought I would be jealous like I was when she went on a walk with him, but I was not. I was just sad.

I am still sad.

When I hear footsteps approaching me, I don't get hopeful. I know her walk. This is not her. Unfortunately, I am also good at knowing the sound of most people's footsteps. I know who is approaching me, and I just want to disappear. My hand tightens around my cup, and I am sure just a bit more pressure would shatter the delicate glass.

"I was not expecting to find you here," Rionn says and sits down next to me easily. He even has the audacity to reach my bottle and take a sip.

I try to suppress the urge to kill him. It would be a horrible scandal. My country will have to go to war if I kill him. I will also

397

create tension with the Moon Kingdom. It is definitely not a good idea.

Although maybe I can just punch him really hard. I feel like I deserve that.

I squeeze my fists at my sides and manage to let out words. "You are really the last person I want to see tonight, Rionn."

He chuckles. "I figured, but I believe you realized my actions do not go with what you want or not."

I grind my teeth. I cannot take the image of him kissing her out of my mind. My eyes would tear if not for the drug that is still in my system. "Did you do it to hurt me?" I ask, revealing the hidden worry deep in me. Now I am actually looking at him. "I didn't love you back. I let things end between us. Did you want to take revenge by having her?"

Rionn stays silent for a long time, that I start to wonder if my question was too absurd. If I am too full of myself. But then his head turns towards me, and he looks so fucking sinister. "That is not the only reason."

"But it is one of them?"

He doesn't confirm again but instead shrugs. "Not everything is about you, Lenora. She is beautiful and graceful, and when I heard about what they made her believe for the last seven years, I thought she was an easy target. Marrying her would be an amazing alliance for me and the Shifters. I was sure she was going to throw herself over to me too. I mean, at least I was at the beginning."

"But then I came," I say, voicing the truth he is too afraid of. Zuraya was attracted to him. He would probably gain her affection if I was not here. She would happily marry him, believing he was the love of her life.

But she knew he was not. I was the love of her life.

I *am* the love of her life.

He can marry her, but he cannot change the fact that she will always love me. He cannot have her like I did. He is bound to have a loveless marriage.

But a marriage, after all.

"I realized she fell for you," he says in a whisper. "I couldn't even blame her. I know how easy it is to love you. I also know how hurtful it can be to lose you. I honestly believe we can bond over that. We can find comfort in each other. You might be easy to love, but Zuraya is too."

I am jealous over his words, but I know I shouldn't be. I shouldn't be selfish. Zuraya deserves to be happy. If I cannot give it to her, someone else should be able to do it. I should want her to fall for Rionn.

My body is all tense, but I have to know. I have to know he will make her happy.

"Do you love her?" I ask, breathless.

Rionn considers it for a moment, but his eyes are soft at the thought of her. I want to poke them. "How can I not love her," he says, fascinated. "I am a Shifter, and she is pure moonshine."

I wait for him to say more. I wait for him to tell me how beautiful Zuraya's smiles are. How strong she is despite being hurt so deeply. I wait for him to tell me how sweet he finds her bratty attitude. How satisfying it is to make her blush. How brave she is. I wait for him to tell me many more loveable things about Zuraya.

But he doesn't.

Rionn fell for me because I was a powerful warrior. I was the Lightbringer. Now he is falling for Zuraya because she is the Moonshine Heir.

I can accept that for myself, but I cannot accept that for her. She deserves someone who will fall in love with every little thing about her. She deserves to be the center of someone's world.

She deserves better than Rionn.

My throat burns, and I ask, "Is it the only reason?"

"Isn't it enough?"

I see red. "Of course not!" I get into his face, wishing I could just punch him. My power makes my palms tingle. I want to explode. "She deserves so much better than what you can give her. She deserves to be truly loved."

Rionn smirks like he is trying to taunt me. "Unfortunately, all she is going to get is me."

My vision darkens, and without even thinking, my power unleashes. I manipulate his mind. I make him feel like there is pressure all over his skin, and it is getting more intense. I want to hurt him.

I want to kill him.

"I want to kill you."

He takes a ragged breath. "Do it then," he says roughly. He is still smiling despite the pain. "If you care about her more than your country, just do it. You can leave with her just after I lose my breath. Or you can push us into a civil war. Kill me if you are brave enough, Lenora."

I can't breathe at his words. I want to do it. I want to end this all and be with Zuraya. I want to not care about anything.

But I am not brave at all. I am a coward.

I cannot let innocent people die for my desires. I cannot fail them for my happiness.

So, I fail Zuraya.

I pull my power back and leave Rionn in the steps. I leave for my room with a broken heart. I know the sight of that bed will give me great pain, but after what I have done, I only deserve pain. I deserve more pain than I have been given since birth.

However my feet go to Zuraya's room instead. I want to get in there and kiss her. I want to hold her and never let go.

The more logical side of me has another plan. I know I should tell her how Rionn doesn't deserve her. I should tell her she cannot be happy with him and that she deserves happiness. I should fix things. I should help her find happiness.

But I can already guess her answer. She is going to tell me no one is going to be able to make her happy. She is going to tell me I am the one that deserves her.

She is going to want things I cannot give, and it is only going to hurt us both further.

I decide she doesn't need me messing with her head. I have no right to interfere with her life when I am not brave enough to be a part of it. She is strong and smart. She can make her own decision without me messing up everything.

Woe in Total Darkness

So, I turn on my heel and march to my own room. I only need to take this for one more night, and then I will leave for the Seelie Kingdom. I will do more research about the Curser. I will focus on my work and hope the thoughts of Zuraya will leave when I don't have to see her anymore.

However, I know I will see her every time I close my eyes. I will until my body is no more than dust on the earth.

49

Zuraya

I pull my cloak closer over my shoulders. The weather is getting too cold to just wear light layers. Unfortunately, I was not in a position to care about that last night. I went to my room and couldn't look at my bed without my lungs turning into knots. I just wanted to get away.

All I saw was Lenora. When she made love to me in that bed, we agreed it was our last night together, but I cannot simply command my heart not to feel. I cannot help but remember each caress and love word whispered onto my skin on that bed.

I don't think I can ever sleep in there ever again. It only reminds me how awful Rionn feels on my body.

I will never welcome his touch.

A breeze hits, and I know I should go back. I have already slept enough, anyway. When I couldn't get in my bed and turned hysteric, I knew I needed support. I needed my best friend. I got out before I could even change my dress. One of my maids put a cloak over my shoulders when I mentioned where I was going, and I am sure someone kept watch over me.

All I cared about was the fact that I got to sleep next to my best friend once more. Whenever I had nightmares, Qyron would come to my rescue, so when the panic surged through me, he was the first person I wanted to come to.

I lied next to the tombstone and signed to him all night long because I knew he could not read lips very well when it was dark.

I told him about how I hated his sister. I told him how she broke my heart. I told him how Rionn's kiss made me want to puke.

Mostly I begged him to come back. I felt like if he came back, everything would be fixed.

"I am so tired," I sign on his tombstone. I like to imagine his ghost is here watching over me. *"I am so tired of accepting my fate. Lenora wants to leave, my father wants me to marry Rionn, and I just go with it. I always have to accept whatever hand life deals me."*

I know he would not appreciate this. He would push me to do whatever I wanted. I wish he could be here and do that.

"I want Lenora," I sign, pouring my deepest desire. This is no secret to my dead best friend at this point, but there is another thing that is also important. *"I don't want Rionn. Not just because of Lenora too. Even if I disregard her presence in my life, I still don't want Rionn. Why do I have to accept him just because she is leaving? I don't think I can ever love someone like I love her, but maybe I can try. I don't have to give up just because she is not brave enough."*

I look at the stone with hope, like it can answer me. I already know what I should do. I have to say "no" to Rionn, not for Lenora but for me. I should be able to live for myself.

I should be better than my father. If I am miserable all the time, how can I be a good ruler?

I can still live for myself even if she is not in the picture. I can do it.

Yes. I have decided. I can do this. I can live for myself while also being a good queen.

"You definitely can," I feel Qyron reply and smile a little to myself.

I get up to go back to my room. I know it is going to hurt when I step inside. I know I will not get over Lenora so easily. But I also know I don't have to punish myself just because she is going to leave me. I walk a little straighter and with a lot more self-confidence.

My steps only falter when I encounter worried servants running around. It is normal for servants to be busy since tonight is the last night of my name-day celebrations, but they seem a little too tense. Also, there are Seelie servants among them, so I get the feeling that this is about something else.

I grab a Seelie servant from her arm, and she stops to look at me with huge black eyes. "What is happening?" I ask.

"Your Highness," she says with a trembling voice. "Princess is giving birth."

Oh.

"Maha," I whisper, and she nods as if to confirm. All the thoughts about myself and my future leave my mind. My whole existence focuses on my friend. I let go of her arm and got a determined look. "Let's go."

I follow the Seelie. I should be with my friend when she is going through something so important. It can be a little scary, but it is also beautiful. Good things should happen around here, and I should be present.

When I step into Maha's chambers, I am immediately welcomed by her high-pitched screams. Servants running around, and some royals are listening in. The door to her bedroom is closed, and I desperately want to get inside. I want to be with her. I want to help her.

First, my eyes look around for Davon. I know he will let me get inside. However, I cannot find him. In the Moon Court, usually, the fathers wait outside with the rest of the court when the mother is giving birth, but I quickly realize Davon probably stood against that tradition. Seelie's have more public births, and Maha most likely wanted her husband there.

I have to let myself inside then. I cannot wait with the displeased-looking royals when one of my few friends is giving birth.

When people realize my presence in the midst of all the screaming, I see the will to approach me in their eyes. That is the last push I need. I open the door to the bedroom and throw myself inside.

Woe in Total Darkness

Maha is in her bed, sweating and screaming. Her eyes are wet with painful tears. There is a midwife kneeling between her legs and two more around her. There are also two servants. Davon is at the head of the bed, one of his hands at the tight clutch of his wife's palm. His attention doesn't even falter with my entrance. He kisses her forehead and murmurs soft words into her ear. His face is full of fear and worry. I don't think I have ever seen him wear that expression before.

One of the servants spots me and bows. "Your Highness, you shouldn't be here."

There is no way I am letting them kick me out. I cannot help but feel like if I leave, something horrible is going to happen. I have to stay here.

Fortunately, Maha spots me between her screams and gives a tired smile. "Zuraya," she says teary. "Please come."

I immediately ran to her side and took her free hand. I smile encouragingly at her. "He is finally coming."

Maha grunts with pain. "I actually changed my mind. He can stay in there a little longer."

"My Flower," Davon murmurs and kisses her head; all the while, Maha takes deep breaths with the instructions of the midwife. "It is all going to be okay. I promise."

"I want it to end," she cries. Every now and then, she screams with pain, and I try so hard to hold back a flinch. I don't want her to hurt. I want her to get better.

Now I wish Lenora didn't train me to hurt people. I wish I had focused on my healing so I could actually help her, but I have no idea about birth. I don't know how I should manipulate her body to help her.

Maybe the midwife can tell me.

"Not much left, Your Grace, I promise," the midwife tells from between her legs.

Maha shakes her head. "I don't believe you. It has been going on forever."

I look at the worrisome General. "When did it start?" *How late have I been?*

"I don't know exactly. She didn't tell me until a little after midnight that she was having contractions because she was afraid it might be a false alarm. She didn't want people to talk about her fake labor again." He gets a murderous look. "I am going to kill everyone who made her insecure about that shit."

Maha's scream cuts his murderous gaze, and he turns back to her with soft eyes. He looks so helpless right now, but I know the second things get better, he sure is going to ruin anyone who gossiped.

I actually have no problem with Davon giving them a lesson. They deserve it for putting Maha in pain.

It can be handled when the baby is out, and Maha is well. It should be soon. Everything should go smoothly.

"Push Princess," the midwife instructs. Maha squeezes our hands and screams again. Her skin looks so pale that I am concerned, but I try not to be. This is a joyous occasion. She is going to have her baby, and all this struggle is not going to matter afterward.

When the baby doesn't come out this time either, Maha lets her head back on the pillow and starts crying. "I can't do this anymore."

Davon looks even more worried and starts leaving kisses all over her face. "You can do anything," he praises her. "You are strong, My Flower. This is nothing for you. Just one more. I love you."

Tears wet her cheeks, but Maha nods to her husband, getting courage from him. Then she looks at the midwife, determined even though she looks so damn tired.

For the hundredth time midwife says, "Push," and Maha does. This time her screams erupt my eardrums, and her fingers squeeze mine so hard that I lose feeling for a second. It happens so fast. Her body falls back to the bed just when the midwife takes out a small blood-covered baby from between her legs.

A smile spreads my lips, and I look at my friend, but Maha doesn't look happy at all. She looks sick and worried. This time I look up at Davon and see him absolutely horrified. Only then do I realize the baby they took away isn't crying, and there is a big pool of blood between Maha's legs. I have never been to a birth before,

Woe in Total Darkness

but it looks too much. It is already too much, and with every passing second, more red spills out.

"What is happening?" Davon roars.

"She is bleeding," the midwife answers like that is any help. "I am trying to stop it."

This time Davon's eyes turn to me. They are hard but also pleading. "Do something."

My eyes pop, and I look down at my friend. She is weakly reaching for the midwife at the corner of the room, murmuring, "My baby." She doesn't even care about herself. She wants her silent baby even though she is dying.

Because I can tell. Maha is dying.

I need to heal her. I put my hands on her arm, trying to feel her body. I can feel her existence. I can feel every part of her. I can also feel that things are not okay in her body.

But I don't know how to fix it.

I know how I can hurt her. I know how to squeeze her muscles and how to poke her skin. I know how to fight. I don't know how to give life.

Tears fill my eyes. "I don't know how," I say helplessly. I don't know anything about birth. The healing I know from before is too basic for what is happening to her right now, and after I came here, I never tried to learn this. I learned how to hurt, not how to heal.

"Zuraya, please," Davon Archard begs me with red eyes. He holds her close and tries to calm her because she wants her baby back. At this point, I am sure the baby is already dead, but Maha is not going to accept it easily.

First, we need to save her. Then we can handle this somehow. She will be sad, but she will get over it somehow. She just needs to stay alive.

I focus more; I try to reach whatever is wrong with her. I want to understand how I can save her, but she just keeps bleeding, and her breathing turns harsher and harsher. "I can't," I cry over her. I can't save her.

I can't lose her.

407

She puts a hand on Davon's cheek. Tears spill out of her eyes, but she manages to speak. "Lenora," she whines. "Bring me, Lenora."

My forehead wrinkles in confusion at her request but Davon looks mortified. "No," he says quickly. "You'll get better. You don't need her."

"Please," Maha cries. I can see her slowly lose consciousness, slowly lose her life. "I am hurting so much."

Davon looks at her with sadness in his eyes for a moment. Then he grits his teeth and looks up at one of the servants. "Get Lenora Mitharaus. Fast."

The servant bows quickly. "She was right outside," she mumbles and goes to take her. Only a few seconds later, Lenora steps inside the room. She looks more confused than anything, but then her eyes go to bed. She sees all the blood, and I can see her heart drop.

"What happened?" she asks, coming next to me and holding Maha's hand. She looks between Davon and me, trying to get an answer.

"I can't save her," I say in tears. I want her to make things better. She is stronger than me. She should be able to fix this.

Lenora looks heartbroken and helpless. "Help me, Len," Maha says to her. "I am hurting."

She shakes her head. "I cannot heal you, Maha," she says with glossy eyes.

"No," Maha says. Her eyes again go to where her baby was taken. She is waiting for a corpse on her deathbed. "My heart hurts. My soul hurts. Make it better."

Lenora's throat moves in a nervous swallow. She kisses Maha's fingers. "You'll get better, Maha. No need for that."

The midwife between her legs looks dreadful but I know none of us wants to accept it. She simply can't die.

Maha doesn't accept Lenora's words. She shakes her head with her last energy. "Let me go happy, Len. Don't I deserve that?"

Lenora doesn't answer, but a tear escapes her eye and slides down to her pale cheek. She puts her hands over Maha's arm, and

Woe in Total Darkness

her skin glows just a little. I don't understand what is happening, but when I look at Maha, I see that her pupils are huge, and she is not breathing so harshly anymore. Davon looks at her with woeful eyes, but he also looks like he is too afraid to ruin whatever is happening.

Maha smiles softly and looks at the midwife again. "I want to see him," she says. "I don't mind if he is dirty."

Davon clears his throat and orders, "Bring the baby."

The midwife looks uncertain for a second but then brings a little bundle. Inside I can see the small blood-covered corpse. Maha doesn't react sadly, though. She takes the body and puts it on her chest. She looks at him with loving eyes and kisses him. "Such a healthy boy," she mumbles.

I only watch, stunned, as she looks up at her husband and says, "He has your hair."

Davon nods while crying. His body is rigid, and he looks lost. "He is beautiful," he answers, his voice cracking, but Maha's smile only brightens.

She kisses her husband and whispers, "I love you." She looks happy. She looks like everything is okay.

"I love you, My Flower," Davon answers, and I cannot breathe hearing the sad tone of this voice.

The Seelie Princess looks back at her baby with a massive smile like it is the happiest moment of her life. She cuddles him close to her chest, and then her head drops back to the pillow. Her eyes remain open, but her body becomes unmoving.

The most lively person I know dies in front of us, and we cannot do anything. She dies with a smile on her face but no one else is smiling.

Davon cups her face shaking his head. "No," he murmurs, crying. "No." And roars in pain, "No!"

His body closes over hers, and he cries. He tries to get a reaction from his wife or his son, but they stay still as he cries for them.

For a second, I reach Maha with my power, but she just feels cold. She is no longer Maha. She is just an empty body like the little baby on her chest. And all we can do is watch Davon Archard cry like he lost his entire world.

Like he would prefer dying with them instead of getting left behind.

50

Zuraya

I lie in my bed and watch my wall with empty eyes. That is all I feel.

Empty.

When they told me Qyron was dead, I got sad. I got devastated. I cried for days. I didn't want to believe it. I hoped for it to be a nightmare.

This time is different. I know Maha is dead. I watched her die right in front of me.

She died because of me. Only if I was a better healer, she could have been alive. Maybe even her son would be alive. I could have saved them.

I know no one is blaming me. I don't have to save anyone. Healing her was not my obligation. It was not my fault, but to me, it feels like it was. Being capable of saving someone and not doing it is the worst thing in the world.

I cannot stop seeing her dead body.

I wish it didn't feel real. I wish I could just ignore it. I wish I didn't feel so empty.

When Maha died, someone took me away from the room. They took me back to my own chambers. I didn't even have time to object. I let them handle everything because I had no idea what to do. I let my maids take off my dress and put a nightgown on me. I let them put me to bed and tell me the ball tonight was no longer happening.

I haven't left since then.

I know what I need. I don't want to feel so empty anymore. I know who I need for that.

Maybe I have been too proud to go see her until now. She was the one who ended things. She left me. I don't want to be the one who rushes into her arms again like a pathetic little girl.

But I need her.

Knowing how short life is only makes it worse. I want to be with her even if she is going to leave in the morning. I want every second I can get. I don't want to lose her any sooner than I need to.

I wonder what Davon Archard would give just to have a few more days with Maha. Or hours.

Or seconds.

I get out of my bed with determination. I get up so fast that my head spins, but I don't care. I don't even care about my pride. I just need her. She is the only one who can make this emptiness inside me better.

When I reach the door to my chambers, I open it in a rush, but the moment they are open, I freeze on the spot. Lenora is standing at the other side of the door. She looks so hurt and helpless. She looks shy.

"I was coming to see you," I say without thinking. If I think I will get cold feet.

Lenora swallows. "I have been standing here for two hours trying to gather my courage."

Is she that scared of coming to see me?

She shakes her head, and her shoulders drop. She looks lost. "I know I have no right to seek you out. I am leaving in the morning, and I know I have already hurt you enough. I just..."

"You don't have to explain," I cut her off. When she looks up at me with hopeful eyes, I reach for her hand, and even that little touch fills something in me. "Just come inside," I say. Because words make everything complicated. We have enough of that for today. We just need to feel.

No explanation is needed.

Lenora lets me pull her inside, towards my bed. I settle in her arms. At this moment, I cannot care that she is going to leave me. I don't care that she has hurt me. She is all I need.

We stay silent for a long moment. Her hands caress my back gently, and my fingers move along her stomach. This is just about comfort. I don't want to ruin it, but the question comes to me. It has been on my mind since I realized what she had done to Maha today.

"You captured her mind," I say. It is not a question. She made her see things differently. She sent her to a reality where her son was alive, and she was not dying. Lenora gave her comfort for her last breath, but how she did it hit too close to home for me.

Lenora's body tenses up, but she truthfully answers, "Yes."

"Have you always known how to do that?"

"Not exactly."

It is not a yes but also not a no. My throat tightens for a second, but I ignore it. "Okay," I answer. It doesn't mean anything now. Nothing does.

Then Lenora just holds me. She caresses my hair, neck, and back softly. Once, she even presses a kiss on my forehead. With her, I feel less empty. With her, everything feels just a little better.

When I am about to fall asleep, she speaks, "I want to give you something."

I look up at her, waiting, and she holds up a hand. I see the single ring she is wearing. It is very different from her normal style. It is a simple silver band, and over it, there is a single crescent. It is a moon ring.

It is my ring.

I push back the sensation of seeing my ring on her finger. I don't want to feel too excited about it. I know I haven't given her this ring. It shouldn't mean anything.

"I took it from Qyron's body," she whispers. I know that. I will always recognize that ring. I gave it to Qyron, and he gave me a sun ring in return. Mine probably got lost during my kidnapping. I have never considered where his must be.

I am actually happy Lenora has it.

I touch the ring lightly and say, "You should keep it."

"It is your ring. You deserve to have something from Qyron."

I shake my head. He was her brother, and I don't mind sharing him with her anymore. I don't mind her keeping my ring. She has held onto something of mine for seven years. I want her to keep it for more years to come.

I want her to have a piece of Qyron and a piece of me.

Softly I press a kiss to the ring and then her fingers. "It is my ring, and I want you to have it. Let it carry the memory of Qyron and the memory of me."

Lenora doesn't answer; instead, she kisses my forehead again and holds me tighter. I let her. I don't push her to speak. Neither of us needs any sad words.

Even without them, we both know I will only be a memory for Lenora after tomorrow. I won't have anyone to comfort me when I am sad. I won't have someone to cheer me up. I won't have the kisses I love so much.

And the worst of all is I won't even have a friend. I have lost everything.

Everyone.

51

Lenora

I leave before Zuraya is awake.

I don't know if it makes me an awful person, but I know I cannot stand to say goodbye to her. I am not sure how to walk away when she looks at me with those huge eyes. I cannot risk it.

Death of Maha only fuels me more. My heart aches thinking of her last moments. I have given her a happy death. I made it good for her, but I cannot make it good for the rest of us. It would only be solved if she was still alive.

It is the same for everyone else. If I leave, the Curse will keep taking lives. I don't want anyone to experience the pain I carry.

I don't want anyone to experience the pain Davon Archard is carrying. I cannot even imagine his state.

I have the ability to save them and protect them, and unlike my mother and King Luran, I cannot ignore that. I cannot turn my back on the ones in need.

Zuraya is going to be here. She is going to miss me, but in the North, she doesn't have to worry about a catastrophe. She will be well protected. They cannot get her again. I can just fight this shit, knowing she is safe now. She can heal.

Sem Thornwood

Maybe if I can catch the Curser and end the Curse, I can come back. Maybe when the threat is gone, we can be together. I don't know if I can do it, and I don't know if Zuraya will wait for me. I cannot ask her to, but if I succeed and she still wants me, then we can leave. If I do my job well, I can have her.

That is the only possible way.

I keep repeating that to myself while making my way to the first courtyard. My soldiers are waiting for me to take off. Our things, the wingless part of my soldiers and the moon spheres, had already started their journey early in the morning as planned earlier.

We didn't change our plans because of what happened. I already know Maha's body must be taken to the Seelie Lands. We can show our grief by attending her funeral. Staying here is not going to bring her back.

Because of that, I decided to see the Seelies first. I wanted to know what their plan is so we can act according to that too. Hashim told me they were in the courtyard, too, so that is why right now, we are both rushing there.

When we step outside, I see my Feyada soldiers, but their eyes are focused on a conversation. It is between the Seelies and Davon Archard. There is a big coffin on a cart. It is not a fancy coffin. Just a sad little chest. I don't want to believe my bright, smiley friend is in there.

I don't want to think how cold her body must be right now.

I just want to ignore it as long as I can, but the sight of the argument makes me realize it is impossible. I have to step in because Maha would definitely not want a fight between her people and her husband.

To me, what she would have wanted still counts.

"Hey," I say, trying to sound soft. I get in between the Seelie guard and Archard. "What is happening?"

Seelie guard answers, "We are taking the Princess's body to the Seelie Kingdom for burial."

"That is okay," I say, trying to hide my confusion. Then I turn towards a fuming Archard. "Maha would want to be buried in her homeland."

He seems to get angrier with my words, but there is a desperation to his posture too. His eyes are swollen, and his shoulders a slumped. He looks defeated but still angry. "I know that!" he shouts at me. "Of course, I fucking know that. The problem is they are saying I cannot come."

My brows furrow. "What does that mean?"

Seelie guard doesn't even react. "General Archard is not welcomed in the Seelie Lands by the Queen's orders."

My blood freezes. This cannot mean what I think it means. It is brutal.

But before I can ask to confirm, Archard explains, "They say I cannot attend my wife and son's funeral." Then he jumps on the Seelie guard.

Both Hashim and I react fast and pull him back, but he is faster. Before we can catch his arms and pull him off of the guard, Archard already lands a punch. Crimson leaks from the guard's nose instantly, and he groans in pain.

"Stop," I whisper into his ear. "Be calm. We'll find a way. They cannot keep you away."

His trashing slows, and his brown eyes turn to me. For a moment, they soften, maybe because I helped Maha in her last moments or because he truly believes I can help. His angry gaze comes back quick, but thankfully he stops and pulls his arms out of our grip.

Seelie guard is holding a handkerchief under his nose right now that turns red very quickly. "You are not helping your case General," he says aggressively.

Archard looks tense, but he doesn't attack him again. "You are keeping me away from my wife and son's funeral," he says again. "Do you understand how ridiculous it is? How barbarous?"

That word really pushes the guard, but he doesn't attack like Archard does. His eyes turn evil, and he gives a sinister smile. "We are not doing that, General," he says.

"What do you mean?" I ask before Archard can. I have a horrible feeling about this.

The guard points to the cart while looking at one of Maha's maids. She goes towards the cart immediately and crunches to the floor. Only then do I see there is another coffin. It is tiny, and it is not on the cart. It just stays on the floor like it is unimportant.

The maid brings the small coffin over to Archard. He looks down at it confused. Then the Seelie guards says, "You can keep your son."

No.

Archard looks at the small coffin with broken eyes, but his body remains tense from anger. "Don't tell me you are saying what I think you're saying."

"We will take our princess for the burial, but we are not interested in your son."

Archard looks up with fire in his eyes. "If you don't want me, I will remain here," he says harshly, letting one fight go for another. "But my son will be buried with his mother. Maha will not be separated from him."

"We don't want him," the guard says.

My throat tightens. I cannot imagine how devastated Maha would be if she knew she was going to be away from her baby in her death. I cannot imagine how sad she would be if she knew the love of her life was not allowed to say his last goodbye to them.

How could the Queen do this? How can she be this hateful towards people her sister loved?

"He is her son," I say to the guard. I know I cannot fix this with him, but how can I stay silent?

The guard looks at me with devilish eyes. "He is the murderer of our princess. We don't want him there."

Archard looks ready to attack again, but the coffin in his arms stops him. He holds it so delicately despite the tension in his body. Right now, he doesn't look angry anymore. He just looks lost.

The sight will break anyone's heart.

The guard and the rest of the Seelies go to their cart and take off without saying another word. Archard just looks after them, and I look at him. His eyes fill with tears, and his fingers flex over the coffin.

"She has given me peace," he mumbles. "And now I am in hell."

Woe in Total Darkness

I touch his arms. "We will fix this," I say. "I promise. I'll speak with the Queen myself. She cannot do this."

Archard shakes his head. "They deserve hell. Now that she is gone, taken away from me, everyone remain deserves hell."

My chest hurts. "Don't do this," I beg.

"Don't push it, Lenora," he says harshly. Then turns his back. "Now, if you leave me alone, I will bury my son."

"Let us come with you."

"No!" he says with rage. "I will do it on my own."

When he starts walking, I move to follow, but Hashim stops me. I look at him with unbelieving eyes, but he just shakes his head. "Let him be."

"She cannot do this."

"She can," Hashim corrects me. "Queen Mav never wanted them married. She never wanted Princess Maha to have a child. She is going to blame him and the baby, and she can keep him away because she is the Queen."

I shake my head. "I'll have to do something."

"When we are back," Hashim says. "Staying here helps no one. Your plan was to visit Seelie Lands anyway. Maybe you can convince her, but right now, you have to be strong and lead us back home."

My throat dries, but I know he is right. I have to be the leader; I cannot be sad or weak. I have to stand strong.

Just when I nod, a voice interrupts us, "Lenora!"

I turn towards the palace and see Zuraya running toward me. She is still in her nightgown and looks like she has been running since her room.

The sight of her only adds to my pain. My body feels like it is going to collapse, and the pain will be the only thing of mine that is left behind.

Zuraya reaches me, breathing heavily, and everybody subtly gives us space. "Were you going to leave without saying goodbye?" she asks, disappointed and accusing.

There is no point in lying. "I am sorry. I didn't know how to do it."

Sem Thornwood

Zuraya shakes her head. "This is not an excuse. I was so afraid I missed you already."

"I need to get going. My duty awaits."

Her throat works up and down. She looks so sad but still keeps her head high. I cannot stop being fascinated by her. "You are really leaving," she murmurs. "You are choosing your duty over me?"

I don't want her to phrase it like that. I don't want her to make me question my morals. I know she holds the power to keep me here, and I am so afraid of her finding out.

Maybe she was right. I need to make her hate me so she can move away.

"It was always meant to be this way," I say. "Our agreement was like this."

"Fuck the agreement," she says, frustrated. "We both know we passed that level already, Lenora. Don't try to play me."

"I have never considered not leaving, Princess."

She gasps. I know it is not my words. She is way too smart to fall for them. She knows I have wanted to goto the Continent with her. She knows I meant it when I said I loved her.

The gasp is for the last part.

I am the only one to call her Raya, and when I don't, I only call her Zuraya. I never call her princess. It is too formal for us.

People who call her princess are the people she was so afraid to show herself to. She knows what I mean by that. She knows I am trying to hurt her to be left alone, and she is not going to let me.

I hope that she won't let me.

"You are not playing fair," she whispers. "You are trying to lose me."

"I am just trying to leave."

"Okay," she chuckles in a mocking way. "If you want it this way, do it this way, but you will regret it. You will not get over me, and you'll be sad we didn't find another way. You will be lost when that happens."

I know I will be, but I don't respond. I don't know how I can respond.

Zuraya gets frustrated, and her jaw flexes. "Farewell, General," she says, her voice cracking, and before I can see her face erupt in sadness, she turns back to the castle.

My heart shatters inside my chest. My pain becomes unbearable. I know I am making a big mistake. I should find a way. I should be able to keep her while still protecting people from the Curser.

I don't know how to survive losing her.

I need to survive.

Maybe I can ask her to wait for me. Maybe we can really find a middle ground. Maybe this can be just temporary, and we can unite soon. Maybe I should be selfish and just keep her any way I can.

I don't even think further. I know I have to have her. I know I cannot leave like this.

So I call out, "Zuraya!" She turns back to me, a little surprised.

Then the catastrophe happens. The Moon Palace erupts into Darkness.

52

Zuraya

I don't hear it happen, but I instantly feel it. I feel how wrong it is. It is not natural at all.

I also see it. I see it on Lenora's face. Her hopeful, determined expression melts in a second. She looks behind me. Her eyes bulge, and terror fills her face. I can even see her breathing get faster.

The sound comes only after that. After I turn my head to see what's happening, I hear screams. People are running away from it. Terrified cries fill the courtyard. In the place of the palace, there is just black. I have never seen anything like this, but I know what it is. It looks like dark clouds surrounding the palace but worse.

It is the Darkness Curse.

It has never come this North. It has never reached any palace.

"No," I whisper, frozen in place. People keep running inside the Darkness. I don't move.

Arms come around me and pull me into a familiar body. "You should go," Lenora says in a panicked voice. When I don't respond, she rotates my body, and I see her terrified face. "Zuraya, you should run," she says, begging.

I see all her soldiers start running toward the Darkness. They know what to do. This is what they do every day.

Woe in Total Darkness

My breath gets caught in my throat, and I look back. People are escaping from the palace. When I focus, I can see that some are injured. It shouldn't be this fast.

This cannot be real.

"What are you going to do?" I ask Lenora.

"I should get in there," she says. Her voice is still pleading. She really wants me away from here. "I have never seen a Patch this big."

That only adds to my terror. I see a monster's limbs as it tries to follow the escaping crowd. I see Hashim flying over to fight it off. I cannot tell what kind of monster it is since its body is not fully visible, but I can tell it is horrifying.

Like Lenora said, I should leave. I know nothing about the Darkness.

I don't even have my dagger.

"Zuraya, please," Lenora begs again. "I need to know you're safe."

Her short nails dig into the skin of my arms, but I cannot look at her. My eyes are glued to the terrible scene in front of me. How does she fight this every day?

I should let her do what she does best. I should runaway too somewhere I can be safe. She shouldn't also worry about me.

But how can I?

This is my country, my palace. How can I become their queen one day if I escape now?

As a princess is my sole duty to marry right?

Wouldn't I be the same as my father and Khan Güne if I refused to use my powers against this?

I had the power to save Maha, but I couldn't use it. I failed her. I cannot fail my court as well.

"No," I murmur, but then I turn towards Lenora and repeat it loudly, "No!"

"What do you mean no?"

"I can't abandon them." I try to pull my body away from her, but she holds me so tightly that I can't. "You have to let me, Lenora."

Her eyes bulge. She looks almost mad at the suggestion. "I won't put your life at risk."

I shake my head. "Let me go, Lenora."

"Never!"

I don't want to do what I do next, but the screams get louder. I know I should get into action. I also know Lenora should be in there. She is the best at this. She shouldn't be arguing with me here.

So, I have to stop her long enough.

She never told me she could capture a mind. She never taught me to capture a body, but I am as good as her. I can do anything if I try hard enough. I can be the best student.

I focus on my power, and I see Lenora's body. I know that body very well, and not just because I have hurt it with my power many times. I know it because I have touched every part of it, kissed every part of it. I love that body.

And now, I want to reach the deepest part of it.

I don't poke her skin or squeeze her muscles. I don't hurt her. Instead, I fill it with my power. Moon replaces her Sun. Every part of her belongs to me. I become her body.

I want to rule over it.

I want to capture it.

Astonishment fills Lenora's eyes. "Zuraya?"

She can only speak because I let her. Her body is mine. I don't focus on how invasive this is. I don't focus on how guilty I am going to feel afterward. Instead, I make her let go of my arms. She obeys my silent command.

She has no other choice.

I don't even have time to be proud of myself for managing this. I cannot think. I just get into action. I take two steps back, not being able to look away. A single tear rolls down her cheek as she watches me and my heart almost stops beating.

I have to save my people.

"I can't hide when they are dying," I whisper to her and, with determination, turn my back to her. In my heart, in my veins, I can

Woe in Total Darkness

still feel her body. She is still under my control, and I don't let her go as I run toward the palace.

People are still running away from it. The crowd hits me on their way to safety, but I don't care. I hesitate only for a second before stepping inside the gruesome-looking black mist. And when I do, all the light in the world disappears.

I don't even need to release Lenora because the Darkness catches my power before I can understand what is happening. Our bond snaps, and I feel like I am going to puke. I can hear people still screaming around me. I can hear the monsters, and I can hear the soldiers who are fighting them.

How can they even fight in this darkness?

The Curse doesn't just blind me, but it wraps me in a very uncomfortable cocoon. It felt wrong before, but now it feels sacrilegious. This thing should not have existed. It is an insult to Tisasa herself.

I have no idea how the cultist think this is a holly phenomenon.

I can feel it over my skin, in my throat, and deep in my stomach. It is choking me. It wants the light inside me.

Then I hear a voice from the outside. It is so easy to miss it between all the screams. It is covered in mist, so hard to pick up. Yet I still know what it is: Lenora screaming my name.

That makes me straighten. I remember why I came here. I don't want to be a burden. I don't want her to rescue me again. Now it is my turn. I reach into my heart despite the smoke filling my lungs. I hold onto my power. I hold onto the light the Darkness wants so much.

Then I start shining. It is dim at first but gets more and more by the second.

I am not sure if it is good or bad because now I can see the horrible scene before me. I understand why everyone was escaping here on foot. One of the monsters looks like a giant hornet but with more limbs like a spider. It is snatching anyone who tries to fly. It takes them into its trap because the hornet can see, but people can't.

Until now.

Almost everybody briefly looks at me, but the terror of the situation is much more important. People focus on how to get out, and soldiers turn back at the monsters. I see Hashim land a good hit at the hornet, and the monster lets others go so it can fight with the Sun Soldier.

Just when my heart drops for my friend, a hand wraps around my arm. "Are you crazy?" Lenora asks. When I turn, I see her eyes look me up and down, assessing me for any wounds.

"I am okay," I say quickly and squeeze her hand. I am breathing a little fast because of the pressure I still feel around me, but I can take care of it. "We have to fight this. Without light, everyone will die."

Lenora shakes her head. "I am taking you out." She looks horrified, like me getting hurt is worse than all these people dying.

I cannot let her act like this. "We are staying," I say harshly. I see a monster coming towards us. "Protect me here," I try another tactic. "Kill them for me."

She looks at where I am looking and immediately takes out her sword. It lights up with warm Sunshine. I realize she has no other light around her other than that. Lenora attacks the monster. "You are going to be the death of me," she says, swinging her sword, but clearly, her words are directed at me, not the monster.

It looks like something between a lizard and a snake, but his tongue is longer than either of them. Its body sways left to right, moving away from Lenora, and tries to stab her with the stinger at the tip of its tongue. It is absolutely disgusting looking, and I lose my breath when the stinger gets too close to Lenora.

"How can I help you?" I shout over the chaos going around us.

Just for a second, her deadly orange eyes turn to me. "Stay the fuck back, Zuraya!" I have never seen her this angry with me.

She swings again, and her sword almost cuts off the monster's entire leg. It doesn't look dependent on them to stand, but it still lets out a painful screech. I can also see how much damage the Sunshine caused. Its skin looks like it has melted.

I wonder if my power can have that effect too. Can I freeze them to death?

Woe in Total Darkness

"I should help," I yell over at Lenora, but before she can answer, I scream because something like a tentacle wraps around my ankle. As it pulls me, I can not resist the power and fall down. The side of my face hits the floor and then scrapes against it. It hurts a lot, and I am sure it is bleeding.

Although it has nothing on the panic I feel.

The monster that grabbed me doesn't look anything like a sea creature. It is the most humanoid looking and smaller compared to others. It has tentacles instead of arms and another one atop its head. It is small, but the tentacles are long.

I try to kick it with my free foot, but nothing happens. "I don't have my weapon," I cry out. I try to focus on my power and maybe manipulate its body, but the panic doesn't let me. I just trash on the floor as it pulls me closer to its mouth, which is filled with sharp teeth.

"No!" I hear Lenora scream. "Don't let it bite you."

I hope it won't because there is not much I can do. I close my eyes and try to see its body. I try to focus on it like I learned, but it doesn't work. It doesn't feel materialized. All the monsters around us feel like mist to me.

How can I capture mist?

Just when I accept my fate, the tentacle around me loosens, and I open my eyes. I see Lenora standing over the butchered monster. I look back at the snake-looking thing she was fighting and see it is dead as well. Lenora is covered in... blood? It is black and too thin to be blood, but nothing is right with these monsters.

She also looks furious.

She grabs me under the arms and puts me on my feet again. "I told you to fucking leave, Raya." She looks mad, but the next moment she wraps me in a hug. Her chest moves too fast against mine. Her hot breath falls over the skin of my neck. I hug her back.

"I am sorry," I whisper. *I am sorry for being a burden. I just wanted to help.*

Lenora holds me closer. All the chaos around us doesn't matter. Only I matter. "I won't lose you," she says.

Her touch and her words make me shine even lighter.

"Just let me handle this," she says, cupping my cheek. "After this, I won't ever leave you."

Her promise causes a sharp sting. It was all I ever wanted her to say for the past few days. I wanted her to choose me over everyone. But things changed. I don't know how much her promise means under these conditions.

I cannot trust she is not going to disappoint me again.

But this is not the time. We can talk later. We just need to survive this.

"What should I do?" I ask. No need for promises under pressure. I just need to know how I can be useful.

Lenora looks around, turning serious from emotional in a matter of seconds. "I cannot close the Patch before we kill all the monsters. It is too powerful when they are alive. I should preserve my light for later. Just keep shining. Try to expand it. Give the people a chance to escape, a chance to fight. Don't let them be blinded."

I nod. I can definitely do that.

"Just focus on that," she says and nods to herself. She looks at me once like she has so many more things to say, but we both know we don't have enough time, so she leaves. As she runs up to a monster, I hear her command, "Protect the Princess."

I know her soldiers. I have trained with her soldiers. So, when I close my eyes to focus on my power, it is all because I trust them. I trust them to protect me. I just need to give them their vision.

My skin glows lighter as I focus on the Moonshine deep inside my heart. Even under my eyelids, I can see. I want to shine so much that this complete darkness is consumed by my power.

And then I think, can I really?

I pay more attention to what I can do. I have the light power, but I am more than a simple candle. Even with my eyes closed, I can see the bodies around me. Even if I don't control them, I can still know their movements. I can know how far I can reach.

The occasional monster sound coming close to me makes me flinch. My light flickers. I cannot have that.

Woe in Total Darkness

I force myself to go deaf. I don't want to be scared. I know they will protect me. Instead, I keep the light going and focus on the movement around me. I can see the soldiers, and I can see the monsters even if they feel like mist. I let my Moonshine guide them.

And soon enough, I can see further. I can see what my eyes could not have if they were open. I feel my power reaching there. Slow but steady. I am lighting up the palace. I am ruining the darkness. I can see the forms escaping monsters. I can see the small startled movements monsters make when my light reaches them. Now they are not the only ones that can see. Now my people are able to run away from them.

Now they can all see because of me.

I am nothing but a statue at my spot. I don't care what is happening around me. I just focus on my power. My light reaches far away, and I can see everything. I can even see the misty figures perfectly. I can feel them.

Quickly I realize what that means.

Just when a monster is about to catch a Feyada, I reach into its skin, its bones. I apply the pressure. I break its bones. I cannot hear it, but I can see how it trashes. I can see how it lets go of its prey.

I can see how it is dying under my palm.

But I don't want to just manipulate the body. I want to capture it. I want to do what I did to Lenora. I want to make them my soldiers so they can fight against each other. So, they can never hurt anyone I love.

Moonshine keeps spreading through the thick walls, brighter every second.

I decide which monster to focus on. Who is my top priority? Who do I want to protect the most?

Lenora is swinging her sword at one of them. She is amazing, as always. She is winning. I know she is going to kill it, but why should I risk it? Her life is too valuable to me to ever risk it. So, I push. I do what I did earlier. I try to reach deep into the monster. I try to get inside its body. I try to become it.

I become the mist.

"Zuraya!" I hear her worried voice despite all my concentration. I can never not hear her.

I push harder. There is nothing to worry about. I will protect us both. I will end this whole thing.

"Stop!" Now she sounds closer. I can see her form turn towards me. She stops fighting the monster since it is now stuck in place, trying to keep me out of its body. It is pathetic.

It let Lenora go. That was all I wanted.

Or maybe it was not. Maybe I really do want the power. I want to be able to rule them.

I feel hands over my skin. "You will drain. Please stop," Lenora begs me.

I hate hearing her sad, but I cannot stop. When I finally destroy this for her, for us, we will be happier than ever. Maybe then people will respect me for real. Maybe then we can truly be together without being scared.

I don't make the monster fight another, but I hold it in place. It cannot move. I keep holding it and attack another. I want to bind them all. They are weak. This curse is so weak compared to me.

At one point, my light reaches almost all over the Darkness because I feel it resisting. I feel it trying to wrap around my light. It feels unearthly. It feels so wrong.

But it doesn't feel stronger than me.

Lenora's hands are still all over my body. At one point, I see her open my eyes, but my vision doesn't return. I still see with only my power. I fight it off. I fight the monsters, and I fight the Darkness.

Pressure builds inside me. Something trickles down my eyes, my nose. The bones in my fingers feel close to snapping. My fingernails feel like they are breaking. My heart beats like it is going to explode inside my chest. My lover keeps begging me in tears.

However, none of it is enough to stop me.

I explode.

My light fills the whole world. It consumes the Darkness and all the monsters within. It brings peace to my people. It brings peace to my lover.

Woe in Total Darkness

Only then do I open my eyes. My body immediately collapses, and Lenora holds me. She is covered in black blood, and her eyes are swollen. She looks at me with fear.

She looks at me with love.

I want to tell her I love her. I want to ask if she is proud of me. I want to ask for a kiss.

But I can't.

Because only seconds after, my eyelids feel heavy. The world remains bright as I get buried in total darkness.

53

Lenora

Wake up.
Please wake up.
Please make her wake up.

I bury my short nails into my palms as I keep everything in. My heart hurts. I still cannot breathe normally. I just want her to open her eyes. I want to know she is well.

Currently, her body is draped over her bed. She has four healers around her. They wanted me out of the room as they worked, so I said, "Make me." No one dared. I am not fucking leaving her side.

One of the healers realizes how fidgety I am and gives me a nervous look. "She is not dead," she confirms.

"Tell me something I don't know."

I probably know more than them. They are supposed to be the best healers in the Moon Kingdom, but they cannot do shit. They just keep checking her again and again. At one point, one even tried to make her smell some oils like that can wake her up.

I want to kill them for being so stupid.

I already know what happened to her. I just don't know how to fix it. That's why when she passed out in my arms, I lifted her and

Woe in Total Darkness

ran around until I could find a healer. It was chaos all over, and everybody was scattered in and around the palace. I still managed to find them and brought them here to her room. I must have had a very deadly look in my eyes since it wasn't so hard.

My eyes fall to her motionless form on the bed. She looks peacefully asleep. I know her body must be feeling so tired.

I tried to stop her.

I failed.

Raya's light was getting larger and larger. I didn't realize how much she pushed herself until it was too late. Shining in a Darkness Patch is hard; it is draining. On top of that, she decided to manipulate the monsters.

She captured them.

I taught her how to use her powers. I never taught her what was pushing the limits. She didn't know what would happen when she used all her power.

In all my years of fighting against the Curse, I have never closed a Patch while the monsters inside were still alive. They made the Patch stronger and more resistant. It is just too much for my power. I cannot overpower it.

But Zuraya did. She closed the largest Patch I have ever seen while the monsters were still alive. She held them back, and her light consumed the Darkness.

I don't think I can ever do something like that, even if I drain my powers to the point of death.

And that was what I thought. I thought she was dead. Those few seconds before I realized she still had a pulse were the worst. Even the thought of her death was enough to choke me into tears.

But she is not dead. She is just drained. All her power, all her energy is drained. She needs sleep, and despite what these healers think, she can only be woken up with light powers. She is going to feel sick when she wakes up, and that can also only be treated by light. The effects are similar to monster bite. The Darkness might have disappeared, but it is still around her. It is making her sick.

The only difference is that she has time. The Curse is not in her blood. It is only skin deep. It can be treated by someone who knows what they are doing.

Unfortunately, none of these healers actually know it. I gave them enough time to try their methods. I knew what she needed the second I brought her here, but I gave them a chance.

I am not a healer. My knowledge is gathered from my experiences and my talks with Andy. I wanted to believe maybe they knew something I didn't. Maybe they had a different way of treating wounds caused by Darkness in here.

Apparently, they don't.

"Don't you have moon spheres?" I ask. "I can lend my powers too if you tell me what to do."

They look surprised, and one asks, "Do you think that would work?"

Oh, sweet Tisasa. "I am not the one that is a healer."

Another healer gives me a desperate look. "This is the first time the Curse came to the North. We don't know how to treat something like this. We are not even sure if waking her up is the right thing to do at this point. She feels too weak."

"She needs rest," I nod. "And she needs a fucking healer who knows what they are fucking doing."

They all flinch. "What do you want us to do?"

"Just leave."

They do.

They won't be able to help her. I feel like maybe I can manage to wake her up, but I don't want to do that now while she is so tired, especially since I don't know what to do afterward.

She needs Andy.

I know what I have to do. Maybe it is just what I *want* to do, but I know it is going to work. That's why I know King Luran is not going to stop me. We both want her to get better.

The only difference is that he wants her to be his perfect little princess after healing, and I want to steal her from here.

Only now do I realize how stupid I was to say not to her. Deep down, I always felt like she could wait for me. I thought she was an

Woe in Total Darkness

option I could come back to after defeating the Curser. I never really saw it as a decision between her and everybody else.

After almost losing her, I know my decision. It is her, and it is always going to be her. I never thought the curse could touch her, but now that it did, I cannot leave her.

I don't care who dies as long as she is well. If that makes me a villain instead of a hero, so be it. I'll be a villain for her.

As soon as she is healed, we are leaving for the Continent. We are leaving for a life we can be together.

I only need to talk to her father now.

———— ‹ ————

"She needs light," I explain to a tired-looking Luran. "She can be healed with moon spheres."

"I don't have the energy to make more moon spheres, Lenora," he says with a sigh. I try my best not to look at him all disgusted. He is disheveled and grumpy because he had to use a lot of power while fleeing the palace.

His daughter saved all these people while he was busy running away, and now he cannot even make an effort to save her.

I look at the bandages on his arms and chest and hope he will die because of them. I know it will hurt Zuraya, but that doesn't stop me. I hate him too much.

"I have moon spheres," I announce like it is news to him. "I also have healers who know how to deal with the damage of the Curse. They can heal Zuraya using the spheres I have."

"You will use them for her?"

I grit my teeth. "Unlike you, I'll do anything for her."

He doesn't even look offended. He just looks like he wants me gone so he can keep being grumpy about his wounds. "How is that going to work?"

"I am going to take her to the Khanate. I believe I can wake her up. I'll make sure she can make the journey. I'll protect her with my life."

King Luran doesn't like that one bit. He looks at my face with narrow eyes. I know he wants to ask me to bring my healers and the spheres here, but my determined look doesn't let him. He just gets more displeased with the situation.

But unfortunately for him, he has no other choice. He has to say yes.

And he does. "Okay. You can take her to the Khanate for her treatment. I trust her with you."

"Thank you."

"But," he says, raising a finger smugly. "I want a soldier of mine for protection as well. Just so I can be sure about her safety."

"That is okay. I'll take whoever you want. We will leave as soon as we can. We don't need to be added to the chaos here."

He nods. "That is okay. You can talk with Davon. Whenever you are leaving, he is going to come with you."

My brows furrow with confusion. "Davon? You are sending your General to guard your daughter on a not-so-dangerous journey."

"I am very concerned about her safety. She needs the best of the best."

I fight the urge to roll my eyes. We both know he is lying. He knows I am going to keep her safe. He wants to send someone just to prove his power over me, and he is sending Davon away because he wants to get rid of him. A grieving soldier is no good to him. I can take care of Davon for him until he is well enough to come back.

Now I really hope he dies.

But I don't argue. I just nod and say, "Very well. Now, if you let me, I need to get my soldiers ready."

He makes a hand gesture for me to leave, and I flee in seconds. I have already made Hashim inform our soldiers. I knew Luran had to say yes. I didn't need confirmation.

I also wanted him to send whoever can go right now. The journey with Zuraya is not going to be fast, so I don't want to drag a crowd. Hashim and I are enough to keep her safe. Now we also have Davon.

I should inform him soon as well.

Woe in Total Darkness

But before, I want to visit my soldiers and see when they are leaving. I also know some of them are injured, but I don't know how badly. I couldn't pay attention to anything but Zuraya. I should show them my support. I also should make the arrangements if any of them are in a condition to not fly.

After those things, we can get ready for our own journey, and I can wake Zuraya up.

I walk along the halls of the palace, trying not to look around much. Every corner is filled with pain and chaos. People are injured, and some are dead. Healers are trying to help everyone. Some cry over a lost one or just because of the trauma of the situation. They were not ready for this at all. They thought they were safe.

They were wrong. Now no one is safe from the Curser.

"Lenora," someone calls out, and I stop in my tracks. I know whose voice it is.

"Rionn," I say, turning around, but I am definitely not ready for what I see. I haven't seen Rionn in the Darkness, but I know he is not someone to run away. He is a fighter. He is also a hero.

The sight of him confirms that he stayed back and fought those monsters. He most probably saved some people.

He did it at a cost.

The right side of his face is in bloodied bandages. I cannot see how bad the wounds are, but I can imagine. He also has a big cut that starts from his lip and goes down to his neck. His lips are almost split in two. I know it is going to heal disfigured. The left side of his head is missing some hair from a claw wound, and I can see that he is missing part of his ear. He has more bandages all over his body, all of them not just filled with red but black blood.

The most handsome man on the Isle of Ae looks destroyed.

I don't want to look shocked. I don't want to offend him, but it is so hard. In all my life, I have never seen someone's face take this much damage after a fight.

"Never seen anything like this" he says, talking about the Darkness.

"I can tell," I say and flinch at how horrible that sounds.

Sem Thornwood

"The healers only patched me back up. They put on some bandages. Turns out their healing magic doesn't work."

Oh no. I know why that can be. "You got their blood on your wounds." Maybe he didn't get any in his veins, but that shit really ruins anything. Now I know his wounds are going to heal even worse.

He nods. His throat moves up and down, and he looks down for a second before turning towards me. "Do you still have problems with the Giant King?"

That is random. I didn't even have time to deal with that recently. "Yes."

"You know he will listen to me if I spoke to him. I am a native ruler. He respects me."

"But why would you do that?"

He smiles like I am stupid. "Northerners don't know shit about the Surse. No Shifter healer will know anything as well. No one will be able to fix me."

"No one but healers from the Khanate," I say, almost finishing his sentence. I say the words, but I cannot understand their meanings straight away. It sounds too ridiculous.

Does he think his life is in danger?

"If you got their blood or their venom in your bloodstream, you would be dead already. You don't have anything life-threatening, Rionn."

"I know," he says. His jaw flexes. "I cannot live looking like this."

I knew Rionn cared about his looks. Anyone who looked like him would, but I never thought he cared this much. "Does it worth it?" I ask, still not fully believing what he is asking of me. Is his beauty really worth visiting the Khanate as the Alpha Shifter?

His kind is not just not welcomed in my lands, but they are deeply hated. We have so many survivors from his uncle's rule. So many escaped from prostitution just like Andy. He will be putting his life at risk by coming there.

But Rionn doesn't step back. "It does," he answers with confidence. "I'll talk with the Giant King if you let me come to the Khanate for treatment."

Woe in Total Darkness

I should just say yes. I really shouldn't take advantage of someone who is this desperate, but my moral compass shattered the second I saw Zuraya in the middle of the Patch. It doesn't matter anymore. "You will leave Zuraya alone as well," I say.

"Done," he answers with a breath.

I cannot help but look surprised. He looks like I can want anything from him, but I don't care about anything else he has. What he offered is already enough. So, I nod. "Very well. You can go talk to Hashim and Davon. We all be going together as soon as we can."

"Okay," he says. Then his voice drops an octave. "Thank you."

I just nod. "Now, if you let me, I need to take care of my girl."

And I leave. I leave for her room.

My plans about seeing my soldiers leave my head. All I want is to see her. I want to make sure she is okay. Hashim can handle everything when I stay by her side. I just want to watch her sleep. I want to let her rest until I have to wake her up.

Then I am going to take her to the Khanate so the healers can use as many moon spheres as they want to heal her. I am going to take her back to my home. I am going to keep her by my side in the Desert.

And she is not going to step into the Sun Khanate as just the Moon Princess. She is going to be welcomed as the Lightbringer.

I will make sure of it.

Epilogue

Davon

I hold the little box in my arms, on my knees, thinking about how I can bury him. I don't want to think of the box as a casket. I don't want to accept I lost both of them.

They separated them.

I know their souls are together. I know Maha is somewhere peaceful with our son. She is holding him, smiling. She is happy. She waited too long for him, and now she deserves to hold him forever in her arms.

I have the strongest urge to join them. Without Maha, nothing makes sense in the world. I was a shell of a person before she came into my life, and now I am even worse than before. She was my love. She was my purpose in life. Most importantly, she was my redemption.

Now I lost her.

Maha was the only thing keeping me in check for years. She knew how to suppress my anger. She was able to make me smile even in the darkest hour. She was always there when I had one of those horrible nightmares.

She was my everything.

She deserved so much better than me. She deserved a better life, but in the end, she chose me. She loved me.

Woe in Total Darkness

My delicate flower.

I just wanted to give her a proper goodbye. I wanted her to be buried next to her beloved mother with the son she loved so much without even meeting him. I wanted to kiss her casket one last time before she was lowered to the underground.

Surely after that, it was not going to be long before I took my own life and reunited with them. My life does not matter without her in it anyway.

My only wish was to know her body was at peace before I died.

They didn't give me that.

And now that is the only reason I stay alive. The only reason I don't bury a big enough grave and get inside with my son's lifeless body is revenge.

A tear escapes and lands on the box in my arms. I can't bear to look at it, so I look up at the palace. I fill with rage seeing the walls that carry so many memories of her.

I know they are going to regret disrespecting my wife and my child.

Now they are going to feel my rage.

Emotions build up inside of me thinking that, and my whole body tingles. I hold the box tighter to my chest. I don't try to suppress my fury for the first time in a long while. I let everything out.

I am thinking about going to Seelie Lands. I think about how much I am going to hurt them. Hate runs in my veins as everything good vanishes, and I decide everyone deserves pain.

In the next moment, the Darkness erupts around the Moon Palace.

THE END

Sem Thornwood

Author's Note and Acknowledgements

Finally being able to share this book with you makes me so happy. My writing career started with dark romance and all my books have a special place in my heart but that was not something I have written before. As a twelve year old my first book was a fantasy book. Well, it was definitely awful but it was from the heart. Since then I always wanted to write fantasy. My first ever real work was also a fantasy book even though it didn't get published. I have worked on a fantasy universe and created so many stories in it. This book was just a little part of it and I hope you will see more about this universe in the future.

When I started publishing my work I started with dark romance because I didn't think I was ready to write a good fantasy book yet. I wanted to learn the process just so I can write fantasy romance in the future. During the process I becamse obsessed with mafia books and will write many many more of them but this book was a dream for me. It was a dream because it is a fantasy book and it was a dream because it is a sapphic romance. I always hated the fact that there was not enugh sapphic romances out there. While writing this book I knew it was going to beeasier to sell this if I made the main characters a man and a woman or two men but I wanted a women story. As a bisexual author writing a sapphic book was very important to me and I finally did it. I have more planned for the future too so don't worry.

There are so many people who helped me during this dream project and I want to thank all of them. Of course firstly I am grateful for all my loyal readers who gave a chance to a small indie author and supported her through her career. I also want to thank to my new readers who gave a chance to me and my book. I hope we will see a lot more of each other.

I want to thank to my beta readers who helped me make this book a lot better and also my ARC readers for helping me in promoting this book. Truly trying to sell a sapphic book is harder than it should be and I am grateful to everyone who wanted to help me reach more people.

I also want to thank my friends for listening to me rant about how anxious I was about this book. I have spent so many days doubting myself and not believing in my book but thankfully I am really happy about how it turned out. I have truly gave my everything.

Now it is time for me to write some more mafia romance but Zuraya and Lenora's story will continue with another book in 2023. I hope you are as excited as I am.

About the Author

Sem Thornwood lives a very simple life of a university student. She is mostly writing or reading. When she is not nose-deep in a book, her favorite activity is to dress up and have vegetarian picnics with her friends. She is trying to spread positivity even in the darkest hour. Most simply, she describes herself as a modern-day fairy, obsessed with cherries and red wine.